No One Saw It Coming

Susan Lewis is the internationally bestselling author of over forty books across the genres of family drama, thriller, suspense and crime – including the novels *One Minute Later* and *I Have Something to Tell You*, which were both Richard and Judy picks. She is also the author of *Just One More Day* and *One Day at a Time*, the moving memoirs of her childhood in Bristol during the 1960s. Following periods of living in Los Angeles and the South of France, she currently lives in Gloucestershire with her husband, James, and her dog, Mimi.

To find out more about Susan Lewis:

www.susanlewis.com
www.facebook.com/SusanLewisBooks
@susanlewisbooks

Also by Susan Lewis

Fiction
A Class Apart
Dance While You Can
Stolen Beginnings
Darkest Longings
Obsession
Vengeance
Summer Madness
Last Resort
Wildfire
Cruel Venus
Strange Allure
The Mill House
A French Affair
Missing
Out of the Shadows
Lost Innocence
The Choice
Forgotten
Stolen
No Turning Back
Losing You
The Truth About You
Never Say Goodbye
Too Close to Home
No Place to Hide
The Secret Keeper
One Minute Later
*I Have Something
to Tell You*

Books that run in sequence
Chasing Dreams
Taking Chances

No Child of Mine
Don't Let Me Go
You Said Forever

Featuring Detective Andee
Lawrence
Behind Closed Doors
The Girl Who Came Back
The Moment She Left
Hiding in Plain Sight
Believe in Me
Home Truths
My Lies, Your Lies
Forgive Me
The Lost Hours
Who's Lying Now?

Featuring Laurie Forbes
and Elliott Russell
Silent Truths
Wicked Beauty
Intimate Strangers
The Hornbeam Tree

Memoirs
Just One More Day
One Day at a Time

SUSAN
LEWIS

No One Saw
It Coming

HarperCollins*Publishers*

HarperCollins*Publishers* Ltd
1 London Bridge Street,
London SE1 9GF

www.harpercollins.co.uk

HarperCollins*Publishers*
Macken House, 39/40 Mayor Street Upper,
Dublin 1, D01 C9W8, Ireland

First published by HarperCollins*Publishers* 2023
1

A catalogue record for this book is available from the British Library

ISBN: 978-0-00-847186-6 (HB)
ISBN: 978-0-00-847187-3 (TPB)

This novel is entirely a work of fiction.
The names, characters and incidents portrayed in it are
the work of the author's imagination. Any resemblance to
actual persons, living or dead, events or localities is
entirely coincidental.

Typeset in Sabon LT Std by
Palimpsest Book Production Ltd, Falkirk, Stirlingshire

Printed and Bound in the UK using 100% Renewable Electricity
at CPI Group (UK) Ltd

For Denise:

Because of you . . .
I laugh a little harder,
Cry a little less,
And smile a lot more

Best friends for more decades than
we'd ever want to admit to

They told me she was dead, but I've found her.

They said my mother was dead too.

She is now.

I'm staring at a photograph of her funeral – who photographs funerals? – and I'm wondering who all the people are. My sister is there, described as the only daughter. With our father being dead – damned straight to hell, I presume (and hope) – she is the chief mourner. She'll be forty-four by now. How time flies.

The last time I saw her she was three years old and screaming not to be wrenched from my arms. I knew better than to scream, but I couldn't help it. It's hard for a ten-year-old to stop themselves, in spite of knowing what will happen if they do.

She's grown into a beautiful woman. That is no surprise. I always knew she would. Our mother was beautiful too.

I more closely resemble our father, but in looks alone. I have nothing of his character. I have done everything in my power to prevent that.

This photograph shows my sister surrounded by people who care for her, and from what it says in the accompanying piece, they all cared for our mother too.

1

They didn't know the woman the way I did.

Apparently she became a paediatrician, a healer of children, which is such a screeching irony that it's as if every instrument in an orchestra is hitting the wrong note.

My sister's life has been very different to mine. I have no idea if she's ever thought about me, if she even remembers me.

I really don't care about my mother dying. I'm glad she's gone. I have no desire to confront what she was, or what she did. She might have ended up doing good, but she was an evil woman once. No one knows that better than I do.

I'm sorry that my sister never came to find me, although there's a good chance she thought I was dead.

I'm not. In fact, finally, after all these years, I'm close enough to see her whenever I choose, although she can't see me. Not yet, anyway, but soon, when the time is right, she will know all about me.

I hope it will bring us both nothing but joy.

PART ONE

CHAPTER ONE

'You know, I can't help wondering how you're feeling right now.'

Hanna Madden blinked with surprise. She hadn't been aware of anyone close by, much less studying her. She had thought she was alone and, for the moment at least, unobserved.

She was standing in the doorway of the Orangery, gazing out over Goldney Hall gardens, where a very elegant evening party was in full swing. Twilight was bathing everyone in an almost dreamlike glow; small bursts of laughter seemed to float above the low rumble of voices, as graceful and captivating as the flowering lilies basking in the Dutch canal. Hanna had always loved this venue, with its lush, flowing lawns, richly foliaged trees and neoclassical statues – a truly splendid oasis at the heart of Clifton, one of Bristol's most exclusive suburbs.

'I'm sorry,' she said politely to the woman who'd joined her, 'have we met?'

The woman smiled winningly and put out a hand to shake. 'Riona Byrne,' she said, 'and I admit I feel as though I know you. Maybe our paths crossed in a past life?'

Hanna took the hand, not entirely sure whether this was

a light-hearted tease, or if Ms Byrne actually meant it. She was Irish, judging by the accent and name, and had a cultured, ironic sort of air about her. Her thick, beautiful red hair was shoulder length and naturally wavy, held from her oval face by a navy velvet Alice band; her eyes, gentle and grey, were humorous and direct. Her smile was friendly and yet Hanna was sensing a hidden hesitancy in its depths, as if she were half-afraid of being rebuffed.

'Now, that's an interesting notion,' Hanna responded with a genial laugh. She was used to putting people at their ease, was good at it, in fact. 'I wonder where the past life might have been?' she mused. 'And was it during this incarnation, or an earlier one?'

Clearly pleased to be taken up on the playful challenge, Riona said, 'I guess the possibilities are endless and not a little fascinating.'

Hanna laughed again, her gentle blue eyes lighting with mischief, her fair-skinned and lovely face flushing with pleasure. 'Seriously, have we met before?' she asked. 'You do seem . . . familiar? If so, I'm sorry for not remembering,' she quickly added. It was rude, pompous even, to have forgotten someone's name, never mind their existence, and she never felt comfortable trying to excuse it with the fact that she and her husband had such a wide and varied network of friends, family and business associates.

'Ah, Hanna! There you are.' Emerging from a nearby clutch of dark-suited men came the man of the hour, her husband, Jack. Though not conventionally handsome – his eyes were too narrow, his nose too large and jaw too prominent to make him so, his imposing height, broad shoulders and high-wattage smile rarely failed to make him stand out in a crowd. They were also known to cause several female hearts to beat a little faster. The fact that he was one of the most prominent businessmen in the region also earned him a great deal of attention, and respect, for he was known to be a tough, but fair-minded and generous employer.

'Are you enjoying yourself?' she asked as he reached her. 'I'd like to introduce you to . . . ?'

'Jack, over here!' someone shouted. It was the newly elected Metro mayor, whose campaign Jack had robustly supported; Jack maintained his smile as he muttered under his breath, 'Is it time yet to let him know who's boss?'

Supressing a laugh as she glanced at Riona, Hanna said, 'Way too early. And don't forget, you like him.'

He grinned. 'Why aren't you mingling?' he asked, already starting to leave.

'I am.' She would have added that she'd just come from the ladies and had made a new acquaintance on the way, but he'd already gone and anyway it seemed a bit presumptuous to make such a claim of Riona Byrne. 'Sorry,' she said to her, 'I'll introduce you later when he's less in demand. Unless you already know him?' No, she couldn't – Jack would never have been so rude as to ignore someone he knew.

Appearing amused, Riona said, 'This is the first time our paths have actually crossed – and is there ever a time when he isn't in demand?'

Hanna rolled her eyes. 'Not really.'

Riona smiled. 'So this evening is to celebrate him taking the title of West Country Businessman of the Year for the fourth time in a row?'

Hanna regarded her openly, enjoying the gentle mockery

that seemed to have no edge to it, only a smooth, easy sense of irony. 'We are indeed,' she confirmed. 'He'll tell you he doesn't put any store by these accolades, but between us, I know he enjoys them.' Then realizing she could be talking to a journalist, she wished she could take it back.

'And what about you?' Riona probed. 'Does it bother you to be famous?'

Hanna had to laugh. 'I'd hardly describe myself as that,' she countered, giving a wave to someone she knew, 'but since you ask, there are times when we'd both prefer a little more anonymity.'

In fact there had been plenty of occasions during the twenty-three years of their marriage when they'd wanted nothing more than to shut out the rest of the world, but she certainly wasn't going to get into any of them now. Her eyes alighted briefly on a male figure in a group beneath the late flowering mulberry tree and her heart contracted. She knew he'd been watching her, had felt it since his arrival, but he wasn't looking her way now.

Riona said, 'I guess I'm hogging your company when I'm sure everyone here wants to talk to you.'

Hanna's gaze roamed the elegantly dressed clusters of people spread out around the lawns and colourful flower beds and said wryly, 'They seem to be managing just fine. Can I ask, are you a reporter?' she said.

Riona's eyebrows rose in surprise. 'No. I'm sorry if I gave that impression.'

Hanna said, 'So what do you do, Mrs . . . Ms . . .?'

'Actually, it's Doctor, but please call me Riona. And is it OK to call you Hanna?'

'Of course. Everyone does, even people who don't know me. Jack often goes for Han, or even Hanny – very annoying.

I tend to call him Jacky if he does that.' She wanted to ask what sort of doctor Riona was, and who she had come with, but was afraid it might sound as though she was challenging her right to be there. She didn't remember seeing her name on the guest list.

In timely answer to one of her questions, Sebastian – Seb – Goodman, Professor of Social and Political Theory from Bristol University, and one of Jack's oldest and dearest friends, came to drape an arm around Riona's shoulders.

'I see you two have met,' he declared. Hanna knew him well enough to tell from his slightly flushed face and glittering blue eyes how attracted he was to Riona Byrne. He was quite a looker himself, with his thick blond hair, chiselled jaw and pretty good physique, but since his wife's passing two years ago, he'd shown no interest in meeting anyone else. 'How are you, Han? Looking great, as uuj,' he said, kissing her lightly on the cheek. 'Did Riona tell you she's a fan?'

Wincing, Riona said, 'It's not exactly what I said. More an admirer,' she informed Hanna.

Pulling a contrite face, Seb said, 'I've obviously mis-spoken, so forgive me, ladies. Can I get you both a drink? Your glasses are empty and I have it on good authority that the vino on offer is pretty easy on the palate.'

It was Badger's Bluff, a chardonnay from a vineyard right here in the centre of Clifton – Jack and Hanna liked to keep things local where they could – and she was pleased to hear Seb, a known wine buff, talking up the vintage.

Aware of Jack's repeated glances in her direction, and others trying to get her attention now, Hanna said, 'Time for me to mingle, but it was lovely to meet you, Riona. I hope you're staying for the speeches.' Her eyes shone with mischief and, to her delight, Riona picked up on it.

'Wouldn't miss them for the world,' she assured her with a dryness that made Hanna laugh out loud.

As she moved away, soon swamped by other guests (a few minutes with her was the next best thing to an audience with Jack), she could feel herself being watched by the man beneath the mulberry tree. She took care to stay away, was determined not to look at him at all, but his scrutiny was like a tether, trying to reel her in. She was strong enough to resist, at least for now.

Everyone was here, from the uniformed High Sheriff (a position both Jack and his now-deceased father had held at various times over the years); all three mayors – Lord, Metro and City; at least two dozen members of the exclusive Society of Merchant Venturers, Jack being amongst their number; at least two High Court judges; several prominent barristers; the *grand maître* of the Bordeaux *Commanderie*; and many of the city's leading businessmen and -women.

As she listened, laughed, commiserated and flirted her way around the party, she found herself glancing about for Riona Byrne. She saw that she and Seb were talking to Bob Reeves, former president of the Rugby Football Union and grower of Badger's Bluff.

'Ah ha! Here you are. I'm so sorry we're late.'

Recognizing the breathless voice of one of her dearest friends, Hanna turned to embrace her. 'Hello you,' she said delightedly. 'Traffic bad?'

'Tell me about it.' Andee Lawrence kept her hands on Hanna's shoulders as they gazed into one another's eyes, wanting to intuit if there were any secrets to be shared, problems to solve, or good news to celebrate?

Andee was around the same age as Hanna, slightly

taller but just as slender and, where Hanna's hair was a delicate strawberry-blonde, Andee's glorious shoulder-length curls were exotically raven. It was her arresting aquamarine eyes that were her most compelling feature, however. They drew a person in instantly, and they also never missed a thing, which had made Andee an excellent detective in the past – and, albeit in a less formal capacity, still did.

She looked around, clocking the other guests, many of whom she knew, if only slightly.

'Where's Graeme?' Hanna asked, referring to Andee's partner; his property development company was currently partnering with Jack's on a Ministry of Defence project based in North Devon.

'He got waylaid as we came in,' Andee replied, 'and I'm sure he's found Jack by now. Who's that over there?' she asked, nodding in the direction of the mulberry tree. 'He seems very interested in . . . you?'

Hanna said, 'I'm sure it's you he's looking at, wondering who you are.'

Andee was amused. 'And he is . . .?' she prompted.

'Hugo Astor. He's heading up our in-house legal team now that Ernst Samuels has retired.'

Andee's eyebrows rose. 'He's very . . . *physical*,' she commented dryly.

Hanna spluttered a laugh. That was certainly one way of describing the man who oozed masculinity to the point of carnality. In fact, in her opinion – despite his looks – he was a pretty loathsome character: cocksure, self-satisfied, egocentric, pompous and, though it pained her to admit it, apparently brilliant at his job.

Wanting to steer Andee away before he realized they

11

were discussing him, she signalled to a waiter and took two full flutes of champagne from his tray.

'Lovely to see you,' she said, clinking her glass against Andee's.

'Likewise,' Andee responded. 'Are you sure it's OK for us to stay for a few nights?'

'Are you kidding? I've been looking forward to it.' It wasn't as if they didn't have the room – they had so much of it at their family home in the Chew Valley that sometimes she and Jack had to text or call to find out where the other was in the house or the grounds.

'Excellent, so we'll have plenty of time to chat.' Andee sipped her drink and made a swift survey of the gathering. 'I see the local high-fliers are out in number,' she commented.

'Still mostly white, over-privileged and entitled,' Hanna muttered, 'but generally good at heart.' She added with a smile, 'So how is life in Kesterly-on-Sea?'

Andee groaned. 'Crazy, but it's that time of year. Tourists fighting for deckchairs and spilling all over the pavements; cafés and pubs struggling to keep up with the crowds; teens beach-partying into the small hours . . . Frankly, it's good to get away for a spell.'

Wryly, Hanna said, 'And presumably no one's gone missing, or been murdered or kidnapped, so your extra-special services are not currently required?'

Andee smiled. 'Correct. Now, who's here that I should meet? Either of the children around, by the way?'

'Leo's is in Italy,' Hanna replied, referring to her and Jack's twenty-one-year-old son, who had recently graduated from Birmingham Uni with a 2:1 in business development. 'And Caitlin's taken the baby to stay with friends in Wales for a while.' Even as she spoke her daughter's name, she could feel her heart tightening and twisting. Their rebellious eighteen-year-old was a uni no-show and regular pot-smoker, as well as mother to adorable eighteen-month-old Sofia. Much of the time Sofia's care fell to Jack's stepmother, Jenny. 'And what about your two?' she asked, certain already that Andee's perfect two – both a little older than Leo and Cait, and from her first marriage – were excelling in their chosen fields.

Before Andee could answer, Jack and Graeme swooped in on them, closely followed by a photographer who wanted shots of the four together – then of Hanna and Jack, followed by just Jack, then Hanna. By the time it was all over, Andee and Graeme had joined other friends, and Jack was talking to the party organizers about where to stand to deliver his speech.

The sun had dropped below the horizon by now, and all attention was starting to focus on Jack as he took his place in front of the Orangery. Hanna walked back a few paces and slipped quietly into the shadows, feeling the pull of her favourite part of the gardens. For most it would be the grotto – a spectacular man-made cave dug into the far hillside. Its walls and ceilings were decorated with hundreds of species of seashells and coral that Thomas Goldney III had transported from the Caribbean during the eighteenth century. There were moves afoot now to rename this historic hall and gardens, given Goldney's links to the triangular slave trade that had firmly placed him and many Bristol merchants amongst the wealthiest men of their time.

Moving past the grotto, Hanna wandered up the gentle slope of the hillside, passing the tower with its smooth stone walls and castellated rooftop. She arrived at a long, grassy walkway raised above the gardens, with the city spread out below. In daylight, and in winter when there were no leaves on the trees, there were spectacular views down to the harbour and all the way across to Dundry Hill in the distance, the start of the Mendips.

She was lit only by moonlight as she slipped in front of the statue of Androcles, the lion wrapped around his sculpted body like a weathered cloak. She inhaled the fresh grassy scent of the nearby orchard and warm night air, and could hear Jack's voice far behind, though not what he was saying. She didn't need to listen; she knew the speech well, having helped to write it. She wondered if he'd noticed her walking away, if anyone had.

She was invisible to the crowd now, melding into the statue's shadow, her pale dress making her appear almost ethereal.

She didn't hear anyone approaching, no footsteps in the soft earth, no whisper of breath or rustle of clothing. She was only aware of him coming to lean against the plinth beside her, when gravity seemed to disappear and her senses began to swim.

Neither of them spoke, or touched, merely stood motionless and silent, the sounds of the party distant and strange, as though they belonged to another world. She could feel the thickening beat in her chest, was aware of her breath, shallow and fearful. She was as alive to him as if his hands and mouth were on her and he was pushing the force of his desire all the way into her.

'You shouldn't be here,' she croaked.

There was a smile in his voice as he said, 'But you knew I'd come.'

She could tell that he was looking at her, but she couldn't look at him. She knew if she did she would lose control;

14

it was already slipping away. She wanted him with an urgency that could so easily override everything else; that always did.

The last time they'd been in these gardens, less than a fortnight ago, at a mutual friend's wedding, they'd walked along this grassy bank to the rotunda, where he'd taken her, swiftly, violently, almost without feeling, his brutal hands clasped around her hips, hawk-like eyes alert to discovery. It had been as if he were doing her a favour, bringing her to a breathless, shattering climax before walking away. It was always like that and she couldn't get enough of it.

She knew already that it was going to be no different this evening.

CHAPTER TWO

Hanna woke slowly, blearily, opening her eyes to a silvery wash of moonlight spreading about the room. It took a moment for her to register that she was in her and Jack's bed, at home. The tall sash windows of their master suite were open to allow in a welcome night breeze, along with the scent of damp, summery countryside.

Beside her, Jack was sprawled out on his back, fast asleep. It took a lot to wake him.

She lay still, listening, wondering what might have disturbed her, certain that something had, but she could detect no unusual sounds. They were quite remote here, on the slopes of the Chew Valley, surrounded by six acres of their own land that rambled and stretched down to the shores of Blagdon Lake. Their boundaries and gates were as secure as they could be made, the large Grade II Georgian property, with its seven bedrooms and bathrooms, was fully protected by cameras and alarms, as were all of the outbuildings.

She'd always felt safe here. Unlike some of their neighbours, they hadn't experienced any break-ins, or gratuitous vandalism, although they were never sanguine about this good fortune; the time could always come when someone decided to target them.

Pushing back the covers, she padded over to a window that overlooked the front drive, not really expecting to see anyone or anything out of place, only to enjoy the cooling air. A fox darted across the lawn and disappeared into the woods that bordered the approach road. Moments later, its eyes appeared from between the trees, yellowy-crimson and staring, as if it knew she was there, watching, and it was watching her back.

Feeling restless, she moved across to the other side of the room to gaze down to the lake. It was a vast, sprawling swathe of black at this hour, with bright moonlight spilling in ripples over its glassy surface. There was no one out there, nothing to see apart from a sprinkle of lights on the far shore and the skitter of a duck or goose breaking the calm of the water. A barn owl hooted and somewhere, at a distance, the roar of a motorcycle faded into the silence.

Reaching for a thin cotton wrap, she slipped it on and let herself quietly out of the room. On the rare occasions when she and Jack were alone in the house, she wouldn't bother to cover up, but Andee and Graeme were with them tonight and she'd rather not embarrass them, or herself, should one of them venture downstairs in search of iced water.

She went barefoot along the landing and took the front stairs, wide and grand, sweeping down to the large entrance hall below. She turned to continue on to the kitchen. It occupied the west wing of the house, with four sets of arch-topped French doors to one side, and three more to the back that opened onto a wraparound terrace, where flower beds and tables with parasols were arranged around a central fountain. A grassy footpath led through the lower garden and snaked on down through a wild-flower meadow all the way to the lake.

The land had been bought by Jack's great-great-great grandfather, back in the early 1800s, but it had been his son, John Madden III, who'd built the first house on the plot based on a design by William Kent. It had been added to and modernized considerably during the ensuing two centuries, but it retained most of its original fireplaces, cornices, pillars, and the typical symmetrical form and fenestration of the original era, while providing all the necessary comforts of a twenty-first century home.

Although Hanna didn't hail from quite such an exalted background, both her parents had been eminent surgeons, highly respected in their fields, particularly her mother, and she herself had gone to all the right schools. As her mother had put it when Hanna had told her she and Jack were to be married, 'Well, he has no reason to be ashamed of you, so let's be thankful for that.'

So typical of her mother.

Finding the kitchen empty, she stood in the darkness for a moment, still uncertain whether she'd been woken by someone or something outside. The valley was teeming with wildlife, so it was no real surprise when a security light was triggered outside the stables. Nevertheless, it caused her a moment's unease as she fleetingly recalled the detestable Marius Hansen triggering the lights one night when he shouldn't have been there. He was the older brother of a girl – Freya – who'd once taken care of the horses, and had disappeared when his sister had left her job a couple of years ago. They might be mostly forgotten now; however, brief moments such as this one could remind Hanna of how uncomfortable Marius used to make her. It was if he was seeing more than she'd ever want him to, or knew things about her that he might one day try to use against her.

18

Shrugging off the unwelcome memory, she turned on a single lamp and gazed at her own ghostly reflection in the night-darkened window. Now someone really was staring in at her: a woman with a pale face and messy, strawberry blonde hair and fathomless eyes. What did that woman out there think of her reflection in here? Would that vague yet watchful apparition have done what she had at Androcles' statue while Jack was giving his speech?

By the time she and Jack had left the party with Andee and Graeme, there had been no sign of the man who'd joined her at the statue. Earlier on in the evening, she'd spotted him talking to Riona Byrne, laughing and flirting as though they might actually know one another. As if sensing her eyes on him, he'd turned and caught her staring. His smirk was despicable, his arrogance appalling, and yet she still couldn't be sure that she wouldn't let him fuck her again.

What was wrong with her? Why was she so drawn to a man she could barely stand? These past weeks since he'd joined the company, it was as if another self was driving her, pushing past who she really was to take over her mind and her body in a way that could be terrifying if it weren't so exhilarating.

She wondered if he might have gone home with Riona Byrne, although why she'd think that when Riona had clearly been with Seb, she had no idea. She wondered how long Seb had known the woman, why he hadn't told her that he was seeing someone. Or perhaps they were colleagues, or simply friends.

Hearing Jack come into the kitchen, Hanna turned around and started to smile. His navy robe was belted loosely about his thickened waist, his hair was tousled and comically on end, while his beloved face was darkened by a shadow beard. In spite of his success and social standing, there was no sense of entitlement or self-importance about him, no prideful enjoyment of his accomplishments and ancestry. The fact that the roots of his family wealth were firmly planted in the slave trade was considered by him to be a source of nothing but shame; it was what drove his remarkable philanthropy.

'Couldn't sleep?' he yawned, putting on his glasses.

She shrugged and tilted her face up for the kiss she knew was coming. 'I thought I heard something,' she said, 'but it was probably just a deer.'

He gazed down into her eyes, his own deep and pene-trating, as if he could see right through to her innermost thoughts.

What was he seeing? What was he thinking?

He arched an eyebrow, kissed her again, and went to help himself to water from the fridge-dispenser.

She loved him and everything about him to the very depths of her heart. True, they'd had some clashes over the years, point her to a couple that hadn't, but she couldn't imagine anything or anyone ever coming between them, in spite of the way they tempted it at times.

She was glad he was awake too. She wanted his company, always did and always would. 'Did you enjoy the party?' she asked as he sat adjacent to her at the island.

'Sure,' he replied. His large hands around his water glass were more workmanlike than elegant, yet she knew how tender they could be, how capable they were in so many ways. 'It was good to see everyone,' he said. 'The award's a bit embarrassing. I think, if they offer it to me again, I should discreetly decline and suggest someone else.'

She smiled. 'And I'm sure you have a suitable candidate in mind,' she teased.

His eyes narrowed, but he didn't deny it. Putting someone else in the spotlight, allowing them the recognition and glory of city-wide success would probably please him far more than achieving it himself. 'Have either of the children been in touch?' he asked, returning to the fridge for more water.

Her heart flipped with as much love as dismay. 'Only Leo,' she replied. 'He's having a great time, apparently, but wanted us to know he was thinking of us tonight. You especially.'

Jack's eyes showed how deeply he felt his connection to their son, their similarities and shared goals. Leo had been nothing but easy since the day he was born and there was no sign of that changing. 'Have you messaged back?' he wanted to know.

'I told him we miss him and we'll send photos tomorrow. No word from Cait,' she added, because Jack would want to know in spite of how it might hurt him, 'but I'm not sure she knew about the award.'

His expression darkened. 'I really don't care about that,' he reminded her. 'It's her not being in touch when she has to know we'll be worrying about Sofia that pisses me off.'

It was pissing Hanna off too, given what an unpredictable and unreliable mother Cait could be, but she said, 'I'm sure everything's fine. If it wasn't, we'd know by now.'

He turned to stare out towards the lake, and she knew he was seeing their tiny granddaughter in his mind – chubby, jubilant, still unsteady on her feet and the most precious part of their lives. It was how they'd felt about Cait when she was small. Leo too, of course, but then Cait had hit her teens, fallen in with the wrong crowd, started taking drugs . . .

'Just get off my case,' she'd shout at them, if they tried to talk to her about it. 'It's only weed, for fuck's sake, and don't tell me you never smoked it because I know you did.'

It was true; Hanna and Jack had, regularly, and it wasn't unknown for them to indulge now, though *never* when Cait was around. Actually, since they'd realized their daughter was using, they'd stopped bringing it into the house, smoked it only when away on what they called their special weekends.

God forbid Cait should ever find out about them.

What really mattered was that Cait adored Sofia. But Hanna couldn't help wondering if Cait was getting high with her friends in some remote farmhouse in Wales right now, while Sofia slept, or watched, or wandered unchecked into the night.

An icy chill went through her merely to think it.

'Are you hungry?' Jack said suddenly.

She thought about it. 'Yes, I am,' she decided.

He went to check the fridge. 'Oh *yes*,' he murmured as something clearly hit his taste buds. He pulled out a tub full of their housekeeper's delicious home-made *saratele*, saying, 'Yes, yes, yes.'

Laughing, Hanna fetched two plates. 'Florina knows you too well. She'll have baked these specially to satisfy your middle-of-the-night munchies.'

Biting into one of the cheesy crackers, he said, 'You know, I think I might have to ask her to marry me.'

'She's already turned you down half a dozen times. Besides, I expect Tomas would have something to say about that.' Florina had been the children's nanny when they were small and had taken over as housekeeper around eight years ago, at about the time she'd married Tomas. He also worked for them now as occasional driver and full-time groundsman. They felt like part of the family, although they didn't live on the property; they had a small place of their own across the lake in Ubley.

He finished his cracker and picked up another. 'When does Jenny get back?' he asked, referring to his beloved French stepmother, who'd moved out of Lake House when Jack's father had died, and taken up residence in the large thatched cottage next to the stables.

'She's due back next Wednesday.'

'Remind me where she went again.'

'To Mâcon – Burgundy – to stay with your aunt Lilian for a few days.'

'Ah, yes. I'm missing her, but it's good for her to get away while she can.'

'And she won't go while Sofia's around – we know that.'

Jenny's attachment to her great-granddaughter wasn't only born of natural love and an innate sense of protectiveness; it also filled the giant hole in her life that had followed the death of Jack's father.

Hanna felt Jack watching her as she popped in the teabags and filled two mugs from the boiling tap. She wondered again what he was thinking, where his mind had ventured in the past few minutes. It was one of so many things that she enjoyed about him: how unfathomable – and sometimes unpredictable – he could be.

'How about you?' he asked as she came to sit down again. 'You didn't say whether you had a good time at the party.' Before she could answer, he said, 'I saw you up at the statue with Hugo Astor.'

Her breath stopped as she nodded slowly.

'I don't think anyone else noticed,' he told her.

She simply looked at him, relieved he thought that, and hoping it was true. She was certain she knew what he was thinking, although he could always surprise her.

'Will it be over soon?' he asked. 'Or should I start to worry?'

'There's nothing to worry about,' she assured him, 'and never will be. Can you say the same?'

Pushing aside his plate, he wiped his hands and mouth on a square of kitchen roll and said, 'You know I can. I love you and only you, Hanny Madden.'

Slanting her eyes, she said, 'I love you too, Jacky Madden.'

He laughed and pressed a kiss to her lips. 'Doesn't it ever turn you on to think of me with another woman?' he murmured.

'Not so much, but I know what it does for you to think of me with a man I don't know, or – even better – don't like.'

His eyes stayed on hers, searching and slightly puzzled. 'Do you really not like Astor?' he asked.

'Not one bit, but he's clearly a good lawyer and I know you're glad you hired him.'

He nodded thoughtfully. 'That's true, he is good. I guess he didn't imagine getting involved with my wife just weeks after joining us.'

With a scoff she said, 'I'd say he expected it. It's how he behaves, anyhow.'

'And you let him?'

'Because it suits me. It'll be over soon. I'm pretty sure it is already.'

He seemed unsurprised. They were well used by now to

the flings one or other of them indulged in from time to time. The only rule was that they weren't kept secret from one another. If they were, that would be cheating, and neither of them ever wanted to go there. They'd seen too many marriages break up because of it, and theirs was far too precious to them to allow anyone to come between them.

'Did you meet the woman who came with Seb tonight?' she asked.

'Briefly. Was it a date, do you think?'

'I'm not sure. She's a doctor, apparently.'

'GP?'

'No idea.'

He regarded her closely. 'Hanna Madden, are you trying to set me up?'

She laughed and play-punched his arm. 'No way. Not if she's with Seb. I just thought I might like to get to know her better.'

'Then call him and invite them over.'

'Mm, yes, I think I will.'

He got to his feet and stretched as he yawned. 'Ready to go back upstairs?'

A few minutes later, they were lying side by side on the bed, hands linked at they stared towards the ceiling and enjoyed the cool night air on their bare skin.

'Do you think we're strange?' she asked after a while.

He shrugged lazily. 'We're just who we are.'

'So, strange?'

Cocking an eyebrow, he said, 'There are a whole world of people out there way stranger than us so, in the grand scheme of things, I'd say we're pretty OK.'

She laughed and settled her head on his shoulder, then

placed a hand on his chest, sinking her fingers into the wiry hair and inhaling the wonderful male scent of him. She listened to his breathing as it deepened, carrying him into sleep, and let her thoughts return to the party and those brief yet erotic moments with Hugo Astor. It wouldn't happen again; she'd made up her mind about that now. He might be surprised and disappointed when he found out – it was possible he'd even try to talk her round – but he'd learn to live with it, if he wanted to stay working for Jack.

CHAPTER THREE

Hello again. I'm sorry, I forgot to introduce myself earlier.

My name is Blanche. It's suits me because my skin is pale, my eyes chalky blue and my lips have little colour. I look as though life has tried to bleach away my physical existence, yet inside my heart vibrates with life and my blood is as rosy red as the varnish painted on Hayley's nails.

I feel oddly hypnotized by those nails as they tap on the table, long white fingers moving irritably up and down, breath coming impatiently, the scent of her skin filling my nostrils.

I only mention Hayley because she is here and a little wild and often has too much to say, although she's not speaking now. She's angered by my stubbornness, frustrated by her need to cow me.

She reaches for the funeral photograph that has my sister at the centre of it. I remove it from her hand and lay it face down on the table.

It takes a while, but finally Hayley leaves. Fond as I am of her, I've no interest in her opinions today.

I keep my hand on the photo and turn to stare abstractedly at the bird-feeders hanging from the trees outside. I've always loved birds, but there was a time when I couldn't name any, and nor could I see them. I could only hear their songs through the walls, sweet and shrill, juddering and sometimes discordant.

I have some memories of the day the police came to take our father away, the chaos, the noise, rage and terror. The smell, too – but with so much adrenalin rushing around did anyone actually notice it? I don't know if anyone was shot, hurt, but I do know that my mother grabbed my sister and took her, leaving me behind. I can still see my sister's treasured little hands reaching for me, clawing, panicking, pleading, desperate for me to hold on to her. Our mother had shown no real interest in her after her birth. There was always too much else going on – too many distractions, demands, rituals; all sorts of comings and goings that burn red and amber and sharp and dark in my mind to this day.

Knowing that my sister is safe and has been for all these years fills me with so much relief and happiness, it's like flowers are floating down from heaven to spread joy and redemption all around us.

Even after so long, she still means everything to me. I'm sure she has no memory – or even knowledge – of how much danger she was in back then. Or of how she used to depend on me, her little stand-in mother. We played, sang, laughed and cried together. I told her stories, all made up from my imagination, because I didn't know there were real children's stories back then. She didn't notice that I couldn't run free the way she did. She was too young to understand where we were and what was happening around us.

And now here we are, like two branches from the same

tree that have grown at the same time, one before the other, but forever joined. We always will be.

I've printed out the photograph taken at my mother's funeral. I made it as large as possible, and then I glued it to a card, leaving a plain white strip down one side. This is where I'm writing in the names of the people surrounding my sister. There are lines drawn to their faces for ease of identity.

Hayley wants to meet them, but I won't allow it. She is too . . . how can I put this? Liberal with her charms. Her libido has a very unreliable off-switch.

In case Hayley comes back, I slide the photograph into a drawer beneath the computer. Billy was working here earlier; I can tell not only by the coffee drips on the keyboard, but by the music website he's left on the screen.

You see, I am not alone here, in case you were thinking that. I never have been actually, not for a long time. These days I surround myself with lively and gentle souls who come and go of their own free will.

I wonder what my sister would make of my friends if she were ever to meet them? A colourful, contrary group of individuals. They are who make up my family today. We are bonded and committed in ways that most families have little sense of. There is only one amongst us who knows everything about my mother and sister. She understands what happened all those years ago. I talk to her often – every day, in fact. I'm sure she'll be back soon.

I realize I am smiling. Warmth is stealing softly through my heart. Having my sister in my life – at least on the periphery – is all I've ever really wanted. Knowing she is safe and loved is all that matters.

I just hope that she really is.

CHAPTER FOUR

Riona let herself in through the front door of a smart detached house in the Westbury-on-Trym area of Bristol. It was Victorian in style, double-fronted with large bay windows on the ground floor, a red tiled roof and white-washed walls. Inside the rooms were spacious, with high ceilings, intricate cornices and cast-iron fireplaces. The well-tended garden surrounding the property was full of trees and flower beds and protected from the outside world by a high brick wall, front and back, and solid automatic gates at the entrance. The pedestrian access was operated by a digital code.

The entry hall was airy and welcoming and as she dropped her keys into a drawer she was listening, waiting for the sound of voices, or music, but all was quiet.

With a small sigh of satisfaction, she checked her reflection in the mirror above the console. She looked tired, she thought, and a little strained around the eyes, but her mood was good. She'd had a call about an hour ago from Seb Goodman, the friendly professor who'd taken her to the party at Goldney Hall last Friday evening. He'd invited her out again, this time to a wine-tasting, followed by dinner, at a vineyard on the outskirts of town.

She was more than happy to go. She'd decided as soon as they'd connected through an exclusive online dating site that she wanted to know more about him. They'd first met at a coffee bar a few days ago near the university, and she'd found herself warming to him in a way that had quite surprised her. He'd seemed to like her too, for he'd asked her right there and then – or after two coffees that had run on to an impromptu lunch – if she'd care to accompany him to an exclusive event that very night. This was where she'd met Jack and Hanna Madden, amongst others, and had listened to Jack's acceptance speech while his wife had been engaged elsewhere.

Riona had no idea if anyone else had noticed Hanna's apparent indiscretion – nor was she sitting in judgement, although it had made her wonder about the Maddens' marriage.

She turned aside, and went through to the kitchen, her low heels tip-tapping on the tiled floor. To her surprise, there was no sign of Blanche. She sighed softly. It was painful even to think about all that Blanche had been through as a child, and since. It was so terrible, unimaginable really, that it rarely found its way into words. To speak of it was to relive it, and there were times when the reliving could be almost as traumatic as the experiences themselves. However, over time, Blanche had developed her own way of coping: strategies, mental exercises and safe havens to help soothe and even displace the fear and anxieties.

She had achieved most of this before Riona had come into her life. Riona's purpose now was to try to prove to Blanche that she wasn't only capable of living a normal life, free of the support systems she'd created for herself and that were actually holding her back, but that she was ready to.

Riona was just finishing a cup of tea when her thoughts were interrupted by Billy, out in the hall, singing along flatly to whatever music was plugged into his ears – *Californication*, she thought. The middle-aged man's look was pugnacious, hard set, almost mean, but he could be very tender with Blanche. He could also be impatient bordering on aggressive. Lately, he'd become mad keen to find himself a girlfriend, and Riona was trying, as delicately as she could, to point out the problems with this, but so far he was refusing to listen.

Hearing another voice taking over the song (Ruby, by the sound of it), Riona felt a flood of warmth. Ruby, half-Italian, half-Scottish, was a dedicated people-pleaser, awkward dancer and easy laugher. She was close to forty, estranged from most of her family, but extremely close to Blanche.

As quiet resumed in the hall, Riona got up and went through to her study. Although she'd drawn up a therapy schedule, it often went forgotten and she rarely tried to enforce it. Freedom to come and go was important, she understood that, and she was always there, at the centre of their world, if anyone needed to talk. Meanwhile, she kept a watchful, in some ways motherly eye on them all, to make sure nothing and no one was going off the rails. She also made regular reports to Dr Emilia Francis, the psychiatrist overseeing this project.

It was a couple of hours later that Riona heard her mobile ringing out in the hall, where she'd apparently left it in her coat pocket. As soon as she saw who was calling, she felt a lift in her heart.

'Hello,' she said warmly, going back into her office and closing the door.

'Hi. Do I have the right number?' Seb asked. 'Is this Riona?'

She smiled. 'It is.'

'Thank goodness. I tried a while ago, but must have misdialled because I got some bloke who . . . Well, any-way . . . How are you?'

'I'm fine,' she assured him, fleetingly wondering if Billy had got hold of her phone and answered it. 'Surprised to hear from you again today,' she said. 'Has something changed about the wine-tasting?'

'No, not at all. I hope you can still make it.'

'I'm looking forward to it.'

'Good. Me too.'

She waited, certain there must be more.

'Actually, you're probably going to think this is crazy,' he said, 'or too much, but I just wondered if you might be free for a quick bite this evening?'

Riona was thrilled that he wanted to see her so soon. 'Where did you have in mind?'

'Oh! Anywhere. Do you have a favourite place? Or I was thinking . . . Rosemarino on York Place, in Clifton. Do you know it?'

'No, but I can find it. Shall we meet in, say an hour?'

'Excellent. Fantastic. I should make sure they have a table. If they don't, I'll call back; if they do, I'll text you with the time.'

Smiling, Riona rang off and sat quietly for a moment, thinking things over and imagining how this new relation-ship might play out. All the signs were good – there was no doubting that – but of course it was very early days.

CHAPTER FIVE

Hanna and Andee were seated beneath a parasol outside the Lazy Lobster on the raised pavement of Chew Magna's South Parade. The sun was blazingly hot today, and the white wine refreshingly cold, while the food, tapas style, was scrumptious. This was one of Hanna's favourite local eateries, and she and Andee always tried to fit in a lunch here while Andee was staying, which wasn't often enough. They got along so well, always had, and Hanna knew if she was ever in trouble, or really needed a friend, she wouldn't have to ask, Andee would drop everything.

She hoped Andee knew the same about her.

'So, let's cut to it,' Andee was saying as she refilled their water glasses. 'Tell me all about Hugo Astor.'

Hanna choked on a laugh and put down her fork. 'I thought you'd never get round to asking,' she countered. 'I saw the way he checked you out when we were at the office yesterday.'

Andee's eyebrows shot up. 'It's the way he looks at you that intrigues me. Are you two . . . ?' She left the sentence unfinished, prompting Hanna to demand in a whisper,

'Please tell me it's not that obvious.'

'It might not be to anyone else, but you can't hide it from me. So how long has it been going on?'

'Nothing's *going on*,' Hanna replied, starting to shell a prawn. 'OK, we're . . . you know, but it's not a relationship. Nothing like. Jack knows, of course.'

'Of course,' Andee echoed dryly.

Hanna had to laugh; she knew that Andee was both intrigued and mystified by the little flings she and Jack indulged in, more so because they never seemed to adversely affect their marriage.

'So is Jack seeing someone?' Andee wondered, taking a sip of wine.

'I don't think so. Or not that he's mentioned, and you know we tell one another everything.' She regarded Andee closely. 'Are you about to reveal something . . .?'

Andee's hands went up. 'I know nothing,' she assured her. 'To be honest, I don't think it's the kind of thing he and Graeme ever discuss. It's all business, sailing and fine wines with them, as you know.'

Hanna did, only too well, and needed no reminding after an entire weekend of it. Which wasn't to say that she and Andee hadn't indulged in things that pleased them every bit as much, such as an eight-mile hike through the Mendips, a dawn horse-ride across the valley fields and lanes, and a thorough examination of Hanna's latest charitable projects while at Madden HQ yesterday afternoon. This was when Andee had been reminded of Hugo Astor's existence, for he'd decided to hand-deliver some files Hanna had requested for an upcoming fundraiser, no doubt presuming that it was a ruse to get him there, until he'd discovered she wasn't alone in her office.

'So, have you told Astor it's not going anywhere?'

Hanna failed to hide a wicked grin as she said, 'We don't do much talking.'

Andee eyed her meaningfully, making her laugh.

'Let's just say I don't think he's got any expectations above the waistline.'

As Andee chuckled she picked up a napkin and used it to fan her neck.

'It's such a shame you have to go home today.' Hanna sighed regretfully. 'I really love having you here.'

'I love coming, and I'd stay longer if I didn't have so much on before we go to Italy.'

Hanna glanced down at the road as a car pulled up, and a woman hurriedly got out. It took her a moment to realize who it was, and another to recall her name. 'Riona?' she cried as the car drove away fast.

The woman looked up and down the street, as though checking traffic before crossing.

Running to the pavement railings, Hanna leaned over and called, 'Riona! Up here!'

The woman turned around and Hanna, startled, immediately began to apologize. 'I'm sorry, I thought you were . . .'

Riona broke into a smile and Hanna blinked. It *was* her, albeit not as neatly groomed as when they'd met the other night, with her russet hair tumbling untidily around her shoulders and her make-up a little smudged . . . 'It is you!' she declared. 'I didn't realize you lived out this way.'

'Oh, I don't,' Riona replied, quickly snapping a scrunchie around her hair. She glanced at the steps a few paces away, went to climb them, and came to shake Hanna's hand with both of hers. 'What a surprise,' she declared. 'It didn't even occur to me that I might run into you today. How are you?'

'I'm great, thank you. Let me introduce you to a good friend of mine, Andee Lawrence.'

Andee was already smiling a welcome as she held out a hand.

Hanna said, 'This is Riona . . . Byrne?'

'Well remembered.' Riona laughed. 'It's lovely to meet you, Andee. But I'm interrupting your lunch . . .'

'No, we're about done,' Hanna protested. 'Why don't you join us for a coffee? If you have time?'

Riona checked her watch. 'Maybe just a quick one,' she said, and sank heavily into the chair Andee had pulled up to their table. 'Gosh, it's hot today, isn't it?' She sighed, using a hand to fan her face. 'Is the food here good? I've heard it is.'

'Very,' Andee assured her. 'They're just small bites, if you'd like to order something . . .'

'Oh no, I've already eaten.'

'How about some wine?' Hanna offered, reaching for the bottle.

'You're too kind, and I'd love to, but I never drink in the day.' She grimaced awkwardly. 'Sorry, did that sound—'

'Don't worry,' Andee came in quickly. 'Nor do we, usually, but today we've made an exception as neither of us is driving.'

Hanna tore her eyes from Riona as a server came to take their order for coffee. How could she say she didn't seem herself when she barely even knew her? 'So what brings you out this way?' she asked, when the server had gone.

Retying her hair, Riona said, 'A patient of mine got into. . . Well, it's a little complicated, so let's just say she needed rescuing.'

Baffled, Hanna said, 'Is she OK now?'

'I think so.' She closed her eyes, as though taking a moment to fully separate from whatever drama she'd just escaped. 'I'm sorry,' she said, 'sometimes things can get a little out of hand.'

'Do you mind if I ask what you do?' Andee put in curiously.

Riona's expression softened as she said, 'I'm a clinical psychiatrist, specializing in trauma and rehabilitation. I'm afraid one of my patients . . . She can be a little over-enthusiastic about making new friends at times. She meets them online and puts herself at risk by going to visit their homes. Fortunately, I followed her this morning, and managed to get her out of a situation before it actually turned into one.' She grimaced awkwardly. 'She's pretty cross with me right now, but she'll calm down. She's safely on her way home now.'

'How do you know she won't go back there?' Andee asked.

Riona frowned. 'I'm trusting she won't,' she replied.

'So where's your practice?' Hanna wondered.

'Oh, in Westbury-on-Trym. We've set up a small clinic there for five residential patients. We can take up to six, but we keep the last space available for emergencies.' With a sudden, near radiant smile she added, 'May I ask what you do, Andee?'

Hanna laughed. 'You'd do better to ask what she *doesn't* do.'

With a playful scowl, Andee said, 'Officially I'm an interior designer. Unofficially I help people who need assistance with police inquiries, or a deeper investigation into something that's happened to them.'

Riona's eyebrows rose. 'Sounds fascinating. Is it?'

'It can be, depending on the case.'

Hanna said, 'Andee is an ex-detective sergeant, and the go-to person in Kesterly-on-Sea if you have a problem that the authorities aren't making headway with. And she's extremely good at finding missing people, as well as answers to difficult questions.'

Riona was clearly impressed, but as she made to respond, their coffees arrived and Andee's mobile rang.

'Sorry, I'd better take this,' Andee said. She got up from her chair and walked along the raised pavement towards the gift shop.

Hanna smiled at Riona. 'Seeing you has reminded me that I was going to get in touch with Seb to invite the two of you to dinner. I mean, if you're . . . Sorry if I'm over-stepping this.'

Riona's eyes shone delightedly. 'Your party was our first date,' she confided in a comical stage-whisper, 'and our second was last night. We had dinner at Rosemarino in Clifton.'

'Oh, I love that place. Was it good?'

'Very, and the company was . . .' She smiled impishly. 'I like him. He's a nice man – and close friend of yours, I believe?'

'He is. We've known him for ever. He's godfather to both our children and his wife was godmother. I expect you know that he lost her a couple of years ago. Cancer, I'm afraid.'

Riona nodded gravely. 'Yes, he told me. So sad, and they didn't have any children?'

Hanna shook her head. 'They were going through the process of adoption when Jilly was diagnosed, so they delayed and delayed, until it was no longer an option.'

Riona's face conveyed her empathy. 'How difficult for them. He really has been through a rough time, hasn't he?'

Hanna nodded slowly. 'Do you mind if I ask how you met?'

Looking faintly embarrassed, Riona said, 'I'm not sure he'd want you to know this, so please don't say you heard it from me. We connected online.'

Hanna gave a laugh of surprise. 'Seb was on a dating site?' she cried incredulously.

'As far as I know he still is. I mean, it's probably a bit soon to be taking our profiles down.'

'Well, good for him is what I say – and I'm going to bet that my son had something to do with it. They're very close, those two.'

'That's nice. I'm sure it's been a great comfort to Seb to have you and your family to turn to.'

Returning, Andee said, 'Sorry about that. It was Alayna – my daughter,' she added for Riona's benefit. 'She sends her love,' she told Hanna.

Hanna smiled. 'How is she?'

'In the middle of moving hell. She didn't want me to help, but now she does, so I guess I'll be going to London in the next day or two. Ah ha!' she declared, looking down the street, 'if I'm not greatly mistaken, it's the cavalry.'

Hanna turned and, spotting Jack and Graeme coming out of the churchyard, she waved to show where they were. 'Did you meet Jack last Friday?' she asked Riona. 'I warn you, he's a bit of a charmer, and once he knows about you and Seb, he'll probably turn it up full blast.'

Riona gave a laugh of surprise.

Getting up from her chair, Hanna put her arms around Jack as he reached her, which probably told him right away that she'd had an extra glass or two.

'Seems we can't leave these two alone for five minutes without the wine showing up,' Jack commented, as Graeme went to drop a kiss on Andee's upturned forehead.

Hanna noticed Riona assessing Graeme admiringly, and couldn't say she blamed her – he had to be one of the best-looking blokes Hanna knew. He was tall, with dark, greying hair, a close-shaved beard and eyes almost as mesmerizing as Andee's – although his were close to black, while hers were a heavenly aquamarine.

After the introductions were made and two more chairs were brought to their tiny table, more coffees were ordered and Jack regarded Riona with frank interest as Hanna confirmed that she was dating Seb.

'We wondered – hoped – you might be,' he declared, 'when we saw you together at the party. I have to say, at risk of making my wife groan, my dear friend always has had impeccable taste in women.'

Hanna rolled her eyes as Andee and Graeme laughed and Riona accepted the compliment with amused grace.

'Riona is a psychiatrist,' Hanna informed him.

Jack's eyes widened with interest. 'In that case, perhaps you could help with our daughter.'

Hanna balked in astonishment. 'Jack! For heaven's sake! Just be glad Cait's not around to hear you say something like that.'

He grimaced. 'I guess it was a bit crass,' he admitted. 'Sorry. Forget I said anything.'

Riona said, quietly, 'Of course. Unless she's suffered a trauma. Maybe I could help.'

Jack glanced at Hanna as he shook his head. 'She hasn't, unless you call having us as parents traumatic.'

He looked up as a woman with a pushchair asked if he could move in to let her pass and, realizing he was blocking the pavement, he scooted his chair over to the next table. Graeme joined him, and Riona submitted to Jack's playful interrogation about her budding relationship with Seb.

Hanna sighed and said to Andee, 'I still don't actually know when Cait's coming back. I messaged this morning, but she hasn't answered. For all I know, she's not even in Wales any more.'

'Is she in touch with Jack or her grandmother?' Andee asked.

Hanna shook her head. 'She knows we're worried about Sofia, and that's probably why she's doing it – to make us suffer.'

Keeping her voice low, Andee said, 'I know how hard you've tried to get to the root of her animosity towards you, but have you thought about counselling?'

Hanna gave a humourless laugh. 'I can imagine how well it would go down if I even mentioned it.'

Andee's eyes flicked to Riona as she said, 'I'm doing a Jack here, but maybe your new friend might have some suggestions on how to approach her?'

Hanna considered it for a moment and began slowly to nod. 'I guess it would do no harm to ask, but we probably ought to get to know her a little better before we start loading her with our family problems.'

Andee looked up as Graeme got to his feet, saying, 'So, my darling, are you coming home with me, or have I lost you to the heady excitement of Chew Magna?'

With a laugh Andee took out a credit card and laid it on the table. 'Where are you parked?' she asked him.

'Behind the church. We're in Jack's car. He'll take us back to the house to pick up our things and then we really should be going.'

'I'll get this,' Hanna insisted, pushing Andee's card aside.

'Already taken care of,' Jack announced, as a server brought the reader to him. 'Where are you off to now, Riona?' he asked as he punched in his number. 'Can we give you a lift anywhere?'

'No, thank you,' she said. 'I'm going to pop into the post office before I head home.'

'In which case, you must give me your number,' Hanna insisted. 'And Jack, we need to figure out a date to invite Riona and Seb over.'

'We must indeed,' he agreed. 'I'm sure you haven't forgotten that I'm going to be in Appledore with Graeme for the rest of the week, and I don't think we can do this weekend, but let's check our diaries.'

'Typical of us to think we're the only busy people in the world,' Hanna said to Riona. 'How are you fixed for time?'

'Oh, I'm fine, quite flexible,' Riona assured her. 'I obviously can't speak for Seb, but I'm sure we'll be able to work something out. It'll be lovely to see you again.'

CHAPTER SIX

I'm closeted with Riona going over what happened earlier today at a stranger's home in Chew Magna.

'Fortunately I stopped it from going too far,' Riona tells me. 'It was a good job I made it there in time.'

I close my eyes, trying to shut out the images she's conjuring of Hayley attempting to seduce someone who apparently hadn't been willing.

'He was pretty shocked when I showed up,' Riona continues.

'What did Hayley do?' I ask, already bracing for the answer.

With a sigh, Riona says, 'She made herself scarce. Do you know where Hayley is now?'

I glance around, as if she might be hiding in a corner of the room – for all I know she is. It's the kind of thing she does.

'Did you know before she left this morning what she was going to do?' Riona presses.

Frustration sharpens my tone as I cry, 'I can't control her!'

Somewhere, at a distance, I can hear the others talking, their voices getting louder as they approach, although as yet I can't make out what they're saying.

'Dr Francis has been in touch,' Riona tells me gently.

I don't reply.

'She wants to come.'

I'm sure she does.

I get to my feet, pull open the door, and walk into the welcoming flurry of chatter.

CHAPTER SEVEN

'Jenny's on line three,' Hanna's PA, Donna, called out from her desk in Hanna's outer office.

'Oh, great!' Hanna responded, always glad to talk to her mother-in-law, and abandoning her computer, she eagerly picked up the phone. 'Jen, are you OK?' she asked. 'Having a good time with Lilian?'

'It's wild,' Jenny responded dryly, her French accent stronger than ever after spending a week with her sister in Burgundy. 'Oh, hang on, she's trying to say something to me.'

As Hanna waited, she walked over to the row of sash windows that overlooked the forecourt four floors below, the main road that passed by their company's boundary wall and the green spaces leading to the Downs. She was feeling jittery this morning, unfocused and even slightly stressed – mainly, although not entirely, because Hugo Astor had requested a meeting with her at twelve thirty. He would be bringing a contract that needed her signature, something his assistant could easily have delivered to Donna, although apparently there were a couple of clauses that Hugo wanted to go over with her before she put pen to paper.

She knew what it meant, and she hadn't refused the meeting.

Her mother-in-law came back on the line. 'So, how are you, *chérie*?' she asked. 'Don't tell me, you want to know if I've heard from Cait.'

Hanna's other reason for feeling anxious. 'Have you?' she prompted.

'Yes, and she tells me she's fine. So is Sofia, who burbled down the line at me for several minutes with her usual, "Anananana".'

Hanna laughed as her heart flooded with love. The child called nearly everyone Ananana, apart from Jack who was Papapapa. That was also what she called her father who, thank goodness, was as good an influence in Cait's life as Hanna could wish for. If only he and Cait would get back together. 'Did you get an idea of when they might be home?' she asked.

'Not exactly. Apparently they've been invited to stay on a while, and Sofia loves it there – according to Cait – so it could be another week or two.'

Dismayed and angry, Hanna said, 'I wouldn't mind so much if we knew anything about these so-called friends of hers.'

'They're musicians, she tells me.'

'So a bunch of pot-heads? Great! Are they in some kind of commune? Is Sofia safe? Is Cait?'

'All I can tell you is that they both sounded fine – in Cait's case, sober and not especially grumpy; in Sofia's, as exuberant as ever. She has a new word, by the way, "woof", so I'm thinking a dog might be coming back with them, although no one actually said that.'

Hanna sighed. 'How's Gaston?' she asked, referring to

the dear old golden retriever who'd belonged to Jack's father and was now Jenny's constant companion.

'He's enjoying France,' Jenny answered, 'but I think, like me, he will be glad to get home. Now, please don't worry yourself too much about Cait.'

'That would be easier if she'd call me, or at least answer my texts. Jack hasn't heard from her either. He's in North Devon for the rest of the week on business, but he's threatening to drive over to Wales at the weekend if she hasn't contacted us by then.'

'Does he actually know where she is?'

'No. Do you?'

'Only that it's somewhere in the Brecon Beacons. I don't have an address.'

'Which is typical of Cait. Still, as long as she's in touch with you, perhaps we can back off a little.'

'And I'll keep the channels open,' Jenny promised. 'Now, I should be back around mid-afternoon tomorrow. Please don't go out of your way to be there – Gaston and I can settle back into the cottage perfectly well on our own, thank you. I am just wondering if you have anything planned for Friday evening?'

Hanna thought. 'Off the top of my head I'm not sure, but I can tell you we've invited Seb and his new girlfriend for dinner the Saturday after next. Why don't you join us?'

'I didn't know he had a new girlfriend. Have you met her?'

'Yes, a couple of times, albeit briefly. Her name's Riona, she's Irish, a red-headed beauty, and she's a psychiatrist.'

'*Oh là là!* Any children?' Jenny always cut right to it.

'I'm not sure about that.'

'Well, yes or no, we can't deny how sad he's been since Jilly passed. It's his turn to have some romance in his life.'

'Says the woman who shuns it at every turn.'

Jenny chuckled. 'No one can replace my beloved David, you know that, and I have everything I need in my family and friends. Have you booked us in for Pilates on Saturday morning?'

'I have.' Hanna glanced round as Donna came to let her know that Jack was on the line.

'I heard that,' Jenny said. 'I'll leave you to it and see you later on tomorrow. Talk to you soon. Love you.'

A moment later she'd connected to Jack only to be told, 'Sorry, hon, I've got another call coming in. I'll get back to you.'

For the next hour and a half, Hanna remained at her desk, making and receiving calls from the various organizations she was involved with, setting up meetings and sending details through to Donna and the events team to make sure their diaries matched.

Jack still hadn't called back when Donna put her head round the door to say she was off for lunch. A few minutes later, Hanna was checking a budget on her computer when she heard her office door close. Her heart gave a heavy thud, her mind seemed to float as her body reacted to Hugo Astor's presence. She didn't have to look up to know he was there.

She ignored him, continuing to appear absorbed in what she was doing, while trying to make herself tell him not to come any closer. He put the contract on her desk and moved around behind her. She was barely breathing as he raised her from her chair and eased her forward, his hands already reaching under her skirt.

CHAPTER EIGHT

Seb and Riona were standing close together, tasting glasses in hand, a variety of bottles arrayed on tall tables in front of them as they listened to a description of an upcoming red. They were at a vineyard close to Bristol where the vintages had won much acclaim in recent years, and the hospitality rotunda was open on all sides to allow in the balmy evening air. The event was well-attended; they always were at this venue, the host being so generous with his product, and the dinner to follow was always worth coming for.

Keeping his voice low so not to be overheard by anyone nearby, Seb said to Riona, 'Do you mind if I tell you you're quite something?'

She leaned in a little closer and she whispered, 'I'm sorry, what did you say?'

Seb put his mouth next to her ear and caught her delicate fragrance, as exquisite as any wine. 'You're quite something.'

To his surprise she blushed as she laughed. It made him like her all the more.

'I've embarrassed you,' he said, his blue eyes full of humour, his smile feeling a little too wide. God, he was smitten.

'Not really,' she whispered. 'I guess it just took me by surprise.'

'So you don't mind that I said it?'

'No, not at all. In fact, I hope you don't mind me saying that I think you're quite something too.'

He was taken aback, not having expected that – then the pleasure of it rushed through him in such an uplifting way that he almost forgot himself and leaned in to kiss her.

Fortunately he was saved by their host's microphone howling as he urged everyone to go ahead and try the Merlot.

Seb quickly consulted his brochure, checked they had the right bottle in front of them and, finding they did, poured an inch into their glasses, followed by equal measures for the small party behind them. Much like everyone else she'd spoken to this evening, Riona had charmed this group into imagining they might already be friends, and while Seb didn't mind that at all, he was also looking forward to having her more to himself.

In fact, he'd been thinking about that a lot since their dinner at Rosemarino, but he didn't want to rush things – although he probably already had. He'd been out of the dating game for so long now that he had no idea what was or wasn't acceptable and, as for taking Hanna's advice to just be himself, that might be easier if he was sure of who he actually was these days.

'You're an extremely eligible, drop-dead gorgeous, wildly intelligent beast of man,' Hanna had informed him playfully. 'She's lucky to have found you and, if you ask me, I think she knows that already.'

Feeling suddenly mischievous, he touched his tasting glass

to Riona's and immediately embarrassed himself by repeating their host's description of the wine. 'Medium body, with a deep resonance and satisfyingly long finish.'

Laughter sprang to her eyes as she tilted her head to regard him. 'Intriguing,' she responded, and took a sip. After allowing the wine to roll around her tongue, she swallowed, waited and murmured, 'Mm, definitely a long finish.'

Seb found himself semi-aroused by the flirtation. To distract himself, he reached for the pencil and order form he'd been given on arrival. 'A case?' he suggested.

Amused, she said, 'Why not?'

'Maybe two,' he decided and, marking it down, he reached for the bottle to pour them another inch or two.

'I thought we were just supposed to taste,' she laughed.

'That's for the professionals. We are not going to allow this to go to waste.' And feeling ludicrously reckless, Seb turned to refresh everyone else's glasses too.

It wasn't until they were shown to a round table for eight in the dining room that he was able to speak to her directly again, although it was still a battle, for it seemed everyone he knew was here tonight and they all wanted to claim his attention. He suspected they were more interested in Riona than in him, and he didn't mind a bit. In fact, he was thrilled to be showing her off, even if this was only their third date. If nothing else, it might stop the match-makers amongst them. They meant well, dear friends that they were, but hadn't yet managed to introduce him to anyone he could get remotely excited about.

How was he ever going thank his wonderful godson? He'd never have joined a dating site without Leo's youthful encouragement (bullying) and now here he was, hardly able to believe his luck. He wondered if Jack or Hanna had told Leo about Riona yet, but guessed not. Otherwise, never mind being in Italy, Leo would have been straight in touch to find out more.

'I thought we might have seen the Maddens here this evening,' Riona commented as they unrolled their napkins and a waiter filled their water glasses.

'We might have, if they weren't at one of Hanna's charity dos,' he replied. 'It's for the local children's hospice, I believe. She's raised quite a lot for them over the years.' An idea suddenly occurred to him and he sat back to look at her. It might be crazy or he could be misunderstanding everything, but . . . 'Maybe you should talk to her about your clinic? I just know she'll be right behind anything to do with mental health. That's if you need funding, of course. I shouldn't have just presumed . . . Sorry, I'm—'

'No, don't be sorry,' she broke in gently. 'It's a lovely idea and really kind of you to suggest it. As it happens, we are fully funded. Actually, I was thinking I might make a donation to one of her causes.'

Thrilled, he said, 'She'll welcome you with open arms. Do you have any thoughts on which one?'

'I don't know what she's involved in yet, but I'll discuss it with her when I can and do my bit to help out where it's most needed.'

Feeling his admiration for her expanding beyond reach, he took her hand and brought it to his lips. 'At risk of repeating myself,' he said softly, 'you really are something.'

Winding her fingers around his, she said, 'There's so much I want to say, and yet I don't seem to have the right words.'

Understanding exactly what she meant, he began wishing

the dinner over and kept his hand in hers beneath the table as their fellow diners drew them into conversation.

A while later, as their starter was cleared away, she turned to him and said, 'If your wine is delivered in time, perhaps we can take some to Jack and Hanna's next Saturday?'

Why did everything she said seem to light him up inside? No one had done that for him since Jilly, back in the early days. 'That's a great idea,' he told her. 'And it could be a good opportunity for you to ask Han about her charities as well. You know, they're very much looking forward to seeing you again.'

'That's nice.' She smiled. 'I'm looking forward to seeing them too. Do you know if anyone else is going to be there?'

'As far as I know it's just family. Leo should be back from his hols by then, and Jenny is sure to be there. No idea about Cait, their daughter.'

'Jenny is . . . Jack's mother?'

'Stepmother. She married his father when Jack was in his teens, so she's very much a part of the family.'

'And Hanna's parents? Are they still around?'

He shook his head regretfully. 'Her dad died when she was quite young so I don't know much about him. Her mother, Catherine, was with us until the middle of last year. She and Hanna were very close. I know she still misses her.'

'That is so sad. She must have been quite young?'

'Early sixties. She was a paediatrician specializing in a certain type of leukaemia. She was also a devoted grand-mother; the children adored her. Actually, we all did.'

Riona's eyes, intense and reflective, remained on his as she took in his words, or maybe she was thinking of some-thing else now, it was hard to tell. In the end she said, 'And what about your parents?'

With a sigh, he said, 'My mother's also no longer with us, and my father's in a nursing home near my sister's place in Canterbury. He has dementia. A wretched business. The last few times I've seen him, he didn't seem to know who I was.'

'Oh, no, that's hard. I'm so sorry. Were you close?'

'Once, yes. He was an economist in his day. He used to appear on the news from time to time commenting on the government's fiscal policies. He enjoyed that. His little bit of fame. He even signed autographs if he was asked.'

Riona smiled. 'He sounds a character.'

'Oh, he was, that's for sure. But tell me about your family. Where are they?'

With an awkward sort of grimace, she said, 'I'm afraid I'm all alone in the world, apart from a couple of cousins in the States who I never see.' She leaned in a little closer, as if to confide something significant, and said, 'I think someone is trying to get your attention over there.'

He turned to find an old colleague on his feet at another table, insisting he come over to sort out some sort of dispute that, when Seb got there, turned out to be about the university's new policy on research ethics.

'You've got to be kidding,' Seb protested, clasping his hands to his head. 'Do you guys never give up? In case you hadn't noticed this is summer, we're all on a break, and this is a social occasion—'

'And he's far more interested in the lady he brought with him,' someone interrupted. 'So give him a break. Let him go.'

'I'm gone,' he told them, 'but nice to see you.'

'Aren't you going to introduce us?'

'I already did,' he called over his shoulder. 'If you weren't there, sorry. Another time.'

'So there'll be another time?'

Ignoring the taunt, though smiling, he returned to the table where Riona was now in conversation with the couple to her left, and the woman to his right, Yolanda Fairburn a lawyer he knew well, was keen to share her latest news.

Seb didn't mind; he liked Yolanda, and her husband Tim. Nevertheless he could hardly wait for the time when he and Riona were out of here and on their way home. He had no idea yet how that part of the evening was going to play out, whether he'd read too much into their flirtation earlier, was expecting too much too soon; he only knew that he hadn't felt this excited, or nervous, since his teens. He wanted her, quite badly, and unless he was fooling himself into believing only what he wanted to be true, he thought she felt the same.

Finally, they were in a taxi on their way to Westbury-on-Trym, circling around the airport to the A370, one of the main arterial roads into Bristol. They sat separately, conscious of the driver, and talked only about the wine and food they'd enjoyed until lapsing into companionable silence. At least he hoped it was that way for her – for his part he was simply tongue-tied and apprehensive.

Eventually they were pulling up outside her gates, where two motion-sensor lights atop the pillars came on. When he'd called for her earlier in a taxi, she'd come out of the side gate, and it didn't seem as though she had a remote control to open the main gates to allow them to drive in.

Feeling foolish, and even slightly panicked, he quickly got out of the car and went round to open the door for her.

'I've had a wonderful time,' she said, stepping out and looking up at him. 'Thank you.'

'Me too,' he said and, putting a hand to her cheek, he leaned in to kiss her. Her mouth was soft and yielding, slightly open and very definitely responsive. He felt the shock of desire pulse through him and pulled her a little closer.

'I'd like to invite you in,' she said softly, 'but my patients will be there. It's a clinic, remember? Things are a little complicated.'

'We could go to my place,' he suggested. 'There's no one else there.'

She looked pained. 'I'd love to, but not tonight. I've already been out longer than I should have.'

Using a tease to hide his disappointment, he said, 'Are you really Cinderella?'

She smiled and kissed him briefly, before going to press in the code for the gate.

A moment later she'd gone through, and it clicked closed. He was left standing in the street, on the one hand admiring her dedication to her work, on the other hoping that she wasn't always going to put it ahead of him.

CHAPTER NINE

I've been thinking about my sister this weekend, regressing all the way back to the early years when our mother, or someone else, would return her to my room, half-asleep, breast milk dribbling from her tiny mouth. I'd snuggle her in to me, needing her warmth and knowing that very soon she'd need mine. I didn't want her to be cold the way I was, or hungry, or unwashed. She wasn't any of those things during her first year, or not often anyway. I don't suppose I was when I was that small, but I can't remember.

Sometimes I sang to her – hummed really, because I didn't know any songs, only chants in a language I didn't understand. My father said they were from his special book; my mother said I had no business knowing anything.

I didn't go to school, but one of my father's friends taught me to read and write and how to do basic sums. I swallowed the lessons hungrily, as needful of the knowledge as I was of the small kindnesses he showed me. He never hurt me; sometimes he brought me extra food or a clean dress that was usually too big for me. He said his name was Isaac, but when he stopped coming my mother said I was lying, there had never been anyone there of that name.

I lived in great fear of them being cruel to my sister as

she grew, that they would chain her too, leave her in darkness and only take her into a false light for their ceremonies. I wanted to save her, but didn't know how. My door was always locked and the only window had been bricked up. I didn't understand about day and night back then, or the change of seasons, or that what I felt for my sister was love.

CHAPTER TEN

Seb and Jack were enjoying a quick pint at the Albion before Jack took off home for the evening and Seb went to meet a long-time colleague for dinner. These get-togethers were as regular as they could make them, half an hour or so for them to spend just being blokes and catching up on each other's news.

It came as no surprise to Seb this evening that Jack was eager to hear more about Riona, and he was just as keen to tell what he could, which wasn't anywhere near as much as he'd like there to be.

'Well, one thing's for certain,' Jack commented, raising his glass, 'she's a stunner. Although, it has to be said you're quite a catch yourself, or so Han keeps telling me, and we know that Han's always right.'

Seb laughed, and was about to drink from his own glass, when a bullish, leather-jacketed youth with greasy dark hair and flinty eyes planted himself in front of their table.

'Hello, Jack,' he said, clearly not entirely sober.

Seb looked at Jack and saw his jaw tighten.

'Marius, what are you doing here?' Jack asked coolly.

The lad shrugged. 'It's a free world, isn't it? Or does this place belong to you too?'

Jack said, 'If you don't mind, I'm having a private conversation . . .'

'As a matter of fact, I do mind. As you know, I've got a lot to mind about.' To Seb, he said, 'I don't suppose he's ever told you about the way he treated my—'

Jack got to his feet, grabbed the boy's arm and marched him outside so fast that even Seb blinked. Jack could be forceful and swift, but this was something else.

As he waited, Seb tried to remember if he'd heard of this Marius before and wasn't sure that he had. He certainly hadn't recognized him, nor had he much liked the look of him. His air of aggression had been almost palpable and, short though the encounter had been, there was no doubt he was harbouring some hostility towards Jack.

A few minutes later, deciding he ought to go and see what was happening outside, he started to get up, but sat down again as Jack came in.

'Everything all right?' he asked as Jack joined him.

'Fine,' Jack sighed, picking up his drink. He didn't appear particularly ruffled, so at least the exchange hadn't descended into fisticuffs, but it had clearly irked him.

'Are you going to tell me who that was?' Seb prompted.

Jack drained his glass and put it down heavily. 'He's someone whose existence I'd like to forget,' he replied, staring at the empty glass, 'but I don't think that sort of good fortune is smiling on me.' He turned to Seb with a dry look. 'Put him out of your mind,' he advised.

'Yeah, I'm really going to do that,' Seb retorted. 'I'm guessing, given his age, he's that boy Leo and his friend beat up a while back, when the friend ended up in prison?' Leo might well have been locked up too, had Jack not called on his influential contacts to make sure it didn't happen.

Jack's eyebrows rose in surprise. 'No, it's not him,' he replied. His tone made it clear that this wasn't an episode of his son's past he much cared to recall. 'Our friend Marius,' he said wearily, 'is someone whose sister used to work in our stables. He was always hanging around, trying to make trouble; Han used to feel quite spooked by him. Since the girl left, he's turned up again a couple of times, threatening to sue me for her wrongful dismissal. He's drunk, as you probably saw, and it's unfortunate that he found us here. I don't think he'll be bothering us again tonight though.'

Seb almost laughed. 'Why? What have you done with him?'

Jack grinned. 'That's for me to know and you not to worry about. So now, shall we have another half for the road? I'm keen to hear more about Riona and you seem to be holding back on me.'

'Ah, I'm afraid it's she who's holding back on me,' Seb confessed, 'and now you're going to tell me I'm expecting too much too soon.'

Jack laughed. 'Never let it be said. You'll win her, no doubt about it.'

With no small irony, Seb said, 'You mean the way I won Han?'

Jack laughed again. 'You didn't put up a big enough fight. If you had, maybe she'd have been yours, and you'd have broken my heart. You also would never have met Jilly and, in spite of everything, I know you'd never have wanted that.' And, picking up their glasses, he carried them to the bar, checking his phone as he went.

For a fleeting moment, Seb couldn't help but think of how easy life was for Jack. He invariably made things work out the way he wanted them to, mainly because people responded to him well, or because it was in their interests to do things his way. As far as Seb was aware, no one ever came off the worse for it, or not often anyway. However, he hadn't forgotten how bitterly he'd detested his best friend all those years ago when he'd swept in and asked Hanna out before Seb could even form the words.

Checking his mobile as it buzzed, he was disappointed to see only a reminder of his dinner at eight. He'd text Riona later, he decided, just to say goodnight, and maybe, if she was still up, they'd message back and forth for a while.

'I *am* listening,' Jack was saying into his phone as he returned to the table with two half-pints, 'but I told you just now, Marius, I'm going to be in North Devon tomorrow . . . Yes, I know where you live and it is *not* on the way. Don't threaten me, son. It didn't work out the last time and it won't again. OK, you do what you have to, just remember what's at stake here and . . . I just told you, don't threaten me. Now grow up, sober up, and go home.' Abruptly ending the call, he dropped the phone on the table and picked up his drink.

'Please don't ask,' he said to Seb after downing the best part of it. 'You're right, there is more to it, but it's too long a story to go into now. All I ask is that you don't mention anything to Hanna.'

CHAPTER ELEVEN

All is quiet in the clinic that's actually a large suburban house converted for the purpose.

I'm in the sitting room where cushions, large and small, are casually strewn around the sofas and floor, and Ruby's dream-catchers are floating whimsically in front of the window. Billy's work boots have been abandoned in the fireplace, and a laptop computer is sitting open on the coffee table. I'm not sure where everyone is, although Riona is certain to be in her office.

It's been a stressful few days with Dr Francis here. She's still here, unfortunately, and she's no faint heart, that's for sure – quite unflappable, in fact. I've known her for a long time and actually I have a lot of admiration for her, although I have to admit I'm envious at times of her easy friendship with Riona. It helps that they share a profession, of course; it means they speak each other's language and have shared goals.

I want to tell them that if it weren't for me, neither of them would have a goal, but I don't because it's not strictly true.

'Please tell me why you won't speak to Dr Francis,' Riona said to me yesterday after the good doctor had popped out for a while.

'There's no need when you do the talking for me,' I told her, not archly, only truthfully.

'But it's you she wants to engage with. I can't always speak for you.'

I merely shrugged, although I could have said, 'Why not?'

Riona has a very gentle, rhythmical way of breathing when she waits for someone to speak. I held out longer, and eventually she said, 'You know Dr Francis is concerned about Billy.'

It wasn't really a question, so I didn't try to answer. Everyone's always concerned about Billy, apart from Billy himself, so what's new?

I could tell she was frustrated, but I took a decision long ago to let her deal with her feelings. I have enough of my own to cope with.

Things are different between us today; they always are after time passes. It's only the past that never changes. The cruel, immutable, intangible and debilitating past. The one in which my sister was ripped away from me and never came back.

I have to admit that the attempted regressions have been hard on me this week. I feel exhausted and not entirely sure how much I might be making up just to persuade the doctors they're making progress. Don't get me wrong, I appreciate their efforts and I'd be totally lost without them, but I'm relieved these intense and invasive sessions don't happen often.

There has been no mention of the photograph showing my mother's funeral and my sister at the heart of her family and friends. I don't want Dr Francis to know about it yet, and fortunately Riona seems to understand that.

I haven't looked at it for a while, but I will later, or tomorrow. It soothes me in a way I can't quite explain, maybe because it gives the impression of time standing still, holding everyone in place where I can easily find them.

I know all about most of them now.

CHAPTER TWELVE

'Jack, at last!' Hanna cried into the phone. 'I was beginning to think you'd never call me back.'

'Sorry,' he groaned, sounding tired. 'I put my damned phone down earlier and it's only just turned up again. Sorry I missed your calls. Are you OK? Where are you?'

'At the office,' she replied, 'and I've hit a midweek lull so I was thinking, if you're going to be down there in Devon until Friday, I could come and join you for a couple of days.'

With a pained groan, he said, 'At any other time that would be wonderful, but it's pretty crazy here. A lot of stress and tempers fraying. I'm hardly getting a minute to myself and my B&B's not quite up to your standard.'

'We could stay with Andee and Graeme, maybe? I know it's a bit of a drive from theirs to where you are . . .'

'Before you go on with that, Graeme's at the B&B with me and I believe Andee's in London helping her daughter move flat.'

Remembering that was true, Hanna said, 'OK, I guess I'll stay here. There's always plenty to do really, I was just . . . missing you, I suppose.'

His tone was tender as he said, 'Then maybe you'll be all the more pleased to see me when I get back?'

'Maybe,' she said lightly, 'but no promises.'

'OK. Is Leo home yet?'

'Tomorrow. His flight gets in at four.'

'Are you picking him up from the airport?'

'Probably.'

'And Cait? No news, I suppose.'

'She's in touch with Jenny, so I'm not panicking yet. Actually, I might give Jenny a call, see if she wants to meet for lunch now she's back from France.'

'OK. Before you go, you know Leo's coming to work for us soon, so have you considered wrapping things up in a . . . certain department?'

Feeling herself flush with both anger and embarrassment, she said, 'Of course.'

'Good. I'll call again later. Love you.'

Her mother-in-law's phone went to voicemail, so Hanna left her a message to call when she was free and returned to her computer, knowing she'd find plenty to do if she tried. None of it would involve Hugo Astor, though, because that was certainly being wrapped up, thank you Jack for the reminder.

She'd seen Astor earlier, in his office, when she'd returned the documents he'd left for her to sign the day before. She'd left his door wide open and had met his eyes as he'd regarded her from behind his desk with that all-knowing, superior smirk of his, as if telling her he knew why she was there and maybe she'd like to turn around and close the door. Instead, she'd spun on her heel and walked out again.

Was there something you wanted? he'd asked in an email a few minutes later.

She hadn't bothered to reply.

Picking up her mobile as it rang, expecting it to be Jenny, she saw it was Seb and quickly clicked on. 'One of my favourite people,' she told him warmly. 'I was hoping to hear from you before this. How did the wine-tasting go at the weekend?'

Sounding amused, he said, 'Yeah, great. I think. It seemed to, anyway.'

She waited. 'OK, I need more than that.'

With a laugh he said, 'You're as bad as Jack.'

'You mean you've talked to him and not me? I'm outraged.'

'Don't be, but if he hasn't already told you about our chat at the Albion on Monday, I'll tell you that being with her is . . . amazing,' and he laughed.

Loving how thrilled he sounded, she said, 'Am I allowed to ask if you went home together?'

Dryly he said, 'No, but you just did, so, what happened was that I dropped her at her place and carried on to mine on my own.'

'Oh.' Not what she'd expected, although it was still early days.

'The odd thing was,' he said, 'that she seemed to be . . . Well, I thought we were on the same page, so to speak, but maybe I just misread it.'

Understanding that he was asking for her advice, or at least her opinion, she said, 'Have you spoken to her since?'

'Only by text. She's got a busy week. The lead psychiatrist of their project is visiting, and apparently that's always pretty intense.'

'But she's still coming next Saturday?'

There was a smile in his voice as he said, 'She says she can't wait, so I guess that's a yes.'

Sensing how happy this was making him, she decided to cut right to it and said, 'Do you want me to prepare a room for you to stay over?'

There was a pause as he considered the offer.

Understanding the dilemma, she said, 'OK, you know the guest rooms are almost always ready to go, and you'll be welcome if you want to make use of one. Or two. Shall we say seven for drinks? Oh, and Jenny has decided to make your favourite dessert because she loves you so much.'

He laughed and, after they ended the call, Hanna sat thinking about how much Seb meant to them all as a family. Handsome, a little shy, madly intellectual . . . She'd always felt a strong bond with him, and a kind of protectiveness, especially when he'd been struggling to stay strong for Jilly. It was quite likely that his wife had no idea about the times he'd come to Lake House, often just for an hour or two, so he could let go in the privacy and safety of what he'd always considered his second home.

Although the initial intensity of his grief was over now, he was still vulnerable, even if he didn't want to admit it to himself, and the last thing Hanna wanted was to see him hurt again.

For a moment she toyed with the idea of calling Riona to see if she might be free for an impromptu lunch, but then remembering what Seb had said about an official visit to the clinic this week, she tried Jenny again instead.

An hour later, she was at a table in Chew Kitchen, checking emails as she waited for her mother-in-law to arrive. She was glad to be out of the office, since she didn't quite trust herself to be around Hugo Astor when the building was half-empty. Walking out on him this morning had been satisfying, enjoyable even; however it had proved almost nothing, for in spite of good sense trying to prevail, she couldn't deny how much she'd wanted him to come after her.

It really did have to stop; she was determined about that, and in fact it shouldn't be too difficult when she actually couldn't stand the man.

How contrary she was.

Spotting Jenny coming through the door, she waved and got up to greet her. At seventy-three, her mother-in-law was a picture of good health and natural-born elegance. Her tall, lithe figure, stylish cap of thick silvery hair and bright, almost youthful, green eyes still managed to turn heads and melted years off her age.

'Shall we choose first?' Jenny said as they settled down. 'A salmon salad, I think.'

'Same here. Now, let's get the boring stuff out of the way – did the plumber come to sort out your shower this morning?'

'He did. Actually, it's the bathroom Cait's using when she's there. All's fine now.'

Hanna grimaced. 'Maybe we should have left it as it was, she'd have had to bring Sofia back to the house then.'

Jenny shrugged. 'At least there are fewer . . . upsets, when she's with me.'

Unable to deny that, Hanna sighed and looked up as a server came to take their order.

'I keep hoping she'll grow out of this *phase*, as you like to call it,' she said when they were alone again, 'but it's been going on for so long now – and I still don't know *why* she hates us so much.'

'She doesn't hate you, she's just trying to work things out for herself . . .'

'And we could help. We *want* to help. Has she seen anything of Ishan lately?' This was Sofia's nineteen-year-old Indian father, who was with his family in Bristol for the summer before returning to Oxford for his second year of law studies. Hanna and Jack had a very real fondness for him, and were afraid that this was what had turned Cait against him. 'Please tell me he's in Wales with them?'

'I'm afraid I don't think he is. In fact, I rather get the impression she's got a crush on her host.'

Having suspected as much, Hanna said, 'Do you know anything about him?'

'Only that his name's Jaden and he's a musician.'

Hanna's heart sank. 'Any idea when she's intending to come back?'

'I'm sure it'll be soon.'

Hanna stared at her water glass and wished it was full of wine. 'You know, Jack's threatening to cut off her allowance in order to try and force her to do something sensible with her life?'

Jenny's eyebrows rose. 'I don't think that would end well.'

'Exactly what I said. He didn't mean it, anyway. He just gets as frustrated with her as I do.'

Jenny regarded her sympathetically, and shook out her napkin. 'Tell me, how is my stepson? Back in Appledore?'

Hanna nodded and sighed. 'He sounded quite stressed when I spoke to him earlier, but at least he promised to be home by Friday.'

'That's good, so we're still on for dinner on Saturday. Florina was asking this morning how many we're going to be. I need to know too, if I'm doing dessert.'

'I'll find out if Leo's going to join us. If he does we'll be six.'

'*Bon.* I'm actually quite excited to meet Seb's new girl-friend. Riona, is that right?'

Hanna nodded. 'He seems quite keen already. I just hope she feels the same because he really doesn't need any more heartbreak.' The mere thought of it triggered all the instinctive protectiveness she felt towards him.

'You know very well that Seb's impossible not to love,' Jenny reminded her.

Hanna smiled to think of how true that was. Sighing she said, 'I just wish you could meet someone—'

Jenny's hand went up. 'No more of that, thank you,' she scolded gently. 'As I've told you before, I loved David with all my heart, but one husband is enough, I think.' Her eyes twinkled playfully. 'To be honest, I am starting to enjoy my freedom. I am only sorry that your dear mother is no longer around for me to enjoy it with. She was a very successful single woman – you have to agree. I was always so full of admiration for her, and affection too, of course. I miss her very much, and I know you do too.'

It was true; her mother's death had hit Hanna hard, in spite of how difficult their relationship had been at times. Catherine Edwards had never been known as an easy woman. Professional, yes; inspirational to her students, certainly; and it went without saying that she'd been adored by many of her tiny patients and their parents. But as far as Hanna knew, she'd always kept her colleagues at arm's length, and though she must have had plenty of male admirers, Hanna couldn't recall her bringing a single one home.

Deciding now was as good a time as any to ask, she said, 'Was there ever a man in her life that she didn't tell me about? You two were such good friends, I'm sure she'd have told you if there was.'

Jenny shook her head as she thought. 'She never mentioned anyone,' she said, 'but she was a very attractive woman, so I would be surprised if there was no one. She was so young when your father died, too young to be on her own for so long, but as you know, *chérie*, she was never comfortable discussing affairs of the heart.'

She'd never been keen on dealing with emotions at all. 'Did she ever tell you anything about my father?' Hanna asked, in spite of already knowing the answer.

'She'd talk about him sometimes. He was a doctor too, I think ten or more years older than her, but you know this.'

'And he left us not long before the heart attack that killed him.'

'I believe this is true.'

'We fell out of love,' her mother had told her once, 'it happens, I'm afraid. You'll find that out for yourself when you're older.'

Hanna could only feel thankful that the prophecy had proved groundless, at least in her mother's lifetime, for the last thing she'd ever wanted to hear was the kind of heartless *I told you so* that Catherine had been so capable of.

CHAPTER THIRTEEN

Billy was shouting at Riona earlier, telling her she shouldn't go out this evening, that it's not a good time to leave me. I didn't hear Riona's reply – she's always softly spoken – but I know she won't give in to him. I don't want her to. She has to have her life and it won't help any of us to try to get in her way.

If we do, she might leave us, and none of us wants that.

When she goes out, she uses the side gate and, though she must feel she's being watched, she doesn't look back. She's wearing a sleeveless white lace top and navy, wide-legged pants. She's slender and elegant, contained in a quiet and dignified way; the kind of person people want to know simply because she's calm and gracious and never judge-mental.

Her laughter is like music for a troubled soul.

She's just how I imagine my sister to be.

I hope she has a nice time this evening. She deserves to after the week she's had.

CHAPTER FOURTEEN

Seb's eyes lit with pleasure as he drove round the corner of Riona's street to find her standing beneath a full-leafed rowan tree, a vision in a simple white top and navy trousers. She looked sensational, and he felt ludicrously proud to know that she was waiting for him.

'No taxi this evening?' she commented as he pulled his quirky old Porsche 365 to a stop beside her.

Quickly going to help her in to the passenger side, he said, 'I hope you don't mind travelling vintage style. You look beautiful, by the way.'

Her eyes smiled into his as she sank into the old leather seat and took the seatbelt he was handing her. 'Thank you,' she said softly, 'and may I say that you're looking extremely handsome yourself.'

He gave a laugh, half-pleasure, half-embarrassment. He wasn't used to compliments; however, he might have earned this one, for he'd changed several times before finally deciding on beige linen trousers, loose-fitting white linen shirt (cuffs turned back over his forearms) and Birkenstock Montanas sans socks.

'I'm afraid there's no air-con,' he grimaced as he folded himself in behind the wheel, 'but with the roof off I don't think that'll be a problem. Do you mind the roof being open?'

'No, not at all,' she declared. 'It's a wonderful car. So different, and . . . stylish.' She turned to look at him. 'Like you I guess,' she teased, and he felt heat in his cheeks as he smiled into her eyes.

'I've missed you this week,' he dared to say as they drove away. Then quickly added, 'Have things calmed down for you now?'

'Yes, thank goodness. It was quite a trial at times, but I'm hoping some good has come from it. And I missed you too. I'm sorry I couldn't see you. Well, I probably could have, but it would have been so snatched . . .'

'Please don't apologize. You're here now, and everyone's looking forward to seeing you. Actually, I should have said before we left that we're invited to stay the night if you'd like to. I realize you don't have anything with you, but we can easily turn around . . .'

'No, please don't do that.' She put a hand on his as though to soften her words. 'As much as I'd love to stay over, I'm afraid I'll have to get back. I can't escape my patients for an entire night, much as I might like to. But don't worry, there's no need to drive me. I'll call a taxi . . .'

'Of course I'll drive you.'

'But then you won't be able to have a drink. No, my mind is made up, I'll take a taxi back.'

He didn't argue, and nor, disappointed as he might be, was he going to let it put a dampener on the evening. He was simply going to carry on being thrilled that she was with him on this wonderful summer's evening, about to share a few relaxing hours with his closest friends.

*

Hanna was in a great mood. The wine was helping, of course, one of her and Jack's favourite Chardonnays, but – even before they'd opened the first bottle of the evening – she'd been feeling good about the way life was going right now, Cait notwithstanding.

To her surprise, Jack had returned from Devon earlier than expected yesterday, and had taken her out for a fish-and-chip supper at Salt & Malt, just the two of them. Leo, now back from Italy, would have joined them if he hadn't already made plans to catch up with friends, which was kind of good, because usually when one of the children was around the conversation became all about them.

After filling her in on the frustrations and small break-throughs in the Appledore project, it hadn't taken Jack long to get round to asking if she'd had any more 'encounters' with Hugo Astor while he'd been away.

She'd countered with, 'Tell me first about Dionne Shore.'

His eyebrows rose in surprise. 'You know I haven't seen her in months. The MOD moved her off the project and . . . that was that.'

'So no contact since?'

He shook his head.

'And no one to replace her?'

'On the project, yes, but he's not my type.'

She laughed and he sighed as he glanced at his phone. Seeming uninterested in the message, he picked up his glass and gazed out of the window. A single boat was drifting along the lake in the twilight, pursued by a small gulp of cormorants.

'Jack?' she prompted.

He turned to her.

'Are you OK?' she asked. 'You seem distracted.'

He appeared surprised. 'Never better,' he assured her. 'Just tired, I guess.' His eyes narrowed slightly, as if he was about to say something, but his phone buzzed again and he took a brief call from the foreman at the North Devon site.

He didn't mention Hugo Astor again, which she was quite relieved about, for she didn't want to lie and say it was all at an end when it actually wasn't. Nor did she want to tell him how Astor, during a brief moment yesterday when they'd passed on the stairs, had asked her to forget wearing underwear to the office on Monday. She had to confess she liked the idea of it; however, it was hardly going to bring things to a conclusion if she went along with it, so she probably wouldn't.

Now, this Saturday evening, she was sitting at one end of the table in their outdoor dining area, where candles in large bulb glasses blended with the subtle glow of the gazebo lamps to bathe everyone in a romantic hue. More lights were secreted around the gardens, inside shrubs, woven through branches, although none was shining brightly yet, for the sun had only just begun to set. The air was balmy, scented by grass, warm earth and climbing roses; the lake was beginning to reflect the orange and lemon hues of the sky.

As everyone tucked into Florina's delicious starter of scallops with chorizo and hazelnut picada, Hanna watched Jack at the other end of the table, apparently enjoying getting to know Riona. Jenny was joining in the conversation while, either side of Hanna, Seb and Leo were chatting about some band Leo had been to see while in Perugia. It was wonderful how relaxed and happy everyone looked, as though they'd known one another for ever – which of course they had, apart from Riona. However, she was fitting in so well, and she really was quite lovely, Hanna reflected. No wonder Seb could hardly keep his eyes off her. She just hoped Jack didn't take the flirtation too far, something he was apt to do when the wine was flowing freely, if only to wind up Seb.

Would she mind if Jack slept with Riona?

Actually, she would, and not only for Seb. She had the feeling that Riona, with her glorious coppery-red hair, sleepy eyes and sensuous smile, was the kind of woman a man could get serious about, and that was the last thing any of them needed.

She looked up as Florina came to clear the plates.

'Ah, this is like *A Midsummer Night's Dream*.' The house-keeper smiled teasingly.

Hanna's eyebrows rose: two men falling in love with the same woman? While she . . . what? Fell for Astor in an ass's head?

She almost laughed.

With a hand pressed to her heart, Riona said, 'Will you just look at the sunset? It's simply stunning.'

Everyone turned to gaze across the lake to where the horizon was a wash of colour. As Jack got up to refill the glasses, Leo said, 'We arranged it specially for you.'

Riona laughed with delight – and to Hanna's surprise she didn't stop, though it surely wasn't that funny.

'I'm sorry,' Riona apologized, recovering herself, 'I'm not used to drinking and I've probably had too much already.'

'As have we all.' Jenny smiled, raising her glass.

'And you've had a tough week,' Seb reminded her, 'so it's good to let go.'

Riona's eyes were soft and glassy as she smiled at him.

Jenny said, 'Please tell us more about you, Riona. It's obvious from your accent that you're Irish, so have you been in Bristol for long?'

Riona regarded her curiously for a moment, as if she'd said something unusual, or surprising. Jenny's smile started to falter, until Riona said cheerily, 'No, not very long, but I must say I'm already quite attached to it.'

'Riona's a psychiatrist,' Seb announced for Leo's benefit. 'She runs a clinic in Westbury-on-Trym.'

'Cool,' Leo responded, raising his glass to Riona.

Raising hers too, she said, 'It is just a small clinic where we're pioneering immersive therapies to treat a certain type of behavioural disorder. It's all quite innovative, and very interesting. I'm quite honoured to be a part of it.'

'Do tell us more,' Hanna encouraged when she stopped.

Looking around the table, as if concerned this might not be scintillating dinner party chat, Riona continued a little more tentatively as she said, 'My colleague – superior, actually – Dr Emilia Francis, and her team – they're based in the States – have secured research funding for a disorder of the mind brought on by early trauma. I was contacted about eighteen months ago and I didn't have to think twice about joining the project. It's a very different approach to the treatment of mental illness than most of us are used to.'

Leo said, 'In what way different?'

Appearing pleased to be asked, Riona said, 'Well to begin with I, as a therapist, am living at the clinic with my patients. Hence the immersive nature of the scheme. We don't have organized sessions, as such, we just talk and live as any other group of single adults might. Of course I am constantly observing them, gathering information for the paper Dr

Francis is preparing for our sponsors, and of course for peer review. I'm her eyes and ears on the ground, so to speak, but my main role is to be there in case any of our patients should experience a difficult episode.'

Looking both fascinated and worried, Jenny said, 'What does "a difficult episode" mean?'

Riona smiled. 'Much the same as for any of us really. Some days are good, others are more of a challenge. With our patients, because of their history, they can occasionally react in slightly more extreme ways.'

'Does that mean they're dangerous?' Leo wanted to know, clearly more fascinated by the minute.

Riona laughed. 'If they were, they wouldn't be able to take part in the trial. They're just individuals who need a little extra support, and the main aim of our treatment is to get them feeling capable and confident enough to deal with life in ways we generally accept to be normal.'

'And one man's idea of normal is another's of crazy,' Jack joked.

Hanna threw him a look. To Riona she said, 'Do you live with them twenty-four/seven? The clinic is actually your home as well?'

'For the time being,' Riona replied, 'but I do get time off, such as this evening and the odd day here and there.'

'And they're OK to be left?' Leo asked doubtfully.

'They certainly are. It isn't an institution and they're not prisoners. They come and go as they please, and so far no one has got into trouble.' She leaned in conspiratorially. 'They're always quite fascinated by my life, I guess much as we all used to be with our teachers' lives when we were at school.'

Wickedly, Hanna said, 'Do they know about Seb?'

81

Riona's eyes filled with mirth as they went to him. 'One or two of them do,' she confirmed. 'In fact, it was Ruby, our resident computer geek and sometime Cupid, who found him on the dating site and brought him to my attention.' She added softly, 'I'm very glad she did.'

Enjoying the way Seb almost blushed, Hanna choked back a laugh as Jack said, 'What were you doing on a dating site, mate? Never had it down as your kind of stomping ground.'

'Look to your son,' Seb told him. 'He did it all, from the photo to the profile. Frankly, even I'd have dated me by the time he was done.'

'This I have to see,' Jack declared, reaching for his phone.

'Not now,' Hanna scolded. 'Anyway, he's probably taken it down since meeting Riona?' She looked meaningfully at Seb.

'He has,' Leo confirmed, 'I checked earlier,' he informed his godfather with a cheeky grin. 'Sad that my great work is no longer available, but I'm thinking of hiring myself out as a profiler.'

'We'll be sure to warn the FBI,' Jack commented.

'Very funny,' Leo retorted.

'Going back to your work,' Jenny said to Riona. 'It sounds so . . . fascinating.'

'You mentioned early trauma just now,' Leo said, 'does that mean your patients are victims of abuse?'

'I'm afraid so in most cases,' Riona replied.

'Oh, isn't this sweet?'

They all looked up to find a sassy teenager dressed in torn jeans and a tight cropped top sauntering on to the terrace, and regarding them all with as much scorn as amusement. Her long, ragged hair was purple and black, her blue eyes thickly rimmed in liner and the piercings in lip, nostril, eyebrows and ears were delicate and almost pretty in comparison to the thick pewter choker around her neck.

'Cait,' Hanna said with an anxious glance at Jack. 'Where's Sofia?'

Ignoring the question, Cait said to Leo, 'When did you get back?'

'Thursday,' he replied. 'Where's my niece?'

'I dropped her at Ishan's. He's been on my case about seeing more of her, so I thought he could have her for the weekend.' Her eyes widened as she looked back at her mother. 'Don't worry, I'm sure if he finds any needle marks in her arms, he'll let you know.'

'Have you been drinking, Cait?' Hanna asked, glancing awkwardly at Riona. 'Please tell me you didn't drive drunk?'

Cait rolled her eyes. 'Ishan dropped me, OK? God, why do you have to make a drama out of everything?'

'Cait,' Jack said, 'if you want to join us . . .'

'No thanks. Hey, Seb, how's tricks?'

'They're good thanks,' he replied. 'Can I introduce a friend of mine, Riona Byrne.'

Cait regarded the newcomer with interest. 'Hey,' she said. 'Nice to meet you.'

'Likewise,' Riona said softly. 'I'm guessing you're Jack and Hanna's daughter.'

'That would be me,' she replied, making Hanna wince with her mimicry of the Irish accent, 'although I'm considering divorcing them. That's a thing,' she said to her father, 'in case you didn't know.'

'Darling,' Jenny said, 'why don't you sit down with us—'

'Sorry, Grandma, not my scene. You've got no shame,

you people, hanging out here in all your privilege while kids are going hungry out there with nowhere to live . . . You make out like you care, with all your *philanthropy*—'

'Spare us the lecture,' Jack interrupted, getting to his feet.

Cait took a step back. 'Don't you dare touch me,' she warned.

Astonished, he said, 'I'm fetching the wine. I'd offer you a glass, but as this isn't *your scene*, perhaps you'd like to go somewhere that is.'

She looked at her mother again and began shaking her head in what looked like pity. 'I don't know how you do it,' she said. 'Why do you stay with him?'

'Cait,' Leo groaned.

'You're blind,' she shouted at her mother. 'Blind to everything . . .'

Leo stood up. 'Come on. I'll take you over to Grandma's. Are you still staying there?'

'Sure. No way would I be staying here with all the lies and pretence and disgusting—'

'Cait, just stop,' he interrupted, taking her by the arm.

'Oooh, being told off by my big brother now,' she mocked, as he steered her back into the house. 'Please don't get like them, Leo. You're too good for all this crap.'

After they'd gone, there was an awkward silence before Jack and Hanna began apologizing together.

'Please, don't be sorry,' Riona interrupted. 'She's obviously not in a great place right now. It happens to a lot of teenagers.'

'Tell me about it,' Jack muttered. 'And she might have an excuse if she'd ever suffered the way your patients—'

'Jack,' Hanna interrupted.

He looked at her in surprise.

'That's not really appropriate,' Hanna told him, wishing the last few minutes could be erased. To Riona she said, 'As you can see, she's quite angry with us, and we've yet to get to the bottom of why. However, it's not a subject for this evening, so shall we move on to something a little more cheerful? Why don't you tell us where you're from in Ireland?'

For the next hour or more as the main course of braised chicken legs, grapes and fennel was served, the conversation flowed freely and lightly, moving from the west of Ireland, Riona's birthplace, to Dublin where she'd attended university. It was a city Jack and Seb had some experience of, thanks to many raucous student and bachelor trips, and they were never shy about reminiscing. Jenny and Hanna had heard it all before, but Riona was apparently delighted by the much-exaggerated accounts, and actually seemed to glow each time she looked at Seb.

Jack opened a dessert wine as Florina brought in six tall glasses filled with luscious strawberry zabaglione, made by Jenny, and they all laughed as Seb swooned.

'There is an extra one for you,' Florina told him. 'I keep one back in fridge for Leo.'

'There goes the diet,' Seb groaned. 'I'll need to work this off . . . Leo!' he cried as Leo returned, 'you'll let me beat you at tennis in the morning, won't you?'

'No way! I'm out of here at seven.'

'You are?' Hanna asked.

'Olivia got back from Spain about an hour ago,' he explained, referring to his girlfriend whose family lived in Dorset. 'I'm driving down there first thing. I'll head straight from Dorset to Appledore on Tuesday to start work with

Dad.' He grinned at his father and Jack couldn't have looked prouder if he'd tried.

'Do you play tennis?' Jenny asked Riona.

'Actually, I was team captain when I was at school,' Riona admitted. 'I even won trophies, but I haven't played in a very long time.'

'Then you must,' Hanna insisted. 'I have plenty of whites . . . Maybe we could do doubles?'

'That would be lovely, but I'm afraid not tomorrow.' She glanced at Seb.

'I should have told you when we arrived that Riona can't stay,' he explained, 'although I kind of hoped she might change her mind?'

'I'd love to,' she assured him, 'but I'm afraid it's not possible. In fact I should probably see about calling a taxi. Do you have a number?' she asked Hanna.

'Yes, of course,' Hanna replied, 'but are you sure we can't persuade you?'

'I wish you could, but I have to honour my responsibilities. I've had a wonderful evening, though.'

'I feel bad for not driving you,' Seb said as Jack got through to a local company.

'I'd feel a lot worse if you did,' Riona informed him. 'This way, we've both been able to have a drink.' To Hanna, she said, 'You have a beautiful home and I've enjoyed the evening immensely.'

Ten minutes later, as Jack released the main gates to let the taxi in, they all got up to say their goodbyes.

'It's been a pleasure seeing you again,' Riona said to Hanna, embracing her warmly and for so long that Hanna was forced to take a step away. 'Sorry,' Riona laughed, 'typical me, overdoing it again. I haven't had a chance to talk to you about donating to one of your causes, but I'd very much like to.'

'That would be wonderful,' Hanna assured her. 'Why don't you come into the office one day this week? Just let me know when works for you.'

'I will.' She turned to Jack. 'I've so enjoyed getting to know you a little, Seb's oldest friend.'

'But not as old as him,' Jack quipped.

'By three months,' Seb informed her.

After she'd embraced Jack and Jenny, Seb walked her outside, leaving the others to retake their seats.

'Well,' Jenny said with an exaggerated sigh as she picked up her glass. 'She's certainly pretty.'

Hanna smiled.

'I like her,' Jack stated, topping up his glass.

'Yeah, she's cool,' Leo agreed. 'I know you won't like me saying this, Mum, but maybe we could ask her to have a chat with Cait . . .'

'She's a psychiatrist, not a psychologist,' Hanna pointed out irritably. 'And anyway, there's nothing wrong with Cait.'

'If you ask me, there's everything wrong with Cait,' Jack argued.

'But she's hardly in the same category as Riona's patients. And besides, she's a new friend, someone we don't really know, so hardly in a position to ask favours of. And Seb is interested in her, so let's stop trying to make this about us and our issues, shall we? How was Cait when you left her?' she asked Leo.

He shrugged. 'As OK as she ever is, I guess.'

'I hope she didn't have any more to drink.'

'She couldn't find anything.'

'I cleared it all out when she moved in with me,' Jenny told him.

'But she'll be smoking weed,' Jack sighed. 'I already feel like I can smell it. Did you see her with any?'

Leo held up a hand. 'I'm not getting into any more of this. She's eighteen and can do as she likes—'

'Not in my house, she can't,' his father interrupted. 'Not when it comes to drugs.'

'Which is why she's at Grandma's . . .'

'I don't allow it,' Jenny protested.

'You're not there right now,' Hanna pointed out. She was checking the time. 'I can't help feeling afraid of how much was smoked while she was in Wales and how can it not have affected Sofia? I wonder if it's too late to call Ishan to make sure she's all right.'

'It probably is,' Jenny said as Seb came back, looking extremely pleased with himself.

'She's something else, isn't she?' he declared, going for the brandy.

'She certainly is,' Jack agreed. 'Just don't fuck it up.'

'Jack!' Hanna protested.

Jack shrugged and went to clap a hand on Seb's shoulder. 'No offence. She's a lovely woman, so she is – and before Han gets on my case again, I apologize for that terrible Irish accent!'

CHAPTER FIFTEEN

I'm with Riona, strolling across the Downs. She's wearing a long white dress fluttering about her calves, and her magnificent hair is tumbling from the confines of a large floppy hat. The sun is warm and inviting, the grass all shades of green, and the trees seem almost secretive in their stillness.

She is being secretive, the way only she can, but we all know she was with Seb last evening.

I think she'd have liked to escape us again today, but we're trailing along in her wake and she's too kind – and professional – to tell us to go away. We all want to know more about the dinner, but I don't think she'll confide in the others – I'm not even sure if she will in me.

Hayley, of course, wants to know if she and Seb had sex. I hope she doesn't ask; her crassness makes me cringe, and I know Riona doesn't appreciate it much either.

Naturally, I want to ask about Hanna, how she looked, what she said, if she wants to meet up with Riona again? I think it must have gone well, judging by how happy Riona seems this morning. I wonder if Hanna's children were there, Leo and Caitlin, and Caitlin's baby daughter, Sofia.

Earlier, over breakfast, Billy tried to make her tell us about the house. 'Is it amazing?' he asked.

Riona simply said, 'It has a beautiful view of the lake.'

I can tell she doesn't want to engage with any of us and I try not to feel offended; after all, I'm not like the others. I have a level of understanding that goes far beyond theirs, an awareness of feelings and situations that almost always escapes them.

Eventually Riona spreads a blanket on the grass and sits down, gazing around at nearby picknickers and ball-players. She turns suddenly at the sound of Billy shouting, and seems embarrassed. But there's nothing to be alarmed about. He's brought along an old baseball bat that a previous owner left behind at the house and he wants us all to play.

It's too hot, so we ignore him.

Riona takes out her phone. I can see there are text messages from Seb, and for a while she occupies herself with reading them before replying. Apparently he's going to be in London for the first part of the coming week so she won't be able to see him. She's disappointed, that much is clear, but it's not as if she isn't busy herself.

I want to urge her to set up a lunch with Hanna, but I know it's best not to say anything while the others are nearby.

Actually, I'm starting to wonder how much I can trust Riona. I've told her everything about me, literally everything, but lately I'm getting the sense she's holding back on me.

I don't think that's quite fair.

CHAPTER SIXTEEN

After parking on the short drive in front of his house, Seb took his holdall from the back of the car, locked up and started to the front door. It was Wednesday evening, so he was back earlier than expected from London, and the best part of that was the fact that he'd be sleeping in his own bed tonight.

He and Jilly had moved into this place thirteen years ago, and it hadn't taken them long to love it almost as if it were a living, breathing member of the family. With its grand Victorian façade, characterful rooms and sunken, sheltered back garden, it was situated midway between Clifton village and the Downs, close enough to the university to allow him to walk to work when the weather was good. Jilly, who'd been an associate professor in French literature, had walked with him when their schedules allowed; for a long time after she'd gone, he'd been unable to face it alone.

Returning to an empty place hadn't been easy either, nor had sleeping in their bed, eating alone at their kitchen table, or working in his study, knowing she'd never be nearby again. Life itself had stopped making sense for quite some time, and yet he'd never once wanted to leave their beloved home. It wouldn't only feel as though he was abandoning a dear old friend; it would feel as though he was abandoning Jilly too. She was still here in so many ways that mattered.

Pushing his key into the lock, he made himself think of Riona and how much he'd like to bring her here. Though they'd never properly discussed Jilly, he felt certain she'd understand how deep a love he had felt for his wife – still did – without feeling competitive or threatened. She simply didn't strike him as the type to harbour futile jealousies over a dead woman. She exuded empathy and under-standing, not surprising really, given what she did.

Jilly would have liked her, he was certain of that, and the feeling would have been mutual.

Dropping his keys on the hall table, he picked up the mail that Mrs Green, the cleaner, must have stacked there, and began sorting through it as he carried on along the mosaic tiled hall to the kitchen. As he passed the staircase he paused and glanced up to the next landing. He couldn't be sure what had caught his attention, only that something had, and he found himself wondering if Mrs Green was still here. It wasn't her day, and she never came at this time; nevertheless he called out, 'Hello! Mrs G. Are you up there?'

The house remained silent and, shrugging to himself, he went on through to put the kettle on, as if he might actu-ally have a cup of tea when he knew he'd pour himself a Scotch before the water came to a boil. He'd been invited to take part in a Zoom call at seven to discuss the consul-tation process he and several colleagues from other universities had endured over the past few days with a cross-party Social Welfare Advisory Committee. Jack's local MP had been the chair, an odious, self-opinionated indi-vidual who unfailingly managed to rub Seb up the wrong way. He had exactly the same effect on Jack, who was already mounting a campaign to get the insufferable bigot ousted at the next election. Seb was already looking forward to sharing some of the MP's most cringeworthy moments with his old friend when they were next together.

As he turned from the kettle he came to a stop, puzzled by what he was seeing. A single dinner plate was on the table and he couldn't imagine – unless it was broken, which it wasn't – why Mrs Green would have put it there. He noticed then that one of the dining chairs had been backed up towards the range, as if someone had left in a hurry. Of course he might well have left it like that himself, but it was surprising that Mrs G hadn't tucked it back under the table.

He moved forward, getting the distinct feeling that someone had been here, presumably since yesterday morning when Mrs Green would have cleaned.

For no earthly reason, the lad who'd accosted Jack at the Albion last Monday shot to his mind. Marius, that was his name. But what on earth would he be doing here, and how would he have got in? More to the point, why would he even want to get in? Seb had no argument with him, had never even seen him before that night, and unless he'd followed Seb home prior to Seb going for dinner, he would have no idea where Seb lived.

He dismissed the thought and reminded himself that both his godchildren, Leo and Cait, had keys to the place and often dropped in on nights when they'd had a few too many to drive home. Or if they just wanted somewhere to crash for a while before meeting friends.

Going back to the hall he shouted, 'Leo! Cait! Are you up there?'

No answer.

Taking the stairs two at a time, he checked the mostly unused formal sitting room first, then the guest bedroom and bathroom, and last of all his study.

All three rooms were exactly as they should be.

He continued up to the next level to find the door of the master suite half-open. Since this wasn't unusual, he barely remarked it, and going in, he looked around. Nothing seemed out of place, and the bathroom and dressing room were much as he'd expect them to be as well. He couldn't put his finger on why he thought someone other than Mrs G had been in the house, he just did, so taking his phone from his pocket, he called Leo.

'Hey!' Leo cried cheerily into his phone when he answered. 'Are you still in London?'

'No, I just got back,' Seb replied, returning to the bedroom. 'Have you been in while I was away? No problem if you have, I just—'

'I've been in Appledore with Dad since yesterday. On my way back now. How did it go with the committee?'

'Oh yeah, it was OK. To be honest I prefer doing these things by Zoom. Less hassle and you don't have to be in the same room as all the idiots. Is Dad with you?'

'No, he's staying on at the MOD site until Friday.'

'So your new job's underway?'

'You could say that. I'll be at the Clifton office tomorrow, starting with the planners. In at the grass roots, as they say. Any chance you're around later in the day?'

'I'll check my schedule and get back to you.'

'Sure thing. Are you OK? You sound kind of . . .'

'I'm good. Well, actually, I think someone might have been in the house while I was away . . .'

'You mean like a break-in?'

'No. Well, maybe. I'll check to see if there's any sign of one, or if anything's missing. I'll text you about tomorrow.'

After ringing off, he went back downstairs and took a thorough look around, but could find nothing to suggest a suspicious entry.

He looked at the photo of Jilly he kept on the kitchen dresser, as if she might have the answer. Of course it told him nothing, apart from how happy she'd been when he'd taken the shot.

His mind went to Riona. He'd like to call her, tell her about this strangeness, get her take on it, but his mobile rang at that moment and, seeing it was Hanna, he clicked on.

'Seb, Leo's just told me someone might have broken into your house,' she said, sounding worried. 'Have you called the police?'

Dryly, he said, 'I think that would be an overreaction.' He put the plate away and went through to the drinks cupboard in the living-room extension of the kitchen to pour himself a Scotch. 'I'm trying to remember if I told someone they could stay here and ended up forgetting about it,' he said.

'What makes you think someone was there?' she asked.

As he told her about the plate and chair, starting to feel foolish now, he became aware of an old memory stirring . . . He couldn't quite get hold of it, but there was something . . .

'Well, I know Mrs Green was there at her usual time yesterday,' Hanna said, 'because her car was outside when I went past.' After a beat she added, 'If someone was there after that, it sounds as though they let themselves in with a key. Who has keys to your place?'

Frowning as he thought he said, 'Apart from me, Mrs G, Leo, Cait and you, no one.'

'Unless, as you say, you gave them to someone and forgot about it.'

He took a mouthful of Scotch, and suddenly the old memory focused. 'You know, there was a spate of pranks a few years ago, when Bristol's answer to the Bullingdon Club decided to break into lecturers' houses . . . If I remember correctly, they moved things around to let the owner know they'd been there, just to spook them, I guess, and left again. Maybe there's some sort of revival. Anyway, let's forget it. I hear Jack's away until Friday.'

'Unless he can get back sooner. I'm meeting Riona tomorrow – did she tell you? She's coming in to talk donations.'

Enjoying the thought of Riona making friends with one of his favourite people, he said, 'Yes, she mentioned it when we spoke earlier. She said she'll be glad to get away from the clinic for a couple of hours. It sounds as though it's been pretty full on for her again this week.'

'I can't imagine it's anything else when you're dealing with mental health issues. Speaking of which,' she went on soberly, 'Cait's gone AWOL again.'

'Oh no. Since when?'

'The weekend. Sofia's still with Ishan, so at least we don't have to worry about her, but heaven knows where Caitlin is.'

'You know she'll come back. She always does.'

With a sigh, Hanna said, 'You're right. Now, are you sure you don't want one of us to come over? Or why don't you come here? It's Florina's night off so Jenny's cooking.'

'As irresistible as that sounds, I've got a lot to catch up

on after being away. And please don't worry. Like I said, I'm sure students are behind it.'

'In spite of them all having gone home for the summer?'

This was a good point, but not one he was going to pursue with Hanna now that the mysterious Marius had flipped back into his mind.

CHAPTER SEVENTEEN

'. . . *depersonalization is a frequently documented symptom of this disorder and is one of two factors of pathological . . .'*

I ask Riona to stop. I don't want to hear about her report to Dr Francis just now. I have other, more pressing things on my mind. Can't she at least sense that, even if she doesn't know it?

I expect her to be annoyed by my interruption, but she seems only curious.

I debate what to tell her.

I have to be honest, I'm having some troubling doubts about her, but I don't feel comfortable mentioning it. It's no good trying to second-guess what she might say – I could get it right, but I don't always, and you know what it's like when you think someone's on your wavelength and they turn out not to be. A lot of confusion and misunderstanding ensues.

Actually, I'm becoming increasingly bothered by her apparent urgency to assess and analyse my so-called psychoses; to 'move me forward', to quote her. It's as if her assessment is all it will take to untangle me from my past.

Or maybe she's just in a hurry to get on with her future.

I decide our early morning meeting is over and start to leave.

She calls me back – I knew she would. I consider not responding, but in the end I tell her, 'You can write as many reports as you like, and read them all out to me, but it won't change the fact that you're allowing your priorities to overtake mine.'

I don't add that she's become all about Seb, while all that matters to me is my sister, but I know she gets the message. She's probably hurt by it, but as I've mentioned before, she has to deal with her own feelings. I have plenty of my own to cope with.

CHAPTER EIGHTEEN

'Annanannana!'

Hanna turned from unloading the dishwasher, breaking into a smile as baby Sofia toddled towards her at speed, crying, 'Ananana!'

'My angel.' Hanna laughed, sweeping her granddaughter up and pressing kisses to her silky soft cheek. 'I've missed you.'

Sofia chortled gleefully while grabbing Hanna's cheeks and blowing a raspberry on her mouth.

Happier to see this child than she ever was to see anyone, Hanna glanced at the door where Cait, as sullen and unkempt as ever, was busy texting on her phone.

'When did you get back?' Hanna asked the toddler, though the question was of course for Cait.

She received no reply, but all that mattered was that they were both in one piece and Cait at least appeared to be sober. At eight in the morning, she damned well should be.

'So did you have a lovely time with Daddy?' she said to Sofia, who'd started to bounce in her arms with all the joy her little soul could muster.

'Annannana,' Sofia gurgled. Her baby-soft curls were the same inky black as Ishan's, her delicate, dusky skin was his too, but the stunning violet blue of her eyes was all her mother's.

'Where have you been for the past two nights?' she asked Cait, knowing even as the words left her lips, snippy and impatient, that she should have started with, 'It's lovely to have you back.'

Cait scowled, but didn't look up. 'What's it to you?' she said shortly.

Hanna was thinking of Seb's possible intruder, while not actually believing it had been Cait. She said, 'Please excuse me for minding about you. I try not to, but it seems to happen anyway.'

'You're hilarious,' Cait responded distractedly. Apparently finishing a text, she looked up, 'If you must know, I've been at Ishan's.' To Sofia she added, 'I was missing my girl, wasn't I?'

Hanna's heart flipped and melted all at once. It was the only time she saw Cait at her best, when she was talking to Sofia. Thank God there was some place left in her that wasn't all curdled up with hostility and resentment.

'Is he here?' Hanna asked hopefully. Relations between her and Cait usually went better when Sofia's father was around.

'No, he dropped us ten minutes ago. I'm sure he'd have come in for breakfast if he'd known you were lurking.'

Lurking? In her own house? Sometimes this was all too difficult.

'Speaking of lurking,' Cait continued, 'I saw that vile Marius when I was coming in. His sister's not working here again, is she?'

'No,' Hanna replied, unsettled by the prospect of that disturbing boy being in the vicinity again. She'd thought he'd gone for good when his sister left; certainly she hadn't seen him since, but she'd heard through the grapevine that he was living near Newton St Loe with his mother and sister (who'd apparently had a child). So he wasn't exactly local. 'Where was he exactly?' she asked, glancing out of the window, as though he might actually be out there watching them.

'He was hanging around by the gates on his motorbike. He took off when he saw us.' Settling Sofia into a high chair with a raspberry yoghurt and plastic spoon, Cait said, 'So, where's Dad?'

Hanna turned back from the window. 'He's not here right now.'

'No shit Sherlock!'

'He's working away for a few days. If you want to call him . . .'

'He's always away.'

'How would you know that when you're hardly here yourself? And he isn't . . . Actually, I'm not getting into this. I need to leave . . .'

'Sure. As soon as I come on the scene, you've always got somewhere else to be.'

Biting her tongue, Hanna said, 'Time's ticking on and, unlike you, I have a job . . .'

'Oh, lovely! Should have seen that one coming. Mummy's very important – but only because Daddy gave her job – while little Caitie is a no-hoper who's screwed up every opportunity she's been given.'

'Annanana,' Sofia chipped in, sounding more unsure than jubilant this time.

Echoing her, Hanna pressed a kiss to her yoghurty face, saying, 'My little angel. Ananana loves you more than anything . . .'

'Definitely more than her own daughter,' Caitlin sniped.

Hanna looked at her despairingly, causing Cait to throw out her hands.

'Just telling it like it is,' she said.

Stifling a sigh, Hanna said, 'Why are you actually here? I thought you were living at the cottage with Grandma . . .'

'I thought you'd want to see Sofia before you left for work.' She flashed a smile. 'See, I'm not so bad after all.'

'I don't think you're bad at all, but for some reason you seem to want to make out you are. Now, would you like some breakfast? There's cereal, porridge, eggs . . . Leo had the last of the bacon, but there's plenty of sourdough for toast.'

'I thought Leo was in Devon with Dad.'

Not commenting on the fact that Cait had apparently already known that her father wasn't at home, Hanna said, 'He came back last night to make an early meeting this morning.'

Cait shrugged and dismissed the subject. 'I can sort breakfast,' she said as Hanna took a box of Coco Pops from the cupboard. 'I'll text Grandma see if she wants to come over.'

'She's already out for a power walk, but text anyway, she's probably not far away.' She returned her attention to Sofia. 'Ananana has to go now, sweetheart. Will you be here when I get home later?'

'We might,' Cait answered, 'depending on how things go down today.' Seeing the expression on her mother's face – hurt, worry, exasperation – she said, 'OK, we'll be here. Does that make you happy?'

Hanna smiled and pressed a kiss to Sofia's curls. It would make her a whole lot happier if she could embrace her impossible daughter too, but at least she didn't seem to have any plans to take off again just yet.

It wasn't until she was driving through the gates that she remembered the ghastly Marius had been hanging about not very long ago. Fortunately, there was no sign of him now.

CHAPTER NINETEEN

An hour later Hanna was in Madden's main boardroom with her events coordination team, going over the many and varied plans they had fixed, or were still arranging, or proposing, for the next three months. There was a lot to get through – there always was – and top of today's agenda was a charity ball in the Great Hall of the Wills Memorial Building; also a summer picnic for friends and families at the Children's Hospice, and a grand fundraising banquet at The Newt near Burton. There were also countless smaller events – tea parties, cricket matches, silent auctions, dance-a-thons on the Downs – all designed to raise money for the Madden Foundation to allocate to those in need.

The time passed – as it always did with her handpicked team – quickly, productively and often hilariously, since a couple of members were natural comedians. It was past one o'clock by the time she finally tripped down the single flight of stairs to her own suite of offices to find it deserted. Clearly everyone had gone straight to lunch. She was ravenous herself, but she had a whole string of emails to deal with before her afternoon meetings got under way, so no time to eat today.

She'd lost track of how long she'd been at her computer when she heard the door to her office close. She looked up and her heart skipped a beat to see Hugo Astor leaning against it, arms folded, expression showing exactly what he was there for.

She stopped what she was doing and stared back at him. This was the first time she'd seen him all week – apparently he'd been in Devon with Jack. She had no idea whether he'd known he wouldn't be around when he'd asked her to forget her underwear when she came to the office on Monday. That day had passed, and she realized it could have been an attempt to humiliate her. There again, he had no way of knowing whether or not she'd met his request.

She hadn't, but she suspected he thought she had.

As he came towards her, the air charged with his purpose. Her eyes dropped to the large bulge of his erection, pressing for escape, then returned to his as he came to a stop beside her.

She had a feeling he was planning on oral sex, but they never articulated their specific desires, simply intuited what the other wanted and did it.

As he began to lower his zip, she put out a hand, not to touch him, but to stop him. 'No,' she said quietly.

He looked surprised. She never said no, was always as hot for it as he was.

He took her hand, used it to pull her to her feet, then pushed it between his legs, rubbing it against him. She removed it and tried to take a step back, but her chair was in the way.

'OK, I get it,' he said softly, and before she knew what was happening, he spun her round, bent her over the desk and pushed up her dress.

'I said *no*,' she seethed, trying to get away from him.

'But we both know you don't mean it,' and, trapping her neck with one hand so that her face was pressed to the keyboard, he forced his legs between hers, tore aside her panties and thrust two fingers inside her.

Using all her strength she twisted herself round, shoved her hands against his chest, and dragged herself upright as he staggered back. 'Don't you dare touch me again,' she hissed at him, so shaken by what had happened that she didn't think to cover herself.

To her astonishment he still seemed to think it was a game, and once again he tried to bend her over the desk, his hands big and strong, his determination inescapable.

'Let me go!' she cried, panicked by her powerlessness. He was forcing her legs apart again, she could feel his erection . . . Christ, was he actually going to rape her? He seemed to think it was what she wanted. Should she scream? What should she do?

The door that should have been locked suddenly opened. 'Hey, Mum, I got you a sandwich . . .' Leo came to a sudden stop. 'What the f . . .?'

Hanna drew herself up as Astor quickly backed away, turning to tuck himself in. 'Get out,' she spat in disgust.

'This isn't what it looks like,' he told Leo as he passed on his way out. His voice was quivering with rage.

Ignoring him, Leo turned to his mother. 'Are you all right?' he said, starting towards her.

Hanna's eyes had fixed on Riona, who was standing just outside her door. She must have seen everything – or enough, anyway. 'I-I, it . . .' she stumbled, pulling her dress down.

'That bloke was attacking you,' Leo declared furiously. 'Jesus Christ, Mum. Who is he? You have to call someone . . .'

'It's fine,' she mumbled, still straightening her clothes. 'It was . . . a . . . mis . . . He's gone now . . .'

'Does he work here? We have to tell Dad . . .'

'Maybe we should call the police,' Riona said, coming into the room.

'It . . . wasn't . . .' Hanna faltered. 'I don't want to make a fuss. Let's just calm down, take a breath . . .'

'I'm calling Dad,' Leo stated, snatching out his phone.

'No! Don't!' Hanna snapped.

Leo gaped at her, flushed and confused.

'I'll tell him myself,' she said, gesturing for him to put away his phone.

Riona came to put a comforting hand on Hanna's arm. 'Why don't you sit down?' she said gently. 'Whatever just happened, it was clearly a shock. Would you like some water? Tea?'

Hanna could hardly make herself think. 'Tea, but Leo can get it.' Having her strapping son towering over her right now, albeit protectively, wasn't helping.

'OK,' Leo said, 'but I want to know his name. If he works here—'

'Leo, please just get me some tea,' Hanna implored.

If Leo hadn't come in when he had, would Astor actually have gone as far as to rape her?

She felt sure the answer was yes and she knew she only had herself to blame. *Except no means no!* If men hadn't learned anything else in these *Me Too* times, surely they had to know that.

Riona said softly, 'You don't have to tell me anything, but . . .'

'There's nothing to tell,' Hanna assured her. 'He just . . . misread the situation.'

'But lucky Leo came in when he did.'

Hanna pushed her hands through her hair and took a

breath. 'You're early,' she said, attempting to move things on. What else could she do?

'I was waiting in reception,' Riona explained. 'Leo saw me and told me to come on up.'

Hanna nodded. 'That's good. Sorry you had to walk into . . .' She gestured to one of her visitor sofas, as if directing them away from what had just happened. 'Shall we sit? I hope Leo thinks to bring you some tea too.'

Apparently sensing they needed to bridge this with something banal, Riona looked admiringly around the office as she walked to the sofa, complimenting the décor, until finally she said,

'You know, we can always do this another time. I can see you're shaken up . . .'

'No, no, it's fine. I've been looking forward to this, and I've got a few suggestions that might interest you . . . My PA's still at lunch, but she's created a file that we can either email to you or put into hard copy for you to take away.'

'That's very thoughtful of you, thank you. So why don't we go for the email option and I'll come again when I've had a chance to read everything through?'

'But I was going to explain why I've chosen the causes I have, and the purpose . . .' She broke off as Marcie, one of the catering team, came in with an immaculately laid-out tea tray.

'Leo said you had a guest,' Marcie told them as she set the tray down. 'I've brought some extra hot water and different-flavour teas in case you're not a fan of regular builder's brew,' she informed Riona.

Riona smiled. 'I'm happy with anything.'

'Where's Leo?' Hanna asked, hoping to God he hadn't

gone looking for Astor. Or called his father. She needed to speak to Jack first.

'I'm not sure where he went after he left the kitchen,' Marcie replied, 'but he turned down a slice of Hetty's carrot cake, which isn't like him.'

Hanna's insides lurched. 'I need to find him,' she said, getting to her feet. 'If you don't mind pouring, Riona?'

'Of course,' Riona said, 'but really, if . . .'

'Leo! There you are,' Hanna declared as he appeared in the doorway. Mindful of Marcie still being in the room, she thanked her and waited until she'd gone before saying, 'Have you called Dad?'

'No. You told me not to, but I will—'

'I'll do it,' she interrupted firmly. 'I want you to put it out of your mind now . . .'

'Yeah, like I'm really going to do that. He was attacking you, Mum . . .'

'And because of who he is, it's going to need careful handling. So please don't go taking matters into your own hands. Dad and I will deal with it.'

Leo's angry, confused eyes went to Riona, as if hoping she might take up the argument for him, but all she said was, 'Things are often not what they first seem.'

Grateful to her for that, Hanna went to put an arm around Leo and kissed his cheek. 'I'm sure you've got a busy afternoon,' she said, 'so let's put this aside and I'll see you at home later.'

After he'd gone, clearly still not happy, she turned back to Riona and said, 'I'm sure I can rely on your discretion over this . . .'

'Of course you can. It's none of my business. I'm happy to drink some tea and get on with the reason I'm here.'

CHAPTER TWENTY

'Oh, Jesus Christ,' Jack groaned when Hanna finished telling him what had happened. 'This is an effing disaster. Have you spoken to Astor since?'

'No,' she replied. She was talking into her phone, staring out of the sitting-room window where her mother-in-law was playing with Sofia on the edge of the pool. They looked so happy and carefree. No sign of Cait. 'Aren't you going to ask if I'm all right?' she said to Jack, annoyed that he hadn't already.

'I'm sorry. Are you?'

She wasn't entirely sure, except *yes*, of course she was. No way was she going to allow Hugo Astor to turn her into a victim. She just hadn't figured out yet what needed to be done, only that whatever it was, Jack had to be involved, which was why she'd come straight home to call him after Riona had left the office. 'I was a bit shaken up after,' she admitted. 'I'd like to say no harm done, but it was pretty horrible.'

Jack was quiet for a moment. She wondered if he was equating harm to the assault she'd suffered, or with the issues it was going to cause at work?

'I always said you were playing too close to home,' he told her gruffly. 'It was never going to end well . . .'

'Don't you dare turn this around on me,' she snapped angrily. 'You didn't mind when you were getting kicks out of it . . .'

'Because you did, but it was always a crazy idea. I only went along with it because I could see you were going to do it anyway. What is wrong with you, Han? Why do you have to—?'

'I'm not listening to any more of this,' she raged. '*You're* the one who started it. You had the affair . . .'

'It wasn't an affair! It was one night with someone while I was in London – and you didn't seem to have a problem with it at the time.'

'That's what you keep telling yourself, but maybe I did. Maybe I was totally fucking devastated . . .'

'Were you?'

She had been at first, but she had to admit that when he'd started to tell her how it had come about, she'd found herself becoming aroused by it . . . And that was how it had all started several years ago. So perhaps there *was* something wrong with her. Other women didn't behave that way, or none that she knew. 'We need to decide what we're going to do about Astor?' she stated. 'I know you can't fire him . . .'

'You're damned right I can't, unless we want lawyers crawling all over it.' He paused again and she heard something in the background that puzzled her.

'Where are you?' she asked, having assumed he was still on site in Appledore. 'Was that a child I just heard?'

'What? Oh, yes. I'm at Steve Colridge's. The site foreman? It's his three-year-old. I need to think about this,' he said, switching back to Astor. 'You should steer clear of him for now – or don't be alone with him . . .'

'Don't patronize me, Jack . . .'

'I'm trying to help here,' he snapped back.

'OK. So what do I do if he apologizes?'

'Do you think he will?'

'I've no idea. When he left the office, he seemed to be blaming me for the way he'd misread things.'

'OK. Tell him you've spoken to me, but for God's sake, if he does come to apologize, don't let your overactive libido get the better of you . . .'

'Did you just say that in front of people?' she cried in outrage.

'Of course not! Everyone else is outside.'

'Apart from the three-year-old?'

'Are you serious?'

Realizing how stupid that was, she said, 'Is there any chance you can get back tonight?'

'I'll make it happen. Where's Leo? Have you talked to him since . . .?'

'Not really. Riona was there . . .'

'*Riona!* Christ, how many people know about this?'

'Stop shouting at me, Jack. It's not helping. Riona was actually very supportive, and meeting with her after gave me the distraction I needed to calm down and make sure I didn't overreact. As for Leo, he's staying at Seb's tonight.'

'OK. I'm sure he'll tell Seb, so be prepared for that. And incidentally, there's no such thing as an overreaction to attempted rape. You just need to be sure that's what it was.'

'How dare you!' she cried, seeing red. 'I thought you, of all people, would know that I'd never make up something like this. I'll grant it might have been a misunderstanding, but I said *no* . . .'

113

'Which he took to be a part of the game. We've done it ourselves, Han, you know that . . .'

'That's hardly the same thing. You'd know if I meant it . . .'

'And he didn't.'

'Are you defending him, taking his part over mine?'

'Don't be ridiculous. I'm just pointing out the way he's probably seeing it so we can decide on how best to go forward.'

'But you're doubting me?'

'No. I just want you to be clear in your mind before we take any sort of action.'

After ringing off, Hanna clutched the phone between her hands and sank down on the sofa. She felt raw, drained, confused. Worst of all, she felt sick of herself. She should never have given in to her attraction to Hugo Astor. She'd behaved as though she had no proper moral compass, a blind, arrogant belief that she could do as she pleased and always get away with it. Was that who she'd become, a woman who hardly cared what she was doing or who it might hurt, even if it turned out to be herself?

She'd never considered what it would do to her children if they ever found out what she was really like – someone who indulged in risky sex with a man she actively detested. A woman who was thrilled by the anonymous sex she and Jack went in for at exclusive Devonshire parties. At least those gatherings did no harm to anyone: everything was consensual, rules were known and not broken. She and Jack got a huge kick out of discussing it after, sharing their experiences and taking them into the privacy of their bedroom. Nothing happened on their own doorstep – Jack had always kept his flings far from home, while she'd brought hers right into the heart of their world.

And now Leo knew.

She couldn't bear even to think of what he'd seen, or of what might have happened if he'd come in only minutes later. Astor had intended to force himself on her, she was sure of it; he'd pushed his fingers inside her, for God's sake. He was so much stronger than her, she'd been totally unable to stop him; he'd had her face pressed to the desk, a hand on her neck, his legs had been between hers, her feet were off the floor . . . The humiliation was insufferable, the degradation and violation, but it was the sense of helplessness that was making her shake all over again.

She must focus on Leo, not herself.

At least he didn't know what had led up to the incident, that she could be said to have brought it on herself. But the truth could easily come out. If it did, he'd no longer be so sure that he'd saved his mother from a sexual assault. He might think he'd managed to come in at the wrong moment – and how repulsed by her would that end up making him feel?

CHAPTER TWENTY-ONE

Seb wanted to drop his head in his hands and let go of a very long, weary sigh, but he knew it would be the wrong reaction. It wasn't what Leo would be expecting, not the reason he'd confided in his godfather over what had happened – or he thought had happened – to his mother today.

Seb had no idea what the truth of the so-called assault was, only that it was probably not as straightforward as Leo seemed to think and, in all likelihood, him walking in on it had made it a darned sight more complicated.

Seb had never understood why Hanna and Jack played outside their marriage the way they did when they were clearly so in love with one another, but he'd never pried. As Jilly used to tell him, 'Everyone has their own fantasies and, as long as no one gets hurt, it's not our place to judge.' It still wasn't his place, but the fact that Leo was so worked up about what he'd seen – and seemed hell-bent on some sort of action – was extremely worrying.

Getting up to fetch two more beers from the fridge, Seb said, 'You have to let Mum and Dad deal with it, son. I understand—'

'I know the bloke's name now,' Leo interrupted. 'It's Hugo Astor. He's the company lawyer.'

Seb had no idea what to say to that, and wasn't proud of the way he immediately wondered if the man would seriously attempt an assault on his new boss's wife? It was professional suicide.

'He can't be allowed to get away with it,' Leo declared, his eyes glittering with purpose. 'I'm not saying Dad will let that happen, but he won't want any bad publicity, we know that, and obvs Mum won't either—'

'You have to trust Dad,' Seb interrupted. 'A lot will depend on how . . . upset Mum is by it, because you're right they won't want the publicity.' He needed to speak to Jack, let him know how rattled Leo was.

His mobile rang and, seeing it was Riona, Leo said, 'Don't mind me. You can tell her I've told you, if you like. She was there, she saw the same as I did.'

Deciding he'd rather speak to Riona when Leo wasn't in earshot, Seb let the call go to messages. 'I'm sure we can rely on her discretion, if it comes to it,' he said.

Leo's handsome face darkened. 'That sounds as though you're all planning to sweep it under the carpet,' he cried, 'but you can't do that, Seb. Things have changed since your day. Men don't get to attack women and walk away like nothing happened. This is my mother we're talking about. I know how much you care for her; you can't just let this go, even if my parents decide they have to.'

Seb didn't argue; the only role he could legitimately play here was to make sure Leo didn't do anything rash before speaking to his father. The last time Leo had taken matters into his own hands, it hadn't ended well, and he was fortunate not to have a criminal record as a result of it. 'Try Dad again,' he said, 'he might be in a better reception area by now.'

To Leo's frustration, his call once again went to voicemail, and since he'd already left two messages, he didn't bother leaving another.

'How was Mum when you last saw her?' Seb asked as Leo put the phone back on the table.

Leo shrugged. 'She seemed . . . OK, I guess. I think Riona being there helped, you know, having another woman to talk to. Riona was actually all for calling the police, but surprise, surprise, Mum wasn't going for that. You know what she's like, the same as Dad, the business comes first, everything has to be dealt with in-house; no way can there ever be any scandal.'

Which was what made Jack and Hanna's lifestyle choices so . . . bizarre, Seb reflected. Call him a traditionalist, unimaginative, unadventurous, it wouldn't change the fact that he was a monogamist at heart who'd never once wanted to sleep with another woman while married to Jilly, and that hadn't changed until Riona had come along.

Leo was busy texting now.

'Have you told anyone apart from me?' Seb asked carefully.

Leo glanced up. 'No way. I need to properly get my head round it first.'

'So you haven't mentioned it to Cait?'

'Are you kidding? She'd go mental if she knew, and I've got no idea in which direction. She wants to come and see you, by the way. Have you heard from her?'

Warily, Seb said, 'No. Do you know why?' The last time Cait wanted to 'see' him was to talk about becoming his live-in housekeeper. She'd even had it all worked out. She and Sofia could move into the guest room, and he'd hardly know they were there apart from when she was cooking and cleaning for him and perhaps once in a while he wouldn't mind babysitting. Fortunately, before he'd been forced to turn down her generous offer, she'd met the Welsh musician and had seemed to forget all about it.

'I think it's to do with Riona,' Leo told him. 'She wanted to know all about her after I shipped her out of the dinner party last Saturday, but hey, you know what Cait's like, it takes some kind of genius to work out what's going on in her head.'

With a smile Seb said, 'Fancy a bite at the Clifton Sausage?'

Leo's face lit up. 'Count me in,' he responded hungrily. 'I'll just text Mum to remind her I'm staying here tonight.'

'OK. Let's leave in ten.' And, picking up his phone, Seb went up to his study to call Riona.

'Hey, how are things with you?' he asked when she answered.

With the usual warmth in her voice, she said, 'Nothing especially interesting to report. How are you?'

'I'm good. Leo's here, so I know what happened today.'

'Ah,' she said shortly.

'Do you think it was an assault?'

'Well, it certainly looked that way to me, and Hanna was quite upset after. However, she was very definite about not wanting to get anyone else involved.'

'Such as the police?'

'Precisely. She said she wanted to talk to Jack first. Do you know if she has?'

'No, but I'm sure she will. So I'm guessing your meeting didn't happen?'

'Actually, she was determined to go ahead with it, and you might be surprised to hear that I think we both ended up happy with the outcome.'

'More pleased than surprised. Perhaps you can tell me about it at the weekend? If you're free?'

'I shall do my best to be. Would you like me to cook for you?'

Thrilled by the prospect, he said, 'I'll definitely sign up for that.'

'At your place?' she added. 'It can get a little noisy around here at times, and to be honest, I'd rather have you all to myself.'

With a rush of pleasure, he said, 'I'm not going to argue with that. Shall I do the shopping?'

'No, I'll bring everything and you can choose the wine. Now, I'm afraid I should probably ring off, but I'll be in touch before Saturday to set a time.'

CHAPTER TWENTY-TWO

'So you've not seen Astor since?' Jack said, passing Hanna a gin and tonic and touching his own glass to hers before drinking.

It was late on Friday afternoon; they were in his office with the door closed, in spite of most of the staff having already gone home.

'No,' she replied, tucking her legs under her as she sank into one of the sofas. 'I didn't exactly go looking for him, but there was no sign of his car in the car park. Have you tried talking to him yet?'

Jack shook his head, looking tired and worried as he sat in one of the armchairs and exhaled loudly. 'I've got to be honest,' he said, 'I really don't know the best way to handle this, and since the person I'd normally turn to for advice is the very person in question, I remain at a loss.' He didn't add, *So cheers, Han, a real fuck-up*, but she heard it anyway, and felt it deeply, along with the bitter shame and regret of bringing them to this.

'We have to hope,' he continued, 'that he's planning to resign with immediate effect, and I of course will let him. But he's a canny operator – it's why I hired him – so my guess is that he won't do anything until I've spoken to him.'

'Are you going to?'

'I would if I knew what the hell to say. I can hardly accuse of him trying to rape my wife . . .'

'It's what happened.'

'Says you. No, listen,' he cried over her as she started to protest. 'It's not that I don't believe you, I do, but it will be your word against his, and given the history you two share . . .'

Her face burned with the mortifying truth of it.

'This could turn really messy, Han,' he continued more gently. 'If the press gets wind of it, you're going to have a very difficult time holding your head up . . .'

'I know that,' she snapped irritably. 'Why else do you think I don't want the police involved?'

He regarded her steadily, his dark eyes narrowed, penetrating, as though he was trying to read her. It took her only a moment to realize what was on his mind. 'You think I encouraged him, don't you?' she said incredulously. 'You think I led him on, let him think it was what I wanted, then changed my mind. Well, that's not how it happened. I told him right away that I didn't want it, I actually said the word "no", but he ignored me.'

Sighing, Jack closed his eyes and let his head fall back against the sofa.

As she watched him, she was recalling how she'd allowed Astor to close the door and get all the way to her desk before she'd stopped him. That could be construed as leading him on.

Oh God, oh God!

After a while, Jack said, 'What if he wants to keep his job?'

Recoiling from the idea, while knowing how impressed

Jack already was with him, she said, 'Are you asking because you want him to stay?'

He raised his head to look at her. 'No, I'm asking because he's in a position to blackmail us into doing whatever he wants, and what I'd like to know is if we're going to allow that to happen.'

Detesting herself more by the minute, Hanna said, 'I know it's all my fault we're in this position, but I'm sure he's no keener to create a fuss than we are.'

'So what, I ask him to go, get him to sign a non-disclosure, and follow it up with a decent pay-off?'

She didn't answer, but it did seem the best solution to her.

His mobile rang, and he went to fetch it. He clicked on, saying, 'Gerard, what can I do for you at this hour on a Friday?'

As he listened to the lobby security guard, he turned to Hanna, frowning in puzzlement. 'The police?' he said. 'Did they say what they want?' After a beat he added, 'OK, put them on.'

'What is it?' Hanna demanded, turning cold.

Jack raised a hand and said, 'Jack Madden speaking. How can I help you?'

Hanna could feel her heart thudding, was hardly able to breathe.

'So where is he now?' Jack asked.

'Oh my God, Leo,' Hanna faltered, starting to get up.

Jack quickly shook his head and put a hand out to stop her. 'Do you know what happened, exactly?' he asked the caller. Then, 'OK, thanks for letting me know. I'll get myself over there.'

As soon as he'd rung off Hanna said, 'What is it? What's happened?'

'Apparently Astor's in hospital,' he replied, sounding as bewildered and worried as he looked. 'A neighbour found him outside his house and called an ambulance.'

CHAPTER TWENTY-THREE

Over an hour had passed by the time Jack and Hanna got through the traffic of Henleaze and Southmead to the hospital.

As they entered the busy main foyer, a tall, short-haired woman in a dark blue suit approached them. 'Mr and Mrs Madden?' she said, not holding out a hand to shake. 'I'm Detective Constable Anna Sterry. Could I have a quick word before you go to see Mr Astor?'

'Of course,' Jack replied. 'Thanks for calling to let me know he was here. What exactly happened to him?'

Gesturing for them to step out of the foot traffic, she said, 'I'm afraid he's been quite severely beaten up.'

Hanna gasped, pressing a hand to her mouth.

Continuing, Sterry said, 'He was unconscious when the neighbour found him last night, and he hasn't been able to tell us much so far, but he was quite insistent that we should call you. You're his employer?'

'That's right,' Jack confirmed.

Hanna's mind was buzzing. Who on earth would have beaten him up? It couldn't have been Leo – it just couldn't. True, he'd done it once before, but his friend had been the real attacker then. Leo wasn't naturally violent; quite the

125

reverse. So it had to have been a mugger. A burglar? How much did Jack actually know about the man's past?

'Mr Astor is saying he didn't see his attacker,' Sterry ran on. 'Whoever it was came at him from behind and fractured his skull with a sharp blow to the head. His collarbone is broken and there are a lot of injuries to his back and legs. Does he have any enemies that you know of?'

As Jack shook his head he looked at Hanna, his eyes warning her to give the same response.

It couldn't have been Leo; this was far too serious for that.

'He hasn't been with us for long,' Hanna explained, 'a couple of months, so we're just getting to know him.' Why had she said that? If it all came out about her relationship with him . . . She couldn't go there, not now.

'We have officers going door to door in the area,' Sterry informed them. 'Maybe someone has CCTV, or a passing dash-cam picked something up. It's a pretty serious assault, the kind we usually see where gangs are involved. Do you have any reason to think he could be engaged in some kind of activity that would end him up like this?'

Jack was clearly thrown. 'Not at all . . . unless he was in debt, I suppose.'

'We're checking that. Any indication of drug use?'

Jack glanced at Hanna as they both shook their heads. 'We only ever see him at the office, or at official functions,' Jack said, 'so I'm afraid we can't tell you much about his personal life. I believe he has a wife, but I think they're separated.'

Sterry noted this down. 'Do you know her name, or where we can get hold of her?'

'I'll have someone from HR check his records. Tell us, just how bad is he? You say you've spoken to him . . .'

'Barely, but he was keen for me to call you. Perhaps,

when you speak to him, you might get a better idea of what happened.'

Hanna could hardly make herself think straight, had no answer to give about anything, so it was left to Jack to say, 'Of course. Can I see him now?'

'I'll check.' Sterry turned away, pressing a number into her phone.

Taking Jack's arm, Hanna led him aside as she whispered, 'Please tell me you're not thinking this is Leo.'

'I sure as hell don't want to . . .'

'But an attack like that? Leo wouldn't be capable. It can't be anything to do with me. It has to be about something else altogether.'

He turned as DC Sterry said, 'If you're ready, I'll show you the way.'

Hanna's hand was on Jack's arm. 'I'll wait here,' she told him.

He pressed a quick kiss to her forehead and followed the detective along the concourse.

Hanna watched, unmoving, barely breathing, a dreadful sense of foreboding stealing over her.

When Jack came back twenty minutes later, he was as grim faced and shaken as she'd ever seen him.

'Let's get out of here,' he said and, taking her arm, he steered her through the rotating doors, and across the road to where they'd left the car.

Once they were inside, he didn't start the engine, simply sat in the driver's seat staring straight ahead, his hands clenched hard on the wheel.

Not really wanting an answer, Hanna said, 'So what happened?'

He took a breath. 'He's in a sorry state, that's for sure, but not sorry enough to . . .' He broke off, glanced at her briefly and started again. 'He's claiming you were up for it until you were interrupted.'

Hanna's eyes flashed with fury. 'That isn't true,' she protested.

'Whether it is or isn't, is irrelevant . . .'

'Not to me it isn't. I need to know you believe me.'

'OK, I do, but that's not our biggest concern right now. He's also saying that he knows the identity of his attacker, and if we don't want him divulging it to the police it will cost us.'

Hanna's heart turned inside out.

'He's claiming it was Leo.'

She began shaking her head, unable to make herself accept this.

Her eyes met Jack's and she knew their minds were in the same place. She thought back to two years ago, when Leo and his friend, Jasper Conlon, had laid into a Bristol uni student who'd dumped Jasper's sister and all her stuff into the dock. The student had ended up in A&E with concussion and several other less serious injuries. Jasper had done a brief stint in prison; it was only Jack's influence with law enforcement that had saved Leo from being charged with GBH too.

'Astor hasn't mentioned any names to the police,' Jack continued, 'but he's told them that his attacker was probably just under six foot, seemed young and athletic, was wearing a hoodie and black jeans and he used some sort of blunt weapon. It happened too fast for Astor to tell what the weapon was, but apparently he heard the attacker say, "Don't ever go near her again."'

128

Hanna sat mute with horror as she imagined her beloved son, usually so mild-tempered and easy-going, beating a man half to death. If it weren't for the previous incident, she'd never have believed it.

Jack said, 'He wants five million to go away.'

She gaped at him as the words penetrated her already stunned brain.

'Five mil and he'll never name the attacker or tell anyone what happened with you.'

As the horror of it engulfed her, she had no idea what to say or do, could only feel tears of hopelessness burning through her outrage. This was all her fault. None of it would have happened if she hadn't thought it might be fun to seduce Astor, as if he were some sort of toy to be played with and cast aside when she'd had enough.

He was playing a whole different sort of game now, and the winning cards were all his.

'You . . . You can't pay it,' she whispered shakily.

Jack's expression was stony as he said, 'I don't see that I have a choice.'

Unable to hold back her emotions any longer she sobbed, 'I'm sorry. I'm so sorry . . . This was never meant to happen . . .'

He reached for her, pulling her as close as the console would allow. 'I know,' he said gently, 'but it has and now we have to deal with it. We need to talk to Leo. Do you know where he is?'

Digging a tissue from the glove box she said, 'I didn't see him around the office today, and he was at Seb's last night. At least I thought he was there.'

Sighing, Jack let her go, reached for his seatbelt and started the engine. As they pulled out of the car park he said, 'Do you know if he's told Seb anything about what he saw on Thursday?'

'No,' she replied.

'Then I think we should probably assume that he has.' Clicking on the steering wheel, he gave the command to connect to Seb's mobile. A moment later Seb answered.

'Jack. Good to hear from you. How are things?'

Avoiding the question, Jack said, 'Is Leo still with you?'

'No. He left this morning. Why? Is everything OK?'

'I'm afraid not. Do you have any idea where he was last night?'

'I was going to have an early dinner with him, but then he took off. I think to his girlfriend's. Have you tried her?'

'Not yet, but I will.'

'What's going on, Jack? You've got me worried here.'

'Did he tell you what happened at the office on Thursday, with Hanna?' Jack asked.

With a barely audible sigh, Seb said, 'Yes he did.'

'Han and I have just come from the hospital. Someone attacked Astor last night and he's claiming it was Leo.'

'Shit,' Seb muttered under his breath.

'What did Leo say to you, exactly?' Jack pressed.

With a groan Seb said, 'You're not going to like this, but he was worried that you – *we* – would end up trying to brush it under the carpet and he was determined the man should pay.'

Hanna covered her face with her hands. This could hardly get any worse.

Seb said, 'I'm going to come right out and ask this . . . Did Leo see what he thought he saw with Hanna, or was there . . .?'

130

Hanna flinched.

'It was an assault,' Jack answered sharply, 'but there was something going on between him and Han prior to that. Yesterday, the man didn't want to take no for an answer.'

'I see. And now he's in hospital. Is he badly hurt?'

'You could say that. We need to find Leo, so I'll ring off now—'

'Seb,' Hanna interrupted, 'did you know that Riona was with Leo when he came into the room?'

'Yes. She's been quite worried about you.'

Jack said, 'Maybe she doesn't need to know what's happened to Astor. Are you OK with that?'

'I guess so, but I know you can trust her.'

'I'm sure you're right, but things have got quite complicated . . .'

Breaking in again, Hanna said, 'You might as well know, Seb. Astor's asking for five million to go away.'

There was beat of shocked silence before Seb said, 'Please tell me you're not going to pay it.'

'This is Leo and Hanna we're talking about,' Jack replied, hitting the steering wheel in frustration. 'My son could end up in prison and my wife's reputation will be trashed. I'm not going to let that happen.'

Hanna's eyes closed as the culpability of it all swamped her again. What the hell must Seb, their dearest friend, think of them now? What sort of damage was this going to end up causing to her and Jack's marriage?

In a calmer voice Jack said, 'I need to get hold of Leo. I'll call you if there's any news.'

Moments later Leo's voice was on the speaker. 'Hey, Dad, are you back?'

'Yes,' Jack snapped. 'Where are you?'

'On my way home. I should be there in ten.'

'Good. We need to talk, son, I think you know what about, so we'll leave it until Mum and I get there.'

CHAPTER TWENTY-FOUR

'I don't believe this?' Leo cried furiously. His fists were clenched hard, his face white with shock. 'You actually think I did it. My own parents . . .'

'Leo—' Hanna broke in.

'I'm not saying the bastard didn't deserve it,' he shouted over her, 'but *you* could at least have asked rather than just presumed I'm guilty.'

They were outside, down at the lakeshore where there was little danger of being overheard and a fine rain was coating them like a cloying mist.

'No one's presuming that,' Jack barked back. 'I'm just telling you what Astor told me. He's claiming it was you . . .'

'And that's enough, is it? What he says counts. Whereas what I say. . .' He stopped suddenly as another realization dawned. 'Shit, I get what's going on here,' he said scathingly. 'You're thinking that – because of what happened with Jasper's sister and the lowlife she got involved with – it stands to reason it was me who did this. It's my MO . . .'

'No,' Hanna protested forcefully, 'that's not what we think, but the police will if Astor decides to accuse you.'

'You might not have been charged the last time,' Jack

continued, 'but that doesn't mean there's no record of the incident . . .'

'For fuck's sake,' Leo cried. 'I'm telling you it wasn't me, OK? Are you at least trying to believe me?'

'Of course we are, and we do,' Hanna assured him. 'There's a good chance Astor was involved in something shady, and that's who came for him, but right now he's accusing you and we have to deal with it.'

'So where were you last night?' Jack demanded.

Looking as though he'd like to thump his father, Leo wiped a hand over his wet face and said, 'I was at Seb's. Then I went to Olivia's. OK?'

'And she can verify that?'

'For fuck's sake!'

'What time did you get there?' Hanna asked.

'I don't *know*. Seven, eight. I wasn't checking.'

'Where were you beforehand?' Jack pressed. 'I mean, after you left Seb's?'

'Driving to Olivia's. Listen, instead of laying into me, you should be focusing on what this a-hole did to Mum . . .'

'It's not forgotten, but we still need to be sure you have a rock-solid alibi for the time of the attack. So where were you around seven o'clock last night?'

'I just told you, on my way to Olivia's.'

'Will ANPR verify that?'

'Of course it fucking will,' but he wasn't looking at them any more. His head was turned away, as he mumbled, 'If it even works on those roads.'

Hanna felt a flutter of unease as she and Jack exchanged glances. Something wasn't right. He wasn't being straight with them.

Jack said, 'Look at your phone, Leo. Were you talking to someone while you were driving?'

'I know I didn't make any calls,' he retorted. 'I was listening to music, OK?'

It wasn't a good enough answer.

'We need to know . . .'

Leo threw out his hands. 'What is this, the fucking inquisition? Why don't you tell us where *you* were last night?'

Jack balked.

'See, you don't like it much either . . .'

'It's not me who's being accused.'

'But you could have paid someone to sort him out. That's how you operate, isn't it? Never get your own hands dirty—'

'That's enough,' Hanna cut in sharply. 'What we're trying to do here is establish that you couldn't have been the attacker because you were somewhere else. Try to work with us, Leo.'

'I told you, I was in my car, driving to Olivia's. Sorry if that's not good enough.'

'But where were you before that?' Jack persisted. 'Did you stop off at the office? Meet with a mate somewhere? We seem to have a tranche of time unaccounted for which unfortunately coincides with the time of the attack.'

Leo stared at him hard, his expression mutinous, his grey eyes flashing with rage and defiance. 'It was you, wasn't it?' he challenged, rain dripping from his hair onto his collar. 'You sent someone in . . .'

Jack threw up his hands in frustration.

'Leo,' Hanna cried quickly, 'you're coming across as if you're hiding something. If you are, we need to know what it is.'

'All you need to know,' he shot back, 'is that my conscience is clear. I never went near the bloke, but if you want to tell yourselves I did, good luck to you.'

Jack stepped in front of him as he tried to walk away.

Afraid it might suddenly turn physical, Hanna moved between them. 'Let's calm this down,' she said, pushing them apart. 'If you say you didn't do it, that's good enough for us, but you need to be prepared for the police asking you the same.'

'And if it gets that far,' Jack continued, 'it'll come out about what Astor did to your mother . . .'

'Good! That's what should happen. I don't want him to get away with it, but apparently you do, and that really fucks me off, do you know that?'

'He'll be losing his job,' Jack informed him tightly.

'Oh *result*! Then he'll be free to go and assault someone else. Let's not call him to account for trying to rape my mother, let's just give him his marching orders and be done with it.'

'You're stepping very close to the line, son,' Jack warned him.

Hanna wasn't sure she could take much more, was even on the brink of confessing how much she was to blame, but seeming to sense it, Jack stopped her.

'You need to know, Leo, that Astor is asking for five million to keep the identity of his attacker to himself. He's claiming it was you and right now you're not giving me anything to prove that it wasn't. So I want you to think about that, then come and find me when you're ready to tell me what really happened last night.'

As he and Hanna walked away, she could feel herself shaking, and wanted desperately to turn back to her son, not to leave him out here in the rain with all this anger and confusion – but she had to support Jack. He was the one who'd get them through whatever nightmare lay ahead; he was the one who loved them both so much he'd do anything to protect them.

Leo suddenly shouted, 'All right! All right!'

They stopped, gave it a moment and turned back. All three of them were soaked through by now, yet showing little sign of noticing it.

'All right,' Leo said again as they drew close, hanging his head. 'I did find out where he lived, and I did go over there, but I swear,' he cried, 'that I just drove by. I didn't do anything; I didn't even see him.' His eyes burned harshly into his father's. 'You can*not* pay him to keep quiet about something that didn't happen. Not where I'm concerned. You just can't.'

Glad he'd finally owned up to this, bad as it was going to be for him, Hanna went to put an arm around him. 'Come on, let's go inside,' she said, 'we can sort things out.'

As they entered the kitchen, Caitlin met them with a bundle of towels. 'I was about to bring these out,' she announced, handing them one each. 'So what's going on? Obviously you don't want me to know or you wouldn't have been out there . . .'

'Leave it,' Leo muttered.

She scowled. 'So I'm supposed to stay in the dark while you lot . . .'

'Not everything has to be about you,' Leo snapped.

'Who's saying it is? But anyway, I *know* it's not all about me. In fact, it's about everyone else, but maybe you don't want to hear that.'

Jack growled impatiently. 'Cait! For heaven's sake.

No one wants to play your games right now. And where's Sofia?'

Shooting him a daggered look, she said, 'If you must know, she's with Grandma doing baby yoga. Or did you think I'd sold her to people traffickers?'

'It's exactly that sort of person who could pick her up the way you carry on, so time to grow up, Caitlin. You're a mother now, look to your responsibilities, the main one of which would be to take proper care of your own child.'

'Jack,' Hanna murmured.

Cait's lip curled as she glared at her father's retreating back. 'You've got a lot more to fear from me, Dad, than I have from you,' she shouted after him, 'just you remember that.'

Used to her childish threats, Jack simply raised a hand and continued on his way.

'That's what I hate about this house,' Cait raged, fists bunched to her cheeks, 'it's all secrets and show, lies, pretence, fucking entitlement and privilege. You're not in a real world,' she shouted into her mother's face and, not waiting for a response, she grabbed her phone and ran off towards the cottage.

Hanna looked round as Florina came into the kitchen, carrying an armful of laundry and an expression that said she'd heard nothing, when she obviously had.

'I picked up your dress from the dry cleaner's,' she told Hanna. 'It's on your bed.'

'Thanks,' Hanna responded, trying to think which dress. As it came to her, she felt her heart sink. She and Jack were attending the Merchant Venturers' Summer Banquet tomorrow evening, a black-tie event that they normally both enjoyed. Jack wouldn't want to miss it, especially when he'd persuaded an old friend, aka an ex-prime minister, to be the guest speaker.

'Mum,' Leo said quietly.

She turned to him.

'Are you OK?' he asked, his eyes showing his concern.

She realized he was referring to what had happened on Thursday, and was deeply touched by the fact that he seemed to understand it was a far bigger deal than she was letting on. She took his hand in hers. 'I'm fine,' she assured him, because she had to. 'It's lucky you came in when you did . . .'

'We can't let him get away with it.'

'Sssh,' she said gently. 'I don't want it going public, I really don't, and it will if we report it to the police. So will you let it be my decision?'

He shrugged, showing that he wasn't at all satisfied. 'As long as it's yours and not Dad's.'

'It is, I swear it.'

Whether he believed her or not wasn't clear, but he obviously still wasn't happy. 'It might be easier to let it go,' he said grudgingly, 'now I know someone's given him a good thrashing.' His eyes came to hers. 'Tell me honestly, do you think Dad was behind it?'

She sighed as she said, 'It's probably best not to ask, or to think about it. What matters is that it wasn't you.'

'So you believe me?'

Did she? She thought so, so she nodded and pulled him into an embrace. She wished with all her heart that this could be an end to it, that they never had to think or speak of it again, but she knew in a way she couldn't explain that this was only the beginning.

CHAPTER TWENTY-FIVE

My memories have been playing me tricks again, swooping and sliding about in my head like movies with the scenes all mixed up. The stories aren't connecting together, the timeline is all wrong, and where there should be certainty there are terrifying patches of darkness. Worst is the way faces seem to morph into one another, turning people I know now into demons from the past and nightmares from my childhood into a future to fear.

I keep wondering if my sister has ever heard me calling for her? Has anyone ever spoken to her about me? Does she know of the times I was taken to the hall to serve my parents and their guests, when I would peer around the room from behind my mask trying to find her. I used to wonder if she was allowed to eat the same food as them, to sleep in a bed, to wash in clean water and dress in warm clothes? She wasn't wicked like me, so she didn't need to be punished for leading our father and his friends into ungodly acts.

There were other children. I remember them well, small, bright faces, large, watchful eyes, but I don't know their names or where they came from. Some were older, some younger, but maybe they were in the foster homes that came later. I can't be sure now.

I keep trying to remember if she was in the hospital at the same time as me. Was it a hospital? My aunt, when she came to take me to her home, confirmed that it was and she was a good person who didn't lie. She told me not to worry myself, that I'd done everything I could for my sister who was in a better place now. For a long time I thought that meant she was dead, but later, when I was well and able to attend school, I made friends who wondered, like me, if my sister had survived and been given to a family who'd changed her name, just as my aunt had changed mine. Everything was done to separate me from my past; it must have been the same for her.

Our family story was – and is – on the Internet for anyone to read, a gothic, ghoulish tale of abuse and sacrifice, of babies being born and allowed to die, of young children being kept in slavery and squalor. There is no mention of our names, but our ages were made much of, with us being so young.

My friends here, at this quiet house in Westbury, as unpredictable and sometimes unreasonable as they can be, understand how much it means to me to have found my sister at last. We have been together for so long that she feels like their sister too.

Riona listens to us discussing this, and she diligently gathers our thoughts to relay to Dr Francis. I believe she is like one of Ruby's dream-catchers; she protects us and only allows good thoughts to pass through the web of care she's thrown around us.

But as gentle and attentive as she is, and loyal, yes, she's always that, I sense that something serious has happened recently, involving my sister, and as yet she hasn't told me anything about it.

I think she'll try to keep it from me.
When will she learn that the bond my sister and I share
will always make her discretion and protectiveness pointless?

CHAPTER TWENTY-SIX

Seb hadn't felt such a ludicrous level of anticipation since his early dates with Jilly. Now, here he was, at forty-three, preparing the house for Riona's visit: changing sheets, putting out fresh towels, and tidying up his bedroom in the hope it might prove a good idea. He opened scented candles from Christmases past and turned Jilly's photo on the kitchen dresser to an angle where it could be more easily noticed. He wanted Riona to ask about her, to get to know her even, and – absurd as it was – he wanted Jilly to see Riona. He just knew Jilly would approve, he'd felt that from the start, and he was sure that Riona understood what a momentous occasion this was for him – another woman coming into Jilly's home, possibly (hopefully) to sleep in her bed, with her husband.

Afraid he might be jinxing things by overthinking it all, he left a pile of cutlery on a work surface ready to be laid out. If he set the table now, attempting to copy the way Jilly had done it, it could look as though he was trying too hard.

With ten minutes to go, he ran upstairs to dab on some expensive cologne, ruffled up his hair a little and undid an extra button on his shirt before quickly fastening it again.

Then he was back in the kitchen, checking to see if there were any more messages from her. She'd sent several this afternoon to find out if he had a high-quality olive oil, some Dijon mustard and enough tabasco sauce for a few dashes. He'd been able to reply yes to all three, and had added emojis letting her know he was hungry. He felt ridiculous about that now; for all he knew, he'd given a different impression all together, but he'd rather not think about what it might have been.

Fortunately there were no new messages; his disappointment would be beyond crushing if she let him down at the eleventh hour . . . But apparently she wasn't going to, for the doorbell was ringing already, which must surely mean she was as keen to see him as he was to see her.

His welcoming smile was so wide as he pulled the door open that it had a long way to fall when he saw who it actually was.

Oh God, oh God, the timing of this could hardly be worse.

CHAPTER TWENTY-SEVEN

Hanna and Jack were standing with a group of friends on the terrace of the Merchants' Hall dining room, sipping pre-dinner champagne and catching up with everyone's news. The evening was balmy and warm; everyone was in their finery, and the sound of birdsong was competing with the low rumble of chat and laughter.

To Hanna's relief, she was feeling more herself than she had over the past few days (the best cure, she'd found, was not to think about Astor at all if she could help it) and she was looking, according to Jack, simply stunning, in her high-necked, sleeveless red gown with a slit to mid-thigh that showed off her slender legs and shoulders. It was good to be relaxing with friends and feeling certain, at least for now, that no one knew what was actually going on in their lives.

Turning briefly to Jack as his hand found hers, she felt a swell of love for him warming her heart. Given a choice, she might have preferred to stay at home tonight, just the two of them, maybe to carry on what had begun during the late afternoon. Making love with him was always better, more deeply satisfying and thrilling than the heady rush of eroticism she experienced with random partners; it even made her wonder why she ever felt the need to do it. She did feel it though, she had to admit that, or she certainly had up to now.

'Maybe the time has come for us to stop our little games,' Jack had said earlier. 'You're enough for me, you know that, and you always will be—'

'And you're everything to me,' she interrupted, meaning it with all her heart. 'I'm sorry about the trouble this has caused . . .'

'Ssh, I don't want to hear you apologizing again. I just want to know you're all right. If you're not, we need to get you some help.'

Her eyebrows rose. 'As in therapy?'

'If that's what it takes. I think you're trying to minimize the effect it's had on you, but no one in this family is ever going to take sexual assault lightly.'

She took some time to consider his words, knowing them to be true, but she couldn't escape the part she'd played in it all. 'I just want to put it behind me,' she said, 'forget it ever happened. Although, I don't suppose we'll be able to do that until Astor can be convinced it wasn't Leo who attacked him.'

'Leave Astor to me,' he said, pulling her to him.

Standing back to look into his eyes she said, 'You know Leo thinks you paid someone to carry out the attack?'

He nodded. 'I'll be talking to him about that.'

'Did you?' she asked, feeling her heartbeat quicken in anticipation of the reply.

Pulling her back to him, he said, 'No, I didn't, but I might have if someone else hadn't beaten me to it.'

Now, as though sensing where her thoughts had strayed, he tightened his fingers around hers, while giving every appearance of being fascinated by whatever the president of the Chamber of Commerce was telling him. She drank more champagne and fell into easy chat with Jay Wells, one of Bristol's leading defence lawyers, whom she'd met a few times before and liked a lot.

She was laughing at one of Jay's wicked anecdotes when she became aware of Jack's phone ringing in his pocket. It was supposed to be turned off, but he'd clearly forgotten, so she reached in and handed it to him.

He appeared surprised at first, until seeing who was calling he said, 'I ought to take this,' and, moving away from their group, he descended the steps onto the grass.

Hanna kept an eye on him as she and Jay were joined by a Chew Valley farmer and his wife, and felt a beat of unease as she realized from the way Jack was talking that something was wrong.

Should she go to him?

If it was the police, some news about Astor, or if it was one of the children . . . Jenny perhaps . . . She wasn't sure what to do, but then he ended the call and turned around to look for her.

Quickly joining him, she said, 'What is it?'

'I have to go,' he told her.

'What? Who was that on the phone?'

'Steve Colridge. The Appledore site foreman. There's been an incident. He's on his way. I've said I'll meet him there.'

'But you can't drive . . .'

'I've only had half a glass of champagne. I'll get Tomas to drive me home so I can pick up my car and he'll come back for you.'

'I'll come with you. I don't want to stay on my own . . .'

He smiled and pressed a kiss to her forehead. 'You'll be fine. You know everyone at our table, they all love you, and there's no point the evening being ruined for both of us. I'll call as soon as there's some news.'

CHAPTER TWENTY-EIGHT

Seb was still on the doorstep, staring at his visitor.

'Cait!' he stated in dismay. 'What are you doing here?'

'Sorry to crash in on you like this,' she said, starting to turn away, then back again. Her face was tearstained and blotched, her eyes half-submerged in running mascara 'I hope it's OK. Can you help me in with Sofia? I didn't know where else to go.'

Realizing he had little choice, he followed her to her car, took the sleeping child from her arms and watched in alarm as she began to unload bags. 'Cait, what's happened? Please don't tell me you've fallen out with your parents again.'

Starting back to the house, she said, 'No, but I would have done if I'd stayed. They don't care about anything except themselves . . . You know what they're like . . .'

'What about Jenny?'

'She's out for the evening.'

As she disappeared inside, he settled Sofia more comfortably on his hip and followed. He needed to tell Cait that now wasn't a good time, that his easy availability since Jilly had passed was coming to an end, but how the heck was he going to do that when he was afraid of where she might go if he didn't let her in?

Closing the front door, he went to lay Sofia on the couch and tucked a couple of cushions around her before returning to the hall to call up the stairs to Cait. 'Are you OK? What are you doing?' he asked, afraid he already knew.

'Just putting my stuff in the guest room,' she called back. Suddenly appearing on the landing, she said, 'Seb, I'm so glad you're here, I don't know where I'd have gone . . .' She broke off as her phone buzzed and, holding up a hand to stall him, she clicked on to take the call and closed the bedroom door behind her.

Angry, worried and exasperated, he returned to the kitchen and stared across to Sofia. He suddenly badly wanted a drink, a Scotch, but he wasn't sure if he could risk it. There was never any telling with Cait how the next few minutes might play out, and there was every chance he could find himself behind the wheel of a car on his way to heaven only knew where.

Realizing he had to warn Riona that the evening probably wasn't going to be quite as they'd planned, he picked up his phone, but got no further than texting *Hi*, when there was another ring on the doorbell.

Jack or Hanna come to collect Cait?

He could always hope.

He hurried to open the door and, seeing Riona standing there looking so beautiful and sunny and happy, he forgot everything in his desire to sweep her into his arms and spin her round and round and round until she cried out for him to stop.

'Hello,' she said, her eyes twinkling merrily.

Stepping forward, he took her hand and kissed it gallantly. 'You look like a dream,' he murmured. 'Am I going to wake up in a minute?'

She laughed gaily, and was about to respond when Cait shouted out, 'Please tell me it's not my parents.'

Riona's eyes came questioningly to his.

He sighed and said, 'Cait, Jack and Hanna's daughter. She turned up a few minutes ago.'

Clearly surprised, Riona said, 'Well, it'll be nice to see her again. Does she know you were expecting me?'

'I haven't had chance to tell her . . .'

Hearing Cait's footsteps descending the stairs, Seb turned round, holding the door wider for Riona to come in.

'Hey!' Cait cried in apparent delight. 'It's Rhiannon, isn't it? Great to see you.'

'Riona,' Seb corrected.

Riona said, 'Cait, this is a lovely surprise. And don't you look a picture? Will you be joining us for dinner? I've brought enough, so you'll be very welcome.'

Quickly, Seb said, 'I'm sure Cait's . . .'

'You know what, I'd love to,' Cait decided, avoiding Seb's eyes. 'I'm starving, and I expect Sofia will be too when she wakes up. So that's really kind of you.'

'Your little girl's here?' Riona exclaimed delightedly. 'Where is she? I'd love to meet her.'

As Seb rolled his eyes, Cait went ahead into the sitting room, and said, dropping her voice to a whisper, 'I think she's still asleep. She's had a busy day.'

'Ah, she's beautiful,' Riona said softly. 'Such an angel. How old is she?'

'Eighteen months,' Cait replied proudly. 'And she can be a little rascal, but we all love her to bits. Don't we?' she added, looking up at Seb.

What else could he say but yes, when it was true? 'Would anyone like a drink?' he offered. 'Wine? G&T . . .'

'I'll take a G&T,' Riona smiled, coming to him in the kitchen, 'but first I'll go and get everything from the car. Chicken and spinach pasta, with lemon cream sauce,' she declared, 'unless you're vegetarian, Cait?'

Cait shrugged. 'Most of the time, but not always, and what you just said sounds fab.' She was engrossed in her phone again, and sank down next to Sofia to start texting.

'Why don't I come and give you a hand?' Seb murmured to Riona.

Apparently realizing he wanted to talk to her alone, she said, 'That would be lovely.' She dropped her purse on the countertop and led the way back outside.

'I'm sorry,' he groaned as soon as they were out of Cait's earshot. 'I had no idea she was coming . . . She seemed upset when she arrived, but apparently no longer . . .'

Putting a finger over his lips, she said, 'It's fine. Honestly,' and going up on tiptoe, she gave him a quick kiss before opening the car to take out the shopping.

'Of course,' she said, handing the bags over, 'I was looking forward to having you to myself for a while.'

Cheered by that, and even more by the wheelie bag she pulled out last, he said, 'I'm glad you're here. That's what matters.' And, managing to feel a lot more optimistic about the evening, he headed back inside.

Riona came in after him, leaving her small case at the foot of the stairs, and she began to unpack the groceries, keeping up a steady, light-hearted chat with Cait. Seb watched the way she moved so easily about the kitchen, as though she already belonged there. It warmed him, and made him glance at the photo of Jilly, as if she too were watching and approving of this new woman in her home.

Once the ingredients were prepared and ready to cook,

Seb topped up their wine glasses and joined them at the table, balking slightly when Cait said, 'So you're a psychiatrist, right? That's what Leo told me. Well, I think I might need you. Everyone says I'm batshit, out of control, raving, but I can tell you: anyone would be in my shoes. So would it be all right to come and have a chat when you can fit me in? I'll pay, obvs . . .'

Seb said, 'Cait, this probably isn't . . .'

'It's OK,' Riona said, putting a hand over his. 'I'd be very happy to help in any way I can, Cait, but my clinic is a residential facility, and we only take on clients who come with a referral, usually from another psychiatrist.'

Cait's lower lip jutted out as she considered this. 'But you'd be OK about having a chat?' she pressed.

'I would, but only to put you in touch with someone who deals with the kind of issues you feel you're having.'

Cait sipped some wine and seemed to be reflecting on this before finally turning to Seb and saying, 'You know about Dad, don't you?' Her tone made it more of a statement than a question.

Not at all sure he wanted to go down this road, he said, reluctantly, 'What about him?'

As Cait started to reply, there was a little thud from the sitting room, and Sofia came toddling towards them, arms outstretched to her mother. 'Ananan,' she gurgled as Cait swept her up and pressed a loud kiss to her cheek.

'Hello, sleepy head,' Cait said, smoothing back her curls. 'Nice of you to join us.'

'Ananan,' Sofia replied happily, and pointed towards Riona.

'She calls everyone that,' Cait explained. 'It was her first word, and Mum naturally thinks it's her.'

Sofia gave a piercing shriek and began reaching urgently for Seb.

'Does she always wake up so fast and in such a good mood?' Riona laughed.

Grimacing as she hauled the baby back from Seb, Cait said, 'Usually. Sorry, my angel, but you don't smell too good. We'd better take you upstairs and sort you out.'

After she'd gone, with Sofia screaming a protest, Riona said to Seb, 'It's wonderful how at home they seem to feel here.'

Seb gave a laugh. 'Leo and Cait have always treated the place as theirs. Jilly encouraged it.'

Riona's eyes found Jilly's photo. 'How did she die?' she asked gently.

He said, 'With courage and dignity.' Then, 'It was cancer.'

She nodded sadly. 'She looks very happy there.'

'It was taken before we knew she was ill.'

Her eyes returned to his as she said, 'Do you still miss her? Yes, of course you do.'

He didn't deny it, only said, 'We were together for a long time.' Then, 'How about you? Have you ever been married?'

She shook her head. 'No husband, no children. What family I have is in Ireland and the States, but what with this immersive therapy and various other things, it's been a while since I got together with any of them. We're in touch though, usually on Zoom.' Getting up from the table, she dropped a kiss lightly on his head as she passed, saying, 'Time to start cooking, don't you think? No, you stay there, I can manage, or maybe you can set out napkins and silverware.'

Happy to follow orders, he added more cutlery to the

pile he'd left on the countertop and dug out a small bowl and spoon for Sofia. 'Incidentally,' he said, 'you don't have to meet with Cait. I mean, I'm sure she'll appreciate it . . .'

'It's no trouble,' she assured him. 'I'll get her number before I leave and send her some times that might work. Do you have any idea what's troubling her?'

He shook his head and went to pick up his phone as it pinged with a text. 'It's from Hanna,' he announced, and read the message aloud. '*Any chance you can throw on your glad rags and come over to the Merchants' Hall? Jack has been called to a site emergency so I don't have a partner. No problem if you're not free. Just thought I'd ask. Hx*'

Riona's eyebrows were arched. 'If you'd like to go—'

'Absolutely not,' he interrupted. 'And if she knew you were here, she'd never have asked.'

'But if she's all alone . . .'

'She'll know just about everyone there. No, I'm not having anything else sabotaging our evening. I'll text back to let her know it's not possible, and I'll send your love.'

Riona nodded. 'Yes, please do that.'

After tapping in the message he said, 'If we'd met sooner we'd probably be there tonight, but I didn't have a plus one when the invitations went out and I'd had enough of turning up to events on my own. There's only so many matchmakers a man can deal with in one evening.'

Laughing, she tapped her wine glass to his. 'Their loss is my gain,' she declared, 'so I'm glad you resisted.'

He was about to pull her into his arms, when Cait made an untimely return with a refreshed and chatty Sofia.

'Ananan, woof.'

'Woof.' Cait laughed back. 'Say puppy.'

'Bubbeee,' Sofia echoed, a beaming smile on her face.

'She wants a dog,' Cait told them. 'It comes from living with Grandma and Gaston, the golden retriever. She's besotted with him. Riona, that smells delicious. I wish I could cook—'

'You're perfectly good at it,' Seb broke in, 'when you want to be. Now, what shall I get Sofia to drink?'

'Oh, I've got all her stuff upstairs,' Cait replied, 'I'll go get it,' but as she made to hand the baby to Seb, Sofia decided she'd rather go to Riona.

Laughing delightedly, Riona took her and began bouncing her around, saying, 'I feel very honoured, you know . . .'

'You'll be rethinking that when she won't let you go,' Cait warned, and with a little tweak of Sofia's nose she was gone.

'I'll carry on with the cooking,' Seb offered, 'if you tell me what to do.'

Eventually, with lots of help and even more distractions from Sofia, the meal was ready to serve. Cait came thundering downstairs when Seb called her.

'Sorry,' she gasped, unloading an armful of baby drinks and other paraphernalia onto one of the countertops. Breaking open a juice carton, she slotted in a tiny straw and handed it to Sofia. 'So, would you guys mind if I went out once we've eaten? I've just been chatting with some friends and they're getting together at this bar on the harbourside and I feel like I haven't seen them in ages.'

'What about Sofia?' Seb enquired, already knowing the answer.

'It won't be for long, and she loves it here, don't you, my sweetheart?'

'Mmm,' Sofia agreed, sucking greedily at her drink. Suddenly she wanted to get down, and once on the floor she ran from the kitchen into the sitting room and back again, squealing with joy.

'She's such a happy little girl,' Riona commented, almost wistfully.

'She's a pain,' Cait said affectionately, 'but we wouldn't change you for the world, would we?'

Off Sofia went again, making a sudden about-turn and coming to bump into Seb's legs. Clinging to his chinos she tilted her head back to look up at him.

'You're a wicked little thing,' he told her, 'who's got us all under her spell.'

'Mmm, woof,' she shouted, and off she ran again.

'So, what can I do?' Cait offered, picking up her glass and refilling it with wine.

'Just sit down. I'll serve,' Riona instructed.

'You won't be driving, will you?' Seb asked, looking meaningfully at the wine.

'Don't worry, I'll get an Uber. Honestly, you can be as bad as Dad at times, but thank God you're not him.'

Sensing some unpleasant rant against Jack looming, Seb headed her off by asking about the place she'd recently stayed at in Wales. Fortunately she was keen to talk about it, and as they tucked into the delicious food, she ran on to the time she'd spent touring southern Ireland with Ishan, Sofia's Dad, before Sofia was born.

'We're pretty sure she was conceived in a place called Abbeyknockmoy,' she informed them. 'Do you know it?' she asked Riona.

'I've heard of it,' Riona replied, 'but I don't think I've ever been there.'

'Yeah, well, not really surprised. Not a lot going on, apart from some Cistercian Abbey that Ishan wanted to see. He's like that, into all sorts of stuff you'd never think of yourself.'

'Are you still together?' Riona asked uncertainly.

Cait shook her head. 'But he's a brilliant dad and Sofes adores him. I mean, I do too, and maybe we'll get back together . . . He wants to, and I suppose I do in a way, it's just not a great idea while I'm dealing with all this stuff up here.' She twirled a finger at the side of her head. 'It's turning me into a basket case.' To Seb she said, 'Did you know that's what they used to call amputees during the First World War? Basket cases? Cruel beyond words. Ishan told me, because Ishan knows all sorts of useless stuff. Doesn't he, sweetie?' she said to Sofia. 'Daddy's way too clever for his own good, but we love him anyway.'

'Daddy,' Sofia declared with a serious frown. Her face was covered in creamy lemon sauce and as she burped she broke into a devilish grin, as if she knew it was naughty.

Cait kept up a running diatribe about all sorts of nothing, alternately feeding herself and Sofia, until finally she blew them all a kiss and headed out.

As the front door closed, Seb looked at Riona and said, dryly, 'Exhausted yet?'

Riona laughed. Sofia was on her lap now, holding a book upside down and chewing on the hard cover. 'I think Cait is nervous about something,' she said. 'But what would she have to be nervous about?'

Starting to clear the table, Jack said, 'Nothing that I know of.' He added, 'All I can tell you is that she's a constant worry to Jack and Hanna, to us all, but she's eighteen, so in charge of her own life . . . Anyway, we're not going to let her hijack the evening completely, are we? Can we talk about something else now?'

Twinkling, she said, 'Of course, anything you like, but why don't we leave all this and make ourselves more comfortable over there?'

'We could,' he agreed, 'but there's a proper sitting room upstairs. Why don't we take our drinks, and Sofia, up there?'

It turned out to be a mistake, because as soon as Sofia saw the TV she wanted to watch it, and since they had no idea what toddlers her age were into, they ended up choosing a Disney movie for them all. Sofia didn't seem to mind, simply settled down on Seb's lap. By the time the film ended all three of them were asleep, Sofia across Seb's chest, Riona with her head on his shoulder.

'Where's she going to sleep?' Riona whispered when she and Seb finally woke up.

Relieved that she hadn't launched straight into saying it was time for her to leave, he said, 'We can put her in Cait's bed. She's used to sleeping with her mother.'

'OK. Any word from Cait to say when she'll be back?'

Still holding onto Sofia as he got up, he checked his phone and said, 'No, nothing. But there's a message here from Hanna sending you her love.'

Clearly pleased, Riona came to take the baby and said, 'Let me see if I can find something to change her into, like a dry nappy, before we settle her down.'

She still hadn't said anything about going home, so he dared to ask if he should carry her bag upstairs.

'That would be lovely,' she replied, heading off across the landing with Sofia.

A while later he was standing at his own bedroom window, gazing out at the night, when he heard her come in. He turned around and felt his heart rate slowing. She was so beautiful, desirable and he wanted her so badly, but he was almost afraid to move. He was so certain he'd do something wrong.

He didn't. Not even slightly. In fact, it all seemed to happen so naturally that it was as though their bodies already knew one another, and their minds were in tune. She was everything he'd imagined her to be: soft, supple, passionate and wonderfully uninhibited. He wondered if he'd ever be able to get enough of her, and it seemed she felt the same about him.

It was a long time before they finally parted and fell asleep in each other's arms.

The room was flooded with light when Seb woke the next morning. He'd slept so deeply that it took him a moment to reconnect with what had happened only hours ago, and as the desire welled up in him again, he turned onto his side, reaching for her.

The bed was empty and cold.

Frowning, he flipped back the sheet and went to put on his robe. Was she in the bathroom? Downstairs making coffee? With a wrench of disappointment, he noticed that her bag had gone. She must have left in the night without managing to disturb him.

He picked up his phone, hoping to find a message, but there were none from her. He glanced around the room – no note either. Deciding it was more likely she'd have left one in the kitchen where there were pens and paper, he dressed quickly in case he ran into Cait, and went downstairs to find out. On the way he noticed the guest room door wide open, a sure sign that Cait wasn't asleep inside, so he stepped into the room to check on Sofia.

This bed was empty too.

A stirring of unease began to work its way into life.

Had Cait come back and left again with Sofia?

Their things were still scattered all over the place.

Continuing down the stairs, he pulled open the front door. Cait's car was there, but Riona's had gone.

Hardly knowing what he was thinking now, he went quickly through to the kitchen. There was no note, nothing to tell him where anyone was.

He was struggling to make any sense of this.

Running back up to his bedroom, he picked up his phone to call Riona. After seven rings he was diverted to voicemail. Without leaving a message, he tried Cait.

No reply from her either. He had no idea if she'd come back in the night, but if she had, and her car was still here, where was she now?

More importantly, where was Sofia?

He checked every room in the house, calling her name in case she'd hidden herself away somewhere, while still trying to get hold of Cait and Riona. Neither was picking up or responding to his messages.

It felt crazy even to think that Riona might have taken Sofia. He couldn't, wouldn't, think it, because there was no way Riona would do something like that.

He stared at his phone helplessly. Why the hell didn't someone call him back?

CHAPTER TWENTY-NINE

I'm staring at Riona's phone on the table. It keeps ringing, over and over. It's Seb, but I can't answer. I wouldn't know what to say to him; I'm afraid of what he might want.

Where is Riona?

She came back, and here's her phone, but where is she?

The others aren't awake yet; I haven't heard them this morning anyway and they're usually so noisy.

Where are you, Riona?

She needs to come now, to answer the phone and speak to Seb.

Where are you? Where are you? Where are you? You need to be here.

CHAPTER THIRTY

Hanna had been trying all morning to get hold of Jack. She knew the reception was poor at that particular site, and that he'd call as soon as he was able, but she couldn't help worrying. It wasn't like him to be out of contact for so long, especially through the night, and if something serious had happened . . .

Best not to finish that thought until she knew that it had.

Nothing had made the news, so she was staying hopeful that no one had been injured, or worse.

As time ticked on and there was still no word, she decided to try Graeme. Although he and Andee were in Italy right now, he was as invested in the project as Jack, so there was a good chance he knew what was going on. Since she didn't have his number, she called Andee's.

'Hi, this is a surprise,' Andee cried cheerfully when she answered. 'Is everything OK?'

'Uh – yes, it's fine.' It didn't sound as though Andee knew anything about the Appledore incident and Hanna wasn't sure now about telling her. 'I just – I wondered if Jack had been in touch with Graeme?'

'Not that I know of. Why? Is there a problem?' Andee said, sounding puzzled.

Knowing she couldn't lie to Andee, at least not outright, Hanna said, 'I'm not sure. Apparently something happened last night at the Appledore site. Jack went down there to investigate and I haven't heard from him since.'

'Really? That's odd. Let me talk to Graeme, find out what he knows. Don't go away.'

As Hanna waited, she wandered out of the bedroom and looked down from the gantry to where Leo and half a dozen of his friends were tucking into one of Florina's hearty Romanian breakfasts. It looked delicious, but she knew she'd be unable to eat if she tried. The nerves fluttering wildly in her stomach had no time for anything but the mounting anxiety that was driving them.

She checked her phone as a call came in and, seeing it was Seb, she let it go to messages. She'd call him back as soon as she'd spoken to Andee again.

Finally Andee said, 'Graeme's getting on to the site now. He says you should try not to worry because if it was serious he'd already know.'

Unsure whether to feel relieved by that or not, Hanna said, 'OK, thanks. I expect Jack'll roll up any minute, anyway. So, are you having a lovely holiday?'

Dryly, Andee said, 'We're trying, but you know, it's so beautiful here and there's only so much one person can take.'

It took Hanna a moment to catch on to the irony. She laughed and said, 'I feel for you, I really do.'

Sounding suspicious, Andee said, 'Are you all right, Han? I'm sensing something . . .'

'I'm fine,' Hanna assured her, suddenly wishing that Andee was right here, right now. She was probably the only person in the world – apart from Jack – she felt comfortable confiding in. Knowing Andee, she would find a way to deal with this awful sense of foreboding that had been plaguing her since the incident with Astor. But she was hardly going to land her paranoia on Andee in the middle of her holiday. 'Life's just been a bit . . . stressful lately,' she admitted. 'I'll tell you about it another time . . .' She turned at the sound of a car coming down the drive and relief flooded through her when she saw it was Jack. 'He's home!' she declared, probably too loudly. 'Please tell Graeme Jack's home, so no need to call me back.'

'OK, that's good. Glad to know he's all right. I just want to feel sure that you are too.'

'I am, honestly,' Hanna insisted. 'Let's get together when you're back. When will that be?'

'The end of next week. I'll call you as soon as we're in.'

As she rang off, Hanna took a breath and let it go slowly. She was feeling anxious again and didn't understand why. Was it part of a delayed reaction to what had happened with Astor? One minute she seemed to be dealing with it; the next all kinds of dark thoughts were crowding in on her. It wasn't over, much as she might want it to be. He was trying to blackmail Jack and Jack wasn't going to stand for it, so how could anything possibly end well?

Hearing Jack talking to the boys, she returned to the gantry and stared down at him. He looked tired, she thought, and the clothes he'd evidently changed into before heading for Appledore were crumpled, as though he might have been in them all night. However, he seemed to have no problem with banter, was in the thick of it with a couple of the drier wits at the table. As usual he ended up letting them score points at his expense. She half-expected him to sit down and help himself to food, but apparently he'd sensed he was being watched because he looked up and found her eyes.

She gave him a half-smile and turned away, going back into the bedroom. He'd know it was a signal for him to join her and he did a few minutes later, closing the door behind him and taking her in his arms.

'What happened?' she asked, feeling stronger just for being held by him.

Sighing he said, 'It wasn't as bad as we feared, thank God, but it's a big setback for the build. An investigation will start on Monday – tomorrow. We've had police and site inspectors, structural engineers, health and safety officials, you name it, there all night. I thought I was never going to get away.'

She pulled back to look at him, her eyes searching his. 'I was worried,' she told him. 'Why didn't you answer my calls?'

Letting her go he began unbuttoning his shirt. 'Sorry, my phone ran out of battery at some point, and the charger in the car isn't working. Are you OK?'

'I guess so,' she replied as he sat on the bed to tug off his socks. 'I just started imagining all sorts of things when I didn't hear from you.'

He looked up and seeming finally to catch on to what was really happening, he came to take her face between his hands. 'You're afraid this had something to do with Hugo Astor,' he said softly, 'but I promise you it didn't, so I want you to put it out of your mind. OK?'

She leaned into him as he pressed a kiss to her forehead. It felt ridiculous now even to have thought it.

'So how was the rest of the evening?' he asked, sitting down again.

'It was fine. I called Graeme just now to find out what was happening.'

He frowned. 'He's in Italy. What did you expect him to do?'

'I wanted to know if he'd heard from you, but he hadn't.'

He stared at her hard, as if trying to puzzle something out, until taking her hand he pulled her to stand between his legs. 'We decided we didn't need to contact him,' he said, 'until we had something definite to tell him.'

'So I did the wrong thing?'

'It doesn't matter. He was always going to find out . . . Obviously. He's probably talking to his main contractor as we speak. Luckily for them, the problems aren't as much theirs as mine, but I'm not going to worry about them now. I need to take a shower and get some sleep; with any luck I might then start to feel human again.'

As he disappeared into the bathroom, she stayed where she was, staring absently at his discarded clothes on the floor, feeling as though something wasn't right about this. Maybe she was allowing paranoia to cover everything with sinister and portentous meaning. She needed to pull herself together, to stop this downward spiral into dark and negative places . . . Whatever had happened last night couldn't have had anything to do with Hugo Astor. The man was still in hospital, at least as far as she knew, and anyway, why on earth would he organize some sort of sabotage of a build site – if he even could – when his attempt to blackmail Jack was still on the table?

He wouldn't, was the answer, so she needed to erase him from her mind now and get on with her day.

CHAPTER THIRTY-ONE

Seb was standing at the front door, watching Caitlin tugging off Sofia's muddy little wellies. Never had he felt so pleased or relieved to see them in his life. They'd turned up a few minutes ago, fresh from a walk on the Downs. Cait was really sorry that she hadn't got his messages, but he knew what the signal was like around here.

It was true; it was appalling.

'I didn't mean to worry you,' she apologized again, leaving the wellies on the doorstep as Sofia raced along the hall into the kitchen. 'The house was so quiet when I left, I assumed you were asleep and I didn't want to wake you.'

'It's OK,' he assured her, closing the door and wanting to hug her just for being safe and having Sofia with her. 'No harm done. I just wasn't sure where you were . . . Anyway, as long as you're both here . . .' He swept Sofia up as she charged back towards him, and blew a loud raspberry on her cheek, making her shriek with laughter. 'Did you have a lovely time?' he asked her, holding her out to see her dear little face.

'Woof,' she replied, her eyes shining with mischief.

'Yes, we saw lots of dogs.' Cait smiled, going through to wash her hands at the sink. 'And we were going to bring some coffees back until I realized I wouldn't be able to manage them with you running all over the place.'

Sofia was reaching for Seb's cheeks. 'Ananan,' she cooed.

Settling her into the crook of his arm, he said, nonchalantly, 'What time did you get in last night?'

Cait shrugged. 'About two, I guess. Sorry to be so late, and if I disturbed you. And thanks for putting my little rascal to bed.'

He took one of Sofia's drinks from the fridge and allowed her to help sort out the straw. 'That was Riona,' he admitted. Then added, 'Did you happen to see her before you went out this morning?'

Cait shook her head. 'No, but she's just texted me her number so we can meet up . . . Sofia! You've just spilled that all over your top. Now what are we going to do?'

'Woof,' Sofia responded as Cait came to take her and stood her on a chair to begin stripping off her hoodie.

Seb checked his phone as it rang. 'It's your mother,' he told Cait, and clicked on. 'Hi, Han. How are you?'

Cait mouthed, *Don't tell her I'm here.*

'I'm fine, thanks,' Hanna replied. 'How are you? I saw you called earlier.'

'Ah yes . . . Uh, it was . . .' He glanced witheringly at Cait. 'I was just wondering how you got on at the banquet last night and if everything's OK with Jack? You said something about a site emergency in your text.'

Cait's eyes rounded as she looked up at him. *All lies,* she mouthed.

Seb turned away.

'It didn't prove as bad as they feared,' Hanna said. 'But it kept him up all night, so he's asleep now. Aren't you two supposed to be fishing this afternoon?'

'At the lake? We are.' He'd actually forgotten, although it was something he and Jack did regularly on Sunday afternoons when neither had anything else on. 'I was wondering,' he said, 'about inviting Riona. I'm not sure yet if she's free today, but if she is . . .'

'She'd be more than welcome. And if the rain holds off, perhaps I can persuade her into a spot of tennis?'

'I'll mention it,' he promised. 'I need to go now, but glad to hear all's OK with Jack. See you later.' Ringing off he said to Cait, 'I wish you wouldn't do that.'

'So what happened at the site?' she asked.

'I don't know. Now I'm going to pop up to my study for a moment. After that, how about I take you girls over to Côte for breakfast?'

Cait's face lit up. 'You're on, because we're starving, aren't we Sofes?'

Once in his study, Seb took a moment before trying to connect to Riona. He was feeling wretched, sick with himself, for the way he'd suspected her of taking Sofia; he couldn't imagine what had got into him even to think it. Panic, he supposed, pure and irrational – but that was a poor excuse after how close they had become last night.

Should he tell her, be honest, see if they could laugh it off?

'That's what happens with children,' she might say, 'all coherent thought goes out the window if you think some harm might have come to them.'

It was true, it did, but he couldn't see it going well if she thought he had so little trust in her. So why risk it, because of course he trusted her.

She answered on the fourth ring in a voice brimming with humour and affection. 'I was just about to call you,' she told him. 'How are you this morning?'

His eyes closed as her beautiful, musical Irish voice washed over him like a balm. 'Yes, good, fine,' he replied. 'A little disappointed to wake up and find you'd already left.'

'Ah yes, I'm sorry about that, it just seemed better than waking you up. I hope you didn't mind too much, but I really had to get back. It's not good for me to be away for the entire night, and I'd forgotten to bring my phone so I couldn't contact anyone. Will you forgive me?'

Too readily, he said, 'Of course.' *That's it, Seb, turn yourself into a doormat.* 'I'm not going to let anything spoil last night,' he told her softly. 'It was very special.'

In the same, intimate tone, she said, 'For me too. I can hardly wait to see you again.'

Without hesitation, he said, 'How about this afternoon? I'm going to Jack and Hanna's and they've invited you to come along. Jack and I will probably do some fishing for a couple of hours, and Hanna's very keen to get you on the tennis court.'

'Oh, how sweet. I'd love to say yes, but I'm afraid it's not going to be possible today. There are things going on here that I need to be around for. I'm so sorry. I hope they won't write me off for another time.'

Trying to quash his disappointment, he said, 'I'm sure they won't. Shall I call you later?'

'That would be lovely. If I don't answer it'll be because it's not easy to speak, but I will call when I can. Please send my love to Hanna, and to Cait. Did she come home last night?'

'She did. I'm about to take her and Sofia for breakfast. Cait's very pleased to have your number.'

'That's good. I hope she calls so we can start getting to the bottom of what's actually troubling her.'

After ringing off, Seb sat quietly with those last words, glad to think Riona was willing to help, but also wondering what Cait might tell her. Should he be worried? He couldn't think why, but he was also asking himself if he should mention it to Jack and Hanna.

On the other hand, Cait seemed to have genuinely connected with Riona – not difficult, he knew – so maybe this was a good opportunity for her to air what was bothering her without the rest of them fussing around trying to work things out – and usually making everything worse.

CHAPTER THIRTY-TWO

At this time on a Tuesday, Hanna was usually visiting one or more of her sponsored charities to assess their ongoing needs and what more could be done to help. This morning, however, she'd received an email from the chair of Giving Chances asking if they could reschedule to next week, and her other appointment with the hospice had also been moved. She wasn't sorry, for she had a lot of reading to get through before her meetings later in the day, which was why she'd asked Donna, her PA, to make sure she wasn't disturbed unless it was something that really couldn't wait.

Apparently something couldn't, for her door suddenly opened and Jack came in, holding up a hand for her to stay seated.

She immediately tensed, feeling certain this wasn't going to be good, especially when he made a point of closing the door behind him.

'I thought you should know,' he said, coming to perch on the edge of her desk, 'that Astor's sending someone to clear out his office in about an hour.'

Her insides gave a sickening lurch at the mere mention of his name. 'Does that mean he's left hospital?' she asked.

'I believe he has, but apparently his brother and a close

friend are "acting as his representatives" in this particular instance.'

Profoundly relieved that Astor wasn't coming in person, she said, 'Have you actually spoken to him?'

'Yes, and he tells me that his offer to remain silent about what happened with you, and Leo, would be withdrawn on Friday unless he's received a positive response to his request.'

She felt the heat of anger rush through her. 'I hope you told him to go to hell,' she snapped.

His eyebrows arched. 'What I said was that he'd be getting a severance payment in line with the terms of his contract, and a personal commitment from me not to press charges against him provided he signed a Non-Disclosure Agreement.'

Hanna's heart turned over. These were the kind of high-stakes games he was so good at; they did nothing but frighten her. 'What did he say?' she asked.

He shrugged. 'I ended the call at that point to give him some time to think things over.'

'Was that wise?'

His smile showed how unperturbed he was by it all. 'My guess is we'll be in a stand-off situation until Friday, possibly into early next week, by which time he'll have come to realize, if he hasn't already, that he can't win this. Not if he ever wants to work again.'

Hanna swallowed dryly, and got up to go and look out of the window. It was raining, chillingly gloomy for a late July day, apart from the mushrooms of colourful umbrellas bobbing along the street outside. The company car park was almost full. It seemed everyone was in today, and she couldn't help wondering, with a wrenching sense of humiliation, how many of them knew what was really going on with Hugo Astor and why his employment had come to such an abrupt end. Even if they had an inkling of the truth, there was no doubt they'd remain loyal to Jack; he was a great boss, fair, generous, and greatly admired for never making enemies – except she'd now managed to do that for him.

'Hey,' he said, coming to put an arm around her, 'it's going to be all right, I promise.'

Wishing she could believe him, she said, 'Will you meet these *representatives* when they come?'

'I have better things to do, but someone from security will be with them to make sure they don't wander where they shouldn't be, or try to take something that doesn't belong to him.'

Out of the window, she could see their son driving into the car park. 'And are you going to tell Leo what's going on?' she asked.

'Not yet. He won't know about Astor's office being cleared, because he'll be in a meeting with me and the chiefs.' This was how he generally referred to his heads of Operations, Finance, Construction, Technology, Marketing, Corporate Strategy, and the various other shareholding executives who made up the board. 'We have to find a new lawyer,' he reminded her, 'and there will be other important points of business to discuss.'

Such as the weekend emergency at Appledore, she thought, realizing she hadn't even asked about it since. But he wouldn't have expected her to; it was his side of the business and he'd obviously have it all well in hand by now.

Wishing she possessed even a modicum of his sang-froid, she moved away from him as she said, 'I'm OK to do this your way, but if he calls your bluff . . .'

'He won't,' he said gently. 'Trust me. By this time next week, it'll all be over. You just wait and see.'

CHAPTER THIRTY-THREE

The sun had staged a spectacular breakthrough in the past hour, making everything – trees, cars, pavements, buildings, gleam and sparkle as if they'd suddenly become brand new. People were smiling again; warmth was spreading through the air and everything seemed to smell good and fresh and enlivening.

Riona and Cait were sipping cappuccinos at a pavement table outside Coffee#1 on Princess Victoria Street. There were plenty of people around, strolling by, or hurrying to wherever they were going, but no one was close enough to overhear their conversation. Not that they were discussing anything of a particularly personal nature, this was more of a 'getting to know one another' rendezvous, as Riona was terming it, although it seemed to be more about her getting to know Cait. But that was OK; it was supposed to be about Cait, and she didn't mind in the slightest hearing all about Sofia, Sofia's father, Jaden, the boyfriend in Wales (soon to be ex), Cait's friends, her confusion over what to do with her life . . . It was all helping to form a clearer picture of the girl, and it might provide a little insight into the nervousness and anger she was suppressing.

The only people Cait didn't seem to want to talk about

were her parents, which Riona found interesting since she was sure they were at the crux of everything. However, there was much less reticence where Seb was concerned, and it touched Riona deeply to learn how much he mattered to Cait. She talked about how he and her father had first met at uni, and the wonderful memories she had of him while growing up – of Jilly too. (Did Riona mind her talking about Jilly? Not at all, Riona assured her.)

'It's great that he's met you,' Cait told her. 'I'm sure he'd kill me if he could hear me saying that – like *pressure*! But I reckon he must find it hard when he's not working so much, like now . . . The summer break probably seems to go on for ever, although he spends a lot of time with Dad. And Mum, of course. Has he ever told you the story of when he and Dad first met Mum?'

'No, I don't believe he has,' Riona replied, keen to hear it.

Cait laughed and grimaced in a way that wasn't altogether pleasant. 'It was typical of my dad. Seb saw her first and he said it was straightaway like no one else was in the room. He reckons she was everything he'd ever dreamt of, a goddess – I know he's teasing her when he says that, or I suppose he is; I mean she's not a goddess, is she? They were at some student party, apparently, so I'm guessing everyone was stoned so she probably did come across a bit other-worldly . . . Anyway, Seb and Mum clock one another and he's pretty certain she's interested, but then Dad sees her and swoops in before Seb can even get past hello. That's the kind of thing Dad does. He has to win, you see, no matter who or what it is. Jack Madden is number one, top dog, the biggest enchilada – the one all the women want, and who all the men want to be. Apart from Seb, thank God.' She finished on a turbulently bitter note and looked away, either embarrassed or wanting to pull back.

'I'm not saying Dad doesn't care about Mum,' she continued, staring down at her coffee now. 'I mean I know he does, but . . .' She shrugged and didn't continue.

Intrigued, Riona said, 'Does the rivalry still exist between your dad and Seb?'

Cait shrugged. 'It might on Dad's part, but Seb's not like that. He's too easy-going, too decent a human being to play Dad's sort of games. Mum blinds herself to them, which makes her just as bad, if you ask me.'

Though it was tempting to ask her to expand on that, Riona decided it was best just to let Cait keep talking, taking it at her own pace, and elaborating only if she wanted to.

She continued to criticize and condemn her parents, mock and cruelly imitate them, and all with a ferocity that didn't quite mask the pain. She thought they were foolish and deceitful, selfish and fake, but it was clear to Riona that she loved them in spite of how hard she was trying not to.

Then quite suddenly, unexpectedly, she said something that Riona had to ask her to repeat.

Cait did, with a look so haunted and raw that Riona was in no doubt that they'd reached the knotted and tangled root of Cait's issues, and now the poor girl was looking to Riona to tell her what to do.

All Riona could think about as she returned to the clinic was how much she wished Cait hadn't confided in her. There was nothing she could do to help, no way of changing the situation, of making any part of it right or acceptable.

However, she'd promised to give it some serious thought before she and Cait spoke again.

'Does Seb know?' she'd asked before leaving.

'I'm not sure,' Cait replied, 'I'm too afraid to ask in case he doesn't.'

Riona wondered if she, herself, should ask Seb, but she didn't want to go any deeper into it; it was bad enough that she knew this much.

Moments after she walked in the door, she could feel herself being sucked back into this troubled world of the clinic. Blanche appeared in the kitchen, looking tense and worried, and Riona felt a deep resistance to being pulled into the dark and tormented depths of Blanche's psyche. To go there was exhausting, debilitating; she selfishly wanted to walk away and leave Blanche to cope on her own.

If only that were possible.

It would be one day; it was what they were working towards, but today the escape felt a long way off, and when she considered what she'd just learned about Jack Madden, she wished with all her heart that she could turn back the clock to a time before Blanche had found Hanna.

CHAPTER THIRTY-FOUR

Friday came and went with no communication from Hugo Astor, although Jack had warned it might go on into the early part of next week, so it seemed that was where they were headed.

Jack, typically, wasn't worried. The day passed without him even mentioning it, and later they joined friends at the Ring o' Bells pub at Compton Martin for dinner, where, as usual, he was the life and soul. Nothing seemed to touch him, and Hanna only wished she could be the same, but she simply couldn't get it out of her mind. If they didn't pay up, Astor was going to go public with everything he knew about her, and twist it around to make it look as though she'd wanted what had happened in her office when Leo had come in. She was going to come out of this so badly she couldn't imagine being able to hold her head up again. And then there was what could happen to Leo if he was charged with the attack on Astor.

How could Jack bear to let it drag on like this?

What made him so confident that they'd win and Astor would just go away?

After spending most of Saturday at the office catching

up on paperwork, Jack called on his way home to let Hanna know that he was dropping in on the Valley Fest, where Jenny had set up camp for the night. She had Sofia with her, and was joined by other friends from around the area. Cait and Ishan were joining them later, as were Leo and Olivia. Hanna was sorry to be missing the big event with its always impressive music line-up, but she and Jack had accepted an invitation to a theatre premiere in Bath before realizing that the dates clashed.

'Listen, I know your heart's not in this evening,' Jack said as they began dressing ready to go out. 'So would you rather stay at home?'

Surprised, she said, 'With you, or on my own?'

His smile was ironic. 'I was meaning with me, but if you'd like me to go without you . . .'

'No, no . . . Do you mean it, you'd stay at home if I said I wanted to?'

'I wouldn't have offered if I didn't.'

She eyed him suspiciously. It wasn't like him to bail on an evening at such short notice, which meant, 'You're not keen to go either?'

He shrugged. 'I'm easy, I just want you to stop stressing over this Astor business, that's all, and I'm not sure whether you'll manage it better if we stay here or go out. What do you think?'

Knowing if that were the deciding factor, it wouldn't make a difference either way, she said, 'If we weren't meeting Peter and Harriet and their daughter wasn't in the play, I'd say let's stay at home. As it is, neither of us will feel good about letting them down.'

'OK, if you're sure.' And that seemed to be the end of it as he checked his watch. 'Seb should be here any time now. We wouldn't want to let him down either. Do you know if he managed to get a seat for Riona?'

'Apparently not, which was a big disappointment for him. I know he's keen to show her off, but I guess there'll be other occasions.'

'I'm sure there will.' Going into the dressing room, he selected what he was going to wear and brought it back to the bedroom. 'She called me earlier,' he said, pulling on his undershorts.

'Who?'

'Riona.'

Hanna blinked in surprise. 'Really? What for?'

'She asked if we could meet.'

Her heart gave a jolt of unease. *Please don't let Riona be falling for Jack; it would totally crush Seb if she wasn't as serious about him as he was about her.* 'I thought,' she said, hoarsely, knowing she wouldn't like it much either, 'that we were ending our little games.'

His eyebrows arched. 'I don't think it was about anything like that, and we *are* ending the games – unless you still want to go to the parties when they come up.'

They seemed part of another life now. 'Do you?' she countered.

Shaking out his shirt, he said, 'I want what you want, and if that's monogamy, then that's what we'll have.'

She felt suddenly light-headed, as if this conversation was moving out of her realm of understanding. 'I'm not sure you sound committed to it,' she accused.

Without missing a beat, he said, 'That would be because you're not seeing anything very clearly at the moment. Hanny, this time will pass, we'll relax again, and when we do we'll be open to all sorts of things, the way we always have . . .'

'Is this you clearing the way to see Riona, *Jacky*?' She could feel how pinched her face was, hear the pettiness and pathetic insecurity in her tone, but this was the last thing she'd expected tonight, considering what they were going through right now.

He regarded her steadily, eyes half-closed, a certain impatience in his manner as he said, carefully, 'I don't know why she wants to meet, but I didn't get the impression it was for the reasons you seem to think.'

'So what did she say?'

'That there's something she thought I should know.'

She frowned. 'Concerning what?'

'She didn't want to go into it on the phone, but she mentioned having met with Cait yesterday. Whether the two things are related, I've no idea.'

'So have you arranged to see her?'

'I invited her to come by the office on Monday at five. You can be there, if you like.'

Thinking she probably would like, she said, 'Are you going to mention it to Seb?'

'I have no reason not to. She didn't ask me not to tell him.'

Certain Seb would feel better if he was at the meeting too, she said, 'You don't seem very interested in whatever she has to say.'

'Not true. I'm intrigued.'

So was she. 'It has to be something to do with Cait. It's too much of a coincidence otherwise.'

Jack nodded. 'I just wonder why it was me she called, and not you,' he said.

CHAPTER THIRTY-FIVE

Seb was in the main guest suite of Lake House, a bright, spacious set of rooms on the opposite landing to Jack and Hanna's, with views down over the lake and on out to the Mendips beyond. He'd always found it calming here, restorative even, and had especially so during the truly difficult months following Jilly's passing.

He was sorry Riona hadn't been able to join them last night, but was even more so about today, for he could imagine how much she'd enjoy waking up to this view and relaxing into a Madden-style Sunday. It was always easy being around his best friends, lingering over breakfast, sometimes going out for it, taking long walks around the valley, or in the hills, playing tennis, and spending a few hours just relaxing with the papers. Riona seemed to have so little time off, and even when she did it was curtailed by her commitments at the clinic.

Still, she'd assured him the project wouldn't go on for much longer, so he remained hopeful that she would be able to spend more time with him in the not-too-distant future. For now he'd satisfy himself with sending her a Good Morning text with a photograph of the view and a wish you were here.

As he stood at the window awaiting her reply, he spotted Jack heading down to the lake in shorts and polo shirt, no doubt on his way to check over the platform he'd installed years ago for their fishing afternoons. Occasionally they found strangers had set up their own camp there, but Jack never tried to move them on. If there was room he'd join them; if not he'd pass the time of day with them before wandering off to find another spot on the bank. After all, the lake and its shores weren't private property, so he was well aware that he had no exclusive rights to fish – or to the platform, even if he had built it.

Hey you, Riona texted. *It looks gorgeous. Really wish I was with you.*

He texted back. *Maybe you could get down here later?*

Let's not rule it out, but things are a little chaotic at the moment. Nothing to worry about. What are you doing today?

Apart from missing you? Just chilling; no set plans apart from fishing with Jack later.

Will you be back in Bristol this evening?

That's the plan. I could be free if you are.

Let's keep in touch about that. How was the play?

Less said the better. He was about to confess to being a little worried about Hanna, who definitely wasn't herself, but decided it might seem disloyal so kept it to himself.

How are Jack and Hanna? Did I tell you I think they're lucky to have you as a friend?

Smiling at that, he typed, *And I'm lucky to have you. Sorry, was that too much?*

Not at all. I like to think of being yours. I'm afraid I have to stop now for a while, but let's text again soon.

She added a row of heart emojis, so he sent the same

back, then sat for a while reading it all over, cringing and laughing at himself for behaving like a besotted teenager.

An hour later, following breakfast, he and Hanna joined a group from around the valley for a five-mile hike, while Jack went to check on the festival goers, taking extra supplies and cash since they'd apparently run out.

He and Hanna didn't get much time to talk as they walked, but he knew he was right to be concerned about her simply from the way she slipped her hand through his arm. She usually only did that when she was feeling vulnerable or anxious – and when Jack wasn't around.

Not until they were finally heading up Awkward Hill at the end of the trek, with the rest of the group far behind, did he say, 'What's happening about Hugo Astor?'

He felt her arm tightening around his. 'I'm not sure,' she replied. 'We haven't heard from him.'

Wishing there was something more he could do to ease her fears, he said, 'Jack won't let anything get out, you know that.'

Her breath caught on a sob as she said, 'I'm sure he won't, but I'm worried about what he might do to stop it.'

Seb had to admit it concerned him too, although Jack wasn't a violent man. He never had been, had no need to be when he was so good at resolving difficult, even impossible situations with charm, persuasion and mitigation. On the other hand, his family had never been under this sort of threat before. No matter what kind of front he put on, Jack certainly wouldn't be taking kindly to that.

Changing the subject as a group of fellow hikers closed in on them, Hanna said, 'How's your dad? When did you last see him?'

With a twinge of conscience, Seb said, 'A couple of

months ago, but I'm planning to drive over there in the next week or two.'

'Is your sister still going in most days?'

'She is, and I'm due to speak to her today so she can give me the latest.'

Hanna's smile was weak, showing that she wasn't really listening. After a while, she said, 'When you next go for a visit, I think I'd like to come with you, if that's OK? I was always fond of him.'

Surprised, and touched, he said, 'As he was of you, but I'm not sure, in his right mind, he'd want you to see him the way he is.'

'No,' she sighed, 'he probably wouldn't.'

They fell silent then and continued to walk, arm in arm, until they finally parted company with the others at the gates to the house.

'Would you do something for me?' she asked as Seb pressed in the security code. 'When you're with Jack this afternoon, will you try to find out what he's planning? You don't have to tell me what it is. I know if it's bad you'll try to stop him.'

'Of course,' he said softly, 'but honestly, I'm sure there's nothing to worry about.'

It was just after two when Seb, after a long chat with his sister, wandered on to the terrace to find Hanna setting the table for a six o'clock Sunday roast. She still felt edgy, but was doing her best to hide it, and was grateful that he didn't mention it. There was no point in them discussing anything further until after he'd spoken to Jack.

'Lord of the manor not back yet?' he asked, helping himself to an apple from the fruit bowl.

'About twenty minutes ago,' she replied, attempting a smile. 'He's taken the tackle boxes and rods down to the lake and left the chairs and booze for you to carry.'

Seb's eyebrows rose. 'I see, it's going to be one of those fishing afternoons, is it?' he said dryly. Going to swing the cool bag up on to his shoulder, he stuck his phone in his shirt pocket and grabbed the picnic chairs. 'What are you going to do for the rest of the afternoon?' he asked.

Her smile was wry. 'You mean apart from preparing a meal for you lot?' She waved a dismissive hand. 'The hanging baskets need dead-heading and I picked up some bedding plants at the nursery yesterday, so I'll probably find somewhere to pop them in.'

'It sounds lonely,' he commented. 'Why don't you go and join the others at the Fest for an hour? If you can find them.'

She shrugged. 'Maybe, but they should be on their way back soon.'

He pressed a kiss to her head, and she could tell he didn't feel great about leaving her, but he descended onto the footpath anyway, following it down to the water's edge where he turned towards the fishing platform.

She had no premonition, no sense of anything at all to prepare her for the way Seb came running back to the house ten minutes later.

His face and hair were soaked in mud and slime; water and weed dripped from his clothes. His phone was clutched in his hand and he was shaking all over.

'What is it?' she cried, her legs almost giving out as she started towards him. 'What's happened?'

'You can't go down there,' he shouted, and grabbed her back as she tried to get past. 'Han, please . . . I've called an ambulance . . .'

'What? Oh my God. Seb, let me go.'

'I can't. I'm sorry. I found him . . . in the water . . .'

Her eyes rounded with horror as she stared at him. 'No,' she said, backing away as she began shaking her head. 'No,' she said again, and wrenching herself free, she began racing down to the lake.

He started after her, caught her, but she broke away again, stumbling as she pressed on.

'I have to let the ambulance in,' he shouted.

She found Jack sprawled next to the platform, half in, half out of the lake, as if he'd been washed in helplessly on a tide. There was a dull red cloud spreading through the water beneath the back of his head. His face was turned skywards and had no colour. His eyes were half-open.

'No, no,' she sobbed defiantly, and sinking to her knees she opened his mouth, pinched his nose and began to breathe forcefully into his lungs. She'd never done this before, had no idea if she was doing it right, but she just kept going. Then she was banging on his chest, trying out CPR, more mouth to mouth, more CPR.

Panic was rushing at her so fast she couldn't stop shaking.

In the distance sirens were wailing, but she kept going.

He couldn't be dead. It wasn't possible. She wouldn't let it be.

'Jack,' she choked, 'oh God, Jack.'

She heard voices, people running, and suddenly she was surrounded. Someone pulled her roughly out of the way and two paramedics dropped to either side of Jack as Seb folded her against him.

'It's not too late,' she whispered fiercely. 'I know it's not. It'll be fine, Seb. You'll see. It'll be fine.'

PART TWO

CHAPTER THIRTY-SIX

The house was full of people, coming and going, climbing the stairs, searching the gardens. Hanna, still damp from the lake, was in the drawing room with Cait and Leo either side of her on a sofa, both leaning into her and holding her hands so tightly that the blood couldn't flow. Every now and again she turned to press a kiss to their heads, dutifully, tenderly, her eyes not focusing. She wasn't going to look at anything properly until Jack came in, laughing and demanding to know what the heck everyone was doing here.

'Let's have a party,' he'd cry, rubbing his hands keenly. 'Han, you sort the nibbles and I'll get the drinks.'

A sob caught in her throat as the image faded, leaving her with the horror of what had happened. It was so hard to process, impossible to believe it was real.

She watched Jenny, white-faced and seeming suddenly aged, put a hand to her head as though to block any more tears. Florina, red-eyed and shaky, was passing around coffee and biscuits. It was her day off, Hanna remembered; she didn't need to be here.

Seb, also still damp from his rescue attempt, got to his feet and walked to the window. Hanna's eyes didn't follow, but she was aware of him, and of her useless anger that he hadn't gone down to the lake at the same time as Jack. It surely wouldn't, couldn't have happened if he'd been there.

There was a Family Liaison Officer in the room with them, a slight, elfin-faced woman with warm brown eyes and curly blonde hair. Hanna couldn't remember her name. Right now she couldn't remember much of what had happened since the police had arrived, only that they'd come in great numbers and in so many vehicles it didn't seem possible to get in or out of the drive. They were all over the grounds, down at the lake and here in the house.

She didn't know if Jack's body had been taken away yet.

She flashed on his head in her lap, wet, muddied, eyes half-shut, lips pale, hair plastered to his skull. His blood still stained her jeans – it was stuck to her fingers – she needed to wash it off.

She couldn't bear this, she really couldn't.

She heard voices coming from the kitchen, but not what was being said. Seb turned to her. 'Maurice Guest has just turned up,' he said.

She flinched. Guest was Avon and Somerset's most senior officer, a friend of Jack's, a fellow Merchant Venturer and keen cricketer, she recalled irrelevantly. It would have taken no time at all for news of Jack's death to reach him, or for him to cancel whatever he was doing and make his way straight here. If she'd thought about it, she'd have known he'd come.

No one had questioned her yet. Maybe he wanted to do it himself, or be there when someone did.

Seb had been with the detectives since they'd arrived. It was only a few minutes ago that he'd come back into the room. He hadn't told her what he'd told them and she was glad. She didn't want the children to hear.

She felt suddenly afraid as Cait got up and went to sit

with Jenny, burying her face in her grandmother's shoulder and quietly sobbing. Why was that frightening her?

She had no idea.

Where was Sofia?

She remembered that Ishan had taken her home with him, and she suddenly wanted to hold the child so much that her arms almost came up to take her.

Leo went to stand with Seb. He was almost as tall as his godfather, not quite as broad; he resembled his father in so many ways that she had to look away.

The door opened; Maurice Guest came in and the FLO stood and saluted. Although he saluted back, his attention was already on Hanna. He was a tall, lean man with a large, hooked nose and unnervingly piercing eyes that currently relayed only shock and concern.

'Hanna,' he said, coming to take her hands as she stood. 'I'm so sorry, my dear. So very sorry.'

She started to speak but nothing came out.

He put a comforting hand on her shoulder and turned to acknowledge Seb, whom he knew, and who then introduced him to the others.

He shook Leo's hand, taking it in both of his. 'We'll get to the bottom of this, son,' he promised. 'No stone will be left unturned.'

'Thanks,' Leo mumbled, and Hanna's heart turned inside out. He looked so young and vulnerable, as if he'd been shattered into a thousand pieces.

He had.

The children's pain might be even harder to bear than her own.

Maurice went to Cait and Jenny and squatted down in front of them. Hanna couldn't hear what he was saying

– probably the same as he'd said to Leo. She was only aware of the tearing anguish in Cait's eyes as they came to hers. She wanted to tell her that it would be all right, that they'd get through this; but it wouldn't, and they couldn't, so she said nothing.

The door opened again and two plain-clothed officers came in: a woman in her late forties and a man maybe ten years younger. There were a lot of detectives here, but this was the first she'd seen of them.

Maurice said, 'Hanna, let me introduce you to Detective Chief Superintendent Elaine Phillips and Detective Inspector Krish Ahmed. Elaine will be the senior investigating officer on the case, Krish her second in command. Two of my best people, but of course my door will always be open if you need me.'

Hanna looked at them, taking in Elaine Phillips's olive complexion and sharp blue eyes. Krish Ahmed's ethnicity made her think of Ishan and she liked him for that.

Elaine Phillips stepped forward to take her hand. 'You have my deepest sympathy, Mrs Madden,' she said. She seemed to mean it, the expression in her eyes said so, but instead of feeling grateful, Hanna wanted to shrink from her. She shouldn't be here. None of them should.

'Mine too,' Krish Ahmed said, also taking her hand. 'I only knew your husband by reputation, but I'm aware of how admired and respected he was. He will be a great loss to our community.'

Hanna wanted to be sick. These words, the sentiments, the kindness was all wrong. It couldn't be about Jack. They were making a mistake; they had to be.

DCS Phillips said, 'Are these the clothes you were wearing when you found him?'

Hanna nodded.

'We're going to need them, I'm afraid. Yours too, Mr Goodman,' she said to Seb.

She looked at Seb, who seemed as thrown by this as she felt, in spite of it being an obvious request.

Maurice said quietly, 'We'll wait here while you change. Then is there somewhere we can talk?'

She took a breath and heard Seb say, 'There's the TV room.'

The door opened and another detective put his head in. 'Excuse me, sir,' he said, addressing his chief constable, 'is it possible for Mr Goodman to come outside again? There are a couple of things he might be able to clear up for us.'

'Of course,' Guest replied. 'They can take your clothes after,' he said to Seb.

Hanna watched Seb leave. Her mouth was too dry to swallow, or even to speak. She wanted to ask if he'd told them that Astor could be the culprit, but it wasn't possible with the police and the children right there.

Had it been Astor?

Florina came in carrying a small pile of clothes.

Realizing they were hers, Hanna felt her heart burn with pain. Florina must have heard the request and had decided to spare her the ordeal of going up to her and Jack's bedroom for the moment.

They went to the laundry room together; Hanna slipped into the fresh underwear, jeans and top and Florina took the others to hand to the police. A detective came in wearing protective gear. He took scrapings from under Hanna's nails, blood samples from her skin and a swab from inside her mouth. Once alone, she turned on the tap to wash her hands and, as she watched Jack's blood dilute in the water, she opened her mouth in a silent scream.

A few minutes later she was in the TV room, where Maurice Guest, DCS Phillips and DI Ahmed were already waiting. Someone had moved the slouchy sofas and capacious armchairs to face one another instead of the giant screen, making it seem as though they were about to have a cosy chat.

Hanna was barely breathing as she sat down next to Maurice, not feeling as though she was the host here at all.

Maurice was the first to speak. 'Officers have already been sent to Hugo Astor's address,' he told her. 'I believe that's who you think is behind this?'

Relieved to know that Seb must have told them that, she nodded and glanced down at her hands, bunched so tightly together her fingers had turned white. 'He and Jack,' she said, then stopped and started again. 'He was trying to blackmail us. He said he'd give us until five o'clock on Friday to come up with the money and if we didn't . . .' She stopped, not sure how to continue.

Krish Ahmed came straight to the point. 'What was the blackmail about?'

She forced her eyes up to his. How much did they already know? If only she could have spoken to Seb before coming in here. 'He accused my son of attacking him,' she said. 'He was beaten badly enough recently to put him in hospital. But it wasn't Leo, we're certain of that. The trouble is we can't prove it. He said if we don't pay him five million pounds to keep it to himself, he'd report it to the police.'

Elaine Phillips frowned as she said, 'That's an extraordinarily large sum for something so . . . relatively minor.'

'Why would Astor think it was Leo who'd beaten him up?' Maurice asked.

Feeling a horrible heat spreading through her, she said, 'There was an incident at the office that Leo witnessed.'

'What sort of incident?'

Realizing there was simply no way she could hold this back, she said, 'Hugo Astor sexually assaulted me. Leo walked in as it was happening.'

Maurice's attention remained focused entirely on her as the others exchanged glances. 'So Astor is claiming that his attack was an act of revenge on Leo's part?' Maurice suggested.

'But Leo didn't do it. I *know* he didn't. Jack didn't believe it either.'

Elaine Phillips said, 'Did you report the assault?'

Hanna shook her head. 'I didn't want to make a fuss. It was over before anything really happened . . .' She kept her eyes lowered, desperate for this to end.

'Did Jack know about it?' Maurice asked, needing to be clear.

'Yes, he did.'

'Did he want to report it?'

'He said the decision had to be mine.'

A moment or two passed, before Elaine Phillips said, 'Mr Astor is a lawyer at your company, is that right?'

'He was.'

'Was? When did he leave his job?'

'Just this week. His brother and someone else came to clear his office.'

'Was he fired?'

'Yes.'

'Because of the sexual assault?'

Hanna nodded.

'And then he was beaten up?'

'That happened before he was fired.'

'So he was attacked outside his home, following the assault, taken to hospital and then . . . Jack fired him?'

'Jack visited him in hospital. That's where he was when he tried to blackmail us. Obviously he couldn't go on working for us after that.'

As Elaine Phillips noted this down, Krish Ahmed took over.

'When the Friday deadline for payment passed, did you hear anything from Mr Astor?'

Hanna shook her head. 'I didn't, no. If Jack did, he never mentioned it.'

'How troubled was your husband by the attempt to blackmail him?' Elaine Phillips asked.

'He felt sure Hugo Astor would back down once he realized that we weren't going to play his game.'

'How long was Mr Astor with the company?'

'He joined us a couple of months ago. Jack head-hunted him from a London firm.'

Elaine Phillips started to speak, but Maurice put up a hand to stop her. 'I think we've taken this line of inquiry far enough for now.' To Hanna he said, 'We'll need a statement from you about what happened today, unless you've already given one.'

'No, I haven't.'

'OK. Thanks for talking to us now. I know it can't have been easy, but you've been extremely helpful.'

As they all stood, Elaine Phillips said, 'Did your husband have any other enemies that you know of, Mrs Madden?'

Hanna blinked in surprise. 'No. He was generally well liked.'

'This is true,' Maurice confirmed.

After he and the senior detectives had gone, Hanna returned to the drawing room to find a search team at work. 'Sorry,' she mumbled, and backed out again, almost treading on Seb who'd come to find her.

'We're in the kitchen,' he said. 'Are you OK? How did it go?'

'I'm not sure. It wasn't very long. They wanted to know about Hugo Astor, and I ended up telling them about the assault. Did you mention it when they talked to you?'

He shook his head. 'I thought it was your place to do that.'

She nodded and let her head fall against him. 'I didn't admit that he and I had been . . . That we have a history of sorts. Do you think I should have? I'm sure he will once they talk to him.'

'Let's cross that bridge when we come to it, but don't forget, assault is assault, never mind what went before.'

Grateful for that, she followed him through to the kitchen where Florina had laid out plates of food for everyone, including the police.

'Mum,' Cait said brokenly as she came in, and half-tumbling from her barstool, she went into Hanna's arms. 'I'm sorry, I'm sorry,' she sobbed. 'I don't want him to be gone . . .'

'Ssh,' Hanna soothed, stroking her hair. 'I know you don't. Nor do I.' He was too alive, too vital, too necessary to them all for everything to end so suddenly and brutally and inexplicably like this.

The FLO stepped forward, phone in hand. 'Mrs Madden,' she said quietly, 'an officer at the gates is asking if someone called Andee Lawrence . . .'

'Is she there?' Hanna cried, turning to the window. 'Let her in! Please.'

The FLO spoke to her colleague, and minutes later Hanna and Andee were embracing at the front door.

'I thought you were still in Italy,' Hanna gasped, holding on tight.

'We got back yesterday. I came as soon as I heard. I tried calling, but I guessed your phone was off.'

'It is. The press . . . Are they out there?'

'I'm afraid so, but there are plenty of police blocking the gates.'

Hanna thought of the fishing platform and how anyone could access it, then she remembered someone saying that the whole area had been cordoned off. 'Come in,' she said to Andee. 'Is Graeme with you?'

'He's gone to Madden HQ to see if he can be of any help there. Han, I'm so sorry. I can hardly believe this has happened.'

'Me neither. I keep thinking he's going to walk in at any minute and ask what all the fuss is about.'

Andee squeezed her hand. 'How are the children taking it?'

'Hard, but we're all still in shock. It's the most difficult for Cait. They've been at such loggerheads in recent times and now she'll never get to make up with him.' As her heart twisted with the awful truth of that, hot tears scorched her eyes. 'I don't know if I can cope with this,' she choked wretchedly. 'I just don't. All the police, the press . . .'

Drawing her into another embrace, Andee said, 'That's why I'm here, so that you won't have to go through it on your own. I'll be your spokesperson, your representative, your adviser, your friend . . . I'll be whatever you need me to be.'

CHAPTER THIRTY-SEVEN

Seb had come upstairs to his room to see if he could get hold of Riona. When he'd tried earlier and his call had gone to voicemail, he'd found himself unable to speak. What could he possibly say? What words were there to describe the nightmare he and Jack's family now found themselves in? How does anyone make themselves say, *my best friend has been killed, murdered?* He was still balking at the truth of it.

This time, to his relief, Riona answered almost before it rang.

'Oh Seb,' she cried urgently. 'I've seen the news. I'm sorry I missed you earlier. I've tried since . . .'

'I had to turn my phone off,' he said. 'The press have my number and they know I'm here.'

'Of course. How are you? How is dear Hanna? I can hardly believe it. You must all be in such a terrible state of shock.'

'We are.' He felt light-headed all of a sudden, unable to attach to a sense of reality, only to a wrenching sense of disbelief and loss.

'What exactly happened?' she asked gently.

He started to answer, then found he couldn't face going over it again. The forensic ordeal with the police was enough, although the image of Jack slumped in the waves wouldn't leave his mind.

'I'm sorry, I shouldn't have asked,' she said tenderly. 'I wish there was something I could do. You will tell me if there is, won't you?'

'Thank you,' he managed. Then, 'A close friend of Hanna's turned up just now, Andee. Never have any of us been so glad to see anyone.'

'I've met her. She's an ex-detective, yes?'

'That's right. She'll know how to handle things far better than we do. The rest of us have only ever met the police in social situations. God, how pompously unworldly that makes us sound.'

'Not at all. Most people don't have dealings with the police, especially of this sort.'

He supposed she was right. How he wished that he, Hanna, the children, Jenny, everyone who knew and loved Jack, were still numbered amongst 'most people'.

'There's a report that the chief constable has been to the house?' she said.

'Maurice Guest. That's right. Jack and I have known him a long time.'

'Then we can surely feel confident of this being solved very quickly?'

Could they? The way time seemed to have slowed, changed direction, turned in on itself, he had no idea what might be possible. 'I'd like to think so,' he replied. 'I know the police are talking to Hugo Astor, so we'll have to see what comes of that.'

'Do you think it was him?'

'I can't think of anyone else. Jack didn't make enemies easily.'

There was a beat before she said, 'Seb, tell me, are you aware of what Cait knows about Jack?'

He frowned. 'What do you mean?'

'Oh dear, I . . . I don't want to break her confidence, I really don't, but, Seb, you need to persuade Cait to tell her mother what she knows about her father. I've no idea if it'll change things, but I can tell you this, Hanna will want to know before the police or the press find out.'

CHAPTER THIRTY-EIGHT

It was just after nine in the morning, and Hanna was standing at the window of her and Jack's bedroom. She knew that everything out there was the same as it always was. Life went on – except it was a different world now. She didn't feel a part of it any more, didn't want to be.

She tried to stop herself picturing Jack down at the lake as she'd last seen him, but the vision was there, bigger and more horrific than ever. She could feel the weight of him in her hands, the shape of him in her lap, the wetness of his blood and the water that had drowned him. Would she ever be able to forget it, or even live with it?

Had he drowned?

Or had the blow to his head killed him first?

He was in the morgue now; maybe he was laid out in a pathologist's lab, naked, lifeless, bloodless, no longer himself, just a body to be examined for evidence.

She couldn't breathe; couldn't stand or sit, couldn't move or stay still. She wanted to close her eyes and sink into wherever he was now to be with him again.

The sun had risen hours ago, and somehow she'd slept through it, after being awake for most of the night. How could that be possible after what had happened? It felt shaming; an unforgivable betrayal. He would have stayed awake for her, she was sure of it, and for the children. So why hadn't she?

The last time she'd seen Cait was here in this room. They'd held each other through most of the night, Hanna cradling her girl as she'd finally fallen into an exhausted sleep. She'd wished with all her heart that Jack could have seen them lying together like that. She knew how much it would mean to him, as it had to her. It was the first time she'd been close to Cait in too long.

No one could ever have imagined it would be something like this that would make it happen.

Now Cait was outside with Seb, halfway down to the lake. As she watched them, Hanna found herself unable to make sense of what she was seeing. They appeared to be arguing, Cait throwing her hands in the air, turning away and back again, clearly shouting, while Seb seemed to be letting her vent. How unlike Jack he was in that respect – Jack would have been yelling back by now, telling Cait to get a grip, grow up, take some sort of responsibility, before storming back to the house having had enough of her nonsense, as he'd called it.

Did Cait have any idea how deeply hurt her father had been by their rift? Why hadn't Jack tried harder to repair it?

Why hadn't she?

Oh Jack. We were so wrapped up in ourselves. When did we stop watching them and start putting our own lives first?

She turned to the bed, half-expecting him to be there, telling her to stop berating herself, it would all be fine, he would sort it. 'It's Sunday. Let's have a lie-in,' he would say.

Today was Monday, and he wasn't here.

Yesterday at this time he had been.

Her breath disappeared. She couldn't pull it in, or push it out. She clasped her hands to her head, and put them down again. The enormity of his loss was threatening to engulf her, but she mustn't allow it. She needed to find out who had done this to him.

As if she didn't already know.

Andee had agreed that Astor must be the prime suspect, but she wasn't ready, she'd said, to rule out other possibilities until she knew the police had.

Who else could there be?

Where was Andee now?

She and Hanna had stayed up talking until after midnight, but Hanna could hardly remember now what they'd talked about. She was more interested, concerned, to know what was going on out there between Cait and Seb.

Pulling on leggings and a T-shirt, she picked up her phone and started downstairs. As she went out to the terrace she almost collided with Leo, who was clearly heading in the same direction.

'What's going on?' he demanded worriedly. 'What are they arguing about?'

'I've no idea,' she replied. 'Cait!' she called out. 'Seb! What's wrong?'

As they turned to her, she felt her heart turn over and almost faltered in her step. Why was Cait so angry and distressed? Her face was deeply flushed and awash with tears. Seb looked anguished too, and moved towards Cait to put a hand on her shoulder.

Hanna wasn't close enough to hear what he said, but by the time she reached them Cait was sobbing into Seb's chest, her hands bunched at her face, her shoulders heaving. 'What is it?' she cried, her eyes on Seb as she turned Cait into her arms. 'What's happened?'

Seb was white, his eyes dark, troubled pools. Quietly, he said, 'Cait has something to tell you.'

Cait pressed in closer to her mother. 'I can't, I can't,' she choked. 'Please don't make me.'

Afraid now, and bewildered, Hanna took Cait's face in her hands. 'You need to calm down,' she said softly. 'Whatever it is, we can deal with it—'

'No we can't. *We can't.*' She looked up at Seb and said, 'You tell her. Please, Seb, don't make me do it.'

Hanna was suddenly fighting an urge to leave them there, to get as far away from them as she could before they shattered her world again. But nothing could be as bad as yesterday; it simply wasn't possible. 'Is it to do with Jack?' she heard herself ask Seb.

When he nodded, she felt her senses spin strangely away from her, as if trying to rescue her from any more heartache. Leo put an arm around her, and she was glad of his support. She felt as though she was in a dream, that nothing was real or to be trusted, not even the sudden inner strength that was making her say, 'Whatever it is, one of you needs to tell me and I'd like it to be now.'

Before anyone could answer, a helicopter swooped overhead, so low that it was no longer possible to hear anything over its engines.

'It's the press,' Leo shouted and, taking hold of his mother, he ran her through the whipping draught back to the house.

Seb and Cait followed, ducking through the currents, holding onto one another, and Cait stayed close to him as they went into the kitchen and closed the door.

Florina and Andee were there, laying out breakfast. There was no sign of the FLO, thank goodness. Hanna had called Maurice Guest last night to tell him she'd rather not have a stranger in the house for the time being, and though he'd tried to explain why it was necessary and how much it could help her, he'd agreed in the end to stand the officer down.

As soon as Andee saw Hanna's face she said, 'What's happened?'

Hanna gave a small shake of her head.

Noticing, Florina said, 'I will leave you now and go home. Just call if you need me.'

'Thanks,' Hanna managed.

After she'd gone, Andee said, 'Would you like me to leave too?'

'No,' Seb and Hanna said together.

Hanna turned to him.

'Andee should hear this,' he said. 'She can only give you the support you need if she knows everything.' Without waiting for a response, he said to Andee, 'Cait told me something about Jack this morning that's important for us all to know before the press or police get hold of it – and they will.'

Fighting another impulse to turn away, Hanna forced herself to sit down, as if rooting herself, and gladly took the coffee Andee put in front of her. Jack might be telling her she needed something stronger, but that was an illusion, he wasn't here, he couldn't tell her anything. 'I'm listening,' she said, her voice low and thankfully calm. It was nothing like how she felt inside, but it was important for Cait and Leo to believe she could cope with whatever lay ahead. 'It can't be as bad as what happened yesterday,' she said, 'so please don't keep me waiting any longer.'

Cait's head went down, and Seb put a comforting hand on the back of her neck. With no preamble, he said, 'You remember Freya?'

Thrown, Hanna frowned.

Leo said, 'Do you mean the Danish girl who worked at our stables?'

Seb nodded.

Hanna remembered her – small, skinny, loved horses, always reliable. What on earth could this have to do with her? She'd left over two years ago.

Cait's head came up, and as her bloodshot eyes came to her mother's, she said, 'She and Dad have a baby together.'

Hanna blinked as her heart seemed to stop.

Leo said, 'What the fuck?'

Hanna started shaking her head.

Andee said, 'Are you sure about this, Cait?'

Cait's breath caught on a sob. 'I-I saw them together,' she told Andee, 'when she was working here. They were in one of the stables . . . I mean, they weren't doing . . . They were just, you know, but I could tell . . . It wasn't right . . .'

Leo turned away; a tight fist pressed to his head.

Hanna was feeling strangely distant, as if everything in her, even her thoughts, had ceased to connect with the here and now.

'When did you see this?' Andee asked gently.

'Just before she left,' Cait replied.

'Jesus,' Leo seethed.

Andee said, 'Did Dad know you'd seen them together?'

Cait shook her head. 'I don't think so. He never said, and I didn't tell him, but' – she glanced nervously at her mother – 'it wasn't the only time. I saw them in his car, after that. I was with Ishan – he saw them too, so he can tell you that I'm not making this up.'

Andee glanced briefly at Hanna as she said, 'No one's saying you are.'

Cait's tone was suddenly angry as she said, 'She's bloody well younger than me!'

Hanna's eyes closed. She needed to shut this out. It couldn't be true; Cait had made a mistake. She'd misunderstood what she'd seen . . . Jack with a girl who was barely sixteen – please God she had been sixteen.

Andee said, 'What about the baby, Cait?'

Hanna started to turn away, but Leo was behind her, putting his arms around her.

Receiving a nod from Andee, Cait said, 'I saw Freya with him – the baby I mean – in Wells, about six months ago. They were watching the swans . . . I was with Sofes and that's what we were there to do. I noticed the little boy straight away, because he was just starting to walk, the same as Sofes. Then I recognized Freya and went to sit on a bench with her.'

She took a breath and continued. 'Her brother was there too – Marius. I didn't see him at first; he was behind us talking on the phone. I never could stand him. I know I wouldn't have stopped if I'd noticed him. Anyway, Freya and I chatted for a bit, mostly about kid-type stuff. I had the feeling she wanted to get away, so to give her an out I said she ought to bring her little boy to the house for a play-date sometime. That's when I realized her brother was there because he said, "Yeah, I bet your mother would love that." I ignored him and told Freya that you'd be OK with her coming and anyway, it was nothing to do with you, it was about Sofia.

'That revolting bloke sits down with us then and says, "We know you saw Freya with your dad when she was working at the stables, she saw you watching, so you can stop the pretence."' Cait's face was ashen. 'I wanted to leave then, I was starting to feel a bit scared, but he pushed me back down and said, "You know she stopped working for your family because of him," and he looks at the little boy and smirks. That was when the penny dropped – or started to, anyway.'

Hanna's mind was a chaos of terrible images: Jack with the girl, that ghastly character tormenting Cait, a little boy hardly walking . . .

'He said Dad knew all about the baby,' Cait went on, 'and that he'd set Freya up with somewhere to live so he could see them as often as he could. Then he made Freya get out a photo of her little boy – his name's Ethan – with Dad holding him.'

Hanna closed her eyes, as if she were being asked to look at the photo too.

Cait said, 'He laughed and I really wanted to punch him. I told him I didn't care about the photo, all it proved was that Freya had bumped into Dad somewhere and he'd made a fuss of the baby. So Marius said I could think what I liked, but they could prove it the same way they did to Dad. They'd send me copies of the DNA test.

'I grabbed Sofes then and got up to walk off, but he came after me, not shouting exactly, but accusing me of being like the rest of my family, thinking I was better than them . . . Then he said . . .' She gasped on a sob, 'He said we'd all think again if it ever got out that the great Jack Madden liked underage girls.'

Hanna felt the words like a blow.

'I got away from him then,' Cait said, 'but about a week later a copy of the DNA results turned up with a note from him saying that you, Mum, probably already knew about Freya and Ethan, but because of Freya's age you were protecting Dad. He called you and Dad terrible names . . . I couldn't stand it, so I ripped it up and tried to pretend I'd never seen it.'

Hanna dropped her head to her hands; her heart was in pieces. She felt so sickened and battered by this, so stunned and lost for a response, that in the end all she could do was look at Andee.

Hanna said, 'If she was underage . . . Even if she wasn't, she won't be a secret for much longer, will she?'

Before Andee could reply, Leo said to Cait, 'I can't believe you kept this to yourself all this time. For fuck's sake, why didn't you ever tell *me*?'

'I wanted to,' Cait cried, 'but I was afraid you'd confront Dad and it would all come out. And it was making me so crazy, because if Mum did know and she was letting him carry on like nothing was wrong . . . I kept thinking, what kind of family am I in? I got so screwed up over it . . . Ishan kept trying to make me talk to Dad, but I couldn't. I didn't want to hear him admit anything, or listen to him trying to lie . . .'

Hanna got to her feet and went to pull Cait into her arms. 'I'm sorry you've had to go through this, my darling,' she whispered shakily. 'I wish you'd come to me . . .'

'But I couldn't!' Cait cried, breaking free to look at her. 'You've got to see that . . .'

'I do, but you shouldn't have had to carry this alone. It's been a terrible strain on you . . . Terrible . . .' She pulled Cait back into her arms and rested her head on hers. This wasn't a time to try sorting through her own feelings, or how she was going to cope with it in an emotional sense. What mattered was what they, as a family, were going to do about it.

As if reading her mind, Seb said, 'Do you know where we can find her or her brother, Cait?'

Cait shook her head.

'Dad's obviously set her up *somewhere*,' Leo stated bitterly.

Hanna said, 'I heard a while ago that they're over near Newton St Loe, but I've no idea where exactly. Or if they're still there.'

Seb said to Andee, 'If we give you all the details we know, would you be able to find her?'

'I'm sure I can,' Andee replied.

'Here's Jenny,' Hanna said, a moment before the door opened and Jack's stepmother came in looking tired – and cross?

'Can't we do something to stop those blasted helicopters?' Jenny demanded as another buzzed overhead. 'Have these people never heard of privacy, or respect? Don't we have . . .' Belatedly catching the mood in the room she looked around as she said, 'What is it? Have they arrested that man? Please tell me they have.'

Deciding Jenny needed to know everything they did, and the sooner the better, Hanna said, 'I'm not sure if this is going to come as news to you or not, Jen, but I've just learned that Jack has a child with . . . someone else. You'll remember her, Freya Hansen.'

Jenny seemed to crumple as she said, brokenly, 'I didn't know. Not about a child . . . I thought . . . He told me, when she left, that it was over. Oh God, my darling girl, I don't know what to say. I'm so sorry . . . I shouldn't have kept it from you. I wouldn't have if Jack hadn't made me . . .'

Leo said, 'It wasn't up to you to tell anyone, Gran – it was up to him.'

'But there's a child?' She looked confused. 'How do you know that?' She was so lost and bewildered that Hanna's heart went out to her. She couldn't be blamed for keeping secrets for her beloved stepson; she'd obviously thought she was doing the right thing and had believed him when he'd said it was over.

'I'll tell you about it later, Gran,' Cait said.

'We're all still trying to get our heads around it,' Hanna added, knowing it would be a long time before she could even begin to. 'It's a lot to take in.'

'But what are you going to do?' Jenny asked. 'What can I do? There must be something.'

'Not unless you know where she lives now,' Andee said.

Jenny shook her head. 'I never stayed in touch with her. Why would I when I was glad to see the back of her? The way she led him on, you wouldn't think a girl her age—'

'It takes two,' Hanna broke in, unable to hear any more of that, 'and Jack was nobody's fool. He always knew what he was doing.'

Cait checked her phone as a text arrived. 'Ishan and Sofia are at the gates,' she said. 'I'll go and let them in.'

Hanna watched her leave, appalled by the fact that Jack had been sleeping with a girl younger than his own daughter, had made her pregnant and apparently continued to see her. What had he been planning? Surely he hadn't believed he could keep it a secret for ever.

So many lies.

Where did they begin and end?

Refocusing them all, Andee said, 'I spoke with Elaine Phillips first thing this morning.'

Hanna took a moment to remember that this was the senior investigating officer in the case that was all their lives were really about right now.

Andee said, 'Apparently they held Hugo Astor overnight, and will continue questioning him this morning. I'm heading into Bristol to see if I can meet with her or one of her team. I'm afraid they need to know about Freya Hansen, and it'll be better coming from us.'

Hanna's heart skipped several beats. 'Do you think . . . Do you think she or her brother might have something to do with what happened to Jack? That lad really is a nasty piece of work.'

Lifting his head from his hands, Seb said, 'He's definitely got some kind of problem with Jack.'

Hanna regarded him in amazement.

'We were at the Albion a few weeks back,' he explained, 'and Marius approached Jack in a way that was . . . threatening? Aggressive, certainly. And he was drunk. I don't know what it was about – Jack hustled him outside before I could get a sense of anything, and he didn't want to talk about it after.'

Hanna's insides sank with dismay.

Andee said, 'Well, unless Astor confesses, I'd say this throws an interesting new light on things.'

CHAPTER THIRTY-NINE

I am staring at the TV where I've frozen the screen on a shot of Hanna and Jack in happier times. They are a very glamorous couple and look so happy, sophisticated, on top of the world. Hanna's laughing. She has such a beautiful, infectious smile; her eyes shine with humour and kindness; her skin is lightly freckled and smooth.

I look at Jack and my heart swells with Hanna's grief. He might not be a classically handsome man, but there is a magnetism to him, I feel, a confidence that is arresting. I can imagine wanting to be a part of his world.

I wonder if Hanna knows his big secret yet, the one that Cait told Riona. Yes, Riona does confide in me from time to time, and she was so upset about this that it all came tumbling out.

How could he have betrayed his beautiful wife like that?

He was, at heart, a despicable man, and yet I have little difficulty imagining how terrible his loss must be for Hanna. I wish I could comfort her, but there is nothing I can do.

Maybe it won't be so bad once she knows the truth.

I release the freeze-frame and find myself watching aerial shots of the house and grounds. It's a stunning place, but thanks to Riona, I already know that.

Where is Riona? She should be here. She's been gone a long time now and I'm getting worried that she won't come back.

I continue to watch the TV. Cars are coming and going from Lake House, having to force a route through the media camp. Police officers are controlling the gates, and combing the lakeside and surrounding area. A white tent is still over the spot where Jack was found; scientists in blue overalls are collecting the evidence they need.

I wonder what they will find and where it will lead them.

Apparently Hugo Astor is still being questioned. No charge has been brought yet. According to one report, his brother and another man are also helping with inquiries.

Apart from that, there seems nothing new to report today, but it doesn't stop the news channels going over and over what they do know and speculating about much more. They keep running old footage of Jack and Hanna. I like to watch that. I want to hear all about her and her children, her charitable works, and the difference she's helped to make to so many lives. They show her coming and going from her office, from parties, charity events, society weddings and awards ceremonies. She always looks so elegant, striking in every way.

I shut my eyes and bunch my hands loosely on the kitchen table.

Where is Riona? Why doesn't she come?

She knows that I can't cope with this alone. She's aware of how afraid I am, so why is she staying away?

CHAPTER FORTY

Andee was with Elaine Phillips in the car park outside Patchway Custody where Hugo Astor was still being questioned. Although the two women had never been colleagues, hadn't even met before yesterday, it had soon become clear to Andee that her own reputation as an ex-detective who'd never really let go of the job had preceded her. She also still had a few high-powered connections within the Force. These would be two reasons why Elaine was giving her the time of day – the other was that as the senior investigating officer of this very high-profile case, she wasn't going to let anything slip by, no matter the source.

They were standing next to Andee's car, a short distance from the adjacent Rolls-Royce building, while Elaine smoked a cigarette and listened to what Andee was telling her.

Andee kept it concise; there was nothing to be gained from over-embellishing a story or detailing emotions. The facts were quite simple: Jack Madden had a child with a young woman by the name of Freya Hansen, who used to work for the Maddens as a stable hand. It was possible the girl was underage when the affair began. She left their employ over two years ago, saying she needed to move on.

No one in the family had heard from her since, apart from the isolated incident when Cait Madden ran into her and her brother in Wells, and more recently when Seb saw Marius at a pub in Bristol.

When Andee had finished, she watched Elaine pinch the end off her cigarette and wrap the butt in a tissue. The woman's face was stern and inscrutable as she finally looked at Andee. 'And Hanna Madden just learned about this . . . *love-child* this morning?' she said, her tone not exactly sceptical, but not entirely believing either.

'I was there when her daughter broke the news,' Andee told her. 'Hanna didn't know anything about it until then.'

'Well, I can see that's what she would want you to think, given the existence of this child. And its mother, and her age, could be viewed by some, such as myself, as a pretty good reason for Hanna Madden to . . . lose it with her husband.'

Andee had been expecting something like that so didn't flinch. 'I realize it'll form part of your inquiries going forward,' she said. 'I'm also sure that you'll be interviewing Freya Hansen and her brother to find out where they were yesterday afternoon around two o'clock.'

Elaine half-smiled and nodded. 'Do you know where we can find them?' she asked.

'I've managed to track down a last known address, which I'll put in a text if you can let me have your number.'

Elaine obliged, and after Andee had sent the message she said, 'Can I ask how things are progressing with Hugo Astor?'

Elaine sighed, leaned back against the car and looked as though she'd like to light another cigarette. 'He doesn't have an alibi,' she said flatly, 'but right now we have nothing to tie him to the scene.' She glanced at Andee and away again. 'Frankly, I'm having a hard time understanding why he'd do it before the blackmail thing played out. The deadline passes on Friday, he offs the bloke on Sunday . . . What's in it for him?'

Having had similar thoughts, Andee started to respond when Elaine continued, 'Five mil to shut him up about the son – Leo? – attacking him?'

'*If* Leo attacked him.'

Elaine looked at her again. 'Either way, you've got to admit it's a princely sum for an offence that's not even guaranteed to end the lad up with a prison term. And considering Daddy's his boss, it wouldn't have much of a negative effect on his record either. So what's this blackmail really about, Andee? And please don't say you don't know, because my gut tells me you do.'

Admiring the woman's instincts, while thinking back over the long conversation she'd had with Hanna last night that had gone on into the early hours, Andee said, 'You're right, I do know, but if I tell you—'

'No conditions,' Elaine interrupted. 'This is a murder inquiry.'

Needing no reminder, Andee said, 'OK. You know that Hugo Astor attempted to rape Hanna in her office and Leo walked in, which basically saved her.'

Elaine nodded slowly. 'And she didn't report it.'

'No, and she still doesn't want to.'

'Why?'

Andee shrugged. 'Think about it, a woman in her position, the kind of publicity it would stir up, speculation, gossip and rumour . . . She and Jack felt it would be better dealt with by letting Astor go. Astor, I'm afraid, threatened to claim, publicly, that he and Hanna had been having an affair and that she was actually a willing party to the fake-rape, unless they paid what he was asking.'

Elaine drew in a breath. Clearly she wasn't liking the sound of this, and Andee had to admit, there was nothing to like about it.

'So *were* they having an affair?' Elaine asked.

Countering, Andee said, 'Does it matter? Attempted rape is attempted rape.'

Elaine didn't argue, but Andee could tell she now believed in the affair.

'Frankly,' Elaine said, 'I'm still not seeing a motive here for Astor to commit a murder. Are you?'

Andee had to agree that she wasn't. 'But you're not ruling him out?' she pressed.

'No. There could have been a lot more going on between him and Jack Madden than we're currently aware of. Or between him and Hanna Madden. We'll have a better idea once we've been through phones and computers.' She checked her watch. 'I need to be getting back, but I appreciate you coming to talk to me. The Freya Jansen thing . . . You've given me a lot to think about.'

Not ready to let her go yet, Andee said, 'Can I ask if there's been an initial autopsy report yet?'

Elaine nodded. 'It was a single blow to the head that killed him. A massive one, in fact, dealt by someone with immense strength, so most likely a man. The only surprising part was that wood splinters were found in the wound, when we'd all assumed he'd been hit with a rock, or maybe a hammer, some sort of metal instrument. I guess a rock seemed more likely, given where he was.'

'So a plank? A wooden mallet? A branch?'

'Any of the above. Forensics are still working on it. No witnesses have come forward with any suspicious sightings, but it's a popular destination for dog walkers, ramblers, nature-watchers, fishermen, from out of the area. So strangers can easily go unnoticed.' With a shake of her head, she pushed away from the car and turned to look Andee in the eye. 'As I said, I'm grateful to you for coming here today. I know we're both trying to achieve the same goal, so I'm going to trust you not to stand in my way.'

'It's not my intention,' Andee assured her. 'I just wanted to try and establish an understanding between us, that I hope will serve us both.'

Elaine nodded. 'Time to go,' she said. 'I'd like to get to Ms Freya Jansen and her brother before the press do, and the way social media works it's going to take no time at all for it to get out there.' She started to leave, but turned back. 'You can tell Hanna Madden that we'll be calling on her again sometime later today.'

'For any specific reason?' Andee asked.

Elaine smiled. 'Without stating the obvious, I know you won't need to be reminded that she and her friend, Sebastian Goodman, were first on the scene. That makes them people of interest, wouldn't you say?'

Andee couldn't deny it.

'Is there anything you'd care to tell me about their relationship?' Elaine prompted.

Andee smiled. 'It's not what you're thinking,' she replied, and with a friendly wave she got into her car.

CHAPTER FORTY-ONE

Hanna's arm was linked through Seb's as they walked through the garden towards a nearby copse. The search teams were still hard at work in the area surrounding the lake and, anyway, neither had the heart to go in that direction. Would they ever want to go there again?

For now they'd just needed to step out of the house for a while, to try to assimilate this shocking news about Jack and Freya Hansen.

If she hadn't been sixteen, surely to God he wouldn't have known that.

But did not knowing excuse it?

And then there was the baby and the ongoing relationship with Freya that he'd never told her anything about.

Hanna felt completely shattered by it all, as if it had torn apart everything inside her. She barely knew what she wanted to say, was afraid that putting anything more into words would somehow make things worse, as if that could be possible. She recalled the girl's pale, sombre face, the pretty eyes and love of horses – and the awful brother's insufferable arrogance; the looks that seemed to suggest he knew something she didn't.

It turned out he did.

As her heart burned with the pain of it, she let her eyes trail over the flower beds, taking in their vibrant summer colours, the butterflies that flitted amongst them, the tiny droplets of moisture on petals left over from the morning spray. She suddenly wanted to plunge her hands into the soil, to dig deeper and deeper, as if she could somehow bury it all away.

As if sensing her surge of despair, Seb squeezed her arm to his side. They paused for a moment to gaze down to the lake, taking in the many shades of blue from the sky, white from clouds and black from shadow. The water rippled softly as ducks paddled around in lazy pursuit of each other and fish broke the surface with small swirls and a splash. How could it possibly have been the setting for something so violent and tragic?

Her eye was caught by a pair of swans gliding under a canopy of overhanging branches, and she was instantly reminded of Cait coming across Freya and her son at the Bishop's Palace moat in Wells.

'I don't know how to feel,' she said to Seb. 'Yesterday he was my husband, the great love of my life, the man I trusted above anyone; today he's . . . I don't know what he is now. I don't even know *who* he is.'

Walking them on, Seb said, 'He's still everything you believed him to be, and there is no doubt in my mind that you were the great love of his life . . .'

'But he lied to me, Seb.'

'He kept a truth from you.'

'Isn't that the same thing? Every time he was with her he'd have told me he was somewhere else, or led me to believe that, anyway. So whichever way you look at it, he was deceitful; he was cheating on me in a way that . . .'

She threw out her hands helplessly. 'I don't know how to describe what he's done, or how the hell I'm ever going to understand it, never mind forgive it. And right now, I *hate* him for not being here to explain himself. Except how can he explain this away?' She was shouting now, as if Seb might have the answer.

He reached for her hand, but she tore it free and walked away, then turned back to him with an anguished groan. Her eyes moved to where a robin was flicking about in a birdbath. 'It's a betrayal that goes so deep . . . *So deep,* Seb,' she said. 'A teenage mistress, a girl who might not even have been sixteen when he first seduced her . . .' She dropped her head to her hands as the enormity of it over-whelmed her.

Pulling her to him, Seb said, 'I'm not trying to defend him, now isn't the time, but I can't help asking myself if he'd got into something with the Hansens that he couldn't get himself out of.'

She stood back to look at him, a hint of colour seeping into her pale face as a new suspicion began taking shape. 'Do you mean . . . Well, support my sister and her child or . . .?'

He nodded. 'It's possible.'

She took a breath as her mind began to race. 'You're right, we need to see her,' she said decisively. 'I'll come with you when we're certain of her address. I want to look her in the eye when she tells me what the hell has been going on.' *And then I'd probably like to kill her.*

'OK, but it might be wiser to let the police speak to her first. If we go, we could end up complicating things in a way that won't help us at all.'

She nodded slowly as she considered this, and as they walked on she felt so much comfort in having him with her, so much stronger and able to cope, in spite of the conflicting emotions tearing through her. 'I'm glad he didn't tell you,' she said. 'I don't think I could have borne it if I thought you'd both been holding out on me.'

With a sigh, he said, 'It's been a terrible burden for Cait to carry. We can see how badly it affected her. She's always had a tricky temperament – we know that – and in this case she simply wasn't emotionally mature enough to know how to cope.'

Feeling her heart twist painfully, she said, 'How terrible it must have been for her to think we were covering up something so awful. I should have tried harder, made her sit down and talk to me . . . I'm her mother, for God's sake, it's my job to take care of her, to protect her, to be there when she needs me, but I was so wrapped up in my own life, in Jack's . . .' She gave a bitter laugh. 'Jack's life. What is that even? What more is there that I know nothing about?' She broke off, shaking her head as though denying her fears, or maybe she was just holding them at a distance for now. 'Did he ever suspect what was really going on with Cait?' she said softly. 'It surely must have crossed his mind that his own actions could be playing a part in the way she turned against us. If so, he clearly did nothing about it. He just let her suffer . . .'

Turning her to face him, he looked tenderly into her eyes as he said, 'We don't know the real truth of anything yet, but whatever it turns out to be, I can tell you this, nothing surpassed the love he had for you and his children.'

She regarded him miserably. 'I wish that made me feel better,' she said, 'but it doesn't.' She attempted a smile and leaned in to rest her cheek on his shoulder. She didn't know whether to thank him or accuse him of being as big a fool as she was. All she did know was that she'd give anything in the world for Jack to come walking towards them now, grinning, teasing, telling them the nightmare was over, time to wake up.

Instead, what she saw as she looked back towards the house made her heart trip with a wrenching pity.

Seb turned round and saw Jenny all alone in her beloved rose garden, seated on Jack's father's memorial bench, her eyes seeming to stare at nothing while she rested a hand on Gaston's silky golden head.

They ran to her, and as Hanna gathered her in her arms, Jenny sobbed, 'I'm sorry, I'm sorry, I shouldn't . . .'

'Ssh,' Hanna soothed, crying too. 'You have nothing to be sorry for.'

Jenny's watery eyes found hers. 'I'm sorry because I don't think I can take any more death. First my wonderful David, then your dear, dear, mother; now Jack and soon it will be Gaston . . .'

'Oh, Jenny,' Hanna wept, holding her close again. 'We're here for you, all of us, and we always will be.'

Sitting the other side of her, Seb ruffled the dog's fur as he said, 'Gaston's not going anywhere for a good while yet, you can be sure of that, but when he does he'll know how loved he's been in his life and that's what really matters to him.'

'I know,' Jenny sniffed, 'and he is loved. We all are, but this terrible business with Jack and now the girl . . . Oh, Hanna, I don't know what to think about anything . . .'

As Hanna started to respond, a helicopter whooshed out of nowhere, roaring overhead and drowning her out.

'Come on,' Seb shouted, helping Jenny to her feet in the ferocious blasts of air. 'Let's go back inside.'

Minutes later, thankful for the calm and quiet of the kitchen, Hanna said, 'I think we could all do with a drink.'

'As long as it has alcohol in it and mine's a double,' Jenny replied.

With a smile, Hanna began doing the honours. Seb's phone buzzed and he picked it up.

'Riona?' Jenny asked, sliding her fingers back into Gaston's fur.

He shook his head. 'Jim Moretti, another of the Merchants, passing on condolences. I can't seem to get hold of Riona at the moment. I hope she's not going through some sort of crisis at the clinic.'

'She'll be worried about you,' Hanna said, 'so I'm sure she'll call the minute she can.' To Jenny she said, 'Do you know where the children are?'

'Yes, a group of Leo's friends came a while ago and they all went through to the TV room.'

'Cait and Ishan too? So Sofia's there?'

Jenny nodded, and took the large gin and tonic Hanna had made her. 'I'm not sure if now's the time,' she said, 'but what are we going to do about the funeral? Do you know what Jack wanted?'

More denial and anguish crashed through her. She turned to Seb, hoping he might have an answer, because she didn't know where to begin.

He said, 'I think the police will let us know when we can start the arrangements, but I'll check on it.'

Hanna nodded and said, shakily, 'I think it should be a small, family only affair. Given what's happened, where we are . . .'

Jenny looked as though she agreed, but said, 'There will be a lot of people wanting to pay their respects . . .'

'We can talk about a memorial at a later date,' Seb said, turning as someone came into the kitchen.

Seeing it was Ishan, Hanna felt her spirits fleetingly lighten. She had a real fondness for this tall, broad-shouldered young man with his dark, intelligent eyes and open heart. Only nineteen and he was already a wonderful father. In spite of how difficult Cait could be, he'd always been there for her, and here he was again today.

He was regarding her with concern as he came to fold her in his arms. 'Hanna, I'm so sorry,' he said, softly, 'about everything.'

Understanding he was including Freya Hansen in his sympathy, she touched a hand to his cheek as she said, 'It can't have been easy for you, knowing and feeling you had to keep it to yourself.'

'I tried to get Cait to talk to you,' he said, 'but she always refused, and I didn't feel it was my place to tell you myself.'

She attempted a smile. 'Well, we know now, so no need for you to worry any more. Now tell me how you are.'

Seeming embarrassed to be asked, as if he was of no significance in the light of everything, he said, 'I'm fine, thanks. My parents send their condolences. They'd like to come and see you when you're feeling up to it.'

'That would be lovely. Please tell them I'll be in touch.'

'Are you going to have a drink?' Seb asked him.

'Thanks, but I've come to get more beers for everyone, and a juice for Sofes.'

Jenny said, 'Are you taking Andee's advice and staying away from TV and social media in there?'

Ishan shrugged. 'I guess. I mean, not everyone, but Leo and Cait have turned off their phones, so we're just hanging out, chatting, watching Sofia's cartoons. Leo wanted to thrash me on the tennis court, but then he worried what the press would make of it if it looked like he was having a good time.'

Hanna's eyes closed in dismay. They were under such relentless scrutiny it was almost impossible for them to do anything.

Coming into the kitchen with Sofia, Cait said, 'Andee's back. Ask me how I know – they filmed her coming through the gates.'

'I thought you weren't watching TV,' Jenny said.

'We're not, just on and off.'

'Dadadada,' Sofia burbled, holding her arms out to Hanna.

'That's Ananana,' Cait said, handing her over.

'Hello, my angel,' Hanna murmured, pressing a kiss to Sofia's velvety little cheek and inhaling the sheer joy of her. 'God, you feel good, do you know that?'

'Woof,' Sofia replied and, sliding out of Hanna's arms, she toddled over to give Gaston a toddler-style throttle.

'Can we stay to hear what Andee has to say?' Cait asked her mother.

Knowing she could trust Andee to hold back on anything it might be best at this stage for Cait not to know, Hanna said, 'Of course. I'll go and let her in.'

'She's here,' Seb said, nodding to where Andee was walking up onto the terrace.

Seeing she was on the phone, Hanna finished off fixing drinks while Ishan took beers through to the boys and Cait began setting out nibbles. Hanna glanced at the clock, but barely registered what it said. It hardly mattered, except that she'd have to contact her and Jack's PAs at some point to find out how they were coping with everything at the office. They'd be fine. Graeme was visiting the various sites, and the 'chiefs' would have taken charge of everything by now, could even be trying to decide who should take over Jack's role for the foreseeable future.

Shutting that thought down, she looked up as Andee came in, and smiled a greeting.

'That is one heck of a scrum at the gates,' Andee commented, coming to give her a hug.

'You know what's really sickening about it,' Cait said, 'is that if we didn't have money, no one would be interested.'

'I'm afraid you could be right about that,' Jenny agreed. 'I think they're going to turn us into a soap opera if they can.'

'A guarantee once they find out about Freya Hansen,' Cait spat angrily. Her eyes filled with tears and, turning her face into Jenny's shoulder, she started to cry.

'Come on,' Hanna said, reaching for her, 'you're going to upset Sofia.'

Regarding her mother with worried eyes Sofia said, 'Mumumum, Dada.'

With a watery laugh, Cait bent down to scoop her up, and held her tightly as she struggled to swallow her emotions.

'We're on the G&Ts,' Seb told Andee. 'Can I interest you?'

'Bring it on,' Andee smiled. 'I don't see any of us having to go anywhere else today.'

As he sorted the drink, Hanna said, 'So how did it go with the police? Have they charged Astor yet?'

Andee shook her head as she sat down. 'I know this isn't going to be what you want to hear, but Elaine Phillips isn't convinced it was him.'

Hanna's stomach dropped.

'He doesn't have an alibi,' Andee continued, 'which obviously isn't in his favour, but right now she's not seeing the blackmail issue as a convincing enough motive. She feels that it hadn't played out yet, so unless it turns out Jack had some contact with Astor that we don't yet know about, it's possible Astor will be released sometime today.'

'On police bail?' Seb stated forcefully.

Andee nodded. 'I believe the other two – his brother and friend – who've been helping with inquiries are also being let go pending further investigation.'

Hanna turned to stare out of the window, crushed by frustration and anger, although in her heart she couldn't deny that Astor attacking Jack now, or at any time, didn't really make sense. It had just seemed to in the first throes of shock, in the desperate need to know who'd done it.

Andee said, 'I told Elaine about Freya Hansen and the child.'

Hanna tensed.

'Someone will be going to interview her today,' Andee continued. 'That is, presuming she's still at the address I found for her. If not, they have plenty of resources, so it won't take them long to catch up with her.'

Hanna glanced at Seb as she said, 'We want to talk to her, so if you could tell us when would be the right time, we'll go together.'

Andee nodded. 'Let the police satisfy themselves about whether or not she and her brother are involved in any way first.' She took a sip of her drink. 'Elaine Phillips told me that the blow Jack suffered was what killed him, and that it was most likely dealt by a man.'

Hanna turned away. The thought, the imagined view of

something crashing down on Jack's head so hard as to end his life unsteadied every part of her world.

After a moment she heard Seb saying, '. . . and so we're wondering if Freya and her brother have been blackmailing Jack.'

'Oh God,' Cait wailed. 'This is so fucked-up.'

Andee said, 'It's a possibility that I'm sure the police are already considering, but I'll call Elaine Phillips when we're done here. For the moment, it's important for you to know two things.' Her eyes moved between Seb and Hanna. 'The police want to interview you both, probably today.'

Although this didn't surprise Hanna, it made her anxious, as though she had something to hide when she didn't.

'This is normal procedure,' Andee assured them. 'They'll be talking to the whole family at some point, and I'm sure you'll all be asked to provide DNA for elimination purposes. The second thing is that – given you have no other alibis – you, Hanna, and Seb, are being termed persons of interest.'

Hanna's eyes rounded with shock as Seb swore under his breath.

'That is just crazy!' Cait protested furiously. 'You can't seriously be saying they think Mum or Seb did this. Why, for God's sake? What possible reason . . .'

Andee held up a hand for her to stop. 'You might not have seen it yet,' she said, 'but I'm afraid someone's lens got shots of you, Hanna and Seb, in the grounds earlier, seeming to argue, make up, argue again . . . I'm sure you don't need me to spell out the spin that's being put on it, but I'm afraid it isn't good.'

Appalled, Hanna turned back to Seb. She couldn't believe that someone out there was trying to make out they were more than just friends. It was cruel, grotesque, when they'd just lost someone they loved in such a brutal and shocking way.

Someone who'd betrayed them both.

'How can we put a stop to it?' Seb said darkly.

'I'm afraid you can't,' Andee replied.

'But if I'm reading this correctly, their insinuations are likely to lead to suspicions that we – or one of us – could be responsible for what happened to Jack.'

The door suddenly crashed open and Leo came in saying, 'Mum! They've just said on the news that I've been accused of beating up Hugo Astor. What the fuck, Mum! I never touched the bloke, I swear it! And who's saying it? Are the police going to arrest me?'

Andee said, 'That's very unlikely, but I'll make a couple of calls to find out what's going on. My guess is that Hugo Astor, or his lawyer, have put it out there to try and deflect attention from him.'

Still looking scared, Leo said, 'If people think I'm some sort of psycho who goes around beating people up—'

'Stop, stop,' Andee cut in firmly. 'You have to try not to let the press get to you, which is why it's best not to engage. Now, I'm going to call Elaine Phillips to find out what's going on there; then, Hanna, could I talk to you alone for a while?'

After she'd gone outside to make the call, Cait said to Leo, 'I need to fill you in on what's been going on here since Andee got back. Come with me while I go and lie Sofia down.'

As she watched them leave, Hanna heard Seb say, 'I'm afraid this is how it's going to be from now on. Our lives are going to be turned upside down and inside out, and apparently there's nothing we can do to stop it.'

Hanna looked at him and said, 'You shouldn't be having to go through this, Seb. You haven't done anything wrong—'

'Nor have you,' he interrupted. 'None of us have, but apparently we're already on trial. Now I'm wondering if we should be contacting a lawyer.'

Hearing his last comment as she came back inside, Andee said, 'That would be a good idea, because I'm afraid to say that Leo, certainly, is going to need one.'

CHAPTER FORTY-TWO

Half an hour later, Hanna and Andee were in the summer room, sun shades lowered to halfway to block out the glare, doors wide open, letting in cool air and the scent of fine rain as it fell steadily outside. The others were in the kitchen with Florina, tucking into the goodies the housekeeper had arrived with a few minutes ago. Hanna had no appetite and it seemed Andee didn't have much of one either.

'I thought Seb might join us,' Andee commented, setting a mug of coffee on the small table beside her.

Surprised, Hanna said, 'I don't think he realized he was invited. Anyway, he's keen to get hold of Riona, and I'm sure he's more than ready for a break from me.'

Andee said, 'So he's still seeing her?'

Hanna's eyebrows rose. 'Why? Did you think it wouldn't last?' Then with a laugh, 'It's only been a few weeks, but they seem to be working out pretty well.'

Andee smiled. 'That's good. And you like her too?'

'As far as I can tell, there's nothing not to like, apart from the awful hours she has to work. But Seb says it won't be for much longer, given how little life it seems to allow her.' She put her own coffee down and tucked her legs under her. 'Cait seems to have taken to her. It was because she confided in Riona about Freya Hansen that we all now know.'

Andee frowned. 'She confided in Riona?'

Hanna shrugged. 'I guess Cait thought she was someone she could trust, who'd give her the right advice. I don't know what Riona told her, but as soon as she heard about Jack yesterday, she told Seb that he must get Cait to tell us what she'd been bottling up in case it had some relevance to what happened.'

Andee regarded her thoughtfully. She looked as though she might pursue the subject, but in the end she said, 'We need to talk about Leo. Apparently someone's come forward with dash-cam footage showing his car passing Hugo Astor's home on the night – and around the time – Astor was attacked.'

Hanna's blood turned cold. Until this moment she'd believed only she and Jack had known that Leo was in the vicinity, at the wrong time on the wrong day.

'It doesn't actually prove anything,' Andee continued, 'but it has raised certain questions, not the least of which is what was he doing there? Don't worry about answering me,' she said, stalling Hanna, 'he can explain it to his lawyer. Jay Wells is going to act for him?'

Hanna nodded. 'She called me straight back when I left a message. Do you know her?'

'Only by reputation, so at least we know he's in good hands. I'm told a detective will be coming here for an initial interview rather than ask him to go in. It'll only give rise to more speculation over Jack's death if Leo is seen going into the station, probably under caution, and at this stage no one wants that.'

Hanna swallowed dryly as she tried to feel grateful for

the consideration – but the idea of Leo trying to prove his innocence, which was what it could amount to, was making her giddy. She thought of Jack and how he was always able to handle these things. He knew exactly what to do and say, and even managed to make them go away, whereas she hardly knew where to begin.

As if out of the blue, Andee said, 'About the attempted rape.'

Hanna's head spun and her heart clenched. Though she'd known this had to be coming, she still didn't feel ready for it.'

'I didn't tell Elaine Phillips about your history with Astor,' Andee continued, 'but I'm pretty sure she worked it out for herself.'

Hanna had stopped breathing.

'It has to be your decision,' Andee said, 'but my advice is that we can, and must, be completely honest with her about *everything*, no matter how hard it is, because likely as not it will come out anyway. And it won't help her, or any of us, if she feels we haven't been straight with her.'

Hanna felt as though she'd lost control of what she was thinking. Nothing was happening in the right order, or for the right reasons. She said, 'I'm guessing the reason they've let Astor go . . .'

'. . . for now . . .'

'. . . is because they think while he has a motive for blackmail, he doesn't for murder?'

Andee didn't deny it. 'Something like that, but if at any point they feel what happened between you two has a relevance to Jack's case, things will obviously change.'

Feeling wretched and once again infuriatingly helpless, Hanna said, angrily, 'He tried to rape me . . .' until, realizing she couldn't go any further with it, she said, 'Should I expect this to get into the press sometime soon so my children can read all about it?'

Sighing, Andee said, 'I wish I could say no, and if it stays with Elaine I'm sure it won't, but if she's forced to pass the information to her team . . . Well, I'm not saying that someone from the lower ranks will leak it, but at the same time I can't guarantee they won't.'

How often her instinct was to fly, and yet she never seemed to have a choice but to stay and fight. Just thank God Andee was here, advising and supporting her in every way she could.

Seb too, of course. She couldn't even begin to think of going through this without him.

Moving on, Andee said, 'It turns out Freya Hansen is still at the address I found for her, and two of Elaine Phillips's team have already paid her a visit.'

Hanna balked. 'That was fast.'

'No one is wasting any time on this case. However,' Andee grimaced slightly as she said, 'you should probably brace yourself for this . . . Freya Hansen is claiming to have been at home all day yesterday, and apparently Jack was with her in the morning.'

Hanna reeled. *He'd been with Freya Hansen as recently as yesterday? On the day he was killed? Was there a connection, something no one was seeing yet?* Then, remembering where he'd actually been, she said, 'But he was at the Valley Fest with Cait and Leo . . . Jenny was there too. They can vouch for that, so he couldn't have been with Freya Hansen.'

'OK, then we need to establish what time he left here in the morning, and exactly when he returned.'

'I can tell you both. He went out at nine thirty to take

some breakfast for the campers, and he came back . . .' Her voice started to falter. 'Around half past one.' Her eyes met Andee's as she said, 'So enough time to call into the Fest, drive on to wherever and then get back to Lake House for his planned fishing afternoon with Seb.'

Andee's expression showed sorrow and regret as she said, 'Freya Hansen is claiming that Jack left her place just after one, by which time her mother had come back from wherever she was and stayed for the rest of the day. So, if the mother can be trusted, Freya Hansen has an alibi for when the attack occurred.'

Of course she did, did anyone seriously think she wouldn't? 'What about her brother?' Hanna asked tightly.

'As far as I'm aware, no one's spoken to him yet, but messages have been left with his sister and on his mobile phone for him to contact the police as a matter of urgency. I'm sure if they haven't heard from him by the end of today, the search will be escalated.'

Hanna got to her feet and started to pace. 'They do realize he's Danish, don't they?' she cried. 'He could be out of the country and halfway to bloody Copenhagen before they do anything.'

'I'm sure all points of exit are already covered.'

Hanna didn't believe it.

'Elaine Phillips isn't going to let anyone get away with anything on this case,' Andee assured her. 'It's too high profile, and she'll be having to report to Maurice Guest on a daily, if not hourly, basis, so you can be pretty certain that the ports were alerted even before I'd left the station.'

Only slightly appeased, Hanna said, 'What time is Elaine coming here today?'

'I'm not sure yet, but others will turn up first – someone

to talk to Leo, someone else to get the DNA elimination underway. Have they already taken the shoes and clothing you were wearing yesterday?'

Hanna nodded. 'And Seb's. Luckily he was staying here for the weekend anyway, so he had a change. I think he's planning to go home tomorrow to pick up some more things. I told him he doesn't need to carry on staying here, that I understand he has his own life to get on with, but I have to admit I'm glad he's insisting – in spite of the conclusions that are being drawn about us.' She flicked a hand irritably. 'What is wrong with people? It's hardly been twenty-four hours and already they're making things up, or twisting them to suit a false narrative, I suppose to boost circulation with sly innuendo and even lies.' She stood motionless suddenly, and sightless, feeling paralysed by her own angst, before turning and slumping back into the chair. 'I shouldn't get so worked up,' she said, 'it won't change anything.'

'You're under a lot of stress,' Andee responded gently, 'and I wish I could tell you it'll get better soon. It will, of course, eventually, but I'm afraid it won't be today.'

Hanna's eyes flicked to her. 'So Elaine Phillips is coming to question me? What happened to just giving a statement? Why do I have to be interrogated?'

Andee's phone rang. She turned it off, saying, 'I know you've already given a statement, so there is no getting away from the fact that you were here, in the house, with Jack, before the attack. You knew he'd gone down to the lake, and they only have your word for it that you had no idea about Freya Hansen and her child before today.'

Hanna stared at her wordlessly, and yet not entirely surprised. 'So, according to them I have a motive?' she said

flatly. 'I followed him, took some sort of weapon with me
. . . Andee, you know I didn't do it . . .'

'Of course, and I don't believe they really think you did,
but they have a job to do, boxes to tick, and Jack was who
he was.'

'You said they think it was a man who struck him.'

'Which is why' – Andee grimaced – 'they're keen to talk
to Seb when they get here.'

Hanna's mouth fell open. 'They can't seriously think . . .'

'I'm sorry,' Andee said, holding up her hands, 'the way
they're seeing it is that you saw Jack leave the house, and
you also saw Seb go down to the lake to join him – and
the next thing you knew, Seb was coming back here to tell
you what he'd found.'

Hanna was still staring at her in disbelief. Was Andee
honestly suggesting that Seb could have done this? And
was she, Hanna, actually starting to see that their best
friend of almost thirty years had had the opportunity (she
had no idea about motive or means). He'd been down at
the water's edge long enough, out of sight of the house . . .
'No,' she said in a whisper. 'That's crazy, Andee, and you
know it.'

CHAPTER FORTY-THREE

'Riona, at last.' Seb half-laughed into the phone, sinking onto the edge of the bed and drawing a hand over his unshaven chin. Now she'd answered, he felt a fool for having tried so often, and yet it would surely have seemed neglectful if he hadn't. 'Are you all right?' he asked.

Her voice was hoarse, hesitant as she said, 'Seb, is that you?'

'Yes it's me,' he assured her, his concern deepening. 'What's happening with you . . . ?'

'I'm sorry . . . I-I don't know where Riona is. I thought she'd have come back by now . . .'

Seb experienced a beat of unease. 'Sorry, I thought you were . . . Who – who am I speaking to?'

'Blanche.'

He wasn't sure what to say. He knew the name – wasn't Blanche one of Riona's patients, a client? Why was she answering Riona's phone? 'I'm concerned about Riona,' he said, 'can't . . .'

'I'm concerned too. It's not like her to stay away this long.'

Thrown again, he said, 'Does someone else there know where she is?'

'I've asked, but they haven't seen her. Billy has gone too.'

Confused, he said, 'Who's Billy?'

'We've all been worried about him. He has a very bad temper and isn't easy to control.'

Seb was starting to be afraid that Riona might have got into a situation with a violent patient. 'Is there someone you can call?' He was racking his brains trying to remember the name of Riona's superior. 'Dr Francis?'

'Maybe Riona and Billy are with her,' she said. 'Billy has become a problem.'

'In what way?'

As if not hearing the question, she said, 'How are you? Is Hanna all right? Such a terrible thing to happen.'

Seb was stunned. Was it possible that Riona had broken their confidence with one of her patients? He struggled for something to say.

'Thank you for ringing, Seb,' she said, sounding hoarse and whispery. 'I know it will mean a lot to Riona. She's so glad she met you. I think you'll make all the difference to her life.'

Minutes later, Seb was still staring at his phone, trying to make sense of what had just happened. It hadn't felt like a real conversation, yet he couldn't quite say why.

And where on earth was Riona? Clearly somewhere without her phone. And with Billy, whoever he was – a patient who was apparently hard to control.

His phone rang and, seeing Riona's name, he paused, not sure he wanted to speak to Blanche again.

'Seb,' Riona said softly when he clicked on, 'how are you? I'm so sorry. Blanche shouldn't have answered my phone.'

'Where were you?' he asked, sounding strained even to his own ears.

'Oh, I'd just stepped out. I wasn't gone long, but she doesn't always have a good grasp of time, or reality. How are things at your end? I heard on the news that the police want to talk to Leo in connection with the attack on Hugo Astor.'

Sighing, as he pulled himself together, Seb said, 'I'm afraid so. I don't know if anyone is drawing any conclusions from that at the moment, but frankly it's not good on any front.'

Sounding worried, she said, 'Do they have any evidence to say it was Leo?'

'There's some dash-cam footage that shows he was in the area.'

'I see. That's not good. Is no one else on the footage?'

'I've no idea. If there is, they presumably don't have a known connection to Astor.'

After a pause, she excused herself and put a hand over the phone. He couldn't make out what was being said at the other end, but there was clearly some sort of altercation going on at the clinic. Finally she came back on the line, slightly breathless, as she said, 'I'm so sorry you're all going through this. You know, if there's anything I can do . . . Remember, I witnessed Astor attacking Hanna? If any of that comes out, I'll be willing to say what I saw.'

'Thank you. I'll tell Hanna, but obviously we're still hoping it doesn't get that far.'

He heard a voice in the background that could have been Blanche's, but he wasn't sure. Riona said, 'Just let me finish this call, please.' Then a pause. 'Are you still there?' she asked Seb.

'Yes. Is everything all right with you?'

'It's fine, nothing I can't handle, but I admit I wish I was with you.'

Warmed by that, and wishing they were together too, he said, 'I'm going home tomorrow to pick up a few things. Can I see you?'

'I'd like that. Will you let me know when you get there?' He heard a male voice in the background – Billy? – but couldn't determine what was being said.

'Are you going to be all right?' Seb asked. 'It sounds as though you have a few difficulties going on over there.'

'They happen from time to time,' she said wryly. 'Things will settle down. What are you doing for the rest of the day?'

Recalling what was in store for him, he sighed despondently. 'The police want to talk to me again. Only to be expected, naturally, but I'm aware that I was at the lake with Jack on my own for a while – trying to save him, of course, but I'm not sure they're fully convinced of that.'

'I can't believe they'd seriously think you had anything to do with it. You were his best friend, you had no motive . . . Just because you were there . . .'

'There were no witnesses, apart from Hanna, but she was at the house, and you can't see that part of the lake from there.'

Sounding troubled, Riona said, 'Has no one else come forward yet to say they saw something?'

'Not that I know of. Right now they only have my word that the attack had already happened before I got to him. By the time the paramedics arrived, both Hanna and I had his blood all over us and our footprints were everywhere.' It was only as he was saying the words that he realized the police were very probably asking themselves if this was something he and Hanna had done together – if they'd had it all worked out beforehand, knowing what they were going to say and how their stories would match.

It made him feel sick.

'Seb, are you OK?'

Swallowing dryly, he said, 'Yes, I think so. I should probably go now, I think the police have just arrived.'

'Good luck,' she said softly, 'and don't forget to call me tomorrow.'

CHAPTER FORTY-FOUR

In spite of the pill she'd taken, Hanna was finding it impossible to sleep. Elaine Phillips had come back to interview her earlier, and now it was playing over and over in her mind, the probing questions and insinuations, the subtle scepticism that had almost made her start to doubt her own mind.

'So Jack had been out for most of the morning,' the detective had said, 'and returned to the house around two. What were you doing at the time?'

'I-I was in the kitchen working out what to cook for dinner,' Hanna replied. 'We usually eat our main meal around six on Sundays. I thought if I was going to do a roast, I should probably start to prepare.'

'Did you and Jack talk when he came in?'

'Yes.'

'What about?'

'Nothing in particular. He said everyone seemed to be having a good time at the Valley Fest and they were intending to be back around five. Then he started to get the fishing tackle ready.'

'So as far as you were concerned, he was at the Valley Fest all morning?'

Reminding herself that Freya Hansen could be lying about him having been with her, she said, 'I had no reason to think he was anywhere else, and the others did see him, so he was certainly there.'

'At some point?'

Hanna didn't respond.

'OK. And how did he seem in himself when he got home shortly after half past one?'

Flashing back to it made her desperately want to live the moments again, to take more notice of what he said, to keep him from going to the lake even. She had to answer the question, so how had he seemed? Distracted? Guilty. Had he avoided her? Truthfully, she said, 'He seemed normal.' *But she'd never detected anything in his manner to make her suspect he was cheating on her, and if Freya Hansen's boy was the same age as Sofia . . .*

'Did you talk about anything else?' Elaine Phillips pressed.

Hanna shook her head. 'He wasn't in the house for long. He was keen to get down to the lake and start fishing.'

'With Sebastian Goodman?'

'That's right.'

'And where was Mr Goodman when Jack came home?'

'He was upstairs in his room, talking to his sister on the phone.'

'Did he come down before Jack went to the lake?'

'No, Jack had already gone by then.'

The detective made a note on her tablet. With no preamble she said, 'Tell me about your husband's relationship with Freya Hansen.'

Tensing, Hanna said, 'I'm sure Andee told you, I didn't know anything about them until yesterday.'

251

'Are you sure?'

'Of course I am,' she retorted. 'Cait, my daughter, told us all in the morning.'

'So that was the first you knew of your husband's relationship with Freya Hansen?'

Flinching at the note of disbelief, Hanna swallowed dryly, as she said, 'Yes,' and even to her own ears she managed to sound unconvincing.

Elaine Phillips made another note, and moved on. 'Did you go down to the lake with Jack before Sebastian Goodman joined him?'

'No.'

'Maybe you followed him there?'

What was that supposed to mean? 'No, I didn't.'

'So you were alone in the kitchen for how long, before Mr Goodman came down from his room?'

'Fifteen or twenty minutes.'

Elaine Phillips looked at her long and hard, her shrewd grey eyes speaking for her in a way that caused sweat to prickle on Hanna's skin. Clearly the detective considered this enough time for her to have gone to the lake, bludgeoned Jack to death, and to have returned without being seen. Hanna started to protest, but stopped, afraid she might end up making things worse for herself when she hadn't actually been accused of anything.

'When Mr Goodman went to the lake,' Elaine Phillips said eventually, 'how long was it before he came back to tell you what had happened?'

Hanna took an unsteady breath. 'Somewhere around ten minutes, I'd say. I can't be certain . . . I just remember him running back to the house and trying to stop me from going down there.'

'Did you notice any blood on Mr Goodman's clothes when he was trying to stop you?'

'I-I'm not sure. He would have tried to revive Jack. I did too when I got there.'

'Which would account for how Jack's blood got onto your clothes?'

'Yes.'

Hanna picked up a note of cynicism again, or maybe it was the way Elaine Phillips always sounded. It could be just a statement of understanding, a little help with an obvious explanation. It was impossible to tell.

She had to stop acting as though she had a guilty conscience.

The interview ended as abruptly as it had begun, leaving her with no idea if the detective had believed her or not. She had a strong feeling she didn't, and it was making everything so much worse. Wasn't it enough that she'd lost her husband in such a mindlessly brutal way and had then discovered he had a child with another woman? Was she going to find herself arrested – imprisoned, even – for a murder she hadn't committed? Was this how people were found guilty of something they hadn't done – just because they were in the wrong place at the wrong time and couldn't prove their innocence?

Late the following morning, they left the house in a convoy of three cars, Andee at the front in her Mercedes, Seb close behind in his vintage Porsche, and Hanna, with the children, at the wheel of Jack's Range Rover bringing up the rear. They'd decided on that order to allow Andee to push a path through the press first, with Seb keeping it open for Hanna to come through. It kind of worked, but the flashbulbs going off in her face, the shouting, banging on the car and bodies diving out of the way as she kept her foot down were beyond unnerving – they were actually frightening. She was unable to take a breath until they reached the bottom of the hill, and even then it was shallow and tentative, as she braced herself for someone to come speeding down the road behind her, or to spring out of nowhere and start it all over again.

'That was fucking surreal,' Leo declared, bringing his face out of his hands. 'They're like animals, for God's sake.'

'I'm so glad we didn't bring Sofes,' Cait said from the back. 'That would have scared her to death. It fucking scared me.'

Wishing they'd stop swearing, while realizing the irrelevance of her annoyance, Hanna watched Andee and Seb drive on ahead, and accelerated to follow. She didn't know why; it wasn't as if they were all heading to the same place. She guessed it just made her feel safer to have them in view for as long as possible.

As they began winding up the hill towards Dundry, she did her best to keep her attention on the road, but yesterday afternoon's interview with Elaine Phillips was haunting her again. Did the detective really think she might have done it? Surely to God not. Andee had done her best to be reassuring when Hanna had told her what had been said, and for a while it had worked, but now everything was starting to crowd in on her again.

Leo shouted, 'Mum, stop! Red light!'

Hanna slammed on the brake, and saw that they'd reached the outskirts of Bristol. There was no sign of Andee and Seb now, but it didn't matter. They were going to different parts of Clifton, while she and the children were heading for the offices of her and Jack's personal lawyer, just off the city centre. She'd emailed ahead to let James Johnson know she was coming and why, and had received a message back within minutes conveying his deepest condolences and saying that of course he would be available for her at eleven thirty.

After parking on a meter close to the Custom House on Queen Square, they walked along one of the cobbled footpaths surrounding the grassy areas. They stopped outside a prestigious, double-fronted Georgian house that at first glance appeared more residential than commercial.

'Are you OK?' Cait whispered, taking her mother's arm as Leo rang the old brass bell.

'I think so,' Hanna replied. 'Are you?'

'Nervous, to be honest. What are you going to do if . . .?'

She got no further as the door opened and James Johnson himself came to welcome them. He was a lean, slightly stooped man in his late fifties, with curly grey hair, close-set eyes and a tight, but not unfriendly smile.

'I'd have come to you, Hanna,' he told her, directing them through the reception area and straight upstairs to his first-floor, senior-partner's office. 'It would have been no trouble . . .'

'Actually, we're glad of an excuse to get out of the house,' she assured him. 'I'm just hoping we weren't followed, or the next thing we know they'll be making up stories about why I've come to see you so soon.'

Scowling his disapproval of the intrusion they were suffering, he invited them to sit on the sofas, while his assistant came in after them to take orders for coffee.

After she'd gone, James closed the door and picked up a file from his desk, before going to sit on the sofa facing theirs. Hanna watched his long fingers turning pages, her heart thudding with unease, and feeling her son's hand slip into hers – a gesture of moral support, she realized – almost made her cry. She didn't want to be doing this, would rather be anywhere else in the world, with Jack, with their family still intact and no more suspicions, fears or betrayals. Just living their normal lives in their haphazard, eventful, but lawful ways.

When he looked up, Johnson's eyes moved between them in a steady, but careful way. It immediately made her wonder if she'd done the right thing when she'd told him in her email that he could speak freely in front of Cait and Leo.

'I'm deeply sorry if this isn't what you want to hear,' he began, 'but Freya Hansen is one of Jack's beneficiaries. She and her child are the subject of a codicil he added back in February of this year.'

As Hanna's head spun, she tried to recall what they'd been doing then, where they might have been, but her mind could grasp nothing. 'Why then?' she asked. 'What happened to make him add the codicil?'

Johnson regarded her regretfully. 'I'm not sure anything happened, as such – he was just putting a few financial affairs in order.'

'Did you meet her?' Cait asked him. 'Freya. Did she come in with him that day?'

Johnson shook his head. 'Paul De Vries came to witness his signature.'

De Vries, Madden's chief financial officer.

'Would he have known what was in the codicil?' Hanna asked, starting to feel betrayed all over again – and foolish for being the only one who didn't know.

'Not unless Jack told him,' Johnson replied.

Leo said, tightly, 'How much is she getting?'

Johnson handed over a page that contained a highlighted figure near the bottom, and Cait gasped out loud.

'That is one fucking great big motive to kill him,' Leo growled fiercely.

Hanna read the seven-figure sum, hid her own shock, and turned to her children, wondering if Jack had ever considered what this betrayal might do to them? Not that this amount compared with what they were about to inherit – but it certainly showed that Jack had wanted to take care of his other son.

Johnson was saying, 'The police have already been in touch with me. A detective is coming here this afternoon. With your permission, I'll make him aware of this codicil.'

Hanna nodded and took a breath, not sure what to do now, if there was any more that needed to be said.

They looked up as Johnson's assistant came in with an overloaded tray.

Hanna didn't want to stay any longer, and sensed the children were ready to leave too, but it would be rude simply to get up and go now. So she took a coffee, declined milk and sugar. She waited until the others had theirs before asking, 'Did Jack ever talk to you about Freya Hansen, James? I mean, did you know about her before the codicil?'

'I didn't,' Johnson replied, 'and we had no further conversations about it after it was signed.'

So, someone else who had no actual details of the relationship; whether it had been loving, or Jack responding to a duty, or to an insidious blackmail.

Fifteen minutes later, they were back in the car heading for home. Cait and Leo sat silently, listening as Hanna spoke to Andee on the hands-free, relating what they'd learned from James Johnson.

Sighing Andee said, 'I'm so sorry. I really am. Are you going to contest it?'

'I think we should,' Cait piped up.

Hanna said, 'It's too early to make that decision when we still don't know what's in the rest of the will. Although James assured us that there's nothing else we wouldn't expect.'

Cait said, bitterly, 'So no more handouts to girlfriends or bastards or blackmailers.' Her voice faltered on a sob and Leo turned to take her hand. He didn't say anything, had hardly spoken at all since they'd left the lawyer, Hanna realized, but what was there to say? This was a terrible, terrifying time for him – not just losing his beloved father, but having the suspicion that he'd attacked Hugo Astor hanging over him. Was it possible in some crazy, warped world that it could lead to a suspicion he'd done the same to Jack?

The detectives hadn't questioned him for long yesterday, but nor, apparently, had they gone away satisfied with his reasons for being in the area at the time of Astor's brutal beating. On the other hand, Jay Wells, his lawyer, had felt confident that a charge was far from imminent.

'They have nothing to show him out of the car, much less on Astor's property,' she'd told them before she'd left the house.

'They're such similar attacks,' Hanna had said. 'Do you think there's a chance they could be linked?'

'It's hard to see how, at the moment,' Jay had replied, 'but certainly the police won't be ruling it out.'

Hanna had sat thinking about Jay Wells a lot after she'd

gone, remembering how the lawyer had gone through her own public humiliation and heartbreak not so long ago. She'd fallen in love with a client who'd been charged with murdering his wife. She'd left her husband for him, had moved into his home in the Cotswolds, but now he was in prison after finally admitting to his guilt. And Jay was back with her husband, Tom. Hanna wondered how Tom could have forgiven her, what their marriage was like now – and she imagined there was probably a lot more to the story than the press had managed to get hold of.

It was easier to think about that than it had been to think about herself, and the fact that she would never be given the opportunity to forgive Jack and find a way forward with him.

'Where are you going now?' Andee asked over the speaker.

Recalling what was in store for them next, Hanna sighed and wished she could drive in another direction. 'Home,' she said flatly. 'Everyone wants to come and pay their respects – the vicar, his wife, a dozen or more Merchant Venturers, all three mayors, the Lord Lieutenant, our local MP – although I've asked him not to come. Jack detested him, and the last thing he'd ever want is that dreadful man using this for his own publicity.'

'I heard him on Radio Four earlier,' Andee said, 'talking about what a tragedy it was and how Jack was such a well-liked and valued member of the community. And how no one will rest until the killer is found and brought to justice.'

Though Leo and Cait groaned in dislike of the man, none of them were able to criticize his words, so Hanna said, 'Are you still at the office?' Andee was using Hanna's desk and PA today to carry out some further research.

'I am, and Donna's being extremely helpful. I'm waiting for a few calls back at the moment, so spending the time going over what we already know. Have you had any responses to the email you sent your extended family?'

Hanna felt guilty for asking them not to come – the first and second cousins, uncles, aunts, godchildren and their parents. Every one of them wanted to be there for her and the children, to feel they were doing the right thing for Jack, but she just wasn't up to facing them all yet. 'I haven't checked,' she replied, 'but I'm telling myself they'll understand.'

'I'm sure they will. Ah, there's my phone and it's Seb. I'll call you later, or call me any time.'

As she rang off, Hanna wondered what Seb and Andee might be talking about, but since it could only be this godawful situation, she let it drift from her mind.

'Do we need to be around when the great and the good come calling later?' Leo asked.

Understanding that he probably didn't want to see anyone now he was being investigated, Hanna said, 'I think it's important that you hold your head up and show that you have nothing to hide. The same goes for me with all these horrible suspicions that have started flying around.'

'I could bring Sofes,' Cait suggested. 'You know how sociable she is, and it'll help stop things getting too morose.'

'Good idea. Jenny should be there too. A united front. It's what Dad would want.' She wasn't sure why she'd added that, when Jack probably didn't have the right to want anything any more. Thinking that deepened all the breaks in her heart. It was so very hard to grieve for him, to know what to think, to say, to do even, when all she really wanted was to be with him. Whether to berate, even hit him for putting them through this, or to feel his strength engulfing her, she didn't exactly know.

'OK,' Leo stated grimly, staring at his phone. 'It's saying that the police have caught up with Marius Hansen.'

Hanna's heart tripped as she glanced at him. She expected to feel relief, even hope that it was all going to be over soon, but she realized she felt nothing, because even if it did turn out to be Marius Hansen, nothing was ever going to bring Jack back.

And what if it wasn't him? She and Seb would remain suspects unless Hugo Astor confessed, and she just couldn't see that happening.

CHAPTER FORTY-FIVE

Seb had been on the phone from the moment he'd arrived home. He made coffee, drank it and made more calls, talking to old friends and colleagues, thanking them for their condolences and assuring them he'd pass their messages on to Hanna and the children. Naturally a good many of them wanted to discuss what had happened, had tried to press him for details while still sounding sympathetic, but he'd managed to avoid it. There was no one he wanted to discuss it with, apart from Hanna and Andee. And probably Riona if they were able to get together this evening. He'd sent a text apologizing for not making it back to Clifton last night, but he was at home now and would love to see her.

No response yet.

'Seb, thanks for getting back to me,' Andee said when he finally got through to her. 'I was wondering if you might have another number for Riona. I've tried the one you gave me, but I keep getting voicemail and she isn't calling back.'

'I'm afraid that happens sometimes,' he replied. 'She gets caught up at the clinic, and it isn't always easy to break away. Have you explained what it's about?'

'I said that it's to do with the incident she witnessed in

Hanna's office. I'd like her to talk me through it, in case she saw or heard something she didn't consider relevant, or worth mentioning before now.'

'Well, I know she's willing to help in any way she can. If she's in touch with me first, I'll be sure to get her to ring you.'

'Thanks, I appreciate it. Have you heard about Marius Hansen, Freya's brother?'

'If you mean that he's being questioned by the police, yes I have. I'd like to be a fly on the wall for that one. Anyway, I was about to call Hanna. Do you know how she got on with the lawyer?'

'Apparently Freya Hansen is very handsomely taken care of in Jack's will.'

Although it wasn't a surprise, it made Seb feel angry, not only because the affair with a young girl was becoming ever more real, but because Jack had kept it to himself for so long. 'So the Hansens have a motive?' he asked tightly.

'It can certainly be viewed as that, particularly if it turns out that some form of blackmail was involved. I'll call Elaine Phillips when we're done here, but before I go, has anyone from the police been in touch with you again since yesterday?'

'No, but I haven't listened to all my messages yet. Are you expecting someone to be?'

'Probably not while they're focusing on Marius Hansen, but I think you should take the advice Jay Wells gave you yesterday and contact her office. It's likely she'll take Hanna on herself, if it comes to it, but you could need representation too. Do you know Ash Baqri?'

'Not well, but we've met a couple of times. I'm really hoping it won't get that far.'

'So am I, but if it does, please don't let them question you again without talking to him first. When an investigation is under this much pressure, a lot of mistakes can be made. We have to be sure that doesn't happen to you and Hanna.'

After ringing off, Seb called Hanna, wanting to check how she was after receiving the lawyer's news, and to let her know that he'd be staying at home tonight unless she was keen for him to come back.

'I must admit, I feel better when you're here,' she told him, 'but I know you're hoping to see Riona. If you do, please send her my love. If she doesn't feel it's too awful a prospect, maybe she'd like to visit at the weekend?'

'I'll ask, and thank you,' he said. 'I feel bad not being with you for the onslaught this afternoon. I can pop back for an hour or two if you'd like me to.'

'It's OK, we'll manage. Perhaps, if you and Riona go out somewhere this evening, you'll be spotted, and our supposed conspiracy of acting together will be put to bed. Poor choice of phrase, sorry.'

He smiled and wished he was with her, for he could tell she was struggling – how could she not be? He felt so torn between her and his desire to see Riona, but at least he'd be back there tomorrow. 'Hopefully there'll be some news about Marius Hansen soon,' he said.

'It would be a relief to know they no longer suspect either of us, that's for sure. Anyway, I should let you go now – Florina needs instructions for our visitors. Hope you get to see Riona.'

As the line went dead, Seb checked his messages. He found nothing from Riona or the police, so put his phone on silent and went upstairs. He didn't feel like talking to anyone else right now, and if Riona did ring . . . Well, he'd call her back, he just needed to lie down on his own bed for a while, to think about what had happened to Jack and how hard he was struggling with it himself.

He was going to miss him so much, already was. He'd been more like a brother than a friend; someone he trusted, respected, loved, relied on, without even really thinking about it. They had always been there for one another through good times and bad, and Jack, with his big, generous heart and easy-going nature, had never thought twice about sharing what was his. Seb was thinking of Hanna and the children, and how they'd always been like family to him and Jilly – but now there was Freya Hansen, whom Jack had never mentioned. Though Seb could only feel glad he hadn't known about the girl – as he'd told Hanna, it was a secret he wouldn't have wanted to keep – he felt oddly betrayed that Jack hadn't trusted him enough to tell him. Why had he kept it to himself? Apart from the obvious reason, of course, that Freya Hansen might have been underage when the relationship started. He certainly wouldn't have wanted anyone to know about that, and could he have opened himself up any wider to blackmail?

It sickened Seb to think of the mess Jack could have been in, to know what it was doing to his family now. There was no way Jack would have wanted that, so exactly how – and when – had he been planning to put things right?

It was the middle of the afternoon when Seb finally woke up, surprised that he'd fallen asleep and for so long. He wasn't sure it had made him feel any better; his head was aching, and the weight of grief seemed heavier and somehow more raw than ever.

Forcing himself up from the bed, he stripped off his clothes, put on his running gear and went downstairs.

His mobile showed eighteen missed calls, twenty-one texts and five iMessages.

Still no word from Riona.

Suppressing his disappointment, he sent another quick message telling her he was worried so please be in touch; then, placing the phone in his armbelt, he set off for a run. It might be drizzling and grey, but it would feel good to be out in the air for a while without being watched the way they constantly were at Lake House.

CHAPTER FORTY-SIX

Riona was seated at her desk, staring at her phone and struggling with the urge to return Andee's call. She had meant it when she'd told Seb she wanted to help, she really had, but since gaining an understanding of what had really happened following the incident in Hanna's office with Hugo Astor, she knew she couldn't.

And now there wasn't just the attack on Astor, there was what had happened to Jack.

Seb's latest text was displayed on her screen now. She longed to assure him that all was fine and that she was looking forward to seeing him later. She'd even typed it out and allowed her imagination to fly with where they might go and what they might do – a romantic dinner somewhere, maybe at his place, or a night at the cinema, before making love the way they had the last time she'd been at his house.

Even now her finger was poised ready to send the message, but she knew she couldn't. She cared for him too much to carry on letting him believe there was a possible future for them, or any kind of relationship at all, when there wasn't.

She hadn't cried in a very long time, but tears were pooling in her eyes as she tried to bid goodbye to him in her heart.

She was surrounded by boxes, each bearing a name in large print on its surface – Ryan, Ruby, Billy, Hayley, Blanche, Riona. There were half a dozen more with no names, just in case they were needed. As yet, there was nothing inside any of them.

No one else was around. The others had taken themselves out of her way a few hours ago, refusing to speak to her, or to engage with anything she had to say. There was so much fear in them – of abandonment, irrelevance, an end to their existence even.

Could she slip out now, unnoticed?

Her heart thudded with the prospect of freedom, of being able to unravel herself from all the complications and demands, unpredictability and imprisonment.

It would be cruel, unforgivable – and anyway, they'd find her. One or more of them would appear at Seb's door, or even inside his house, and she couldn't allow that.

Getting up from her chair, she moved quietly to the door.

The place was silent; no sound coming from anywhere, not even the tick of a clock. This was her only opportunity. She could pick up her phone, walk outside and drive away. She didn't have to take anything with her, she didn't need anything other than the keys to the car.

Knowing they were on a hook in the kitchen, where Billy had left them, she tiptoed across the hall, as if any slight noise might disturb them, even though they weren't here.

She was alone. She kept telling herself that. *You are alone. They aren't here.*

The kitchen door was ajar. She pushed it gently, took a step inside and felt her heart whoosh with shock as she walked straight into Blanche.

CHAPTER FORTY-SEVEN

Jack must have left the banquet that Saturday night at the Merchants' Hall to be with Freya.

Hanna couldn't get the thought out of her head. Now it was there, it was refusing to leave, to stop tormenting her, even though she had no idea if it was true.

Freya had rung him; he'd taken the call, they'd spoken for only a few minutes, and then he'd left. That was the sort of power she had over him – she called, made her demand, and he went running, no matter where he was, or what he was doing. She'd never known him to be controlled like that, and it made him feel like a stranger, someone she'd despise rather than respect.

She realized that if she was right about that Saturday, then he'd fabricated a pretty extravagant lie about an emergency at the Appledore site. Graeme hadn't seemed to know anything about it when she'd called the next morning to find out if he'd heard from Jack, and Jack, having failed to be in touch with her throughout the night, hadn't even rung on his way home.

She could check easily enough; all she had to do was ring Graeme or Andee and ask the question outright, for they'd be sure to know by now. However, in this moment, she didn't have the heart to catch him out in yet another lie. There was already too much to deal with; even if he had gone to Freya Hansen that night, what difference did it make now? Probably none, but she had to know.

Opening up the closet in his dressing room, she inhaled the powerful scent of him and pressed her face to the jacket hanging closest to her. She suspected everyone would think she was losing her mind if they realized she was burying herself in him like this, but after the hours of small talk this afternoon, the terrible sense of loneliness that had overcome her as dignitaries, friends and neighbours conveyed their condolences, she'd wanted him so desperately that this was where she'd ended up. Everything in here was his, was exactly as he'd left it, and if she closed her eyes, she was sure she could hear him.

Hanny, I love you more than anything or anyone, you know that. Don't listen to what's being said; it's not real; it's being twisted in a way that will be bound to hurt you if you believe it. So don't, my darling. Believe in me, please. Believe in us.

She inhaled deeply, as if the very essence of him could move through her with answers, explanations, truths that were bearable. As if being in this windowless room meant that nothing outside existed any more. She imagined his hands on hers, his breath on her face, his smile curving against her lips.

'Mum! Are you in here?' she heard Leo call from the bedroom door.

She didn't answer, remained completely still.

'I don't know where she is at the moment, Andee. Can I get her to call you back?'

Knowing she ought to leave now, she closed the closet

doors and leaned back against them. For a wrenching moment, it felt as though she was closing the door on him. She bowed her head and inhaled deeply, letting the breath go steadily, quietly, soothingly. She knew that anger and confusion would come to darken her mind again soon, that resentment and bitterness would find their places too, but right now, in these moments of quiet despair, she felt calm and close to him.

She found Leo a few minutes later in the TV room with Ishan and Sofia. The child, with a chocolatey face, was asleep next to her father; Leo and Ishan were watching a cricket match on Sky Sports.

'Mum, there you are,' Leo said, looking up when he realized she was there. 'Are you OK?'

'I'm fine,' she nodded. 'Glad everyone's gone at last.'

'What a shitshow,' he grumbled, 'but I guess they all meant well.'

'Where's Cait?' she asked, going to peek at Sofia.

Ishan said, 'Over at Jenny's having a private yoga session with Jenny's instructor. They tried to find you to see if you wanted to go too.'

Hanna smiled. 'Thanks for staying here with Cait,' she said. 'I think it's making a lot of difference, having you around.'

His expression was ironic as he said, 'I'll tell her you said that, then sit back and watch her trying to prove you wrong.'

With a half-laugh, Hanna turned back to the door.

'Andee wants you to call,' Leo told her. 'I left your phone in the kitchen.'

Going to find it, Hanna spoke for a while with Florina who was still clearing up following the reception, or afternoon tea, or whatever it was supposed to be called when people visited after the murder of a husband.

'The police have called me and Tomas for more questioning,' Florina tentatively announced as Hanna was about to leave the room.

Hanna turned back, worried, curious, for they'd already been interviewed once, why was it necessary again?

'I think it's about Freya Hansen,' Florina said gently. 'They didn't know about her when they talked to us before.'

Feeling her throat turn dry, Hanna said, 'Is there anything you can tell them?'

Florina's large green eyes were steeped in sorrow as she said, 'We didn't know about the child until yesterday, and we only found out then because I overheard you talking. I'm sorry, I wasn't meaning to eavesdrop—'

'It's OK,' Hanna assured her. 'Everyone's going to know soon enough.'

Florina nodded. 'It's already on social media.'

Hanna's heart stopped. 'I didn't know that,' she said.

'It just came up on my feed. I'm sorry. Please don't think it was me or Tomas who leaked it. We never said a word, I swear.'

'I know that,' Hanna reassured her. 'Did you know that Jack was . . . involved with her, when she was here?'

Florina's cheeks reddened. 'Not for sure, but I thought . . . Maybe there was something. Tomas said it was what she, or her brother, wanted us to think, and I always told myself he was right until we found out about the baby.'

Hanna's eyes drifted as she took this in, not sure how to process it, or if she even needed to.

'Mr Jack loved you very much,' Florina said softly.

Hanna attempted a smile, and holding up her phone said, 'I need to make a call.'

A few minutes later, she was in the summer room, her eyes absently following a flock of Canada geese landing on the lake as she said to Andee, 'I hear it's broken about Freya Hansen?'

'Have you seen it?'

'No. Do I need to?'

'Not really. I can tell you if you prefer.'

'I do.'

'OK, an online news service has posted a video of Freya Hansen outside her home with the child.'

Hanna felt suddenly sick. 'What's she saying?'

'That the rumours are correct; she and Jack have a little boy together and Jack adored him.'

Hanna's head began to spin. She hardly knew what to say, what even to feel, apart from unbearably humiliated, and furious that the world was finding out at all, never mind this way. 'So now everyone will think I had a good motive to kill Jack?' Before Andee could reply, she said, 'What's happening about the brother?'

'I'm afraid his alibi for Sunday checks out.'

Tight-lipped, Hanna said, 'So where was he?'

'Playing football for a local team. The kick off was at one p.m. The game ended a couple of hours later and he was on the pitch the whole time.'

Of course he was. It was never going to be so simple as to charge him with the crime and have it all go away. 'Why didn't he come forward sooner?'

'I'm afraid I don't know the answer to that.'

'Have they let him go?'

'I believe so.'

273

Hanna watched the geese taking off again, flapping their wings, skimming the surface before soaring to the sky. There was a whole other world going on out there, one that she dearly wished she belonged to; anywhere rather than here. 'I'm guessing this means Seb and I are back to being the main suspects?' she said hoarsely.

'I can't say I've heard that, but it's possible. Even so, I don't imagine they have any more evidence now than they did yesterday or they'd have been in touch about it.'

'I think it's enough for them, and the press, that Seb and I were here at the time and we already know they think we have a motive. I suppose Seb staying in Bristol tonight will make it seem as though we're trying to create a distance between us to throw them off the scent.'

'Do you know if he's seeing Riona?'

'I haven't spoken to him for a couple of hours, but even if he is and they're together, it'll either be construed as a set-up – or they'll say I acted alone. At least that would get Seb off the hook, I suppose.' Despondently she added, 'We seem to be running out of suspects, unless someone who works for Jack, one of his colleagues, or a business rival, is hiding something.'

'Well somebody is, somewhere,' Andee retorted, 'and after the digging around I've done today, I know who's at the top of my list.'

Hanna braced herself.

'I'm not going to say any more until I've had the chance to explore it further,' Andee continued, 'because I really don't want to make any mistakes with this.'

Knowing this was exactly what her friend excelled at, and feeling thankful a thousand times over to have her onside, Hanna said, 'Do the police know about it?'

'I shouldn't think so. They wouldn't have any reason to be looking in this direction yet. But if I find I'm right, they'll be the first to know.'

CHAPTER FORTY-EIGHT

Seb had spotted two photographers during his run the day before, so it wasn't a big surprise to find himself featured on the inside pages of a couple of newspapers this morning. It was, however, an intrusion into his personal life that he found offensive and unacceptable – not that he could do anything about it.

He guessed he just had to feel thankful that no one had written anything particularly salacious about him, and that he'd realized he was being followed before he'd crossed the Downs into Westbury-on-Trym. In fact, it had probably saved him from making a fool of himself by just turning up at the clinic, hot, sweaty and soaked to the skin, to make sure Riona was all right.

She still hadn't got back to him, and apparently she hadn't returned Andee's calls either, so she surely had to understand how worried he was by now. His biggest fear was a patient had injured her in some way and she had been unable to call for help.

Maybe she'd decided she didn't want to see him any more and thought ghosting was the best way to handle it.

For the moment, though, uppermost in his mind was Freya Hansen's appearance on breakfast TV only minutes ago, proudly showing off Jack's son while struggling with her grief over what had happened. She'd been at her home, near Bath, so the cameras had obviously gone to her, while he, Hanna and the children had been on the phone with one another as they'd watched in revulsion and disbelief.

'Of course, I'm devastated by what's happened,' Freya Hansen had told the interviewer, her small round face and mousey hair surely making any viewer wonder what a man like Jack had seen in her. Certainly it was what Seb had thought, ungallant and shaming as it was. He'd never have said this girl was Jack's type; maybe the hint of a Danish accent had had an appeal, and of course there was her youth, but he'd rather not think about that. (The one positive was that no one had yet questioned how old the girl had been when the relationship started.)

'How did you hear about what happened?' the interviewer asked.

'From the news. I'm not in touch with Jack's family. They haven't wanted anything to do with me since I stopped working for them.'

'I don't believe it,' Hanna muttered down the line. 'Were we supposed to stay friends? We barely even knew her.'

The interviewer said, 'Have you had any contact from them since Jack's death?'

'No. I had hoped Mrs Madden might reach out, but she hasn't so far. Of course, it's still early days and she will be trying to come to terms with it all herself.'

Freya's mother jumped in. 'It's a terrible thing that's happened, and I'm sure knowing that her husband was planning to leave her hasn't helped at all.'

Seb heard Hanna's intake of breath, or maybe it was his own.

'That is such bullshit,' Cait seethed. 'No way was he planning to leave.'

'She's a fucking liar,' Leo growled. 'And that mother – she's a witch, she's making it up.'

'She is,' Seb heard himself say. 'Hanna, you've got to believe that this is not true.'

Hanna hadn't replied, had simply continued to listen as Freya Hansen's mother said, 'Jack was worried about his daughter's mental health problems, that's why he hadn't already left.'

'I don't believe this!' Cait yelled furiously. 'I want to kill her.'

'Obviously, he didn't want to hurt his wife,' the mother continued, 'but they'd been married a long time and he was ready to start a new life with Freya and Ethan.'

Freya said nothing, just gazed down at her son.

'Ethan loved his daddy, didn't you, sweetheart,' the mother ran on, 'and now he's going to grow up without him.'

At that point Seb said, forcefully, 'Turn it off. Now! As Cait said it's all bullshit, so we don't need to hear any more. I'll be there in less than an hour.' As if his arrival at the house could change anything, or even begin to make it better – he simply didn't want to think of them going through this alone, especially when he knew that Andee had already left for the day.

'I need to make a short trip,' she'd explained when she'd woken him with a call about five thirty this morning. 'I'll be back by this evening, but if you can be with Hanna and the children while I'm gone, I think it would be a good thing.'

After assuring her he'd be there, he said, 'Did you hear back from Riona?'

'No, I didn't. Did you?'

'No,' he replied, and would have weighed in with how worried he was if he hadn't realized his love life was the least of her concerns right now.

Since it remained a serious concern for him, he detoured to Westbury-on-Trym first on his way to Lake House. Not that he was intending to go in, or even ring on the gate bell – apart from anything else he couldn't be sure that Riona would let him in. His intention was simply to park down the street, with her gates in view, and then send a text asking her to come out to reassure him that she was OK.

So that was what he did.

I'm outside. Please do something to let me know you're safe. If you don't want to see me again, that's fine, but I need to know you're OK. If I don't see you or hear from you in the next few minutes, I'm going to call the police. Sorry if this seems extreme, but that's how worried I am. Sxxx

He sat staring at the gates, blinking only when a car or a jogger passed, or as a young mother hurried a pushchair by, presumably on her way to nursery. There was a moment when he thought he saw the gates starting to open, but if they did they quickly closed again.

A triumph of hope over longing.

His eye was caught by a movement in an upstairs window. The twitch of a curtain? The shadow of someone passing? It wasn't possible to tell; there was nothing there now, no signs of life from the upper windows at all.

Then he saw the side gate open and a woman in baggy jeans and a hoodie stepped out onto the street. He couldn't tell if it was her, was unable to see her hair, but she was the same height and build, although he'd never seen her dressed that way. He started to open his car door, but her hand went up, abruptly, as if telling him to stay where he was.

He fell back into his seat and watched. She was looking around, as though checking to find out if anyone else was making her the focus of attention. He wanted to tell her it didn't matter if they were; all he cared about was that no harm had come to her.

She turned as if to go back inside. Then, quite suddenly, she was staring down the street right at him and his insides went into freefall. It wasn't Riona, only someone who looked unnervingly like her – the same colour hair, identical pale skin and slender limbs, but so strikingly, shockingly different that he was unable to make sense of it.

The gate closed and she was gone.

He continued to sit where he was, unsure what had just happened, or what he should do. He wondered if it had been Riona dressed down, drained from overwork, stressed beyond caring how she looked. He checked his phone, hoping a text or call might arrive, but minutes ticked by and it remained silent. In the end he sent a message himself.

I don't understand what just happened. Who was it who came out into the street? Please call. I have to go to Hanna's now, but phone will be on.

By the time he arrived at Lake House she'd replied.

Saw the girl on TV this morning. She means Hanna harm; she isn't to be trusted.

He sat staring at it. He didn't disagree with what she'd said – for it was clear that Freya Hansen and her mother were trying to create trouble for Hanna – but it was nothing like the kind of message he'd expected. What on earth was going on?

CHAPTER FORTY-NINE

Seeing Seb pulling up outside in his car, Hanna ran downstairs and across the hall to tug open the front door. She didn't care how many cameras were capturing this scene from the gates or what inferences might be drawn from her urgency – she just needed to see him.

'Hey,' he said, getting out of his car. 'What's the hurry?'

Grabbing his hand, she pulled him inside and slammed the door. 'I want you to take me there,' she declared, her face flushed with anger, eyes glittering with intent. 'I need to see that girl face to face—'

'Hang on, hang on,' he interrupted. 'I'm not sure it's wise . . .'

'I don't care what it is, Seb, I have to do it.' She spun on her heel and headed into the kitchen, where Jenny was feeding Sofia. Cait, with tears on her cheeks, was going through a large pile of sympathy cards.

'Hanna, let's just talk about this,' Seb said, going to drop a kiss on Sofia's head and giving Cait a shoulder rub. 'This is an open case, the police won't—'

'I'm not interested in the police.' Hanna was stuffing her phone in her bag. 'They can do or think what they like, but I'm not letting that girl get away with what she said this morning.'

Cait said, 'I told her she should talk to a journalist herself, put her side of the story . . .'

'I am not playing this out for the public to salivate and speculate over,' Hanna snapped at her. 'Leo's gone ahead,' she told Seb. 'He's not going in; he's just checking to see if there's any media outside. As soon as it's clear, I intend to knock on the door. It'll give her the shock of her life and she'll probably try to slam it in my face, but I won't be leaving until I've got her to admit the truth.'

Jenny said, 'It was disgusting what she said on TV, she needs to be confronted . . .'

'But not by Hanna,' Seb tried to argue. 'This could end up doing you more harm than good,' he warned her.

'Then so be it. I can't sit here just waiting for the fall-out from it . . . Or the moment when she decides to reveal she was under sixteen when they were first together. We don't even know if that's true.'

'It isn't,' Cait stated decisively.

'Have you spoken to Andee?' Seb asked. 'Does she think you should go?'

'I can't get hold of her, but whatever she thinks, I'm doing it. If you don't want to drive me that's fine, I'll drive myself . . .'

'No, I'll take you, but, Han, I need you to know that I really don't think this is a good idea.'

'I hear you, now can we please leave? I have the address already in my phone. It shouldn't take much more than forty-five minutes to get there.'

As they drove out of the Chew Valley, heading in the direction of Bath, Hanna sat staring mutely, furiously, at the passing countryside, feeling so close to murderous as she recalled what Freya Hansen had said that morning on TV that her hands kept clenching. She knew in her heart that Jack would not want that outrageous interview to pass unchallenged, so she was doing this as much for him as for herself and the children. She was going to make that girl admit she'd lied when she'd said Jack wanted to leave his family; that he'd never discussed Cait's state of mind with her; that the only relationship he'd had with her and the child had been forced on him, probably through blackmail.

And while they were at it, she wanted to see these famous DNA results that apparently proved the boy was Jack's. The originals, not copies, because for all she knew they were fake.

Had Jack checked? Surely he would have. It didn't matter – she needed to check too.

They were finally closing in on the village when Seb said, 'I thought we were being followed just now, but whoever it was has just turned off.'

Hanna was thankful for that.

Leo rang, and she clicked on her phone. 'Are you there?'

'Close enough,' he replied. 'She's definitely at home, and so far no sign of any press. There are a couple of cars on the front drive, an Audi A1 that's got a baby seat in the back – she just came out to get something from it, so that must be hers – and a black Mini that could be the mother's, or the brother's.'

'Have you seen him?' Hanna asked. Marius Hansen was the one person she really didn't want to come face to face with – just the thought of it was turning her insides to liquid.

'No, but there's a motorbike on the street that could

belong to the next house. It's closer to their drive, but I guess it could be his.'

'Where are we going to find you?' Seb asked as they passed the welcome sign for the village.

'OK, she's got an end-of-row property – they're all detached on this street, not grand, but kind of smart. There's a T-junction opposite with a pub about twenty metres along. I'm in the pub car park.'

'What's the name of the pub?' Seb asked.

'The Rose and Crown.'

After following the GPS through several old and cobbled streets behind a quaint market square, they came to a small estate of newer builds. As their destination was announced on the mobile, Seb quickly swung the car to the right and found the pub.

Leo got out of his Golf and came straight over to the Porsche, going to the passenger side. 'Are you OK?' he asked his mother as she stepped out.

Not sure what that was any more, Hanna said, 'I just want to get this over with. I need you to wait here. Seb will come with me.'

He looked about to protest but Seb said, 'The fewer of us involved in this the better, and you've already got enough going on.'

Leo flushed slightly, but didn't argue. 'Don't take any shit from her,' he advised his mother, 'and if the brother's there, you can tell him from me I'm not convinced by his alibi.'

Hanna attempted a smile, knowing she wouldn't do that. She squeezed his hand, then looked at Seb, ready to go.

'How are you going to start this off?' he asked as they approached the house. 'What's your strategy?'

Wishing she actually had one, she said, 'I'm simply going to ask her to take back what she said about Jack leaving, because I know it's not true. I don't care what she says he told her – I *know* that he was not planning to go and live with her.'

'Well, I have to agree with that, but I'm not sure you're going to get her to take it back just by asking. She's put it out there now. Everyone heard what she said . . .'

'Seb, if you don't want to do this with me, then go and wait with Leo.'

'No, you can't go there alone. I'm on your side, Han – I just don't want you to end up even more hurt than you already are.'

Feeling a horrible surge of nerves go through her, she braced herself as she looked at the house standing ahead of them like an immovable threat. It was red brick and double-fronted, with blinds at the windows and a bright yellow front door. There was a toddler bike and scooter on the path, and a small trampoline on the grass. It was presumably all provided by Jack. She tried to imagine him here, his car parked outside, using his own keys to get in, sweeping the little boy up in his arms . . . How often had he come? Was this where he stayed when she'd thought he was on site somewhere? One, two, three nights in a row. Did he have clothes here, his own special chair . . .

For a horrible moment she felt the enormity of it closing in on her, but she took a gulp of air and felt Seb's reassuring hand on her back as they reached the gate.

'You still don't have to do this,' he said softly.

But she did, because the front door was opening and a heavy-set, middle-aged woman with a tight blonde ponytail and hostile expression emerged.

Freya's mother.

'What are you doing here?' she demanded, planting her hands on ample hips and filling the doorway. 'You have no right to be here. This is intimidation . . .'

'I want to see your daughter,' Hanna called out, too loudly. 'There are things we need to discuss . . .'

'She has nothing to say to you. We don't want you here. You're trespassing on private property.'

Seb said, 'If Freya doesn't have the courage to come and face us herself, maybe you'll tell her that we—'

'I'm not scared of you,' Freya Hansen declared, moving past her mother to face them. 'I just don't have anything to say to you.'

'He couldn't wait to leave you,' the mother growled. 'He talked about it all the time. He was always here, every chance he got.'

'You're lying,' Hanna cried, knowing she couldn't allow herself to believe it, not now, not here, like this.

'I don't care what you believe. All that matters to us is what you did last Sunday to stop him from leaving. You're an evil, wicked woman, Hanna Madden, who deserves to go to prison for the rest of your life.'

Stepping in front of Hanna, Seb said, 'As I understand it, you only have each other as alibis for last Sunday afternoon, so if I were you, I wouldn't be so free with your accusations.'

'They were here.' Marius Hansen manhandled his mother out of the way and came forward, arms bulging, short hair standing in spikes, narrow eyes raking Hanna up and down in a way that made her skin crawl. 'They wouldn't even know how to get onto your property . . .'

'Freya would,' Leo shouted. 'She worked there long enough.'

286

Hanna spun round as Leo joined them, clearly ready to muscle up against Marius.

'So why did you do it, Freya?' Leo challenged. 'Or was it you!' he snarled at Marius. 'My guess is he'd had enough of your blackmail; he was cutting off funding—'

'You need to leave,' the mother yelled over him. 'If you don't, I'm calling the police.'

'I want to see the DNA results,' Hanna cried angrily.

'I sent them to your daughter,' Freya told her. 'She has them. She knows.'

'What you sent was a copy. We have no way of knowing if you doctored them, or paid someone for them—'

'That's it! Call the police,' the mother instructed her son.

Taking out his mobile, Marius kept his eyes mockingly on Hanna's as he pressed three keys and put the phone to his ear.

Having no idea if he was bluffing, and not really caring, she turned away. There was nothing to be gained from staying; Seb was right, she'd been out of her mind to come.

Seb held his ground. 'Our lawyer will be in touch for the DNA results,' he informed them, 'and I know that the police have more questions for you, Marius, so I'm sure they'll be glad you're in touch.'

An hour later, they were back at Lake House, grouped around the kitchen table, mostly not eating the lunch Florina had served. Hanna felt nauseous simply looking at the food, and making her feel even worse was the dreadful, misguided confrontation that kept replaying in her mind. How could she have thought it was what Jack would have wanted? Why had she told herself that? It hadn't been him speaking to her, it had been her own voice, her own fury and need to hit back that had propelled her into making such a goddamned fool of herself.

'You know you can't believe a single word they uttered,' Seb said, reasonably. 'There's no way Jack wanted to go and live there. In that house? On that estate? I'm not being snobbish – maybe I am – but this was his home. He grew up here . . .'

Hanna said, 'I'm sorry, Seb. You were right, I shouldn't have gone . . . I . . .'

He raised a hand. 'Maybe it wasn't such a bad thing. It's certainly given them something to think about.'

'What? That we suspect the child isn't Jack's?' she countered, aware of Cait's and Leo's eyes on her, feeling how much this was hurting them too. 'We both know Jack would have checked that himself before putting the boy in his will . . .' She suddenly clasped her hands to her head in frustration. 'Jesus, why didn't I get that into my head before going? What is wrong with me?'

Jenny said, 'Hanna, you're being too hard on yourself. You're still in shock over it all.'

As if she hadn't heard, Hanna said, 'The little boy meant something to him. You only have to think of the codicil to know that. He must have had a relationship with him, with them both . . . He's obviously been supporting them since she left here.'

'But he could have threatened to cut off funding,' Leo put in lamely, 'and if he did they'd have wanted him dead before he had the chance to change his will.'

Shuddering at the thought, Hanna said, 'He was with them the day he died. He came back in a good mood, not like someone who'd just had some sort of showdown.'

Hanna looked at Sofia as she began banging a spoon on the table.

Removing it from her hand, Jenny said, 'I have to say, the fact the police think it was a man who did it bothers me, especially with Marius Hansen having this rock-solid alibi.'

'I reckon they got someone else to do it,' Leo retorted as if he knew all about how these things worked.

'They can't know for certain it was a man,' Hanna pointed out. 'It's just their impression. A woman is equally capable of delivering a lethal blow, particularly if she's heavy and has the strength of a man.'

'The mother's a bit of a bruiser,' Leo commented.

Seb said, 'I think we should let Andee know that we've been there. I'm sure she'll advise that we inform the police, so let's find out what she has to say.'

On speakerphone, several minutes later, Andee said, 'OK, it wasn't the best move you've ever made, Han, but I'm not seeing that too much harm was done. As far as we know, there was no one around to witness it, and it was a good thing to challenge the DNA results. That needs to be done. I'll leave you to speak to James Johnson, the lawyer, and at the same time you might request a further test is carried out for reasons of probate.'

Hanna gave a small groan of misery to think of all that would entail.

Andee was still speaking. 'I'm seeing Elaine Phillips later,' she said, 'so I'll probably tell her about the visit, if she doesn't already know. It could be interesting in the context of other things I've discovered in the past twenty-four hours.'

'You mean about the Hansens?' Hanna asked, experiencing a frisson of mixed dread and hope.

'Indirectly, yes. I've been trying to make certain connections . . .' There was a pause and the sound of a public address system in the background before Andee said, 'I'm sorry, I have to go.'

'Where are you?' Hanna quickly asked.

'At Heathrow, meeting a flight, and the person I'm waiting for has just come through. I'll call you later.'

CHAPTER FIFTY

Several hours later, after dropping a jet-lagged passenger at the Avon Gorge Hotel, Andee was at the other side of Clifton village on the top floor of Madden headquarters, in Jack's office. With her were Elaine Phillips and Krish Ahmed, both managing to look as relaxed as if they spent most days in this sophisticated and welcoming environment, when the opposite was more likely true.

Taking a sip of the soft drink Jack's PA had provided prior to leaving for the day, Andee said, 'So the Hansens didn't get in touch with you about Hanna's visit this morning?'

'Nothing's come through,' Elaine replied, 'and I'm sure it would have by now if they'd rung in. So what happened?'

'From what I can tell it was an unpleasant doorstep scuffle that didn't end up serving anyone well. You will have seen the interview Freya Hansen did this morning on breakfast TV?'

Elaine's expression showed that she hadn't been particularly impressed by it.

'So you'll understand how upset Hanna was, and when you're in that frame of mind you don't always make the wisest choices.'

'Which means?' Elaine prompted.

Andee sat forward in her chair. 'Before we get into that, would you be willing to tell me if Jack Madden was making regular payments to Freya Hansen that could be construed as child maintenance?' In any other investigation, the detectives probably wouldn't have that sort of information at this stage – but in this one she knew they might.

Elaine's eyes went to Krish's, a silent instruction for him to reply.

He said, 'One of his accounts shows a monthly transfer of five thousand pounds, in her favour. It was set up in April two years ago.'

Andee's eyes widened, not at the transfer itself, but with surprise at the huge amount. 'So they began around the time Freya Hansen left the Maddens' employ', she stated for clarification. 'Can I assume Jack's personal accounts are now frozen, but the transfers were happening until that happened?'

'Correct,' Krish replied. 'It's also thought that the brother has made a few attempts to set up a nice little arrangement for himself, but there's still a way to go on that.'

That was interesting. It could account for why Marius had told Cait about Freya and the child – a warning shot across Jack's bows? 'Obviously you know by now,' Andee said, 'that Freya Hansen and her son are very well taken care of in the will.'

Both detectives nodded.

'So Ms Hansen stands to benefit . . .'

'Where is this going, Andee?' Elaine wanted to know.

'OK, we've all been drawn into the Freya Hansen narrative, including Hanna, and I'm sure you're going to look more deeply into it, but now I'm going to give you a different scenario.'

Elaine didn't bother hiding her interest; clearly she too was someone who liked to think outside of the box, but hadn't yet worked out how to do so with this one.

Andee said, 'I collected a doctor from Heathrow today, a psychiatrist based at a clinic near Baltimore, and who specializes in a very specific disorder. She has a lot to tell us that could turn out to be very relevant to this case. Her name is Emilia Francis. I'm going to outline quite a lot about her and her work now, but please feel free to look her up after we leave here.'

CHAPTER FIFTY-ONE

The following morning, Hanna was in her home office, next to the TV room, working on ways to increase the Madden Foundation's victims' support initiatives. It wasn't only a distraction, because as grief-stricken and discombobulated as she was, she couldn't and wouldn't lose sight of how fortunate she and her family were to have the kind of financial and social support they had. Most people didn't have anything like their contacts or financial security. So, for the moment at least, she was determined that something good should come from this that would benefit society's victims who were largely ignored. And never again was she going to have it said about Cait that losing a father might not be so hard, just because Cait had been photographed at the pool yesterday with Ishan and Sofia. It was such a stupidly cruel and petty thing to spread over social media, as if the only way Cait's grief could be real was if she came from a deprived background, or shut herself away like some apostolic nun.

She was so engrossed in sending an email to her PA that she didn't hear footsteps approaching, only knew that Leo was there when he barged in holding out his phone and looking as angry as she'd ever seen him.

Her heart went into freefall. 'What is it? Who is it?' she cried, springing up from her desk. Please God, no more bad news, not another TV interview.

'It's Jay Wells, my lawyer,' he told her, tightly. 'Apparently someone vandalized Freya Hansen's car last night and the police want me to go to the station.'

Stunned, Hanna grabbed the phone. 'Jay. What's going on? Why do they want to speak to Leo?'

'I don't have all the details yet,' Jay replied calmly. 'I just got a call from DC Crabbe asking him to go in.'

'I don't know that name. It's not who interviewed him before.'

'No, Crabbe is one of Elaine Phillips's team, but I don't want to read too much into that at this stage. Leo tells me he was at home all night, last night.'

Turning to him, Hanna said, 'That's right, he was.' Her eyebrows were raised in a question. Could he have sneaked out after they'd all gone to bed? Not to cause damage to anyone's car, but to see a friend?

'What?' he growled, throwing out his hands.

Jay said, 'Crabbe is claiming that Leo was at Freya Hansen's house yesterday.'

Hanna's eyes closed in despair. If only he'd done as asked and stayed outside the pub . . . 'Yes, he was with me and Seb, but he also left with us. Jay! He didn't vandalize anyone's car. He'd never do something like that, any more than he'd ever have attacked Hugo Astor. I realize you don't know him well, but if you did—'

'It's OK, I believe you, but he still has to be interviewed. Can he get to Patchway in an hour?'

'I should think so. I can bring him . . .'

'I can drive myself,' he protested.

'He'll be there,' Hanna assured Jay and rang off. 'Where's Seb?' she asked Leo, starting for the door.

'He got a call from Andee about half an hour ago and went into Bristol.'

Hanna paused, wondering what that could be about. Nothing significant, surely, or one of them would have told her.

'If you ask me,' Leo said hotly, 'Hansen trashed the car himself just to cause me trouble.'

Hanna didn't argue; that thug had always struck her as being capable of anything. 'Are you sure you want to drive yourself? Is Ishan still here?'

'I think so, somewhere, but I'll be fine. They can't pin anything on me when I *know* I wasn't there.'

It wasn't until after he'd gone that Hanna recalled those words and felt a chill go down her spine. He hadn't been there, she was sure of it, but what if he'd taken a leaf out of his father's book – or what he believed to be his father's book – and sent someone else to do the job for him?

That's not who your father was she wanted to yell after him, but he'd already gone – and actually, how did she really know who Jack was any more?

CHAPTER FIFTY-TWO

Seb hadn't spoken in what felt like an hour or more. His throat was dry; his head was aching with all that he'd heard, all he couldn't make himself accept. It was as if he'd stepped into some sort of other world, and at some point he would be let go, returned to where he belonged, to reality.

When Andee had asked him to come to Jack's office, this was the last thing he'd been expecting. What he'd heard had completely blindsided him. In fact, nothing about it would ever feature on a scale that began to make sense for him, an intelligent man.

The woman Andee had asked him to come and meet – Dr Emilia Francis – was someone he felt he'd ordinarily be pleased to meet. She had a calm and gentle demeanour, wore the air of someone experienced in her field – he had a lot of experience of such people – and she had a way of talking that didn't demand attention, yet quietly asserted her authority. He'd say she was in her mid-sixties and her accent was mid-Atlantic. Her silvery fair hair was neatly cut, her cobalt blue eyes clear and steady. For long moments he found himself transfixed by her voice, as if the movement of her lips, the sound of her words was something apart from their meaning. Although he didn't move, every now and again he found himself wanting to turn away from her engaging smile.

Everything about what she was saying felt wrong, the produce of some sort of fantasy, or drug, but as he continued to take it in, he was aware that the cognitive part of his brain was storing it, tucking it into everyday considerations, as though he could put it away like food after shopping. It was all for later, and yet it was right here, and right now, and Dr Francis had finally stopped speaking, was looking at him as though expecting him to respond.

He glanced at Andee, knowing that if she weren't here he wouldn't be believing this, in spite of how convincing Dr Francis was. In truth, much of it was going over his head – he'd had no experience of this sort of situation in his life, wasn't even sure he'd ever heard or read about it. Well, probably he had, but he'd never expected it to touch his life, least of all the way it apparently had.

How was he going to be able to face Hanna after this?

'I realize,' Dr Francis said, 'that this has been very hard to hear, and I'm sure you have a lot of questions, which I'll be very happy to answer.'

He got to his feet without knowing why, perhaps to escape her, or somehow to connect with Jack, who surely to God had to be hearing this and feeling the way he did right now.

Turning to Andee he said, 'What did she do, for God's sake, to make you think you couldn't trust her?'

As sorrowful, regretful as he'd ever seen her, Andee said, 'Putting it down to instinct sounds trite, but I'm afraid that's all I have to offer.'

The answer annoyed him, made him want to challenge

her, rage at her, even stoop to belittling her and her bloody instinct, but he forced himself not to. Just because he didn't like the truth – detested it, actually – didn't mean it wasn't a truth. And what the hell was to be gained from shooting the messenger?

Andee said, 'The police are there now. We can take you. DCI Phillips has cleared it.'

He stared at her with eyes that hurt, that felt as though they didn't belong to him. He wasn't sure if he'd taken a step back, but felt he had. Was Andee mad? Why would he want to go there now?

In the end he said, 'Hanna needs to know.'

Andee and Dr Francis exchanged glances, before Dr Francis said, 'I'm very happy to talk to Mrs Madden, but before I do that, I think I should tell you the part that she and her now dead mother have played in it all.'

CHAPTER FIFTY-THREE

By the time Hanna arrived at Madden HQ, less than an hour after receiving the call from Andee, she was working hard on centring herself, trying to remain calm and strong no matter what was in store. Nothing could be as bad as losing Jack, or having to walk into the office for the first time without him, in spite of the awful betrayal. Not having him any more – and knowing she never would again – continued to surpass everything else. She still loved him, and couldn't imagine a time when she wouldn't miss him with every fibre of her soul.

As she took the lift to his floor, her biggest fear was that Andee had uncovered something truly horrific about the company.

Why else would they be meeting in Jack's office?

As soon as she entered the room, her heart jolted to see DCI Elaine Phillips already there. Andee hadn't mentioned anything about the detective coming, so whatever was about to be revealed it seemed the police already knew.

This wasn't good. It had to be terrible.

Andee came to greet her and spoke so no one else could hear. 'I'm afraid this is going to be a shock, but it'll explain a lot.'

Hanna immediately felt worse.

Andee was saying, 'I thought it was best to ask Elaine to sit in. I hope you don't mind.'

Hanna's eyes met the detective's – at least she didn't appear hostile, but she wasn't smiling either. Then she noticed there was another woman in the room, older, maybe around sixty. She was getting to her feet and coming to shake hands. There was nothing unfriendly about her; the reverse, in fact: she had a gentle, calming appearance.

Andee said, 'This is Dr Emilia Francis who's going to be doing most of the talking today.'

'Mrs Madden,' the doctor said warmly. 'Thank you for coming to meet with me.'

Hanna looked at Seb, who was perched on the edge of Jack's desk, as though he might tell her how worried she needed to be. For a horrible moment, she thought he was going to avoid her eyes, but then he was coming to her, embracing her, taking her to a sofa to sit beside her, and keeping one of her hands tucked into both of his.

Irina, Jack's PA, came in with coffee and sandwiches.

Andee poured from the cafetiere, but no one wanted to eat.

'Please don't keep me in suspense,' Hanna said as the door closed behind the PA. 'What on earth is going on?' She was looking at Elaine Phillips, but it was Andee who replied.

'We're assuming,' she began gently, 'that you've never Googled Riona Byrne?'

Hanna balked. 'No. Why?' She glanced at Seb as if he might tell her.

'I didn't either,' he said quietly. 'At least only superficially. So I guess I saw . . . what she wanted me to see.'

Becoming increasingly confused, Hanna turned back to Andee. 'Why are you asking this?' she demanded.

Andee said, 'Before we get into the detail, I should explain that Doctor Francis – Emilia – is a psychiatrist specializing in a particular type of disorder—'

'You work with Riona?' Hanna interrupted, addressing the doctor. 'I recognize your name now; she's talked about you. Don't you head up the project she's running for people with . . .' Her voice trailed off as Dr Francis raised a slender hand for her to stop.

'I do indeed treat people with behavioural disorders,' the doctor said, 'but Riona is not a colleague. I could say she was a patient, but that wouldn't be strictly true either, at least not in the conventional sense. Because, you see, the bright, lively and very admirable woman you know as Riona Byrne is an alternative identity for my actual patient, who is called Blanche.'

Hanna blinked, not following.

The doctor didn't seem surprised. 'I'm afraid to say she knows practically everything there is to know about you. We'll come on to how and why, later. First, let me explain that Blanche has, for many years, suffered with a condition known as Dissociative Identity Disorder.'

Hanna tried to think if she'd ever heard of it, but couldn't be sure that she had.

'There was a time,' the doctor said, 'when it was more commonly known as Multiple Personality Disorder. Both are often confused with schizophrenia. Blanche is not schizophrenic; she is what we call "the host" for several different identities, Riona being the most dominant amongst them. Riona is what we in the profession call "the gate-keeper", meaning, more or less, that she is who Blanche would like to be.'

Hanna was dumbfounded, could only stare at the doctor.

302

Emilia Francis was apparently leading them into a world they had never before encountered, had barely even knew existed. She had no idea how it was relevant to anything, but obviously it was or no one would be here.

'During my time treating Blanche,' the doctor continued, 'I have met all her different identities on many occasions. They're also known as "alters", or "alternates". Some have stayed with her for long periods of time, others come and go, and there are those who just hang around in the background, not really doing very much. Let's say, they're there if needed, but there is little call for them. Riona has been a constant alter in recent times and I've probably had more conversations with her than with Blanche.'

Hanna glanced at Seb again, trying to gauge if he was finding this any easier to comprehend than she was, but his expression was inscrutable.

'As I said a moment ago,' Dr Francis continued, 'Riona is who Blanche would like to be. In fact, I've no doubt that Blanche would be that person today, had her early life not created the mental condition she now suffers from.'

Unsure whether she was more fascinated or discomfited, Hanna tried to imagine how this must be affecting Seb – because if she was following this correctly, then the doctor was saying that the woman he'd fallen for, had even made love to, wasn't real. For her it was defying any level of understanding, so it surely must be the same for him.

Dr Francis pressed on. 'I first became aware of Blanche when she was fourteen years old. She was a frightened, skinny little thing on the day her aunt brought her to my clinic. She couldn't look at me; couldn't even speak for herself for a good part of our time together. I had been warned by her aunt that she would be like this. I had also, prior to our meeting, been filled in on the details of her background.

'Knowing what she suffered as a child isn't going to serve us here today, and as you can't unknow something, I would rather spare you the experience of hearing it. However, it's pretty certain that her mother was an undiagnosed schizophrenic, and we know that her father was a religious zealot and leader of a commune based in a remote part of County Clare in the west of Ireland. Most of what I've learned about those early years has come from the police and social workers who managed to get her out of the commune when she was around eleven years old. By then, Blanche believed herself to be the vessel into which everything bad was channelled in order to cleanse her father and his followers of evil. I'm afraid it included rape, also starvation, appalling neglect, slavery and imprisonment. She was hospitalized for some time after the rescue, as were other children found to be there, but none were in as poor a state as Blanche. At this point, by the way, her name was Brianna; her aunt changed it to Blanche when she brought her to England.

'All the children were put into foster care following extensive rehabilitation, and continued to be closely monitored by social services. This was where Blanche stayed until a social worker managed to track down an aunt in Kent. The aunt willingly took Blanche into her home – until then she hadn't even known she had a niece – and set about doing all she could to help Blanche, now aged thirteen, to find her way into a normal life.' The doctor paused, took a sip of coffee and continued.

'From the time Blanche was brought out of the commune,' she said, 'she kept asking about her baby sister. It has been established since that Blanche's mother did have another child, a girl, who Blanche, aged around seven, was left to care for. This care took place in a basement of the commune with no windows or warmth, and for most of the time they remained unwashed and meagrely fed. Blanche taught her sister to talk and walk, and shared a love with her that neither child experienced with anyone else. The baby was around three years old when she was suddenly removed from Blanche's care. We don't know why. Blanche was told her sister had been set free thanks to her holy act of self-sacrifice. It's not known what this act entailed, and unfortunately no one's been able to find out what actually happened to the baby, whose name was Anna. She could have been sold for adoption – I believe that was a practice of the cult – or she may have been killed, possibly by accident, and buried. Bodies of small children were found around the commune, although none have been identified as relating to Blanche.'

Hanna's hand was pressed to her mouth. This was beyond horrific; that poor little child, fighting to keep herself and her sister alive in conditions no one, least of all a child, should ever have to endure.

'When the commune was broken up,' the doctor said, 'Blanche's father was arrested along with a half a dozen or more of his followers, and her mother took her own life. Incidentally, Blanche's mother and aunt were both English, her father was Irish. He too is dead now, he died in prison.

'It was Blanche's fight for survival that led her to seek refuge in alternative personalities. Her earliest self-alteration would probably have happened around the time her sister was taken from her, but there are no records to tell us this was the case. These alternates, as they grew in number, became her saviours, her friends, in an extremely unpredictable and violent world.'

Dr Francis paused again as Andee came to refill her coffee.

Hanna watched the simple act as though it was happening in a parallel world.

'It was when her aunt realized how frequently Blanche was losing herself in other personalities that she sought professional help. Thankfully, her GP wasn't inclined to write Blanche off as a problem teen who might be helped with anti-depressants or some sort of cognitive counselling. He listened when the aunt explained about Blanche's background and recognized right away that she required a psychiatric diagnosis. I was younger then, of course, and I wasn't actually specializing in DID at the time, but it had been the subject of my PhD dissertation while I was at Cornell University in the States. And the GP and I happened to be old friends.

'I was in the process of setting up a practice with two other psychiatrists in Boston, when the GP contacted me, so I flew to Britain, and to make a long story short, I've been treating Blanche ever since. As an aside, I no longer charge for my services, though it might interest you to know that Blanche could well afford them, as her aunt left her extremely well provided for.'

Hanna's voice was hoarse as she said, 'So her aunt is no longer alive?'

'She passed when Blanche was in her mid-thirties. Blanche took it very hard. She was suicidal for a while, there were several attempts, but then one day, out of the blue, "Riona" reappeared. I hadn't seen her since Blanche was in her teens, when she'd manifested as a charming, chatty young thing who was fascinating to listen to and quite endearing to watch. I'd hoped then that she would stay around and gradually give Blanche the confidence to be this way all of the time, but I'm afraid it didn't happen. There were other alternate identities, however, who did stay around, and more have come and gone over the years.

'Back in her teens, Blanche didn't have anything like the kind of control over them that she seems to have now – it's this control that makes her case of particular interest to those of us who specialize in the disorder. In the early days she suffered a lot from amnesia, which is common in sufferers of DID, meaning that when another identity manifested, she remembered little or nothing of it after she had returned to herself.

'These days she tends to remember quite a lot, although she, as Blanche, will not be "present" during the dissociative intrusion into her executive functioning.' She grimaced slightly. 'I'm sorry, I should keep this in plain English. It was Riona who helped Blanche cope with the grief of her aunt passing in a way that Blanche wasn't able to manage alone. She talked to me a great deal as Riona during that time. She likes Riona, is proud of her, and is working on building up the courage to be her all of the time. If you talk to her as frequently as I do, either during visits or by phone, you could believe that she and Riona have finally become one. Or perhaps I should say that Riona has taken over completely.'

Seb said huskily, 'Except she isn't real.'

Regarding him sympathetically, the doctor said, 'Not in the sense you mean it. However, to Riona and Blanche, she is very real. As are the others who fulfil different roles for

Blanche. There is a cook; a girl with loose morals; a computer geek; a musician . . . Sometimes it can be hard to keep up, but the important thing to remember is that each and every one of them believes themselves to be real, and they don't want Blanche to "get better" or they will cease to exist. Riona, on the other hand, who considers herself head of the house – actually "psychiatrist in residence" is what she calls herself to me – wants nothing more than for Blanche to let herself go so she can be Riona and nobody else.'

Hanna sat back against the sofa, not sure how much more of this she could take without starting to feel as though she was losing her own mind.

Seeming to understand her concern, Dr Francis said, 'If you'd like to take a break . . .'

'No, no,' Hanna interrupted. 'I just . . . I'm not sure how well I'm processing this.'

With a smile of understanding, the doctor said, 'It's difficult, I know, a great deal to take in.'

Elaine Phillips looked up from her phone. 'I'm sorry, doctor, but I'll need to get back to the clinic soon and if Mrs Madden is up to coming with me . . .'

Hanna started, unable to imagine why she would want to go there.

'Yes, of course,' Dr Francis said. She returned her gentle blue eyes to Hanna and said, 'I need to explain why you are so important to Blanche.'

Hanna's insides clenched; she surely couldn't have heard that right. How could she matter to a tragically damaged woman whom she'd never met in any real sense?

'As I mentioned just now,' the doctor said, 'Blanche's name was changed when she was brought to England by her aunt, but her surname stayed the same. Edwards. Her mother was Catherine Edwards.'

Hanna stopped breathing. Long moments ticked by before she managed to say, 'That was my mother's name.'

The doctor nodded; clearly she already knew that. 'Blanche's baby sister,' she went on, 'the one that disappeared, was called Anna. Blanche believes that the child is still alive, grown now, of course, and her name has been changed, as hers was. Anna is not so very different from Hanna. Hanna Edwards. Your name before you were married. And as you say, your mother was called Catherine.'

Hanna looked at the others, half-expecting them to protest on her behalf, or even explain what the heck this all meant, but they only looked sorry, and as though this wasn't crazy at all. 'I'm not related to Blanche,' she told them, 'and nor was my mother.'

'No,' Dr Francis agreed, 'you aren't, but I'm afraid Blanche has convinced herself that you are. This isn't the first time she's found someone she believes to be her sister. It happened a few years ago, when she was still in Kent. The Anna Edwards in that instance didn't have a mother called Catherine, but the same name was enough for Blanche to convince herself she'd found her missing sibling. I can put you in touch with the woman, if you like. She'll be able to tell you that Blanche never tried to harm her in any way, didn't even go near her. However, her constant phone calls, all of them made by "Riona" – though basically sweet and charming – became enough of a nuisance for Anna Edwards to end up contacting the police. Blanche was given a warning and told that if she didn't stop harassing Ms Edwards she would be served with a restraining order.

'It upset Blanche a lot. She didn't want to let go of Ms Edwards, but when I explained that, if she didn't, it might become difficult for her to continue living independently, she made herself stop. For a while after she refused contact with me. I couldn't force it on her, but I know that she didn't break her promise, because I asked Ms Edwards to let me know if Blanche got in touch again. She never has.

'Then one day, just over two years ago, "Riona" rang to tell me that Blanche had sold her aunt's house and was going to start a new life, in a new town. She, of course, had every right to do that – she's a private citizen who's as free to move around as the rest of us. Naturally, I was concerned, but I'm afraid I was going through some personal difficulties at the time – my husband and I had broken up – and so I admit I probably wasn't as attentive to this news as I should have been.

'So she moved to Bristol and, after a while, we resumed contact via video link. We spoke most weeks, and there was never any knowing who might pop up on the screen from one session to the next. Usually it was Blanche as Riona, and it sounded as though they were settling in well. Riona, Billy, Ruby, Hayley . . . I was assured by Blanche herself that all was calm; she was enjoying the quiet and finding lots to do in the house to occupy her time.

'It never crossed my mind that she might have found another Anna Edwards who, it turns out, she believed had been renamed Hanna. In fact the first I knew of it was when Andee contacted me. I flew straight over and yesterday Elaine took us to the "clinic". What we found needs to be looked into a lot more closely, but from what we've seen so far, it appears Blanche has spent over a year doing her – I suppose she'd call it research, on you. Neither Blanche as herself, or as Riona, had ever mentioned that finding you was the reason for moving to Bristol, and of course I had no idea until yesterday that she'd worked out a way of meeting you, even becoming a part of your life through Riona.'

Hanna's mouth was dry; she was unable to move, even to think much beyond saying, 'So I'm not related to her?'

The doctor shook her head. 'No, not at all – but in her mind, you are.'

Hanna had no idea how to respond to that, could find no words or understanding that might begin to make sense of it. In a way she felt afraid, but couldn't say why. It was beyond imagining that all this time she had been the focus – the obsession – of a tragically damaged woman who could have harmed her at any time. She'd been haunted, watched, analysed, stalked . . . She felt nauseous and bewildered, as if she'd become unanchored from her own life.

'Are you saying,' she finally managed, 'that when she met Seb . . .?' She turned to him and, seeing how stricken he looked, she had her answer. Apparently Riona (or Blanche) had used him to get to her. Turning her hand in his, she squeezed his fingers tightly, and felt guilty for the relief of knowing that she wasn't the sole victim in this.

Dr Francis said, 'It's important at this stage for me to stress that Blanche has never meant you any harm and still doesn't. I'm absolutely certain that her only purpose in getting to know you was to keep you safe. All she's ever wanted to do for her sister is to keep the bad people away.'

Hanna could sense a terrible darkness starting to gather at the edges of her mind. She had an idea now of where this was going and all she could do was hope, pray she was wrong.

Dr Francis said, 'Whether Blanche is herself, or Riona, she is passive, peaceful, would never harm anyone. The alternates are much the same, although livelier in some cases, perhaps more forthright, but Billy, he's—'

'Billy? A man?' Seb interrupted. 'How can he be a man?'

Clearly having expected the question, Dr Francis said, 'It's not unusual for alternates to be of the opposite sex. Blanche has one other that I know of – his name's Ryan. He's kind, not very talkative, a good cook. Occasionally he and Billy appear as one, which I've seen Billy struggle with. When he has the limelight, he doesn't want to share, or be held back by Ryan's generally more docile and agreeable nature.'

'But in reality,' Seb said, needing to get this straight, 'they're both Blanche having some sort of struggle with . . . who she wants to be?'

The doctor nodded and Hanna felt her head starting to spin.

'I appreciate this isn't easy to understand when you haven't had dealings with it before,' Dr Francis said, 'but something it's very important for you to know about people with DID is that, when another identity takes over, they become that person. In Blanche's case she may, or may not, be in the background during "alternative" periods, aware of what's happening, but she won't be driving it. Often she's not there at all, and so won't remember what's occurred while she's spent time away from herself.'

Elaine Phillips shifted in her chair, her expression taut, showing how unimpressed she was with that last statement.

Hanna was becoming increasingly bewildered, and fearful of what this was leading up to.

'To give you an example of how powerful and individual

alternates can be,' the doctor continued, 'it's not unknown for one of them to speak Spanish, or another to excel at maths, sport, music, for example, while the host themselves has none of these attributes. There are even cases of an alternate suffering with diabetes and requiring insulin when the host has never shown any signs of the disease.'

Apparently realizing she might be going too far, she said, 'I can give you websites to help your understanding. Many papers have been published about it, some written by me . . . Actually, there is a book, dating back to the Sixties, called *Sybil*. It tells the true story of a young woman whose experiences of DID aren't so very different to Blanche's. I'm sure you can still get hold of it. It might help to explain things better than I've managed in this short time.'

Hanna saw Andee make a note of it, and turned back to Dr Francis as the doctor said, 'Of course it's not possible for an alternate to change their host's appearance completely, but they are able to alter it in a way that can be quite dramatic. If you see Blanche, you might think she vaguely resembles Riona, a kind of watered-down version of her, if you like. In Billy's case, she appears very masculine and harder faced. In Ryan's, she's lean and shy. Ruby is youthful, vibrant, *seems* shorter than Blanche and chunkier, though of course she isn't. Hayley is bright, attention-seeking – she wears a lot of make-up, something Blanche ordinarily shuns. I don't get to see Hayley often, but I know that she is quite highly sexed and has at various times worked as a waitress, a hotel receptionist and an estate agent.'

'You mean Blanche – or these alternates – go out to work?' Seb asked incredulously.

'Yes, but none of them are able to hold down a job for long, for obvious reasons.'

Andee said, 'I had no idea the human brain could do something like this.'

With a smile that seemed almost sad, Dr Francis said, 'It's extraordinary, isn't it, and of course it's capable of an enormous amount more that we don't even know about yet. In Blanche's case it all began with protecting a little girl who suffered dreadful trauma and neglect, and grew into providing herself with friends that she didn't have the confidence to make on her own.'

'Is it new?' Elaine Phillips asked. 'I've never heard of it before.'

Turning to her, the doctor said, 'The first diagnosis of Multiple Personality Disorder was as long ago as the eighteen hundreds, in France. DID wasn't recognized until the 1980s, so in that sense you could say it's new, but we've come a long way since then.'

And all without any of us knowing, Hanna was thinking, *unless someone in your family has it.* How frightening that must be.

Unconsciously holding tighter to Seb's hand, she said, 'You must be going into so much detail for a reason, and I'd really like to know what it is.'

Putting aside her coffee cup, Dr Francis said, 'I understand from Andee that you had an unfortunate experience in your office with one of your husband's employees and that Riona witnessed it. And then the man concerned was attacked and ended up in hospital.'

Hanna swallowed dryly. 'Are you saying Riona – Blanche – did that?' she asked incredulously.

'If asked, Blanche would tell you it was Billy, and in her world it would be the truth. Someone had hurt you and they needed to be punished. Billy would have assumed control in order to make it happen.' She gave Hanna only a moment with that before saying, 'Riona was aware that your husband had a child with another woman. She also knew that you had never been told of the child's existence. For Blanche, this meant that Jack was someone else who had hurt you.'

Hanna tensed all the way through. She knew what was coming next, and it was like a speeding truck.

'I'm afraid,' the doctor continued, 'that Blanche – Billy – is almost certainly responsible for what happened at the lake.'

Hanna felt herself recoil. She flashed on a weapon smashing down on Jack's skull, him falling forward into the water having no idea what had happened. That anyone had even been there.

She tried to breathe. It was time for her to leave, to get away from this madness, to go back to a world where people like Blanche or Riona or Billy didn't exist.

She heard Elaine Phillips say, 'We're also looking into the possibility that "Billy" vandalized Freya Hansen's car.'

Hanna stood up, walked to the window on featherlight legs and stared out at normality. In that other, parallel universe, traffic was waiting at the pedestrian crossing; people were strolling through shade and sunshine; a van pulled out of a street opposite and drove towards the Downs. She was thinking of so many things – her and Jack in this office together; their wedding day; the children's birthdays; the arguments and making up; their home; their love for one another . . . It began to blur, memories running into one another, as if stirred from their natural resting places and losing their way.

She put her hands to her face and felt tears wet on her

cheeks. Her shoulders began to shake. Huge, violent sobs tore through her. This couldn't be why Jack had died. Please God it couldn't.

Andee came to wrap her in her arms, murmuring soothing words against her hair as Hanna struggled to regain control. It was all too much. She knew what she'd heard, understood the words and even, God help her, believed them, but at the same time she simply couldn't accept them.

Seb came to put a hand on her back, rubbing it gently. She turned to look at him, saw his own devastation and let her head fall against him.

The others sat quietly, saying nothing at all, clearly understanding that Hanna and Seb needed this time before either of them could face what more was to come.

In the end it was Hanna who spoke first. 'Where's Riona – *Blanche* – now?' she asked Elaine Phillips.

The detective shook her head slowly as she sighed. 'That's what we'd all like to know,' she replied.

CHAPTER FIFTY-FOUR

Riona was feeling quite cheerful as she sped along the motorway towards the Bath turn-off. Everything was going to be all right. She was back in control and thankfully neither Blanche nor the others were fighting her. They'd gone very quiet this morning, as though finally understanding the need to back away, to fade like ghosts at dawn so she could take over and sort things out.

It was heartbreaking to her that she couldn't undo what Billy had done to Jack. Damn, damn Billy! He was such a hot-headed fool with little or no sense of what was appropriate. Yes, he could be kind, very sweet with Blanche and the others, but he was also wild and impulsive, with no real sense of his own strength. Still, at least he'd finally admitted to her that he'd been responsible for what had been done to Jack.

'I should have guessed of course,' she said out loud as she indicated to join the slip road.

Actually, she had, but she'd ignored it because she desperately hadn't wanted it to be true. Not only had Billy destroyed Jack's life, he'd destroyed those of many others too, including hers. She'd truly believed that one day soon she'd be able to explain things to Seb, to confess the complexities of Blanche's disorder and how she, Riona, was managing to beat it, but that wasn't going to be possible now.

Stupid, stupid, demented Billy.

Blanche should have ignored him, pushed him away, stifled him, locked him up in a place that he couldn't escape. She'd never allowed any of them to be violent before, so why now? Blanche needed to explain this, but she was shying away, speaking to no one and apparently hearing nothing, which was fine with Riona as long as it stayed that way.

She had things to do now that Blanche must *not* be a part of, as she could clearly no longer be trusted.

CHAPTER FIFTY-FIVE

Hanna couldn't believe what she was seeing. Actually she didn't want to believe it. Every wall in this otherwise lovely kitchen was covered in photographs of her, many of them dating back to her teens, all of which were on Facebook. It was completely disorientating finding them here in a stranger's house, larger than life, as if something about her had been caught in a parallel world.

As she continued to look, she recognized shots from magazines and newspapers of events she and Jack had attended together. There was one of her opening a new centre for special needs learning; another showing her shaking hands with the mayor at a school fête. There she was, beaming with pride at Leo's graduation; and looking very glamorous as she sipped champagne at a society wedding. Then she was finding things that she hadn't seen before, not because they weren't in the public domain, but because she'd never trawled the media for images of herself.

Blanche didn't appear to have missed anything.

'Take a look at this,' Andee said quietly. Her hand was gloved and the especially large picture that she was passing, printed onto a flimsy board, was already covered in a transparent evidence bag.

As Hanna stared, transfixed by the shock of it, the forensic team continued moving around them like ghosts, clicking cameras, dusting, covering, bagging . . . There was some sort of commotion going on outside, but she barely registered it. A baseball bat had been found.

'Jesus,' she heard Seb mutter as he came to look over her shoulder and realized the photograph's significance.

'What's the occasion?' Dr Francis asked, joining them.

'It's my mother's funeral,' Hanna murmured. She was feeling light-headed now and slightly nauseous. 'We're all there and . . .' She didn't have to say any more, they could see for themselves . . . At the side of the photograph, on a white strip, was a list of everyone present, with an arrow drawn from their name to connect them to who they were in the shot: her, Jack, the children, Jenny, members of their extended family; three of the 'chiefs' and their wives. Seb's name was the only one that was underlined.

Elaine Phillips said, 'We think she might have been tracking everyone in this photo for some time, trying to find a non-threatening way to you, Hanna. It looks as though she decided you provided it,' she said to Seb. 'Can I ask how you met?'

Thinly, he said, 'It was online.'

'OK, that follows. She'll have set up alerts for everyone probably – we'll know more once we've analysed her computer. Basically, it means she'll have been notified whenever you signed up to something. A dating site would have been a gift for Riona.'

Feeling as sickened by that as Seb clearly was, Hanna slipped an arm through his in a gesture of comfort.

'There's more in the office next door,' Elaine Phillips continued, 'and a framed photograph of you, Hanna, was found next to one of the beds. It must be the room she was using, because the others are empty, although there are names on the doors relating to the alternative personalities Dr Francis told us about.'

The doctor said, 'The boxes we found yesterday, in the office? Did any of them turn out to have anything in them?'

'Only the one marked Riona. Forensics have it now, but I'm sure we can get a list of the contents if you think it'll be helpful in finding her.'

'What I'm thinking,' the doctor said, 'is that if it was still here then it doesn't seem likely that she's run away.'

Raising her eyebrows, the detective said, 'The entire place has been searched top to bottom, including attic, basement and garden; there's an APB out on the car; units are currently checking Mr Goodman's home, also Mrs Madden's, so if you can suggest something else . . .' She broke off as her phone rang and walked away to take the call. At the door she came to a sudden stop.

'When?' she demanded, tension seeming to radiate from her. 'Is anyone there yet? OK, I'm on my way.' Ending the call, she turned and fixed intense eyes on Andee.

'Freya Hansen's little boy,' she stated. 'Apparently a neighbour saw a woman with reddish hair putting him into the back of a white Ford Fiesta. Units are on their way to Freya's address now.'

Dr Francis said, 'Blanche would never hurt a child, and I think you know Riona wouldn't either.'

Phillips rounded on her. 'How can you say that when you've told us yourself that a bloody monster exists inside her?'

The doctor took a pace back.

Because he had to, Seb said, 'Riona drives a silver Lexus.'

Phillips eyed him sourly then, gesturing for the doctor to follow, she left the room saying, 'If it's not her, I'll resign.'

CHAPTER FIFTY-SIX

After rapidly stripping off their protective clothing, Hanna and Seb ran to his car. Andee had left ahead of them, catching a ride with Elaine Phillips and Dr Francis. Though not invited to follow, Hanna and Seb were going to do just that. If necessary they'd wait in the pub car park, out of the way, but neither of them was prepared to sit around waiting for news as if they were simply on the periphery of this.

They left Westbury-on-Trym, heading for the city centre and on to Keynsham. Hanna rang Cait.

'Mum! What's going on? Why did you make Leo—'

'Listen,' Hanna interrupted. 'Are you all at Ishan's?'

'Yes, but why? Where are you?'

'I'm with Seb. There's a lot I need to explain, but for the moment it's important that you stay where you are and keep Sofia indoors.' Why was she saying that? She had no reason to believe Blanche wanted to take Sofia – but how were any of them to know what Blanche or any of her alters wanted?

'What!' Cait shrieked. 'You're . . . Mum! You've got to tell me . . .'

'Certain things have come to light about Riona. I'll

explain everything when I get home, but whatever you do, if she calls, or turns up there, you must not speak to her. You just call me. OK?'

Cait fell silent.

Hanna turned cold. 'Please tell me she isn't there.'

'No. I'm just . . . This is doing my head in. What's wrong with her, for f's sake? I thought we all really liked her.'

'I'm sorry, my darling, I have to go. Andee's trying to get through, but if anything happens your end, call me right away.' And clicking off, she tapped to connect to Andee.

'Han, Dr Francis is saying that you and Seb should be with us, so can you get to Freya Hansen's?'

'We're already on our way.' She'd ask later why the doctor wanted them there. 'Is there any news about Ethan yet?'

'No. Can you put this on speaker so Seb can hear?'

'OK, done.'

'Seb,' Andee said, 'did you ever see Riona in another car besides the Lexus?'

'No,' he replied, 'but I never got past the gates, so I don't know what vehicles were there. I take it there's no car outside her house now?'

'Actually, yes, it turns out there's a silver Lexus in a car port around the back, so we're waiting to find out if there's a Fiesta registered in Blanche's name. Or Riona's. We don't know yet what sort of ID she has for her alters, if any.'

As the call ended, Hanna stared straight ahead and said, almost to herself, 'No one could have seen this coming. They just couldn't. Could they?'

'No,' Seb assured her. 'No one.'

They drove on in silence, taking the bypass and heading

on towards the outskirts of Bath. Hanna used her phone to Google the term 'Dissociative Identity Disorder'. The first results were quite reassuring – apparently most sufferers *weren't* violent – but the further she went, the more alarming it became.

'Oh God,' she groaned, 'it says here that up to seventy per cent of DID sufferers have violent self-states . . .'

'Put it down,' Seb said gently. 'You don't know how accurate that is, and it's not going to help . . .'

'They have to find that little boy,' she said, feeling a terrible desperation starting to build. 'They bloody have to. He's just an innocent child, and there's no knowing what she might do.'

CHAPTER FIFTY-SEVEN

There were police everywhere when they got to Freya Hansen's house. Helicopters were flying overhead; the media was starting to turn up. Neighbours had gathered on doorsteps looking appalled, wanting to help, and even making cups of tea.

Seeing Dr Francis standing at Freya's gate talking to Andee, Hanna leapt out of the car and made straight for her. 'How dare you?' she cried as she reached them. 'How bloody dare you let that woman out into society when you *know* she's dangerous? I looked it up, seventy per cent of sufferers have a violent self-state, so you have full responsibility here, and culpability. My . . .'

'Mrs Madden—'

'. . . husband would still be alive if you'd done your job and no one would be out looking for an innocent little boy because *you* decided that some crazy woman was safe to be on the streets. Well, let me tell you this, *Dr* Francis, you are going to pay for what she's done to my family, and if any harm comes to that child, I swear I'll do everything in my power to make sure you never work again. You're a disgrace, a fraud, an accomplice to murder . . .'

'Han,' Seb murmured, taking hold of her, 'the press—'

'I don't give a fuck about them,' she raged, snatching her arm free. 'Let them hear what I have to say. They need to know what's been going on here – what *she's* allowed to go on.' Stepping closer to the doctor, she said, 'No self-respecting psychiatrist would have allowed this to happen so why the hell did you?'

Dr Francis's face was white, as she said, 'I understand your anger, Hanna . . .'

'No you don't! You've got no idea what it's like to lose someone you love, to feel like your life is over because the man at the centre of it is no longer there . . . But he would be if that psychotic *creature* hadn't been allowed to roam free. Two minutes on Google told me that she had the potential to be dangerous, and yet *you* in all your professional wisdom saw fit to let her come and find me, someone she doesn't even know except inside her deluded head.'

Keeping her voice steady, Dr Francis said, 'Blanche has been a patient of mine for over thirty years, and in that time neither she, nor her alters, have ever demonstrated a tendency for violence. And contrary to what you read, most people with DID don't have a tendency . . .'

'Except the seventy per cent that do.'

'I'm afraid that information is false. The fact that Blanche has never hurt anyone before, or even spoken about it, means that she has the right to lead a normal life . . .'

'*Normal!* What the fuck is normal about someone who goes around pretending she's someone else? Who has to hide behind God knows how many personalities just to make herself function? That's not normal, Dr Francis. In my world it's totally bloody abnormal . . .' As her voice faltered, shredded by grief, Seb turned her to him and held her tight. His own eyes were hostile as he looked at the doctor.

'She's right in everything she said,' he told her. 'None of us should be standing here today.'

Andee said, 'Now isn't the right time for this, but I'm sure you realize we still need a lot of answers.'

The doctor nodded, and turned to Elaine Phillips as she came out of the house.

'How are things going in there?' Andee asked.

Phillips's expression was grim as she said, 'About as well as you might expect. The poor girl's distraught, terrified, even more so now I've explained what I could about Blanche Edwards.'

'Jesus Christ,' Hanna muttered furiously, 'how is she supposed to understand that?'

Addressing the detective, Dr Francis said, 'Did you show her a photograph? Has she ever seen Blanche, or anyone resembling her?'

'She doesn't think so,' Phillips replied, 'and she hasn't noticed any strangers hanging around. No suspicious phone calls either. Apparently she just popped inside while Ethan was playing with some bricks in the front garden and by the time she came out, a couple of minutes later, he was gone.'

Hanna clasped her hands to her head, feeling as wretched for Freya as she might if one of her own children had been taken.

'Any news on the white Ford Fiesta?' Andee asked Phillips.

The detective shook her head. To Hanna she said, 'She wants you to go in.'

Hanna balked in surprise.

'There's a FLO in there with her,' Phillips said, and turned away to take a call.

Andee said, 'Would you like me to go for you?'

Hanna glanced at the house. She felt exhausted, drained, and yet adrenalin was racing through her so hard she was physically shaking. 'No, I'll go,' she said, 'I just hope that awful brother's not there.'

Seb came to the front door with her and waited as she stepped into the hall where a uniformed officer – the FLO – pointed her towards a room on the left. She found Freya sitting alone next to an overflowing toy box, looking as fragile and traumatized as anyone would in her position.

'Where's your mother?' Hanna asked, going further into the room.

Lifting red-rimmed eyes, Freya said, 'She flew to Copenhagen with my brother this morning. They were going to visit my grandma, but they're on their way back now.' Her small, round face was blotched by desperate tears; her hands were tearing apart soggy tissues.

Feeling wretched for her that she was having to go through this without her family, Hanna started to speak, but Freya said, 'I thought it was you. When Kylie, my neighbour said,' she sobbed on a breath, 'she saw a woman with red hair putting him into a car, I-I thought you'd done it to punish me.'

'Oh, God,' Hanna groaned, going to kneel in front of her. 'I'd never do such a thing, no matter how upset or angry I might be. I'm a mother myself, I know what it would do to you and no one, no one deserves that.'

Staring down at their joined hands, Freya said, brokenly, 'I knew it wasn't when they said the woman's hair was bright, kind of coppery; yours is closer to blonde.' More tears welled up to choke her. 'Then I just didn't know what to think.' Her mouth trembled, her breath was shallow and ragged. 'They'll find him, won't they?' she pleaded. Her tortured eyes came to Hanna's. 'Please say they will.'

Wanting to give hope, no matter how small, Hanna said, 'I have no doubt of it. Everyone's looking for him.' She added with a note of wryness, 'He's Jack's son. That gets him all the police attention anyone could wish for.'

Freya nodded, although it wasn't clear if she'd heard. 'They told me about this woman, Blanche something-or-other,' she said. 'It was so weird; I didn't understand it. Why would she want my baby?' She bunched a fist to her mouth, 'Will she hurt him, Mrs Madden? Do you know her? What does she want with him?'

More afraid of that question than she'd ever want the girl to see, Hanna said, 'I-I'm not sure.' How could she voice the fear that Blanche, Riona, Billy, whoever, might want to end Ethan's life because his existence was painful for Hanna, a sister who wasn't a sister at all? It made no sense, and yet here they were.

Thinking only of Riona, and what little she knew of her, she said, 'It's possible she's trying to keep him safe . . .' Seeing Freya's shock and incredulity, she quickly added, 'OK, I realize how that sounds, but in her mind, the way things are for her . . .' How the hell was she going to explain this, when she knew next to nothing of the mental disorder? 'There's a doctor outside,' she said. 'She's been treating the woman who probably has Ethan. She can tell us what's likely to be happening now.' She glanced over her shoulder and quickly back again as Freya's hands tightened on hers. 'Don't leave me,' the girl said plaintively. 'Please . . . I . . . If Jack was here he'd sort it all out . . . I know he would. Maybe he knows what's happening, wherever he is, and he'll keep him safe?'

330

In the face of such blind and desperate faith, all Hanna could say was, 'If that's possible, you're right, he will.'

Freya slumped forwards into Hanna's arms. 'He's just a baby,' she sobbed. 'Just a baby who loves everyone the same as Jack . . .'

From behind them Seb said quietly, 'Han, there's been a development.'

CHAPTER FIFTY-EIGHT

Riona couldn't decide whether this was good or bad. So many blue flashing lights closing in on her, blocking the road, not letting her go any further. But it was OK. She would speak to them, make sure they understood everything properly, because it was quite possible they didn't. She would explain that as long as the little boy was with her – fast asleep in the back, so adorable and cute – the others couldn't get near him. They couldn't even exist as long as she stayed in control.

She pulled over and quick as a flash jumped out of the driver's seat and slipped into the back beside the child. She needed to be with him in case he woke up. He might feel afraid and want his mother; she could comfort him and tell him everything would be fine.

She smiled tenderly as she looked down at him – Jack Madden's son. He was dark-haired like his father, or maybe he took after his mother. Blanche didn't know because she'd never seen Freya Hansen. It was a pity Jack Madden had ever seen her; Blanche wouldn't have got them into this mess if he hadn't.

She raised a hand to smooth the boy's cheek, but stopped

herself in time. It would only disturb him, and best not to do that until everything was sorted out.

She looked around, surprised the police hadn't reached her yet. No one was even close. They were keeping well back, watching her, speaking into radios and moving people away from the area. They were in the Chew Valley, on a causeway with water, lakes either side of them. Very close to Hanna's house, probably only a couple of miles away.

She caught her reflection in the rear-view mirror and tilted her head to one side. Blanche had long wanted to let her poor damaged-self go along with the others, and now, at last, the time had come for her to be only Riona.

'You shouldn't have done this,' Blanche said, but Riona wasn't listening.

CHAPTER FIFTY-NINE

The departure from Freya's house had happened so swiftly and with such urgency that Hanna could only feel grateful she and Freya had ended up in the same car with Elaine Phillips at the wheel. Dr Francis was in the passenger seat; Andee and Seb were following in his Porsche, with blues and twos leading and bringing up the rear.

They were heading full speed towards the Chew Valley, where apparently the Fiesta had been stopped on one of the causeways. Apparently the occupants were still inside the vehicle: one was a child, the other a woman fitting Riona's description.

Or Blanche's? How different were they?

'He'll be all right, won't he?' Freya kept saying, biting into her nails as they sped through the country lanes, rocking from side to side and lurching as Elaine Phillips accelerated and braked with breathtaking skill. 'I know he will. He's so brave. I expect he's made a new best friend. He does that all the time. You should see him . . .' She choked and laughed. 'She won't hurt him, because she already loves him. She does. Honestly. You can't help it. If you knew him . . .'

With all her heart, Hanna hoped it was true. She felt certain Riona would love the boy, but what if it was Blanche, or, God forbid, this Billy, who'd taken him? She felt sick at the mere prospect of that. She just hoped Dr Francis knew what to do when they got there, and please God they wouldn't be too late – but she couldn't allow herself even to think that.

Realizing Freya was speaking again, she tuned back in.

'. . . and he was never going to leave you. I know you know that, but I feel I have to say it. We weren't together any more or anything like that. He didn't want to see me, really; he only wanted to see Ethan. He'd come to see me more often recently – once a couple of weeks ago, and then the night before he . . . But he only came because Ethan's been ill and he was worried about him. And I'm sorry for all the things my mum said on TV. She can be really . . . Anyway, for the record, I was seventeen when Jack and I—'

'It's all right,' Hanna interrupted, putting a hand over the girl's. 'We don't need to discuss this now.' Maybe a time would come for them to talk – she was sure it would – but all that really mattered right now was the boy.

Eventually they sped through Bishop Sutton, veered sharply right, and the causeway between Chew Lake and Herriot's Mill Pool stretched out in front of them like a runway. A long, two-lane stretch of road with no traffic, no sign of runners or hikers, and the regular bird-watchers, fishermen and ice-cream sellers nowhere in sight. However, there was a crazed panoply of blue flashing lights belonging to a dozen or more vehicles, including an ambulance and fire engine.

Elaine Phillips said into the radio, 'We've just arrived, has anyone approached the car?'

'Negative,' came the reply.

Hanna didn't hear what else was said, as Freya surged forward, pointing, crying out, 'There they are. It's a white Fiesta. Is he in there? I need to get to him.'

'We need you to stay where you are,' Elaine Phillips barked sternly as she brought the car to a stop at the edge of the scene. There were so many people, some in uniform, others not, and everyone had the Fiesta firmly in sight. It was like a still life; a frozen moment in time that could animate at any second.

Hanna's heart was thudding so hard it hurt. She held onto Freya, watching, fearing the officers might be armed. *Please, please, don't let any weapons be needed.* If they shot Billy, they'd kill Riona and Blanche . . . She couldn't make sense of how that made her feel, apart from supremely strange.

Elaine Phillips and Dr Francis got out of the car. Phillips glanced back inside. 'Freya, I need you to stay calm, OK?' she said. 'The situation is under control, but the doctor needs to talk to Blanche before we can let you approach.'

Hanna could feel Freya's fear pumping through her as she forced herself to nod. Hanna closed her arms around the girl and held on tighter than ever. Neither of them spoke, barely even took a breath as they watched Elaine and the doctor start towards the Fiesta. It felt unreal. How could this be happening in their tranquil valley, right at the centre of the place she called home?

As the two women reached the car, a uniformed officer approached Elaine Phillips, spoke to her briefly, then stood back as Dr Francis crouched down to see into the back seat. The door was open, shielding their view of what might be happening, they could only see that Elaine Phillips remained standing alongside the uniformed officer.

'What are they doing?' Freya muttered frantically. 'Why doesn't she just hand him over?'

Wishing she would, Hanna caught a movement at the corner of her eye and glanced round to see Seb and Andee standing a few feet away from them, watching proceedings. Keeping an arm around Freya, she helped her out of the car and took her to join them. There was nothing any of them could say or do as they waited for the moment Ethan would be passed into Dr Francis's arms.

Long seconds ticked on. Still no one on the causeway moved. Swans drifted silently around the Mill Pool below; purpling clouds gathered overhead, silent witnesses to events unfolding. Hanna felt rain in the air; birds cawed and flapped; over on the lake everything was still. The sailing dinghies and fishing boats must have been ordered to clear the area.

'What's happening?' Freya pleaded as Dr Francis stood up and spoke to Elaine Phillips. The doctor turned and started towards them, her pace not quite a run.

'Why hasn't she got him?' Freya sobbed wretchedly. 'Is he really in the car? Does anyone know . . .?' She tried to break free, but Hanna and Andee grabbed her back.

'Hanna,' Dr Francis said as she reached them, 'you need to come with me. She wants to speak to you.'

Before Hanna could respond, Freya cried, 'I want to come. I need to see him. Is he all right?'

'He's fine,' the doctor assured her, patting her hand, 'but you need to wait here.'

'I'm his mother,' Freya shrieked. 'He needs me . . .' As she broke free of Hanna, Andee caught her again and held her close. 'It'll be all right,' Hanna heard Andee murmur. 'We just need to do as the doctor says.'

With a disorienting pounding in her ears, Hanna fell in beside Emilia Francis to walk back to the Fiesta. She had no idea what was expected of her now, only knew that there was next to no time to ask.

'It's Riona,' the doctor told her. 'Just treat her the way you usually do, be friendly, understanding – we don't want to give the others any reason to try and take control.'

Though her head spun, Hanna tried not to feel intimidated as she said, 'Are you sure Ethan's OK?'

'Yes. Bewildered, wants his mummy, but he's unharmed. Riona wouldn't hurt him.'

Hanna said nothing; that argument had already been had, and to no satisfactory end.

They were so close now she could see Elaine Phillips's tension. She wondered what she was walking into? How was she supposed to know what to do when she'd never confronted anything like this before in her life?

As they reached the car Elaine Phillips said, 'Hanna's here,' and the detective stood aside to make room for Hanna to crouch down beside the rear seat.

Her breath was almost stolen by how normal everything looked. Riona, in a pale yellow dress and gold pumps, sitting closest to the door, looking for all the world like the mother or guardian of the little boy standing on the seat beside her. She had a protective hold on him as he bounced and pointed through the back window to his mother. Hanna's heart didn't have time to fold around the fact that he was Jack's as he cried, 'Mum, Mum. Want Mum,' and Riona, calm, almost serene, turned to smile at her.

'Hanna, thank goodness you're here,' she said, in her gentle Irish voice. 'I've been trying to explain that I was on my way to your place. I'm afraid I took a wrong turn somewhere and ended up here, but no matter, everything's fine, thank goodness.'

'Why – why were you coming to me?' Hanna heard herself ask.

As if it were the most obvious answer in the world, Riona said, 'Because I know this little treasure will be safe with you.'

Responding the only way she could, Hanna said, 'But he's safe with his mother.'

Riona shook her head. 'His mother tried to steal your husband, and now they have a son whose existence is extremely hard for you . . . Blanche doesn't want that. She needs to know you're happy and that anyone who hurts you is stopped or punished. I'm afraid the others support her in this, especially Billy. It shouldn't have been a surprise to me, what he did, but I'm afraid I had . . . other distractions.'

Hanna was barely listening, only had eyes for the child. Her overriding instinct was to make a grab for him, and yet she knew she shouldn't. No matter how reasonable Riona seemed, this situation had the potential to change in a heartbeat.

'When I learned that he'd vandalized Freya's car,' Riona continued, bringing Hanna back to the moment, 'I knew I had to act before he did anything worse. And the only answer that made sense was to bring the boy to you. If Blanche or Billy or any of the others knew you had him, maybe I could persuade them that you'd accepted him, that you weren't sorry he'd been born.' She quickly caught Ethan as he lunged towards the front seats, trying to escape her, not knowing how. 'Careful,' she murmured, 'or you'll fall.'

Turning back to Hanna, she said, 'I can't always stop them, you see. I try, but I'm afraid they can be very head-strong, especially Billy. He's taken on Blanche's anger towards Freya Hansen for what she did to you, so it's possible Freya is in danger.'

Hanna could only stare at her. There was too much to unravel, but all she could really think was that Riona, the gatekeeper, had taken Ethan in order to protect him from Billy, or Blanche, who were actually right here, in this car, and could emerge at any moment. It was so bizarre, so beyond anything she could begin to understand that it was a long moment before she realized she needed to give the right – acceptable reaction – to what had been said.

'Thank you for looking out for Ethan.' She smiled, feeling the skin around her mouth stretch and tremble. 'We're all deeply in your debt, but you need—'

'You understand, I'm sure,' Riona interrupted, 'that it was Billy who attacked Jack. And Hugo Astor. He also broke into Seb's house, a few weeks ago. I'm afraid his temper has become a lot worse recently. We've been working on it, but I know he still frightens Blanche with how *fiercely* he protects her. I've seen her cower from him when he shouts . . . It's quite alarming. It's all him, not her. She's not a wicked or vengeful person; she's sweet inside, kind, consid-erate, full of love for her sister . . .' She paused, sighed softly and said, 'Of course I know you're not really her sister, but I'm afraid I haven't been able to persuade her of that yet.'

Hanna had no idea what to say. She just wanted to take the child and get away from here, to return them both to a world they understood, but Riona was still holding him and Hanna still didn't dare risk what might happen if she tried to snatch him.

Riona was staring ahead now, seeming lost in her thoughts. 'I know this won't help you,' she said, 'but Billy didn't mean to kill Jack. He just wanted to punish him for what he'd done to you. The problem is that he doesn't always know his own strength.'

Hanna's mouth was dry, her heart was crying out as she said, 'Can you hand Ethan over to me now? I'll take him home. Like you said, he'll be safe with me.'

Riona nodded and her eyes moved to the boy. 'Yes, he will, because I know you'll never blame him for what his father did. You're not that kind of person.'

'I won't,' Hanna assured her, and reached out her arms.

Riona kept hold of him.

'You need to get his mother to safety too,' she said. 'I accept and understand that you wish her ill, but . . .'

'I don't. Really, I don't,' Hanna insisted. 'And of course I'll keep her safe.' *From you – except you don't realize that, do you? You have no idea that you're warning me about* YOU.

Riona smiled and looked so beautiful, so peaceful and satisfied that Hanna felt she might be the one losing her mind.

'Can I take him now?' she asked, putting her arms out again.

Riona's smile fell away, and her lips started to droop, and her whole demeanour seemed to shift. Hanna found herself watching in appalled fascination. Riona's complexion was dulling before her very eyes; her jaw hardened, her eyelids sagged and her sweet air of grace and femininity was overtaken by one of bullish menace and confusion.

Ethan howled as the grip on his arm tightened.

Hanna gasped as Riona spoke in a voice that wasn't hers. 'She's trying to shut me out, but she can't.'

Dr Francis suddenly snapped, 'Billy, please step out of Riona's way. We need to speak to her.'

The altered Riona's eyes darted to Hanna and stayed there, piercing, watchful, enquiring and mistrustful.

Hanna didn't dare to move.

'Riona,' Dr Francis called out, 'you need to come forward.'

'She's not here. She's gone.' There was a laugh and a cough followed by long, tense seconds, until, without Hanna even seeing it happen, Riona was there again.

'You see how forceful he is,' she said, 'but you have nothing to fear from him, Hanna – it's you he wants to protect.'

Without thinking, Hanna said, 'Please tell him it isn't necessary. He's already done enough damage . . .'

'Don't antagonize him,' Riona advised. 'And try to remember he only does what he thinks is right.'

'How can he think it's right to go around attacking people and even killing them?' Hanna cried savagely. 'And you! You've taken a child from its mother, for God's sake.'

'I've already explained that it was for his own good. And please don't shout – you're upsetting him.'

Seeing that she was, Hanna bit back her anger and said softly to the boy, 'It's all right, sweetheart. Everything's going to be fine.'

'Yes, it is,' Riona confirmed, 'but before I let him go, I want you to promise me you won't persecute Blanche over this. She isn't to blame for anything. She's a victim – you must see that. What happened to make her the way she is

342

wasn't her fault, so please assure me that only Billy will be held to account.'

Ready to agree to any sort of madness just to get the child away, Hanna said, 'You have my word. I'll do anything I can to help you . . .'

'Not me, Blanche.'

'Yes, Blanche. I won't let anyone persecute her, I promise.'

Riona regarded her for a long, excruciating minute, and Hanna could see the muscles in her face starting to twitch, the struggle darkening and narrowing her eyes, the tension seeming to expand her body, until eventually, in one swift, fluid movement she lifted Ethan over her lap and passed him into Hanna's arms. 'Take him quickly,' she said.

Clutching the child to her, Hanna stood, swayed, and was steadied by the doctor. She turned away, her vision blurring, then half-ran towards Freya, who was already racing to meet her, ready to grab her precious boy into her arms.

'Thank you, thank you, thank you,' Freya sobbed over and over. 'Oh God, my baby, my boy . . . I was so scared . . . Are you all right? Let me look at you . . .'

Hanna's eyes went to Seb as he reached them, flicked to Andee as she came too, but it was Seb she was looking at until he wrapped her in his arms, as though shutting out the terrible last few minutes.

She clung onto him tightly. He was strong, she knew that, he bore things silently and stoically, but there must be cracks all the way through him right now. He'd truly believed Riona was someone who could make him happy after Jilly; a beautiful, lively, kind and intelligent woman he could share his life with. He would never have dreamt it would end like this – but who would?

Looking up at him, Hanna said, 'Are you OK?'

He seemed surprised, then faintly ironic as he said, 'It should be me asking you that.'

She turned to Freya and Ethan. Two paramedics were with them, but Freya wouldn't let go of her son. Hanna went over to see if she could help.

'They want to take him to hospital,' Freya explained, 'to check him over.'

'I'll come with you,' Hanna said.

'Yes, no . . . My mum's on her way back. She's going to meet us there. One of the detectives said he'd take us. I don't want to go in an ambulance.'

Elaine Phillips joined them, looking as relieved as any police officer would with this outcome to a child abduction. 'You're a special boy,' she said, touching a finger to Ethan's rosy cheek, allowing them a glimpse of her softer side. To Hanna she said, 'Thanks for what you did back there. There was no knowing how it would go, but it seems the doctor was correct in the understanding of her patient.' She seemed to want to say more, but whatever it was, she kept it to herself.

Hanna turned to look back in the direction she'd just come from, and saw Riona being taken from the Fiesta towards another car. It had tinted windows and blue lights that were, inexplicably, still flashing. From this distance Riona seemed calm; her hands hanging loosely at her sides, her flame-coloured hair tumbling around her shoulders, her gold shoes catching a glint of sunlight. Dr Francis was beside her, a gentle hand on her arm, and when Riona got into the car, the doctor slipped in beside her.

'Where will they take her?' Hanna asked Elaine Phillips.

'To Keynsham custody,' the detective replied. 'It's the

nearest. I'm just glad I won't be the one to interrogate her. We have specialist officers for that,' she explained when Hanna's surprise showed. She went on to say, 'Whether they've come across someone like Blanche Edwards before . . . I guess we'll find out.' She glanced at her phone when it buzzed, and said to Hanna, 'I'll be in touch. With you too,' she told Seb. 'You'll need to give statements.'

As Elaine walked away, Hanna leaned in to Seb again, resting her head on his shoulder and feeling the faint beat of his heart. Standing alone on the gravelled edge of the causeway, they watched two detectives put Freya and Ethan into the back of a car; an ambulance drove away behind them. The vehicle containing Riona and the doctor left next, blue lights still flashing, but no sirens howling.

Andee came to join them. 'Someone's going to take me to collect my car,' she said. 'Have you been asked to go to the station?'

Hanna shook her head. 'Not yet, so we'll go back to the house.'

'I'll call the children and Jenny,' Seb said, 'get them to meet us there.'

Hanna's heart twisted. She wasn't sure she was up to explaining all this to them yet – except of course she would; she had to. Jack was no longer here to take care of things the way he always had, with little fuss, a lot of energy, and often with humour. She wondered how he'd explain today, what words he'd use to describe the indescribable, how he'd achieve a level of understanding that virtually defied it.

She remembered him saying once: *there is nothing more reliable in its random acts of cruelty than life itself.* She tried to think why he'd said it, but it was eluding her, and anyway, it wouldn't have been anything as cruel or point-less as this. The way he'd lost his life would never make any sense to her, no matter what kind of explanation anyone tried to give.

She recalled the brief glimpse she'd had of Billy just now: strange, pugnacious, intrusive; kind of lost, now she came to think of it. She imagined him stalking Jack beside the lake, a woman in a man's body, or was it the other way round? *He didn't mean to kill Jack*, Riona had said, *he doesn't always realize his own strength.*

If only it had been just an injury. All they'd be dealing with now would be his recovery and the possibility that their lives could eventually return to normal. As it was, they had somehow to get used to the unthinkable reality that they were never going to see him again, that whatever they did going forward would be without him.

It was unbearable; he was going to miss so much and it was suddenly all crowding in on her. The children's accomplishments, whatever they might be, their ambitions, relationships, weddings, owning their own homes . . . He wasn't going to see Sofia grow up or ever hold any other grandchildren they might have. The house was going to be so empty without him; the company would change and grow with Leo at the helm and Jack would never see it.

She could hardly breathe. She needed to make her mind stop.

Seb's arm went around her and she leaned into him for a moment, so glad he was there, crying inside for how much he was going to miss Jack, too. She walked with him to the car and thanked him as he opened the door for her to get in. She had no idea how she'd have got even this far without him; she just hoped she was helping him, too.

As they drove away, her gaze drifted to the empty lake where Jack had sailed countless times over the years, since he was a small boy. He'd loved the tranquillity and fun of those Sunday afternoons with a passion – the days he'd been on duty, all the friends he'd made along the way. He'd taught numerous youngsters to sail, Leo and Cait included, and had never minded about mistakes or damage as long as their hearts were in it and they tried again. It was hard not to love something when Jack did; his whole heart and soul would go into it in a way that drew everyone along with him. So many people were going to be lost without him, but for his family the loss was immeasurable. They'd be too sad to move on for a long time, and too afraid to embrace life the way they used to, now they knew how little it could be trusted.

As they left Chew Lake behind, she found herself wondering how Jack might have managed if she'd been taken suddenly. Perhaps she could learn something from that. What advice would he give if she could ask him how best to cope?

It wasn't until later, as the children arrived home and came to sit with her and Seb in the TV room that she realized what Jack would say if he were here: *It's not only about you, Han. Nothing ever is, because things don't happen in a vacuum and time doesn't always play by the rules. So why not think about what happened to Blanche as a child, what it must have been like for her to have become what she is today?*

TWO MONTHS LATER

CHAPTER SIXTY

Hanna had left far too much time to get here, worried she'd be late, that they wouldn't let her in if she was, that there would be roadworks or an accident along the way. Instead, it seemed she'd arrived before anyone else. So all she could do was sit in the car and wait. Fortunately she was sheltered from the wind, sweeping across the surrounding landscape and carrying rank countryside smells along with it.

As she stared at the building in front of her, she tried to imagine what was going on inside – all the suffering, fear and vain hope – and asked herself again if she should have come. She hadn't been certain she would; right up until she'd left the house an hour and a half ago, she had thought she might not.

Seb had wanted to accompany her – so had Leo, and Andee – but for a reason she couldn't quite explain, she had decided to come alone. She hoped she wouldn't regret it; she didn't think she would. However, the past few months had been so full of the unforeseen, and she knew only too well that anything was possible.

During the times she was alone, which was often these days, she talked to Jack in her mind, and felt sure he was listening, was even right there in the room, watching her and responding in ways that sometimes made her smile or even laugh. There was always so much to tell him. She wanted him to know everything, for their connection to continue as if it had never been broken. The children said they spoke to him too; occasionally they even thought they heard him. It was as if the house was still full of him, and they all wanted it that way for as long as they could keep it going.

Something that had gone smoothly – in spite of the fact that it shouldn't have been happening at all – was his cremation and the burial of his ashes in the family crypt. In the time since, it often felt like a bad dream, until it was suddenly so real that she wanted to scream to try and wake herself up. Life without him didn't feel like a proper life at all. Thirty chosen guests had attended the service; hundreds and hundreds more had donated to the Madden Foundation. Sometime in the next few months, there would be a memorial service, and anyone who wanted to remember him and celebrate his life would be welcome. At the time of the cremation, neither she nor the family had been able to face everyone else's grief.

Cait in particular was suffering now. As soon as the police had stopped coming and the press had forgotten them, the reality of losing her father – and the role she felt she'd played in his death by confiding in Riona – had hit her hard. For weeks there had been no way of consoling her; her grief and guilt were consuming and loud and at times terrifying. Hanna had been afraid she would try to take her own life to try to escape the pain, or to punish herself.

Thankfully she'd been persuaded to undergo counselling,

and after a few sessions, when she'd finally started to calm down, Ishan had returned to Lake House with Sofia. All three were living there now, back in Cait's room, although Ishan was due to leave next week to begin his final year at Oxford. Hanna wasn't looking forward to that. She'd come to depend on the soothing influence he had on Cait, and besides, she and the children might be too lonely on their own, now that Jenny had gone to stay with her sister in Burgundy. Jenny hadn't said yet when she might be back, but she was in touch most days, especially keen to hear about how Leo was throwing himself into the company, eager to learn everything the chiefs could teach him, ready to take over from his father. Sooner now, rather than later.

Coming back to the moment, Hanna watched other cars beginning to arrive. She stole glimpses of the drivers and passengers and was reminded of her plans for a victims' support scheme. She'd already viewed two properties as prospective refuges with the Madden architects, and she was soon to start talks with the local authorities. It would happen, she was in no doubt of it, although it would be a year or more before they could start officially helping their first families. It was this project, perhaps more than the many others she had on her desk, that was helping her to get through the constant, debilitating might of her grief. She knew now that the shock of a sudden death, whether through accident, murder or suicide, was almost impossible to push through. It never made sense to those left behind. Now every day felt wrong, and very often she couldn't imagine anything ever feeling right again.

She continued to watch as men, women and children began making their way to the visitors' centre. She wondered if Emilia Francis had been here since Blanche's transfer to custody following her appearance at the magistrate's court. She hadn't thought to ask when the doctor had returned her call two weeks ago.

'Hanna,' the doctor had said, 'how are you?'

It had taken Hanna a moment to assemble her thoughts, to remember how she wanted this conversation to go. She began with, 'I'm sorry for the things I said to you on that awful day when little Ethan was taken.'

'There is no need to apologize. It was an extremely difficult time for you and tensions were running high for everyone.'

An understatement if ever there was one but, having no desire to dwell on it, Hanna moved on. 'I want to ask about Blanche and whether it might be possible to see her?' She felt her heart jolt as she spoke the words, as if the request had shocked her rather than the doctor.

There had been a pause before – sounding curious and cautious – Emilia Francis said, 'Is this in response to a letter you've received from her?'

Frowning, Hanna said, 'No.'

'Ah. She told me she'd written, but maybe she hasn't sent it. Can I ask why you want to see her?'

Steeling herself, Hanna said, 'I've been thinking about her a lot – well, of course I have – and I've been wondering . . . If I knew more about her and what she . . . experienced, maybe it would help me to understand why my family and I are where we are.'

The doctor was quiet again, presumably thinking it over. In the end, she said, 'I can see why you think this might be a way of helping with your grief, but it's unlikely it'll give you the answers, or the peace of mind, you're seeking.' She went on to say, 'You might remember me telling you that you can't unknow something, and if you were to hear the details of what Blanche suffered . . . Well, I don't think the images it'll conjure are something you'd want to live with after.'

Hanna said, 'Perhaps not the full details—'

'She needs to focus on what we're trying to achieve for her,' the doctor interrupted. 'As you probably know, the prospect of prosecution hasn't gone away. We're hoping it will – Elaine Phillips is with me on this – to quote her, "a trial could very easily descend into farce if Blanche is allowed to go to court". In fact, it certainly will if she enters a plea of not guilty, which she intends to. As far as she's concerned she, Blanche Edwards, did not commit the crime.'

'But on some level she must know she did.'

'I'm afraid this is the power of alters. They are as real to Blanche as I am to you, or you are to me. Actually, neither Elaine nor her superiors believe it will go to court, but until the prosecution's psychiatrist has delivered his assessment on whether or not she's mentally fit to stand, we can't be sure.'

Taking a moment to consider this and what it actually meant, Hanna said, 'So it's highly likely that no one will be held accountable for Jack's death?'

'I'm afraid not in a court of law. However, Blanche isn't denying that Billy was culpable . . .'

'But Billy doesn't bloody well exist,' Hanna cried in a rush of anger. '*She* did it. *She* was the one who hit him so hard with a baseball bat that she killed him outright. And please don't tell me she was acting as Billy, using his strength, his *persona* . . . *She* is the one who did it.'

'I fully understand how frustrating this is for you . . .'

'Frustrating doesn't even begin to cover it. I've lost my husband, my children have lost their father, because that woman . . .' She stopped herself, realizing she was venting at the doctor all over again, blaming her, hitting out at anyone she could possibly hurt, when she knew it was never going to change things.

She hadn't intended the conversation to go this way.

Dr Francis said, gently, 'Why do you really want to see her, Hanna? How do you think it's going to help you, or her?'

Realizing she had to be honest now, in spite of how foolish or wrong-headed it might make her sound, she said falteringly, 'I think Jack would want me to. I can't explain why, I just . . . feel that he would.'

'And if Blanche decides she doesn't want to see you?'

Unprepared for that, Hanna said, 'Do you think she will?'

'I honestly don't know. She has become very withdrawn since being sent to the prison – obviously not the right place for her, but the justice system being what it is . . .'

'You said she wrote me a letter.'

'That's what she told me, but if you haven't received one, I can't know if that's true.' Before Hanna could respond, she said, 'Blanche needs a lot of help right now, more than ever before . . . Punishing her through the legal system for what she did is one way of dealing with her, but I'm sure you can see that it's not the right way.'

Knowing she couldn't disagree with that, much as she might want to, Hanna said, 'I still want to see her.'

'OK, I'll ask her if she's willing, but please bear in mind that she has the right to say no.'

*

Blanche hadn't said no, and now here Hanna was, in the visitor centre of HMP Eastwood Park, the secure women's prison north of Bristol, sitting opposite Jack's killer, who, unsettlingly, could so easily be Riona Byrne, and yet not. It had felt like a punch to the stomach when she'd first laid eyes on this faded, neglected version of a once-beautiful woman. She was like the portrait in the attic. Gone was the vibrant red hair, the glossy curls that had fallen to her shoulders; what remained had no lustre, was shorn bluntly and scraped behind her ears. The mesmerizing green eyes had been leeched of life and colour. This woman – Blanche – was thin, scrawny, her skin blotched and grey. It was as though the ghost of Riona was retreating, trying to leave as little of herself behind as possible.

At the same time, she was looking at the woman who'd killed Jack. It seemed incredible, impossible, and yet it was true.

Finally realizing she needed to speak first, Hanna said, 'Thank you for agreeing to see me.'

Blanche kept her eyes lowered, watched her index finger pressing against the table as if she were trying to push something into the fake wood. Her nails were blunt, bitten, her knuckles red raw. Had she been fighting, trying to tear down walls? It looked more like eczema. Hanna had never noticed eczema on Riona's hands. Maybe this was an example of what Dr Francis had said about alters having their own conditions.

She wondered if Blanche was going to speak at all, if it would even be Blanche who answered. What would she do if it wasn't? It was nerve-wracking in a way that made her want to get up and leave. She didn't want to become entangled in the chaos inside this woman's head, dragged into the kind of confusion she'd never be able to navigate.

Then why was she here?

Blanche's eyes were still lowered as she said, 'I knew her.'

There was so much noise around them that Hanna had to lean in slightly as she said, 'I'm sorry?'

'I knew her,' Blanche repeated, more clearly. Her head came up and a flash of defiance passed through her eyes as she said, 'I loved her. She meant everything to me.' She gave a hoarse laugh, making it sound like a marvel, she said, 'I had a sister. She was mine. I was told to take care of her and so I did, with all my heart and soul. No one ever hurt her – I made sure they hurt me instead. That's what you do for your sister. You keep her safe, you make sure she knows she's loved in spite of everything.' Her eyes dulled as they met Hanna's and tears began to well from their depths. 'I want you to be her,' she said brokenly. 'Please be her.'

Hanna opened her mouth but no words came.

'I'd know then that she got away, that no harm ever came to her,' Blanche explained. 'If it did it would be my fault, and I did everything I could to keep her safe.' She pressed a hand to her mouth as her face contorted. 'They might have buried her alive,' she choked, 'or set fire to her . . . She was only three . . . Please be her. *Please.*'

Trying to swallow her emotions, Hanna said, 'I'm sorry. I can't be someone I'm not.'

Blanche turned sharply aside, as if rejecting the words. 'That's what Riona says,' she muttered. 'That you can't be someone you're not. But I think – I *know* – you can be anyone you want to be.'

Hanna thought of the tragic way she'd used those words,

and how they'd led her to reinvent and protect herself with delusion and disassociation. She hoped she was saying the right thing when she asked, 'Is Riona with you?'

Blanche's eyes drifted to nowhere as she slowly shook her head. 'She's not here,' she replied. 'This is no place for her. She'd hate it, but maybe she'll come. I miss her.' After a beat, she focused on Hanna again and said, 'I think she's with Seb. She's very keen on him, you know, and she deserves to be happy. He could be very good for her.' She blinked a couple of times, slowly, deliberately. 'You haven't seen her?'

Having no idea how to answer that, other than to ask how she possibly could without coming here, to the prison, Hanna said, 'What about the . . . others? Are they with you?'

Again Blanche's gaze moved away and her hands clenched and unclenched on the table. 'Billy shouldn't be here,' she stated. 'He's a man and this place is only for women, but it's good that he stayed. He helps me sometimes; he's much stronger than I am, you see, and very protective.' She sighed quietly. 'Hayley, Ruby and Ryan have gone. I don't know where. I never hear from them now. They might come back. I hope so; Ryan is an excellent cook and the food in here isn't so good.'

Bizarrely, Hanna found herself on the edge of understanding why the alters might have been so important to Blanche. They helped her to create a world that was just about bearable.

'I hope you know,' Blanche said, turning back and seeming a little more animated, 'that Billy is very sorry for what he did. *Very* sorry. He should tell you himself, of course, and I'd like him to, but he won't. He says he'll tell everyone when he goes to court. He's going to plead guilty if they give him the chance, but at the moment they're holding *me* responsible for everything.' Her eyes were wide with disbelief as she continued. 'It wasn't me,' she stated. 'I would never have hurt Jack, in spite of the way he betrayed you. He shouldn't have done it, of course, it was very wrong of him to have a child with someone else. I agreed with Billy that he needed to be taught a lesson, the same as Hugo Astor, but Billy took it too far. He doesn't know his own strength.'

Recalling Riona uttering those very same words, Hanna felt a shudder go through her. She was realizing now, too late, too late, that the doctor was right: coming here wasn't going to help her, or Blanche. Unless she'd wanted proof for herself that this wretched, broken woman really wasn't fit to stand trial.

In the end, realizing there was no more she could say or do, she got to her feet and looked down at Blanche as she said, 'Thank you for seeing me.'

Blanche stared up at her, seeming neither upset nor surprised that their visit was over. 'If you decide you are my sister,' she said, 'please come again. If not . . .' She shrugged and bowed her head.

Hanna turned away, but hesitated as Blanche said, 'And should you happen to see Riona, please tell her I miss her.'

Hanna stilled for a moment, but knew there was nothing to be gained from attempting an answer. She would never be able to connect with the cognitive impairments that overwhelmed Blanche's ability to reason, so she said nothing, simply walked away and returned to the car.

She had no reason to think she'd ever see Blanche again, nor did she want to. She didn't hate her, didn't wish her ill, but there was no getting away from the fact that the woman, however she wanted to present herself, had taken Jack's life. And no amount of delusion or regret would ever bring him back.

For that she despised Blanche, detested her with every fibre of her being, and yet at the same time she couldn't wish her any more torment than she'd already been in for years.

CHAPTER SIXTY-ONE

A week later, Hanna was in her study, working from home, when Elaine Phillips rang.

'I thought you should be the first to know,' the detective said after very little preamble, 'that the CPS-appointed psychiatrist has declared Blanche Edwards mentally unfit to stand trial.'

Hanna sat back in her chair, feeling oddly winded by that, as though it were a surprise when it wasn't.

'I'm sorry,' Elaine continued, 'I know this probably doesn't feel like proper justice for Jack—'

'No, no,' Hanna interrupted, 'I just . . . I was expecting it, obviously, maybe not quite so soon, but actually it's good to have a decision.' That was true, she realized, although she still needed time to process it. 'What will happen to her now?' she asked, glancing out at the rain that seemed not to have stopped for days.

'Emilia Francis is working to get her into a secure facility in the States,' Elaine replied. 'Apparently, there's a better understanding of the disorder over there. It's possible the doctor will be successful, but I've no idea when it might happen.'

Hanna found herself suddenly pitying Blanche. She had

no one apart from the false protectors, or friends, in her head, and Dr Francis, of course. Thank God for the doctor, or Blanche's future could turn out to be even lonelier than her childhood.

After thanking the detective for the call, she checked for messages from Cait, who was at playgroup with Sofia. Finding none, she rang Andee.

'Well, I guess it's closure of a sort,' Andee commented when Hanna finished telling her the news. 'Does it feel that way?'

'I suppose it does. At least the awful prospect of going to court isn't hanging over us any more, and that can only be a good thing.'

'How do you think the children and Jenny will take it?'

'They'll probably feel quite relieved too. Jenny said as much when we spoke last night – she just wants it behind us so she can come home and we can get on with our lives. I'll be glad to have her back, I know that, especially with Ishan leaving tomorrow.'

'That's come round already? How's Cait coping with it?'

'Actually, she and Sofia are going to help settle him into his new flat for a couple of weeks, and when she comes back she tells me she's thinking about enrolling on a course at Bath Spa or UWE.'

'You must be pleased about that. What does she want to study?'

With a dry laugh, Hanna said, 'Cait being Cait, she hasn't made up her mind yet, but actually I think she's serious about doing something. She wants to make her dad proud, she says, which makes me want to cry, but fortunately I manage not to. We'll have to work out childcare, of course, but now we won't be doing so much entertaining, Florina has said she'd like to take it on. Speaking of entertaining reminds me, are you and Graeme still coming to the charity dinner next Saturday?'

'Absolutely, we wouldn't miss it. It'll be good to see you.'

With a smile to try to cover her trepidation about attending a big event for the first time without Jack, Hanna said, 'It'll be good to see you too. Apart from anything else, it'll give me another opportunity to say thank you for everything you did at a time when you couldn't have been more needed.'

'You don't have to thank me. It's what friends are for. Now tell me, how's Seb?'

Hanna's heart twisted slightly as she said, 'OK, I think. I've hardly seen him these last few weeks. I mean, he calls quite often to check on us all, and Leo gets together with him for lunch now and again, but he's busy with his university commitments now the academic year is getting back in swing.'

'But he's coming to the dinner?'

'As far as I know. Yes, I hope so.' She gave an awkward laugh, 'I won't have a plus one if he doesn't, and I'm not sure how well I could cope with that.' Worried about how self-pitying that might sound, she quickly added, 'But of course I'll still go.' She didn't want to admit that she was afraid Seb was actively avoiding her. She was probably being overly sensitive – or needy. However, he certainly wasn't coming here as often any more and nor were they meeting up in town.

Deciding she'd try to speak to him about it next week, she finished her call with Andee and did her best to get on with some work.

*

The following Saturday she could tell as soon as Seb opened his front door to let her in how pleased he was to see her. And wow, was she pleased to see him, even more than she'd expected to be. She could have gone on hugging him for an hour; it felt so good to remember how connected they were in so many ways. She wondered how he was coping now with Jack's loss. She knew he'd never stopped missing Jilly, and his best friend's death would have left as big a hole in his life as it had in hers. She hadn't been a good enough friend to him since it had all happened, she realized; she should and would try harder.

'You look stunning,' he told her, his eyes showing his appreciation as he took her wrap and draped it over a chair in the hall.

Pleased, she gave a little twirl to show off her sky blue, figure-hugging gown with fishtail hem and sequinned shoulder straps. She'd bought it especially for this evening, knowing how much Jack would love it. He wouldn't get to see it now (or maybe he could – she liked to think that was possible on whatever level). Anyway, it buoyed her a lot to know that Seb admired it.

'You're not looking so bad yourself,' she informed him teasingly, checking out his exquisitely cut dinner suit with dark purple cummerbund, matching shirt studs and bow tie. True, most men looked gorgeous in formal dress, but some could carry it off better than others; Seb was near the top of the game.

Clearly enjoying the compliment, he gestured for her to go through ahead of him, saying, 'We can wait for Andee and Graeme to arrive before I crack open the champagne, or we can have a glass now.'

'Are we celebrating something?' she asked, glancing over her shoulder.

'No, I just thought it would be a good way to start the evening.'

Agreeing that it would, she said, 'I'm sure they won't mind if we go ahead.'

As he went to take a bottle from the fridge and set out four glasses on the countertop, she sat down at the table and helped herself to an olive from a dish of hors d'oeuvres. 'It's crossed my mind,' she said, trying to keep her tone light, but wanting to get this out of the way, 'that you've been avoiding me.'

When he simply continued to open the bottle and fill two glasses, she realized with a thud to her heart that he wasn't going to deny it.

Maybe he hadn't heard that Blanche wasn't to stand trial.

Of course he had.

She wished now that she hadn't brought it up. She was obviously sounding needy, maybe resentful, even judgemental.

Coming to the table, he handed her a drink and clinked his glass to hers as he said, 'To you.'

She smiled and took a sip, feeling the bubbles tickle her nose.

He sat down on the opposite side of the table, stretched out his long legs, crossed them at the ankle and said, 'I admit I was. Avoiding you.'

Her eyes widened as her embarrassment deepened.

'Not,' he continued, 'because I wanted to, but because I felt we both needed some space; some time to try and come to terms with what had happened – and the part I played in it.'

'The part *you* played?' she echoed in surprise.

'I brought Riona into our lives,' he reminded her, 'or at least I was duped into doing so. If I'd been less desperate, more discerning, I'd have known right away that something was wrong.'

'Oh, Seb, we were all taken in by her, including Jack, never forget that, and not for a single minute have I ever thought you were to blame for anything. No one has, because you weren't. God, I'm really sad to think you stayed away because of that. We've missed you, you know. *I've* missed you.'

He smiled and she could see how much it meant to him to hear that. 'I've missed you too,' he told her, 'however, I hear you've been busy. Leo keeps me up to speed with everything – the new refuge, all the upcoming fundraising efforts . . . He also tells me,' he added, half-frowning, half-incredulous, 'that you and Cait have been seeing something of Freya and Ethan?'

Hanna smiled as she nodded, glad to have the opportunity to tell him about that. 'I thought we should,' she said. 'He's Jack's son, after all. And he's a dear little boy. Very noisy, loves to charge around the place as fast as his legs can carry him. Sofia's besotted with him, and you'd be amazed to hear the way she's starting to speak now. I think because of him. So many words all at once – oh, and we have a puppy arriving for her next week. Surprise, surprise, she wants to call it Ethan – or Eesh, as she says it – but we're trying to talk her out of that.'

Laughing, he said, 'What sort of puppy?'

'A golden retriever,' she said, certain he'd already guessed the answer. 'I thought it might help Jenny a little, when Gaston finally goes, if there's another dog to take care of. We know it's her favourite breed.'

367

He nodded, clearly approving of the decision. 'How is she?' he asked. 'Where is she?'

'Fine, and coming back from her sister's on Tuesday. I thought I might give a little dinner to welcome her back. If you're free, I know she'd love to see you.' *Please say yes. Please. It won't mean as much without you.*

'I'd love to come,' he assured her, 'just let me know the date and time and I'll be there. Are you staying here in the guest room tonight, by the way? Did you bring an overnight bag?'

'Yes, it's in the car. I should probably go and bring it in, but first tell me about you and what you've been up to all this time. I guess you've been busy now everyone's back.'

With an ironic raise of his eyebrows he said, 'My calendar is already full of committees, seminars, departmental business . . . However, the big news I want to share with you is that I've decided to go to UBC.' Apparently realizing she had no idea what he was talking about, he said, 'University of British Colombia. Canada.'

Her mouth turned dry and she struggled to keep her smile in place as she said, 'That's wonderful. They're very lucky to have you.' Universities from all over the world were forever offering him positions, but Jilly had never wanted to leave Bristol. Now he had nothing to keep him here, and she couldn't bear the thought of him going. It would be too much so soon after losing Jack; in a way it would be like losing him all over again. But she had no right to keep him here.

'I've already accepted,' he said, glancing down at his glass, 'and I was thinking . . .' He paused, frowned as he looked at her, then shocked her to her core as he said, 'Why don't you come?'

She stared at him, sure she couldn't have heard right.

'You'll love Vancouver,' he told her.

So she had heard right. 'But my home is here,' she protested. 'Lake House, the children, the Foundation . . . Seb, as much as I . . . You must know I couldn't possibly leave them. I don't even want to.'

He appeared baffled for a moment, then laughed as he said, 'Han, it's only for a month.'

Now she felt truly embarrassed. She'd thought he was asking her to move countries with him.

'They want me to chair an international conference on migration as an adjustment to environmental stress,' he continued, reminding her without trying of his international standing in the academic world. 'I'll be given a house and a car for the time I'm there,' he continued, 'and the schedule doesn't look too pressing so I thought . . .' He shrugged. 'Well, I thought it would do you good to get away for a while. A change of scene, a recharge if you like, and when the conference is over maybe we could do a tour of the Rockies, Banff National Park, Calgary . . . Anything we like. So what do you say? Are you up for it?'

She hardly knew what to say. This was the last thing she'd expected when she'd come here this evening, yet here she was, looking at the prospect of a trip to Canada, exploring places she'd long wanted to visit with Jack. Nevertheless, the idea of it was starting to grow on her. But she needed to think about it, discuss it with the children, make sure all her Foundation commitments could be met.

'When do you leave?' she asked.

'Two weeks on Monday.'

That soon. Really no time at all to think. 'OK, I'll come,'

she declared suddenly and started to laugh. 'I'll come,' she said again, as if to prove to herself that she meant it. He was right, she did need to get away for a while, Jack would want her to – *she* wanted to – and now she felt so excited she could hardly wait.

'That'll be Andee and Graeme,' he said as the doorbell sounded in the hall.

'I'll pour their drinks,' she offered as he went to let them in.

Canada! She'd just agreed to go to Canada for a month. What were the children going to say? Knowing how much they loved Seb, it would probably be something along the lines of: 'I'll help you pack,' or 'I'll drive you to the airport.'

Would they think it was a romantic trip? No, it was too soon for that, and she should probably reassure them it wasn't before she went. Not that she could rule out the possibility of being involved with Seb some time in the future – who could, when he had so much going for him? And she'd loved him for ever and never wanted to think of him not being in her life.

She was getting ahead of herself, of everything.

'Hello, hello, sorry if we're late,' Andee declared, coming into the room.

'You're not,' Hanna assured her, 'and you look gorgeous. Red is a great colour on you.'

'Ah, but you are outshining us all, Hanna Madden. Come here, let me hug you.'

'My turn,' Graeme insisted as he came in, looking as handsome as Seb in his dinner suit, and as stylish.

As they embraced, Seb finished pouring the champagne and handed Andee and Graeme their glasses. 'Taxi's due in ten minutes,' he announced, 'but enough time for a toast.

370

To Hanna, who's remarkable in every way bar none, and who's just agreed to come to Canada with me for a month.'

Andee's face dropped in surprise and immediately lit up. 'You're kidding,' she cried, knocking her glass against Hanna's. 'That's the most wonderful news! It's somewhere I've always wanted to go. So have you,' she reminded Graeme, turning to him.

'This is true,' he agreed.

Seb said, 'So, why don't you guys join us?'

Hanna almost choked as Graeme tilted his head thoughtfully, then said, 'If you're serious, I reckon you could count us in.'

Andee turned to him in astonishment. 'Just like that? What about all your work commitments? The break we'd planned in Cornwall . . .'

'Canada's more exciting.'

'You don't even know when they're going.'

'When are you going?' Graeme asked Seb.

Seb gave him the date.

'That works,' Graeme declared, 'and if it doesn't we can meet you there?'

Laughing as he slipped an arm around Hanna, Seb said, 'Absolutely. Come whenever it suits you. I'll email you all the details tomorrow.'

In spite of the ache in her heart that Jack wasn't enjoying this moment with them, Hanna couldn't stop smiling. He really would want her to do this, she knew that beyond any doubt, and he'd be thrilled to know that Andee and Graeme had decided so rashly – even more rashly than she had – to come too. And if she couldn't go with Jack, who better than with Seb?

'OK, that'll be the taxi,' Seb said when the doorbell

sounded again. 'A little early, but there'll be plenty of champagne when we get there.'

As Andee and Graeme headed outside, Hanna picked up her wrap from the chair in the hall and noticed Seb's answerphone was flashing on the table next to it.

'Looks like you've got a message,' she told him as he joined her.

Surprised, he said, 'Really? No one ever rings me on the landline these days. Must be a cold call.'

'Do you want to check?'

He shrugged. 'OK, press play.'

She did, and a moment later their eyes met, as a voice they'd thought never to hear again said, 'Hi, Seb. It's Riona.'

ACKNOWLEDGEMENTS

A huge thank you to Paul F. Dell, PhD from the Psychiatric Clinics of North America. His expert knowledge and extensive papers on the subject of Dissociative Identity Disorder were simply invaluable in pulling this story together. If I have misrepresented the condition in any way the fault will be entirely mine.

Love and thanks to my best friend, Denise Hastie, for taking me around the Chew Valley and bringing it all to life in such an inspiring and detailed way. A truly beautiful part of the West County – I now want to move into the house I created for Hanna and Jack.

Also much love and thanks to my husband, James, whose incredible patience and support saw me through this book when I was going through a very difficult time. As many of you will know, losing a dog is absolutely heartbreaking – I lost both of mine, Coco and Lulu, within 16 hours of one another. I then had a horrible accident that took me some time to recover from. The kindness and sympathy expressed by so many Facebook followers during those months really helped to buoy me, so a huge thank you and very much love to all of you who got in touch.

Last, but never least, in fact probably the most important of all, love and thanks to my wonderful agent, Luigi Bonomi and to my editor Kimberley Young. It's true to say that I really couldn't do it without either of you.

Read on for a sneak peek of Susan's new novel
– her 50th book to be published!

Coming 2023 . . .

She didn't hear any footsteps approaching, but she wouldn't have. She had ear buds in, listening to music as she worked, and was so focused on what she was doing that even a fire alarm might not have disturbed her.

She was alone in a meeting room, a glassed-in space tucked away from the main office and close to the lifts. The walls were cluttered with books of all genres and sizes and brightly coloured posters, most of them promoting an upcoming TV series. There was a large blank screen at one end of the room and a coffee station at the other.

She hadn't made herself a drink yet, but she might when she'd finished. Or more likely, she'd head home as it was close to 7.30 p.m. and everyone else had already left for the day.

No one had popped in to say goodnight on their way past; this didn't surprise her, but it upset her. It was awful being disliked.

She only had herself to blame, she knew that, but it didn't make it any easier. She shouldn't have given in to him, should have steered well clear, but he'd been so very hard to resist. He'd made her feel breathless every time she saw him, caused wild and greedy flutterings in every part of her; his eyes when they met hers seemed to set her on fire.

He said she did the same to him.

He couldn't resist her either.

She'd stopped it now, told him they couldn't continue, but it was already too late to repair the damage she'd caused.

He'd taken their break-up hard and his wife had gone to pieces.

His wonderful, beautiful, talented wife who, some were saying, had already met someone else. So maybe she hadn't been that broken-hearted after all.

Her task this evening was to pack up the props that had been used for a promo shoot the day before. It had been for a book soon to hit the screens in a major new horror series. The props had been returned from location all bundled up in a sheet like dozens of little corpses. Apparently they'd been on loan from a doll's hospital. Who even knew there was such a thing? Did people really take their broken dolls to have limbs repaired and faces remodelled? It seemed so sad – and weird.

For two hours yesterday the dolls had been positioned around a deserted, cobwebby house in the countryside, perched ghoulishly on shelves and chairs, laid out on the floor and twisted into odd shapes to suggest violence and thwarted escape. Some had been placed face down, or up, in a bath and one – blonde-haired, ruby lipped and nude – was hung by its neck from a dusty chandelier. All those miniature bodies; the grisly suggestion, the turbulence of grotesque innuendo. It had been as spooky as hell. She'd been very glad when the camera stopped and it was time to get out of there.

This evening she was carefully wrapping each of the dolls in tissue before laying it gently into a large, padded box. Even in this setting they somehow remained disturbingly real. It was as though they were inside their own doll-world, looking back at her through hard, unblinking eyes, grimacing and grinning; a few even had teeth. They were thin and brittle, fat and rubbery. Some were made of porcelain or china, others were moulded from plastic, even from wood. She sensed them watching and listening, breathing silently and knowing everything.

She didn't hear the door open behind her, had no idea anyone was there until they were standing right beside her. She started to look up, to say, 'Aren't they creepy?' or, 'I thought you'd already gone home,' but before any words could form on her lips, the pages of her life suddenly flew by, the movie unreeling, taking her from where she was in her story straight to the very end.